SEALED WITH A LOVING KISS

After the death of her parents, Mary Jones discovers a secret in the pages of her father's diaries. Her search for the truth brings her to Cliffehaven. Here, she finds work at the Kodak factory, shifting through the Airgraphs which are being sent from all over the world by people in the armed forces. With the help of Peggy Reilly, Mary starts to build a new life for herself. But events that happened eighteen years before still echo, and should a promise Peggy made then be broken, it will have a devastating effect not only on Mary, but them all...

SEALED WITH A LOVING KISS

SEALED WITH A LOVING KISS

by

Ellie Dean

Magna Large Print Books
Long Preston, North Yorkshire,
BD23 4ND, England.

British Library Cataloguing in Publication Data.

Dean, Ellie
Sea of rememberance...

A catalogue record of this book is
available from the British Library

ISBN 978-0-7505-4261-6

First published in Great Britain by Arrow Books in 2015

Copyright © Ellie Dean 2015

Cover illustration © Elizabeth Ansley by arrangement with
Arcangel Images

Ellie Dean has asserted her right to be identified as the author of this
work in accordance with the Copyright, Designs and Patents Act, 1988

Published in Large Print 2016 by arrangement with
Random House Group Ltd.

Magna Large Print is an imprint of Library Magna Books Ltd.

Printed and bound in Great Britain by
T.J. (International) Ltd., Cornwall, PL28 8RW

Acknowledgements

Jim Reilly's voyage to India and the contents of his many airgraphs would not have been so realistic if I hadn't had the privilege of being entrusted with the diaries of Kenneth Douglas Fowler who made the same journey. I'm indebted and hugely grateful to Jean Relf and her brother David Fowler for lending me these precious memoirs, for they have given me a real insight into the language of the day and the experiences these men went through during their service to their country.

I would also like to acknowledge the help, advice and encouragement I've received from my brilliant agent, Teresa Chris, who has never faltered in her enthusiasm to do her best for me so I may reach my goals.

Thanks also go to Georgina Hawtrey-Woore, who has been a wonderful editor throughout the series. Her enthusiasm and encouragement have been a great spur, and it's marvellous to have an editor who sees things in the same way that I do.

Last, but never least, I need to thank my darling husband, Ollie, who has provided coffee, suppers, a shoulder to lean on and an ear to listen. I couldn't have achieved any of this without him.

Author Notes

The airgraph was invented in the 1930s by the Eastman Kodak Company in conjunction with Imperial Airways (now British Airways) and Pan-American Airways as a means of reducing the weight and bulk of mail carried by air. The airgraph forms, upon which the letter was written, were closely inspected and censored before being photographed and then sent as negatives on rolls of microfilm to all the theatres of war. At their destination, the negatives were enlarged and printed on photographic paper and delivered through the Royal Engineers (postal section), also known as APS (Army Postal System).

The use of the airgraph was not rationed, and its postage was set at three pence (3d) for civilians, but free to members of the armed forces. It proved to be instantly popular, with approximately 2,000 being processed an hour. Yet, because of its size – approximately 4ins x 6ins – and the lack of privacy, it was limited, so when sufficient aircraft capacity became available, its use declined in favour of the air letter.

A historical note: a similar system was employed during the Franco–Prussian War, when carrier pigeons were used to send primitive microfilm strips across German lines. The creator of microfilm was the British scientist John Dancer in 1839, and it was the French optician René Dagron who added his first microfilm patent to Dancer's work in 1859.

Chapter One

Cliffehaven, 1942

Peggy Reilly was restless after her long, intimate talk with young Mary Jones, and she lay awake staring into the darkness, thinking of the tangled web of lies and secrets that she must keep to herself. It had been imperative to dissuade Mary from continuing to ask about Cyril Fielding, for the truth, if told, would cause lasting hurt not only to little Mary but to others who'd been innocently drawn into Tommy Findlay's deception. And yet she'd hated the subterfuge, for it went against her open and honest nature, and she knew how easily lies could be uncovered – and when they were, they inevitably brought more hurt than ever.

Her thoughts whirled and she eventually became impatient with them. There was nothing more she could do except keep an eye on the girl and make sure there was no further trouble from Tommy Findlay, for Mary was determined to stay in Cliffehaven, and she would have been deeply suspicious if Peggy had forced the issue and tried to persuade her to go back to Sussex.

She climbed out of bed. Pulling her old dressing gown over her long winceyette nightdress, she put on her slippers and quietly checked on Daisy before she left the room. Her baby was almost a year old now, born on the terrible day that Pearl

Harbor had been destroyed and Malaya had been invaded, but she could sleep through anything, and was thriving despite the restrictions of rationing, the noise of air raids and the absence of most of her family.

Beach View Boarding House was silent but for the occasional creak and groan from the Victorian timbers, and Peggy closed the kitchen door before turning on the light. The kettle was always left filled in case there was a bombing raid and the water supply was cut off, so she placed it on the hob of her Kitchener range and waited for it to boil.

She had lived at Beach View for most of her forty-three years, and it was so much a part of her that she couldn't imagine living anywhere else. Her parents had started the boarding house business shortly after the railway line had reached Cliffehaven and the popularity of seaside holidays soared. When they had retired, Peggy and her husband, Jim, had taken over and raised their family here. The day trippers and holidaymakers had stopped coming once war had been declared, and so Peggy had decided that to make ends meet she would have to take in permanent lodgers.

But the war had brought huge changes to Peggy's family, for they were now scattered to the four winds and she rarely saw them. She regarded the photographs with longing, for they were lined up on the mantelpiece below the framed picture of the King and Queen. Jim looked handsome in his army uniform, the twinkle in his dark Irish eyes undimmed as he gazed back at her. He'd been called up and was on his way to India now, and she was waiting impatiently for his next airgraph.

Her two young sons, Charlie and Bob, were down in Somerset on a friend's farm with her eldest daughter Anne, who'd recently had her second baby. Peggy had yet to see Emily Jane, and little Rose Margaret would be changing so fast that she was probably unrecognisable from the toddler she'd said goodbye to all those months ago.

There was a photograph of Anne and her husband, Commander Martin Black, who looked very handsome in his RAF uniform – but she knew how Anne worried about him, even though he was flying a desk now he'd done more than his share of sorties over enemy territory. Their enforced separation had come shortly after Rose Margaret had been born, and Peggy knew just how deeply they both suffered from it.

The photograph of Cissy, her middle daughter, showed a laughing, fair-haired girl of twenty-one in a WAAF uniform. She'd once had dreams of joining ENSA and becoming famous like Vera Lynn, but thankfully she'd grown out of such silliness and had settled down very nicely at Cliffe aerodrome, where she drove an Air Vice-Marshal about.

Peggy gave a sigh as she ran her fingers through her dark curls. Cissy was in love with Randolph Stevens, a young American bomber pilot, but there were almost continuous raids over Germany now, and too many of those brave young boys had not made it home. As Cissy had already lost several friends to this terrible war, Peggy fretted that her daughter would suffer even more heartache should anything happen to Randy.

Unwilling to dwell on such dark thoughts, Peggy looked at the small black-and-white snapshot of the lovely girls who were lodged with her at Beach View Boarding House. It had been taken in the back garden at the beginning of the summer, and despite the restrictions of wartime and the long hours they worked, they looked happy as they gathered around a smiling Cordelia.

Cordelia Finch was well into her late seventies – her age was a closely guarded secret – and she'd been living at Beach View for years. Small and birdlike, with a propensity to twitter, she was aptly named, and had become an intrinsic part of Peggy's family. All the girls adored her and were very patient with her when she tangled her knitting or switched off her hearing aid, which could lead to some very odd conversations.

Peggy looked at them all and smiled. They were her chicks, and she adored them. There were Cordelia's great-nieces, Sarah and Jane, who'd escaped from Malaya just before the fall of Singapore; Irish Fran with her wild mop of autumnal curls; and her friend and fellow nurse, Suzy, who was fair and elegant and about to marry Peggy's nephew, Anthony.

Then there was little dark-haired Rita, who'd been Cissy's childhood friend and whose father was away with the army. She'd lost her mother while still very young, and had come to live at Beach View after the slum housing behind the station had been smashed to smithereens by fire bombs and she'd been made homeless. Rita was a tomboy who liked nothing better than to race about on her motorbike, but when the photo-

14

graph had been taken, she was wearing a pretty dress instead of the usual WWI flying helmet and fleece-lined leather jacket, boots and weather-proof trousers.

Rita too had found love amongst the ranks of the airmen up at Cliffe, and she shared the same fears as Cissy every time they heard the squadrons leave the runway. Matthew Champion was a Spitfire pilot and also under the command of Anne's husband Martin, and, to Peggy's mind, was far too young to be doing such a dangerous job. Yet despite his youth, he was a dedicated and skilful pilot, and Martin had nothing but praise for him.

Peggy snapped out of her thoughts and let her gaze alight on Kitty Pargeter, who stood on the edge of the happy group. She'd come to Beach View after she'd lost her leg in a plane crash, and had left this house a bride shortly before Jim had come home on embarkation leave last month. She was married now to Roger Makepeace, who was her pilot brother's wingman, also at Cliffe, and had returned to the ATA, where she was still delivering aircraft all over the country. There had been a letter from her only the other day, saying how happy she was despite the fact she and Roger rarely managed to get time off to be together.

Peggy made the pot of tea and then sat looking at each of the photographs, remembering all the other girls who'd come to her for shelter. She still heard from most of them, but it had been a while since she'd heard from Danuta, the Polish girl who'd come to Beach View looking for her brother. He'd been killed whilst on a raid over Germany, and Danuta had stayed on for a while before she left for some mysterious posting in London. There had only been a few letters from her, but in the past months there had been nothing, and Peggy was beginning to worry that something might have happened to her.

Peggy's musing was disturbed by the sound of her father-in-law's snoring, which was accompanied by the deep snuffles and snorts of his large, shaggy lurcher, Harvey. Ron shared his basement bedroom with Harvey and two ferrets, and Peggy had long since given up trying to keep it clean and tidy. The ferrets, Flora and Dora, were housed in a large wooden cage, but Harvey was no doubt stretched out beside Ron, shedding dog hairs, slobber and muck all over the bedding.

The pair of them frequently tried her patience, for they were scallywags and always up to some mischief or another. But their heroic rescue of that mother and her baby from the bombed-out boarding house the previous weekend made up for it all, and like everyone else at Beach View – and indeed in Cliffehaven – Peggy was very proud of them.

She stirred a few grains of precious sugar into her tea as she sat at the kitchen table and then reached for the scrapbook she'd been putting together for when Jim came home. There was so little she could write in the cramped space of the airgraph, and she'd decided to start the scrapbook so that Jim could have some idea of what had been happening during his absence. Turning the pages, she came to the cuttings she'd taken from the newspapers.

The headline in the local *Recorder* was large and glaring: 'HERO AND HIS DOG RESCUE

16

WOMAN AND BABY FROM INFERNO', and the article went on to describe the destruction of the Grand Hotel and the two boarding houses during an enemy raid where at least ten people had lost their lives. The reporter urged the public to support the newspaper's call for Ron and Harvey to be awarded some kind of recognition for their bravery – and in the following issues there had been a deluge of letters in favour of this idea.

The story had even reached the national press, and the clamour to reward Ron and his dog had grown. Ron had found the whole thing extremely embarrassing, and he'd hidden away from all the fuss on the allotment with his friend Stan, or out in his garden shed, hoping it would all soon die down and he could get on with his usually quiet life.

But it was still going on, and Ron was getting grumpier by the day, constantly muttering that it was a lot of fuss about nothing, and that he'd only done what any other man would do in the circumstances. For all his blarney and swagger, Ron was actually a very modest man, and as Peggy regarded the terrible picture of him and Harvey she couldn't help but smile, for as awful as it was, it had actually caught the very essence of both of them.

Ron was dressed in his disreputable corduroy trousers which were held up with garden twine, a sweater that had more holes in it than a sieve, filthy wellingtons and his long poacher's coat. He was glaring at the camera from beneath the bill of his stained cap, and no doubt about to tear the reporter off a strip for daring to take his picture.

Harvey's brindled, shaggy coat looked as if he'd been rolling in something, despite the fact she'd actually hosed him down earlier that day, and his paws were bandaged to protect the cuts that he'd sustained during the rescue. But his ears were pricked, there was undoubted intelligence in his eyes and he seemed to be grinning at the camera. Harvey was definitely not shy, and, unlike his master, thoroughly enjoyed it when people made a fuss of him.

Peggy felt a pang of frustration that was heavily laced with affection. The pair of them looked disgraceful, and hardly a good advertisement for her housekeeping skills – but then they had never conformed to any rules, and were now far too set in their rumbustious ways to change.

She flicked through the next few pages which held newspaper photographs of Cliffehaven's Spitfire, and an article about Rita's sterling efforts at fund-raising for it, as well as a piece about the new WVS mobile refreshment truck that had been donated so generously by the Queen. She set the scrapbook aside and drank her tea. It was rather nice to have the house to herself for a change and to sit still before the usual chaos of the day began. But it was now two in the morning, and if she didn't get any sleep, she'd be fit for nothing by tonight when she would have to go with Mary to the Anchor.

The girl was playing the piano there tonight, and although she didn't have an inkling that Tommy Findlay was the Cyril Fielding she'd been searching for, and therefore her father, she'd had a most unfortunate confrontation with him when he'd tried to pick her up one night. Not surprisingly, she was very wary of him – and as he was Rosie Braithwaite's younger brother, and now living at the Anchor during his term of bail, it was all horribly awkward.

Peggy knew she wouldn't sleep yet, so she lit a cigarette and continued to sip her tea as her thoughts raced. Cliffehaven before the war had been quite a small town, the community close-knit, with a fair share of people who couldn't mind their own business. It hadn't changed that much, despite the fact the town was now inundated with newcomers who worked at the many factories that had sprung up since the war had begun – which was why it had been so important to keep Mary's secret hidden. There were still some who had very long memories, and even if they didn't know the full story their imaginations had filled in the gaps, and it was surprising how close to the truth a few of them had come.

Rosie Braithwaite had taken over the Anchor almost twenty years ago, and although she'd had to struggle against prejudice and suspicion – and various men who'd tried their luck – she'd made a great success of it. Ron had fallen for her, and after several years of trying, had finally managed to persuade her that although he might be a scruffy old Irishman, he was the right man for her.

Rosie's younger brother was quite a different kettle of fish, for Tommy was like a bad penny that kept turning up to cause trouble. He'd been involved in various fraudulent scams over the years, had spent at least three terms in prison, and regarded women as a soft target for his questionable charms. He was an all-round rotter.

Tommy had just been released from his latest spell in prison, and because he suffered from mild asthma had managed to evade being sent straight into the army as other prisoners were. He was out on probation, the terms of which meant he had to have a permanent address and must report for warden and fire-watch duties each day. His ex-wife and two children would have nothing to do with him, so he'd played on Rosie's rather misguided sense of family loyalty and was now ensconced at the Anchor for at least six months.

Peggy knew that Ron had already been to the Anchor to warn Tommy to keep his hands to himself and not bother any of the girls who came into the pub – and had even told Rosie about how her brother had tried to pick Mary up the night he'd arrived back in Cliffehaven from prison. According to Ron, Rosie had been furious, and had told her brother straight that if he didn't behave, he'd be out on his ear. Knowing Tommy's preference for a comfortable, easy life, Peggy suspected he would toe the line. Even so, Mary needed her support tonight, and she mustn't let her down.

Stubbing out her cigarette, she turned off the light and went back to her bedroom. Mary had stayed overnight because she was billeted with Peggy's sister, Doris, who lived on the far side of town and it wouldn't have been wise to let her walk home alone in the dark. Cliffehaven was usually a quiet little town, but since the arrival of the allied troops – and Tommy Findlay – it could be a little daunting late at night for anyone as nervous and young as Mary.

She glanced at the bedside clock and realised everyone would be getting up in less than four hours to have breakfast and go to work. She had done enough thinking and her poor head was aching with it, so she climbed back into the empty, tousled bed and pulled the covers up over her shoulders.

It still felt strange not to have Jim's long, strong body curled around her, and she missed him most in these lonely hours. Yet her weariness finally overcame any such sadness and within seconds she was fast asleep.

Mary woke and turned over in the narrow, single bed, wondering for a moment where she was. Then she remembered she was at Beach View, and that she had a longer walk to the Kodak factory from here than she had from her billet in Havelock Road. She rolled onto her back and stretched, listening to the sounds of the waking house.

The light patter of footsteps running down the stairs was probably Jane, who began work at the dairy very early so she could groom and feed the Shires before starting her milk round. Mary liked Jane, for she was a sweet, rather innocent girl, who worked hard not only at the dairy, but as a part-time bookkeeper at the uniform factory. She was very close to her older sister, Sarah, who'd joined the Women's Timber Corps and spent her days in the Corps office on the Cliffe estate – but that was hardly surprising, as they were far from their home in Malaya, their mother was living in Australia with their baby brother, and there was still no news of their father or Sarah's fiancé, Philip, after the devastating fall of Singapore to the Japanese.

Mary didn't envy their situation at all and couldn't imagine how they managed to cope with the dreadful uncertainties. But she did envy their living here at Beach View, and in a way she regretted turning down Peggy's offer of a permanent room. Peggy reminded her of Barbara Boniface, who'd taken her in after the rectory and church had taken a direct hit during a bombing raid and both her parents had been killed. Both women were motherly and warm and always ready to listen and give sensible advice, and Mary counted herself very blessed to have had such sterling support during her darkest hours.

The girls were terrific company too, and dear little Cordelia Finch was like the grandmother she'd never had. And yet her billet with Peggy's sister Doris was very comfortable and she'd become friends with Ivy, the Cockney girl with whom she shared a room – and although she and Ivy had come from very different backgrounds, they'd got on immediately. Probably because Doris was so bossy and snobbish that they had a common battle to fight and shared the same sense of humour. There had been a lot of giggling over the past week, and her spirits had been lightened considerably.

Mary yawned and slowly sat up. She ran her fingers through her long dark hair and thought how strange it was that she'd become so settled in Cliffehaven after such a short time. She'd left her village in Sussex only a week ago, but so much had happened in those few days that it felt as if she'd been here for much longer.

She drew back the blackout curtains and looked down through the taping on the window into the garden at the rear of Beach View. Long and narrow, it had been turned into a vegetable patch, and even the turf on top of the gloomy Anderson shelter was sprouting with winter seedlings. A washing line hung forlornly across the path that led to the gate and flint wall, and from up here she could see straight across the twitten into the back gardens and windows of the terraced houses opposite. It was a far cry from the rambling grounds and woods that had surrounded the rather isolated rectory.

The memory of what had happened on the night of her eighteenth birthday chilled her and she pulled on her dressing gown. Her parents' deaths had left her not only bereft of home and family, but of everything she had ever believed about herself. The discovery of her father's diaries and the document hidden within them had revealed that she wasn't Gideon and Emmaline's daughter at all, but the illegitimate and unwanted product of a seedy affair between the married Cyril Fielding, and some girl he'd met during his rounds as a travelling salesman.

The gentle Reverend Gideon Jones had taken her in and loved and cared for her, but Emmaline's puzzling coldness towards her had finally been explained, and Mary could understand now how difficult it must have been for a proud, self-centred woman to take on the responsibility of such a child. Yet, despite the fact there had been little affection between them, there was still a part of Mary which mourned the fact they could never talk again or make peace with one another – and it was this sense of things being unfinished between them that was the hardest to bear.

It had been that document and those diary entries that had brought Mary to Cliffehaven in search of answers, and although she'd suspected there could only be disappointment ahead, she hadn't been prepared for how swiftly her search for Cyril Fielding was concluded – or how devastating the truth had been.

Dear Peggy, she'd done her best to soften the blow, but there was no escaping the fact that her real father, Cyril, was a cheap crook, a liar and a thief who'd spent time in prison and didn't think twice about living off the different women who'd fallen for his dubious charms. As for her mother, there was no news at all, and as she'd abandoned Mary within days of her birth and effectively disappeared, Mary could only conclude that she must have been very young and not willing to tie herself down to motherhood – or Cyril.

Mary shivered and drew the belt of her dressing gown more tightly round her narrow waist. She'd had a lucky escape, for although Emmaline had found it impossible to be a loving mother, she and Gideon had given her a home, an education and a firm basis for an honest, fulfilling life. How different it might have been for her if Cyril had not done that one decent thing in his disreputable career.

Her hand strayed to the long gold chain that hung from her neck, and she carefully drew the gold locket out and nestled it in the palm of her hand. Barbara's son, Jack Boniface, had given it to her on her birthday just before he'd left on the troop train, and she'd treasure it always. His letters of love and support had bolstered her spirits during those dark days of anguished loss, and his parents, Barbara and Joseph, had gladly taken her in and given her the affection and warmth she'd needed so badly. They were her family now, and when Jack returned from the war, they would marry and move into one of the farm cottages so that Jack could begin to take over from his father.

She sighed and tucked the locket away. There seemed to be no end to this terrible war, and it could be months, if not years, before they saw their dreams realised. All she could do now was continue with her job of sorting through the airgraphs at the Kodak factory save as much money as she could, and make the best of things until it was time to take up her place at the teaching college in Lewes.

She had to admit that she was quietly revelling in her independence after a lifetime of being carefully guarded against the world beyond the rectory walls – and although Gideon and Emmaline would definitely have disapproved of her playing the piano in a public house, she saw no harm in it, and thoroughly enjoyed entertaining the servicemen and women who could forget their responsibilities for a few hours and sing their hearts out.

She tensed at the thought of having to face that horrid Tommy Findlay this evening. He'd tried to pick her up as she'd been walking from the factory in the gloom of a wintry afternoon, and the episode had given her quite a scare – to the point where she'd actually hidden from him down an alleyway when she'd seen him again last night talking to that woman, Eileen. But Peggy had assured her he'd been warned by Ron and Rosie to be on his best behaviour and never to approach her again, so she had to believe she was safe from any further incidents.

She squared her shoulders, opened the door and headed to the bathroom. She was eighteen, earning her own living and, come next September, would be starting her teacher training course. It was time she toughened up and became more like her new friend Ivy, who was more than capable of dealing with unwelcome advances and the rigours of life. Ivy might have come from Hackney and been exposed to such things from very early on, but there were lessons to be learned from her, and Mary knew instinctively that it would be wise to follow her example if she was to survive this new and rather exciting life.

Mary finished preparing for the day and carried her overnight bag down the stairs. Leaving it in the hall with her overcoat and gas-mask box, she went into the kitchen to discover that she was the last one down.

Suzy and Fran were in their nurses' uniforms and preparing to leave for Cliffehaven General as Sarah reached for her heavy overcoat to wear over the green sweater and khaki jodhpurs of the Women's Timber Corps. Ron was surreptitiously feeding Harvey bits of toast, while Rita drank the last of her tea and dragged on the Fire Service issue coat over her black uniform jacket and trousers.

Mary smiled at sweet little Daisy, who was gurgling with laughter and clapping her hands as Harvey snaffled bits of her breakfast from her high-chair tray, whilst Peggy tried to stop him from doing it at the same time as coaxing Daisy to eat her eggy soldiers. Cordelia was taking no notice of anyone as she read the newspaper, and Mary wondered if she'd switched off her hearing aid – which Peggy had told her was a common occurrence.

'Help yourself to porridge, dear,' said Peggy, who looked a bit tired this morning. 'There's tea in the pot and plenty of bread for toast.'

'We'll all see you tonight then,' said Fran as the girls headed for the concrete steps that led down to the basement and back door. 'To be sure, there's nothing I like more than a good sing-song. It reminds me of the bars at home, where there was always good craic, and I do wish I hadn't left me fiddle behind in Ireland.'

'You can play the fiddle?' asked Peggy as everyone stared at Fran in astonishment.

'Ach, we all play one instrument or another where I come from,' she replied dismissively. 'Me da was a terrific fiddle player, and me mam wasn't at all bad on the penny whistle. They used to take me and me brothers and sisters to the local bar every Saturday night, and there was always a farthing or two for us if we performed well.' She gave them all a cheerful wave and hurried off down the steps to be swiftly followed by the others.

'Did you know about that?' Peggy asked Ron.

'Aye, she did mention it a long while ago, but I'd forgotten about it until now. But to be sure,

27

she's right about everyone learning to play something, even if it's only the spoons.' He puffed out his chest. 'I used to be a dab hand at them in my younger days,' he added proudly.

'I'd have thought you'd have preferred blowing your own trumpet,' said Peggy with a teasing light in her eyes. 'To be sure, you have a great talent for it.'

'Ach, Peggy girl, it's too early in the morning for that sort of talk. I'll take meself and Harvey off for our walk, and hope you'll be kinder to an old injured soldier by the time we get back.' He stomped off down the steps with Harvey at his heels.

'Don't take any notice of Ron,' said Peggy as she finished feeding Daisy and cleaned her face with her bib. 'He has a good sense of humour and I think he rather enjoys all the ribbing he gets. As for the wounded soldier malarkey, he uses that as an excuse to avoid any jobs I might have for him to do about the house.'

Mary smiled and ate her delicious porridge. She liked Ron, even though he had rather alarming eyebrows and looked as if he slept in clothes that had never been washed, and it was lovely to sit in this homely kitchen, and to share in the warmth and affection of the people who lived here.

'It's a shame Fran can't get her hands on a violin,' she said as she put a thin smear of the horrid fishy margarine across the wheatmeal toast. 'Does anyone else in the house play an instrument? Only it would make for a very special evening at the Anchor if we could persuade people to come and join in.'

'That's a marvellous idea,' said Peggy. 'I can't

think why Rosie hasn't thought of it before. She's usually very sharp when it comes to getting more customers in.' Her bright smile faded. 'But I doubt Rita or the others have such a talent – they didn't mention it when Fran told us about her fiddle.'

She put Daisy on the floor so she could crawl about and pull herself up on the furniture. 'Mind you, there's no guarantee that Fran can play the fiddle with any expertise, and even if we found one for her, it could end up sounding like tom-cats having a set-to.'

Mary laughed. 'You may well be right. But, you never know, she might surprise us.'

Peggy sat down and poured herself a cup of tea. Then she suddenly snapped her fingers. 'I've just remembered where there is one,' she said excitedly. 'Doris went through a phase of hoping that Anthony might prove to be musical, and she bought a violin, a recorder and then the piano – all to no avail, of course. Anthony is tone deaf and couldn't string a tune together if his life depended on it.'

She puffed furiously on her cigarette as the idea took hold. 'My sister's a hoarder, never throws anything out. I bet she's stuffed it away somewhere to gather dust along with all her other brief flights of fancy.'

Mary finished the toast and returned Peggy's bright smile. 'I'll ask her about it tonight. If she's in. I've never known a woman to be so busy with committee meetings.'

'Bless you, dear, they aren't all such things. She goes to see her husband in his flat above the Home and Colonial Store he manages. She and Ted have been separated for a few months after he had an affair with "the floozy", but she's agreed to forgive him enough to go round there occasionally for a game of whist and a glass of sherry.'

Peggy tapped ash into a saucer. 'I think that now Anthony has virtually moved out again, she's getting a bit lonely. My betting is that it won't be long before she lets Ted return home to Havelock Road. After all, she has to keep up appearances, what with the wedding getting so near, and Suzy's parents being so well connected.'

Mary raised an eyebrow at this as she sipped the last of her tea.

'Oh yes,' said Peggy as she settled back in her chair for a good gossip. 'Suzy's grandfather went to prep school with Winston Churchill, you know, and Churchill was a frequent visitor to their home before the war. Her father is something very important in the Foreign Office and her mother is a society hostess and very well connected.'

She shot Mary a rather naughty grin. 'Doris has a great deal to live up to, and is busting a gut to put on a grand show at this wedding.'

'Oh dear, it doesn't bode well for any of them, does it?' said Mary.

Peggy shook her head. 'If Ted has any sense at all he'll keep well out of it until all the fuss is over. She's been a complete nightmare to poor Suzy and Anthony, taking over the arrangements, inviting people they don't want – making all sorts of plans that are really none of her business.' She stubbed out her cigarette and went to rescue Daisy, who was chewing on a lump of anthracite she'd plucked from the coal scuttle.

'Did Suzy tell you she and Anthony asked me last night if I'd play the church organ for their ceremony? I agreed, of course, but I'll have to go and ask the vicar's permission to practise. Our church organ back in Sussex was out of action for over two years, so I'm a bit rusty.'

'That would be wonderful,' sighed Peggy. 'The organist is a lovely old dear, but she gets flustered too easily and keeps forgetting to put on her reading glasses so she can see the music. She fumbles about, pulls out all the wrong stops and has difficulty reaching those pedal things with her feet, because she's so short. It can be terribly hard to follow anything she's trying to play.'

'In that case I'll have to go and see her as well as the vicar,' said Mary as she glanced at the clock. 'I wouldn't like to upset her.' She got up from the table. 'I'm sorry, Peggy, but I'd better get a move on, or I'll be late for my shift.'

She quickly washed her crockery and left it on the wooden drainer as Peggy cleaned Daisy's face again, removed the coal scuttle out of her reach and put her back on the floor. Cordelia was still occupied with the newspaper and seemed oblivious to anything going on around her.

'How are the rehearsals going for Doris's charity concert on New Year's Day?' asked Peggy.

'Slowly but surely,' replied Mary. 'It's all a bit haphazard because the orchestra is made up of civilians as well as servicemen, and not everyone can get the time off. But it's coming along nicely considering we can only rehearse once a week, and it feels marvellous to be playing with a proper orchestra.'

Peggy beamed. 'You're very brave,' she said. 'I wouldn't have the nerve to do anything like that.'

Mary smiled back. 'It's far less stressful to be a part of an orchestra than sitting behind the piano on my own, believe me.' She glanced at the clock again. 'I'm sorry, Peggy, but I really *do* have to go.'

Fetching her coat, gas mask and overnight bag from the hall, Mary returned to the kitchen and gave Peggy a big hug. 'Thank you for everything,' she said. 'I do appreciate how difficult you must have found it to tell me such things last night, and I'm very grateful.'

Peggy pushed her dark curls away from her face. 'I'm glad you feel like that, Mary. It can't have been easy for you either. But as long as you're able to put it all behind you and get on with your new life here in Cliffehaven, then I'm happy.'

'I'll see you tonight then. Seven o'clock outside the Anchor.'

'We'll be there, dear, don't you fret. Now run along and have a good day.'

Mary waved goodbye to Cordelia, who'd finally looked up from her newspaper, and then ran down the steps and out into the garden.

It was a bright, brisk morning, with the sun shining from a clear sky, and the wind holding the saltiness of the sea. White gulls swooped and hovered above the rooftops, their wings gilded by the sunlight as their mournful, raucous cries heralded a new day.

Mary took a deep breath and began to walk down the twitten towards the street that led up the hill, and eventually to the factory estate. She was freed from her search into the past and although she still deeply mourned her father Gideon's passing, she could now forget about Cyril Fielding and the feckless girl who'd given birth to her, and look forward to this new life in Cliffehaven.

Chapter Two

Rosie Braithwaite pushed back her platinum hair and heaved a sigh of exasperation. She'd just collected up the dirty glasses, scattered newspapers and a full ashtray from her sitting room and carried it all into the tiny kitchen. On seeing the mess there, she immediately stormed into her brother's bedroom without knocking.

'I will *not* have you turning my home into a pigsty,' she snapped.

Tommy was lounging in bed having a cigarette and quickly pulled up the bedclothes over his bare chest. 'I'd appreciate it if you'd knock before you came crashing in here,' he protested.

'And I'd appreciate it if you showed some respect for me and my home,' she retorted, her horrified gaze taking in the clothes flung on the floor, the dirty cups and plates, discarded magazines and overflowing ashtray.

'Aw, come on, Sis,' he drawled, flashing her one of his most charming smiles as he ran his fingers through his brutally short hair. 'I've been out with the ARP all night, and what with having to report to the police station every day and do a shift with the Civil Defence Service, I can't be expected to turn my hand to housework as well.'

Rosie could no longer be moved by that smile, for she'd long since learned it was utterly false. She folded her arms and looked at him with little affection. Her younger brother had been the bane of her life ever since he'd discovered he had a talent for charming people out of their money. Now, because of her stupid sense of family loyalty, she was stuck with him until his term of probation was over. It was going to be a long six months.

'Get up and put on some clothes,' she said crossly. 'Then clean this mess and sort out my kitchen – you've got time before you have to report in to the police.'

The charming smile faded and the indolence disappeared as he sat up. 'I don't appreciate being ordered about as if I was a kid,' he retorted. 'I had enough of that in prison.'

'Then start behaving like a grown-up. For goodness' sake, Tommy, you're forty-five, and your bad behaviour has led you to my door, yet again. Pull yourself together and at least try to make an effort.'

'It's not easy,' he replied, stubbing his cigarette out in the ashtray. 'People have long memories, so how am I supposed to be able to start again with a clean sheet?'

'There are no clean sheets as far as you're concerned,' she said wearily. 'And if people have long memories, then I'm afraid you're just going to have to put up with it and show them you really mean to mend your ways.'

'That's all very well,' he grumbled, reaching for his pyjama jacket. 'But someone's been asking questions about me, and I don't like it.'

Rosie frowned. She was afraid this would happen, for Tommy's past was littered with wrongdoing and she suspected there were several people who would have liked to get their revenge on him. 'What sort of questions?' she asked.

He suddenly looked shifty and gave a nonchalant shrug. 'Just asking about me.'

'Well, you only have yourself to blame,' she said with a sigh. 'Though why anyone should be asking after you when most people in the town know you're living here is a little odd. If they have something to say to you, then why not just come out and say it?'

He shrugged again and his gaze slid away from her

She recognised the evasion and knew he was hiding something. 'I don't want any trouble, Tommy,' she warned. 'This is a respectable pub and it's taken me years to turn it into a good business. If you have people after you, then you can settle any disputes outside these four walls. Is that understood?'

He nodded, his expression sour.

'And what were you doing with Eileen Harris last night?' She saw he was about to deny it and hurried on. 'I saw you meeting her outside and going off with her – and I will *not* have you bringing her in here.'

'Which is why we met in the street,' he said sulkily. 'We had things to discuss, that's all.'

Rosie took a deep breath. 'Just keep her away from me,' she said coldly. 'Now get dressed and sort out your mess.' Not waiting for a reply, she left the room and slammed the door behind her, which made the poor brindled pup, Monty, cringe.

Deciding she couldn't stand being indoors any longer, she soothed the pup and clipped the lead to his collar, then fetched her coat and flat shoes and went downstairs. Once she'd reached the pavement, she took a deep breath of the crisp morning air and felt instantly better.

Monty pulled on the lead so he could sniff at everything before he watered it, so it was a while before Rosie reached the end of the road and tried to head towards the seafront.

Monty had other ideas and began to pull in the opposite direction. His sire, Harvey, lived up the hill with Ron at Beach View, and that's where he wanted to go.

'Come on, Monty, we're not visiting him today. We're going down to the prom so you can chase the gulls.' She stroked his brindled head before rather forcefully dragging him down the hill. He was only a few months old but already large and ungainly, and could pull ferociously hard on the lead, so when he decided he rather liked the idea of the seafront and took off at a gallop, she almost had to run to keep up with him.

The promenade had been closed off from the mined beach by huge coils of barbed wire and several gun emplacements, and now it was deserted. Rosie let Monty off the lead and watched as he raced back and forth, barking at the seagulls. He was a sweet dog, but a ruddy nuisance at times – just like Harvey – and yet he'd become an intrinsic part of her rather lonely life these past few months, and now she couldn't imagine not having him.

A bit like Ron, really, she thought with an affectionate smile. Darling, scruffy, naughty Ron – with his twinkling Irish eyes and stout heart; how she adored him. And how very much she would have liked to start a new life with him.

She ran her fingers through her platinum hair and lifted her face to the weak sun as she fought the regrets. Her poor sick husband would never leave the asylum, and all the while he was alive, the law forbade her to divorce him – so she was stuck in this half-life of being alone and yet not free to follow her dreams.

Her conscience bothered her frequently, for although she and Ron had never slept together, she was guilty of being unfaithful to her husband, for she'd given her heart to Ron. But the real guilt lay in the knowledge that she couldn't find the longed-for happiness with him until her husband died – and yet to wish him gone was a terrible sin. She gave a wry smile and began to slowly follow Monty down the promenade. Once a Catholic, always a Catholic, and there were none so adept at feeling guilty about everything.

She determinedly pushed these thoughts aside, for she'd survived the situation for two decades and would continue to do so until things were resolved one way or the other. Her husband could live for many more years and Ron could get tired of waiting – or he could die and Ron might change his mind about marriage. After all, he'd long been a widower, was very set in his ways, and would find it extremely difficult to settle down to a new way of life with her.

Their relationship, as it was, gave them both a deep, loving friendship with the added spice of secrecy and stolen kisses in their moments alone. It could change radically if they lived together, for she liked order, and Ron was chaotic at the best of times.

Rosie pulled up her coat collar against the wind, and after a brief, sorrowful glance at the piles of rubble that had once been the Grand Hotel and two boarding houses, she continued her walk.

It was good to be free of her brother's company and the rigours of running a busy pub for a little while. Yet, at fifty-two, the late nights were beginwing to take their toll, and although she still loved the camaraderie of a full bar and the ring of her till as the money poured in, she knew that she'd come to rely increasingly on darling Ron's continuous and unstinting support.

Not that she was ready to sell up and retire – the thought of living in a small flat or bungalow with nothing to do all day was deeply depressing. But no one realised how much it took to run a pub – especially in wartime – for there was far more to it than standing behind a bar and chatting to the punters while you pulled pints.

There were licences to fill in, orders to make, stock checks and pipe-cleaning to be done so the barrels of beer didn't spoil. There were unexpected visits from the inspectors and police to check she was keeping a respectable house and wasn't serving under-aged drinkers or trying to sell black-market booze. Restrictions on everything meant that supplies of beer and spirits were getting lower by the month, and the busy lunch-time sessions and the much longer evening ones took time to clear up once the door was shut behind the last customer.

It was a matter of pride to plaster on a smile, put on her make-up, tight skirt and frilly blouse, and to slip on her high heels, for she saw her role as landlady much like the leading part in a theatre production, and the clothes and shoes were her props. Yet, at the end of the night, her feet were aching, her clothes stank of cigarette smoke and spilled beer – and the empty bed upstairs was not at all inviting.

She watched as Monty began to chase a seagull, and then realised in horror that he wasn't looking where he was going. 'Monty, stop! Stop now!' she shouted as she began to run towards him.

Monty chose not to hear her, and was so intent upon catching the gull that as it flew above the coiled barbed wire, he took a great leap after it. With a howl of pain he was instantly snared.

'Monty, oh, God, Monty,' panted Rosie as she reached him. 'Keep still or you'll hurt yourself even more.'

Monty howled piteously and squirmed even harder.

Careless of the damage the sharp barbs would do to her hands, Rosie tried to ease back the wire and grab his collar so his flailing paws couldn't reach the mined shingle. 'Keep still,' she begged as he continued to whine and yelp and wriggle.

But his long legs were caught, the barbs sticking more firmly into him every time he struggled. Rosie was almost in tears.

'Let me help.'

Rosie shot a glance at the woman and froze. It was Eileen Harris. 'I can manage,' she said stiffly.

'No, you can't, and your poor dog's suffering,' she replied as she held back several coils of wire with her gloved hands.

Rosie didn't stop to think. She grabbed the other side of the wire and together she and Eileen managed to extricate Monty. Clipping on his lead, Rosie ran her torn and bloody hands over him. There were tears and scratches and he'd lost several clumps of hair, but he was pulling on the lead, ready to chase another gull. 'I think I'm worse off than he is,' she said ruefully, her voice unsteady with relief as she looked at her damaged hands.

'You'd better get them seen to before they get infected,' said Eileen, patting Monty.

'Thanks for your help,' said Rosie awkwardly as she found a clean handkerchief to dab at the wounds. 'I couldn't have got him out on my own.'

Eileen nodded, her expression giving nothing away. 'It wasn't all my fault, you know,' she said quietly into the tense silence that had fallen between them.

Rosie felt the prickle of dislike raise the hairs on her neck. 'Why should I believe you?' Her voice was flat with loathing, for this woman had lied to her and betrayed her in the worst way possible.

'Because it's true,' Eileen replied. She reached out her gloved hand and quickly withdrew it again as Rosie flinched from it. 'If you'd only let me explain,' she began.

'I've heard enough of your lies to last me a lifetime,' snapped Rosie. 'Thank you for helping me with Monty – but don't think that's earned you even one more second of my time.'

Ignoring the pain in her hands, she tugged on the lead and marched away from Eileen, furious that she'd had to rely on the woman for anything after all the terrible hurt she'd caused in the past.

Mary had spent the day sorting through the airgraphs to categorise them into separate piles according to the service or theatre of war of the recipients. It was tedious work, made a little less so by the radio programmes being piped into the vast warehouse, the company of Jenny and the other girls who worked beside her, and the thought of all the men who would receive these letters from their loved ones. One day, she too would be sending and receiving such letters, for even if Jack didn't pass his test for the commandos, he would still be sent abroad. The thought didn't thrill her, for she dreaded the moment they would have to part – and the doubtlessly long periods of time they would be separated until this war was over.

She emerged from the Kodak factory at five, to find Ivy waiting for her, and they walked past the guard at the gate of the enormous factory estate, and down the hill in the darkness.

'There's that woman again,' Ivy muttered.

Mary glanced across the road to the shadowy figure they'd seen waiting there the past two evenings. 'I wonder who she's waiting for,' she replied without much interest. 'She must get very cold standing about like that.'

Ivy shrugged and dismissed any further discussion on the subject. 'I'm really looking forward to tonight,' she said, her elfin face lit with excitement. 'All me mates are coming, so it should be a good turnout.'

Mary's feelings about the evening ahead were mixed, for although she was looking forward to being an intrinsic part of a happy evening, she definitely wasn't keen on the idea of bumping into Tommy Findlay.

She shook off the doubts and smiled at her friend. 'The more the merrier,' she said lightly. 'Peggy and everyone from Beach View are coming too, and there might even be a bit of added entertainment tonight.'

She went on to tell Ivy about Fran and her fiddle.

'Cor, that would be good,' Ivy exclaimed. 'We 'ad ever such good nights at the Dog and Duck back in 'Ackney. The landlady were a dab 'and at the Joanna, and there was more'n a few locals what could get a good tune out of penny whistles and a squeeze box.'

'Let's just hope Doris kept the violin and that Fran can actually play it, otherwise you'll just have to put up with me,' Mary said.

They carried on walking and Ivy chattered away about what they'd wear, who they might meet and which songs were the most popular. As they crossed the humpbacked bridge, they waved to the stationmaster, Stan, who was standing outside his Nissen hut ticket office having a gossip with one of his elderly pals, and then they hurried on down the hill to Havelock Road.

'Take off that filthy footwear immediately,' said

Doris as they came through the front door. 'I will not have you traipsing dirt through my house.'

Duly chastened, they shed shoes and boots and hung their coats on the rack in the hall. 'I was wondering, Mrs Williams,' said Mary, 'if you still happen to have your violin?'

Doris frowned and looked down her nose. 'How do you know about that?' she asked suspiciously.

'Your sister remembered you'd bought one several years ago – and I wondered if you'd be kind enough to lend it to me,' replied Mary carefully.

Doris's eyes lit up with almost greedy excitement. 'You can play the violin? But why didn't you say? I could have arranged for you to–'

'No, no,' interrupted Mary hastily. 'It's not for me, but for a friend. I couldn't play a violin to save my life.'

Doris thought about this and then sniffed. 'And who is this friend?'

Warned by Peggy that Doris didn't like Fran, Mary knew she would have to fib. 'It's a girl I met the other night,' she hedged. 'She's from Dublin, and when she heard I was playing at the Anchor, she said that if only she had her fiddle she'd have loved to accompany me.' Well, it was a sort of truth.

'And is this girl a respectable sort?'

'Yes, very,' said Mary firmly.

'My violin is not a fiddle,' Doris said snootily. 'It is of very good quality and I bought it in London when my Anthony was a boy.'

'I'm sure it is,' said Mary rather breathlessly. 'And I promise to take very good care of it.'

Doris seemed satisfied with this. 'I have no intention of getting covered in dust and spiders' webs, so if you want it, then you'll have to go into the attic to find it.' She pointed to a hatch in the ceiling above the upstairs landing. 'But you will come directly down without poking and prying into my private things – and if there is even a single scratch on that violin after today, I shall be seeking reparation,' she warned.

'Thank you so much, Mrs Williams, that's incredibly generous of you.'

Mary realised she was laying it on a bit thick, so she stopped babbling and ran up the stairs. She detached the wooden ladder from the hooks fastened to the wall, drew it out to its full length and made sure it was firmly balanced before she climbed up to push at the hatch and slide it to one side.

'Hold on tight to the ladder, Ivy,' she called down as it wobbled a bit.

She balanced on the top rung and hauled herself up. There was a cord dangling to her right, and when she pulled it, the attic was flooded in light. It was a large space beneath the roof, and there seemed to be few cobwebs although everything was covered in a thin layer of dust.

Mary looked round at the neatly stacked boxes and suitcases, and saw several large, ornately framed paintings, a child's rocking horse, some broken chairs, hat boxes, a dressmaker's dummy and two trunks. Sitting on top of one of the trunks were three cases – one for a violin, one for a trumpet and one for a flute. Poor old Doris had certainly done her best to encourage her tone-deaf son into being a musician.

'What's she got hidden up 'ere?' asked Ivy in a stage whisper as she emerged through the hatchway.

'Nothing much,' said Mary, 'but I have found the violin and more besides.' She walked back to the hatch. 'We'd better get back down, she's bound to be watching and listening, and actually there's nothing up here of any interest,' she said softly.

'Blimey, you're no fun at all, are yer?' Ivy grumbled as she reluctantly withdrew from the hatchway.

Mary turned off the light and handed Ivy the three cases before replacing the cover over the hatch and descending to the landing. She put the ladder back and they hurried into their bedroom to examine what Mary had found.

'It's a good-quality instrument,' she murmured as she lifted the violin out of the silk-lined leather case. 'And looks as if it has all its strings as well as spares, and the bow is almost brand new.' She grinned at Ivy. 'If Fran really can play this, then we could do some Irish jigs.'

'Yeah, well, don't get too carried away,' said Ivy as she gave the flute and trumpet a cursory examination. 'Singing's one thing, dancing's quite another. There won't be room to swing a cat in that place now word's got out you're playing again tonight.'

Mary settled the lovely violin back in its bed of silk and shut the case before she inspected the flute and trumpet. All three instruments seemed to be in excellent condition, but of course she couldn't really tell until someone played them.

She returned them both to their respective cases, dusted off the leather with her handkerchief, and thought perhaps she should find a little present for Doris by way of thanking her.

Supper was a vegetable stew, which Mary and Ivy ate in the kitchen as Doris had gone out. Mary had wanted to ask her permission to borrow all three instruments, but as she wasn't there, she decided to risk taking them anyway.

They washed their dishes and cleaned the kitchen, then grabbed their coats, gas-mask boxes and instrument cases and headed for the Anchor.

Peggy was waiting for them outside the pub. 'Goodness me,' she said as she saw what they were carrying. 'My sister must have been keen on getting poor Anthony to play something.' Her smile broadened. 'I haven't said anything to Fran, because I didn't want to disappoint her if Doris had sold the violin.' She gave a little shiver of pleasure. 'Oh, my word, we shall have some fun tonight.'

Mary hesitated as Peggy opened the heavily studded oak door. 'Is...? Will...?'

Ivy, who knew all about what had happened with Tommy Findlay, gripped her hand. 'He won't be no bother, gel – not with me about. I got a very sharp knee,' she said darkly.

Peggy smiled at Ivy. 'That won't be at all necessary, Ivy – not tonight, anyway. He's out and not expected back until late.'

A sense of relief flooded through Mary, and she followed Peggy and Ivy into the crowded bar quite happily. She was greeted warmly by everyone as she squeezed past them to get to the table by the inglenook fireplace. Rosie, Cordelia and all five girls were sitting there chatting and they beamed with pleasure as she greeted them.

Rosie gave her a swift hug, mindful of her bandaged hands. She waved away Mary's concern and explained about Monty and the barbed wire. 'It looks worse than it is now I've cleaned them up,' she said dismissively. 'Now, I understand you might have a bit of a surprise for us tonight,' she added excitedly, her glance taking in the instrument cases.

Mary looked across at Fran and held out the violin case. 'You said you liked to play, so I brought this along,' she said, and smiled.

Fran leapt to her feet with an excited squeak and grabbed it. Fumbling to undo the catches, she drew the instrument out and sighed with pleasure. Her green eyes lit up and she tossed back her tumble of russet curls as she rested the violin on her shoulder and began to tune it with expert ease.

Mary and Ivy sat down and watched breathlessly as the notes became clearer, and an expectant hush fell over everyone in the bar.

Fran shot them all a playful smile. 'And to be sure, I'm betting none of you believed I could play, did ye?' Then she drew the bow across the strings and the sweet, haunting melody of 'I'll Take You Home Again, Kathleen' filled the room.

Mary noticed there were tears in many of the boys' eyes, and her clear soprano soared as she joined everyone in the chorus.

'Oh! I will take you back, Kathleen,' she sang along with Ivy and the others. 'To where your heart will feel no pain, and when the fields are

47

fresh and green, I'll take you to your home again!'

There was a stunned silence at the end, and then the place erupted with the clapping of hands and the stamping of feet as they called for more.

'You don't need me at all tonight,' shouted Mary delightedly over the noise.

'Ach, 'twould be a shame if ye didn't join in,' shouted back a flushed and happy Fran. 'For it looks like we have someone to play the trumpet as well as the flute, and if I'm not mistaken that American has a harmonica, Ron's got spoons, and I can see at least two penny whistles. All we need now is a set of drums and we'll be well away.'

Mary looked round at the gathered servicemen and laughed. 'I can see you lot came prepared,' she said.

'Aye, we have that. So let's get going and set this place jumping,' yelled a sandy-haired Irish guardsman.

Mary and Fran grinned at one another and headed for the piano as more people crowded into the pub and Rosie shot off to help her two middle-aged barmaids serve them. The crowd parted like the Red Sea under Moses' command, and those with instruments stood by the piano awaiting instructions.

'We should start with something lively after that,' said Fran. 'How about "Wild Rover"? There's quite a lot of Aussies in here as well as Irish and Americans.'

From the moment she and Mary played the intro the others joined in, and soon the old rafters of the Anchor were ringing with the sound of music and song. Ron played the spoons quite expertly; one of the Americans was beating out a drum rhythm with his hands on a wooden stool; another was playing his harmonica with rather more enthusiasm than skill – and the two boys on the penny whistles were fairly dancing a jig as they played. Considering that none of them had practised together, and the tune wasn't familiar to everyone, they were coping remarkably well.

As they played one tune after another the crowd around them grew, the beer flowed and a young boy pushed his way through to stand by Fran with his banjo. He couldn't have been more than fifteen, and shouldn't really have been in the pub at all – but for once Rosie turned a blind eye, for he could play his banjo superbly, and before long, Mary found she was being led into unfamiliar American folk songs. She stumbled a bit at first, but soon found the refrain and got through them.

A long while later Rosie appeared at her side with a laden tray of drinks for the musicians. 'There's a cup of tea for you on the table,' she said quietly to Mary. 'Go and have a break.'

Mary gratefully went back to Peggy and the others and sat down to drink the very welcome tea. She was hot and perspiring, for the temperature in the room had risen considerably with so many people crowded into it and the fire burning in the hearth.

She looked round expecting to see Fran coming to join them, but there was no sign of her, and poor Rosie and her barmaids were frantically trying to serve the customers who were lining the bar three deep. Ron had given up on the spoons and was lending a hand too, and Ivy had deserted her to go and flirt with a rather dashing American airman.

And then silence fell as the sweetest notes began to fill the room and all eyes went to Fran, who'd been lifted onto a table, the violin nestled beneath her chin, her glorious hair tumbling down her back as she closed her eyes and played 'Danny Boy' with no accompaniment.

There wasn't a dry eye in the house and the previously raucous voices were hushed as they softly sang the melody, for the blood of the Irish ran strongly through many of them, and this song touched a chord deep within them all, for it was a call from their loved ones, and the dream of returning home.

Mary blinked back her own tears and smiled at Peggy, who was busy dabbing her eyes with a handkerchief. 'She's wonderful,' Mary breathed. 'To be able to hold an audience like that is a talent that can never be taught.'

Peggy watched Fran in awe. 'I would never have guessed,' she murmured. 'She looks so at peace and so beautiful – and the way she's playing...' She faltered and blinked away her tears. 'Goodness me, how very silly. I'm getting all emotional.'

So was Mary and just about everyone else in the room. As the song came to an end and the final haunting note drifted into silence there was a long pause, and then everyone was on their feet to applaud and beg for more.

Fran looked over at Mary, raised a finger to signify she would play one more before she took a rest, and then with a nod to the boy beside her and the other musicians, she led them all into a lively Irish jig.

As the admiring crowd clapped their hands and stamped their feet in time, the old walls shook and the brick floor shuddered, making bottles and glasses dance across the tables. 'She'll literally bring the house down in a minute,' shouted Peggy in delight.

'I think it's been standing long enough to weather it,' Mary shouted back.

Cordelia was beside herself with excitement and three glasses of sherry as she gripped Mary's hand. 'What fun it all is,' she twittered. 'My goodness. Is it going to be like this every weekend?'

'Only if Fran and I are off at the same time,' said Mary. She eyed the flushed little face and the empty glass Cordelia had pushed towards her. 'Wouldn't you prefer a cup of tea now?'

'Oh, no, dear. I want another sherry,' she replied firmly as she nudged the glass nearer.

Peggy looked over Mary's shoulder and her happy expression instantly became one of dislike. She reached for Cordelia's glass. 'I'll get it,' she said.

Mary frowned and looked round to see what could possibly have brought such a change to Peggy's happy mood. And then she saw him and went cold.

Tommy Findlay was leaning in the doorway to one side of the bar, his hands in his pockets, his blue eyes trawling the throng of people and settling speculatively on Fran before slowly moving to Ivy and her friends.

A shiver of apprehension ran down Mary's

spine as she saw Peggy approach him. Whatever she said to him made him shrug nonchalantly before he went back to his creepy surveillance.

Mary seemed to be momentarily frozen in her seat as those feral eyes settled on her for a lingering moment. She felt trapped, the perspiration chilling on her skin as her pulse raced so fast she could barely breathe. And then she told herself not to be so silly and found the courage to stare back at him, coldly, defiantly, bolstered by the knowledge that she wasn't alone and he wouldn't dare approach her.

His steady gaze broke as Ron pulled on his arm and turned him away from the door, virtually pushing him into the hallway that led to the upstairs rooms. Ron had him against the wall, his finger jabbing angrily at Findlay's chest as he spoke to him.

Mary found she'd been holding her breath, and she let it out in a deep sigh as she turned away and picked up her rapidly cooling cup of tea. She had survived the encounter and would do so again if necessary – though she didn't relish the thought of ever bumping into him on a dark night.

She drank the tea and looked across at Ivy, who winked and jerked up her knee. Grinning back, Mary relaxed. A knee was certainly a good weapon, and she'd make sure to use it should he accost her again.

Peggy returned with Cordelia's sherry and a large glass of water for Mary. 'Sorry about that. Rosie's banned him from the bar, so he shouldn't have even been there. Ron's giving him a right ticking off, I can tell you.'

Mary drank half the glass of water and stood up. 'Thanks for that, Peggy. Now I really must get back to the piano and give poor Fran a rest.'

Chapter Three

Over the following two weeks there had been several more nights when Mary and Fran had entertained an ever-growing number of admirers and musicians at the Anchor. There was an Argentine airman who'd brought a set of bongos, which were very exotic for Cliffehaven; more penny whistles and a couple of recorders; and dear old Reg Farmer, who was as ancient as the hills and used to play in revues on the end of the pier, and could still get a jolly good tune out of his accordion.

Having spoken to Peggy first to get her advice, Rosie had relented and allowed Tommy to serve behind the bar. She'd found she and her barmaids hadn't been able to cope with so many customers, and Ron couldn't always be there due to his Home Guard duties – neither could she find anyone willing or able to step in who she could trust. And to Peggy's relief, it seemed that Mary had got over her earlier fear of him and could now carry on as if he wasn't even there.

Peggy collected the post and went back into the kitchen where a rather fragile Cordelia was nursing a hangover. 'I did warn you that another sherry wouldn't do you any good,' she said fondly.

'My headache has nothing to do with the sherry,' protested Cordelia as Daisy hung on to her hands to keep her balance. 'It was all that noise. As lovely as it was, I left the Anchor with my ears ringing.'

Peggy seemed to remember that she'd left the pub happily singing as she leaned very heavily on Ron's arm. But she let it pass. 'There's another letter from Canada for you,' she said instead.

'My word,' Cordelia breathed. 'Things are changing.'

Peggy was glad to hear it. Cordelia's two sons had emigrated to Canada many years ago, and up until quite recently there had been few letters and cards. Yet, with the war on, their consciences must have been pricking, for they'd not only sent a wonderful parcel stuffed with tinned goodies, material, knitting wool and dried fruit, but had sent several letters these past weeks.

She retrieved Daisy, who was now very unsteadily trying to climb up Cordelia's legs, and put her in the playpen so they could both read their letters in peace. Daisy was into everything now she could crawl and pull herself up on things, and it meant having to watch her every minute.

Daisy stood at the railings and threw her toys out at Harvey, who was lying in front of the fire. He gave a little groan of annoyance, sneezed and went back to sleep. He'd had a long walk with Ron and Monty this morning and, after their late night, just wanted to be left in peace to dream of chasing rabbits.

Peggy sat down and sorted through the airgraphs to work out which was the earliest one, then eagerly opened the plain brown envelope. Measuring only four by five-and-a-bit inches, and restricted to just over two hundred words, Jim's usual scrawl was cramped as he'd tried to cram in everything he wanted to tell her.

The seas had been very rough during the first part of the journey, and although he was feeling a good deal better now, he was still suffering from a cold. The days had become much warmer as the convoy headed for their first port of call, and he'd seen many strange and exotic sea birds along the way. They'd been escorted for a while by a school of porpoises, which had been a magical sight, and one he'd never forget.

When he wasn't doing his batman duties for the Brigadier and the Colonel, he'd spent most of his time on the poop deck reading. There was a concert organised each afternoon, but on the whole the time was passing very slowly and it was getting extremely hot and uncomfortable below decks at night.

The second, third and fourth airgraphs described the long days at sea, the various concerts put on by the men who had a talent for such things, and the games of housey-housey, at which he'd had no luck. They'd been offered lessons in French, German or Hindustani, and because he was so bored, he thought he might try one of them – which made Peggy smile, for he had enough trouble with the King's English, let alone some foreign language.

There had been lectures over the Forces' radio, and he'd managed to snaffle one of the Brigadier's Players cigarettes, which had been a real treat after the Woodbines they sold on board. It was extremely hot in the hammocks below decks now the blackouts had been put over the portholes, so everyone had stripped off and the place stank of sweaty feet and more besides.

There was a sweepstake being run on how many miles the ship travelled every day, and frequent calls to midnight musters on deck. Orders went out for every man to wear tropical kit, but they soon became soaked with sweat, which was most unpleasant. But they'd seen shoals of flying fish, and used seawater hoses to keep cool – and to keep them from getting too browned off, there were boxing matches and tugs of war between the various services on board, as well as a singing competition which he'd entered and come third. Most of the men, Jim included, had taken to sleeping up on deck during the night now they were approaching the equator, for the temperature below had soared above a hundred degrees.

Peggy carefully slid the airgraphs back into their envelopes and placed them in the shoebox she kept in her wardrobe. She could have done with lazy days and a bit of heat herself, for it was a bitterly cold December, and with Daisy's first birthday, the wedding and Christmas looming, she didn't have time to sit about.

She returned to the kitchen and set about heating up the vegetable soup they would have for lunch. There was a ham bone for tonight – not that there was a lot of meat on it – and she had left it to simmer with some pearl barley and the rest of the vegetables. If there was any soup left after lunch, she'd throw that in as well. With so many people to feed, it was a huge help to have Ron's garden out the back, and his shared allotment with Stan. However, the potatoes were almost gone until the next lot came up, so she'd soon have to go and stand in some endless queue to buy more.

She watched through the kitchen window as Ron carefully lifted his onions out of the cold ground and tied them together with string. They would be hung up in the dry shed until they were needed.

Her larder was actually looking fairly respectable for once, for she and the girls had gone in search of blackberries earlier in the autumn, and having saved enough sugar, there were now several jars of jam in her larder. Ron's crop of beetroot had been boiled and pickled, and she'd made endless jars of onion and tomato chutney. Cordelia had found a recipe for parsnip wine, and the result was now fermenting up in the airing cupboard – which gave Peggy many a sleepless night, for she suspected that if the bottles weren't watched carefully, they'd explode all over her clean linen and towels.

The herbs had been harvested and dried, then placed in yet more jars, so the bland meals could be given a bit of flavour, and the very last of her bags of white flour had been carefully stored away until the time came for her to add it to the mixture for the wedding cake, which was now in a large bowl in the larder, protected by a strip of muslin.

She had begged, borrowed and saved her rations as well as she could, and with the dried fruit that Cordelia's family had sent from Canada, she knew, from the heavenly smell of it every time she'd stirred a few drops of Ron's brandy into the mixture over the past couple of weeks, that the cake would be rich and flavoursome. The bag of icing sugar that Rosie had donated was an absolute treasure, and Peggy was already planning on how to do the icing – although she still didn't know where on earth she could find the appropriate decorations to put on top.

As she stirred the soup, Peggy thought about all the things still to do before the wedding. Suzy's parents would be arriving on the 18th. At first they had insisted upon booking into the Grand Hotel for the night, but since that had been reduced to rubble, and there were no other hotels that hadn't been requisitioned by the forces, Peggy had asked them to stay with her instead. She'd made it clear that her accommodation was not as posh as they might be used to, but that they could be assured of a warm welcome. She'd also rather reluctantly extended the invitation for them to stay over for a few extra days – which would have stretched her housekeeping to the limit. Thankfully, they'd declined as they already had pressing engagements back in London.

Doris, of course, had made a terrific fuss about these arrangements. She'd insisted that such important people shouldn't be staying in Peggy's tatty old boarding house, and had even overridden Peggy's invitation by issuing one of her own.

Having heard about Doris from Suzy, and how she'd tried to take over everything, and driven both her and Anthony to distraction in the process, Mr and Mrs James had tactfully declined, citing the fact that they wished to spend time with their daughter and wanted to be with her on her wedding morning so that her father could escort her from Beach View to the church.

Peggy kept stirring the soup, her thoughts occupied by all the changes that would have to be made to accommodate them. Sarah and Jane had willingly offered to give up the large double room at the front of the house and would move into the smaller one at the back. As they were sisters, they didn't mind sharing the double bed just for a couple of nights. Yet it would mean stripping beds, emptying cupboards and giving the room a jolly good spring clean.

As she simply couldn't expect such important visitors to eat in the kitchen, the dining room would also have to be cleaned and polished, and the floor given a good waxing. The sweep was coming tomorrow to deal with the chimney – she didn't want any falls of soot spoiling the proceedings – and she would have to hunt out her best china and glass and make sure they were thoroughly washed. Her mother's lovely hand-stitched linen tablecloths and napkins needed a wash and iron, and the dust and cobwebs had to be beaten out of the long velvet curtains and swept from the cornices and ceiling rose.

Harvey would have to be hosed down and made sweeter-smelling with his special shampoo and flea powder. Ron would have to be bullied into taking a bath and putting on decent clothes for a change and then be persuaded to have a haircut and shave – and the ferrets must be firmly locked in their cage and kept out of sight. It was a huge upheaval for just one night, and with less than a week to go, Peggy was feeling rather beleaguered.

'Oh, how lovely,' sighed Cordelia as she came to the end of her letter and took off her half-moon reading glasses.

'Good news?' asked Peggy distractedly.

'They've asked if I would like to go to Canada to live with them for the rest of the war. They're rather concerned about my safety here, being so close to the Channel.'

'It's a bit late in the day for them to be concerned,' said Peggy with some asperity. 'You were more in danger during the Blitz.'

'I know, dear, but the thought is there, and it was very kind of them to offer.'

Peggy studied her friend as she put the letter back in the envelope. Cordelia's expression was one of sadness and longing, and Peggy's heart went out to her, for her family had virtually ignored her until now, and she wondered rather cynically if this new concern was entirely altruistic. Cordelia had a fair amount of money tucked away in the bank as well as the ownership of a bungalow which she'd inherited, and was still in possession of several very nice pieces of antique silver and valuable jewellery.

'You're not actually considering going, are you?' she asked with some alarm.

'Of course not, dear,' Cordelia replied. 'My home is here with you, and if they'd really been concerned about my welfare, they'd have issued their invitation back in 1939.'

Peggy gave a sigh of relief. 'I'm glad they asked you,' she said as she went to put her hand on the older woman's shoulder. 'But this old place just wouldn't be the same if you weren't here.'

'Bless you, Peggy.' Cordelia patted her hand. 'I can think of no place I'd rather be – and the thought of going on some convoy across the Atlantic with U-boats hunting us down makes me go cold.'

'But you'd like to see your sons again, wouldn't you? And meet all the grandchildren and so on?'

Cordelia nodded. 'But I'm far too old to start thinking of going all that way, war or not. Perhaps they'll come and visit me when it's all over.'

Peggy heard the wistfulness in her voice. 'Well, they'll get a warm welcome,' she said firmly. She turned to the stove and gave the soup a final stir. 'Could you lay the table and slice some bread, Cordelia? Lunch is ready.'

She shouted down to Ron to wash his hands and come up, and then gasped in delight as a wonderfully familiar figure came through the back gate. 'We've got a visitor, Cordelia,' she said excitedly. 'Lay another place, would you?'

Before Cordelia could ask who it was, Martin Black came running up the cellar steps to be greeted by a joyful Harvey, who put his front feet on Martin's shoulders so he could lick his face, thereby knocking off his gold-braided peaked hat.

'Get down, ye heathen beast,' growled Ron, making a grab for his collar. 'Sorry, Martin,' he said as he retrieved the hat and gave it a rub with his dirty sweater sleeve. 'I hope he hasn't damaged your uniform jacket.'

Martin took the hat, ruffled Harvey's head and looked at everyone with a beaming smile as he smoothed his handlebar moustache. 'No damage done. My word, it's lovely to see you all again.'

Peggy threw her arms about him and hugged him tight. She adored Martin, for he was not only the perfect son-in-law, but one of the bravest men she knew. 'We don't see enough of you,' she said. 'How lovely you could snatch some time off.'

'We're on ops again tonight, so I can't stay long, unfortunately.' He unbuttoned his blue jacket and loosened his tie. 'But I had a couple of hours to spare, so I thought I'd trundle over.' His gaze fell on Cordelia, who was in a lather of excitement. 'And how's my special girl today?' he boomed.

'All the better for seeing you, you naughty boy,' she twittered. 'Now come and give this old lady a kiss before she melts right away with longing.'

Peggy smiled as he duly obliged, then remembered the soup and quickly took the pot off the stove. 'You timed it well,' she teased as she reached for an extra bowl. 'We were just about to have lunch.'

'That soup smells wonderful. Just what the doctor ordered on such a cold day.' He rubbed his hands together in eager anticipation and then went to pluck Daisy out of her playpen so he could give her a hug.

Peggy watched him and her heart twisted, for she knew how very deeply he was missing his own children.

Having amused Daisy for a while, he placed her carefully in her high chair and tied the bib around her chubby neck. Then he reached into his pocket to draw out a packet wrapped in newspaper.

'This is a little something to put away for the wedding. Be careful with it, though,' he added as he handed it to Peggy. 'It's quite delicate and only on loan, I'm afraid.'

Peggy unwrapped the packet and gasped in delight, for he couldn't have brought anything more useful. She admired the small plaster bride and groom standing hand in hand beneath a trellis arch, and the length of lovely blue ribbon which held two perfect little silver bells.

'Oh, Martin,' she breathed. 'They're perfect. But how on earth did you find them? I've been scouring the shops for days.'

'One of my pilots got married the other week to a lovely girl whose father owns a patisserie in London. I knew from Anne's letter you were having trouble finding anything to put on the cake, so when I asked, they very kindly said I could borrow them.'

'I'll write a note to thank them before you have to go back to the airdrome,' she said. 'How kind and thoughtful to let us have them. Suzy will be delighted – and I promise we'll take great care of them.' She quickly wrapped the decorations back in their paper and put them safely away in the top drawer of her bedroom chest.

They sat down at the table and tucked into the soup and bread, while Peggy fed Daisy and Harvey sat by Martin's knee in the faint hope he might get something to eat as well.

'So,' said Ron as they ate and discussed the war news. 'Is Malta as badly damaged as the newspapers say?'

Martin nodded. 'It was one of my chaps who flew that special reporter out there, and he said it defied description. Seventy-five percent of Valetta has been destroyed, and the rest of the island has been virtually reduced to piles of matchsticks and rubble. They reckon that even with normal supplies and facilities it will take sixty years to rebuild Malta's towns and villages.'

'The casualties must have been very high,' murmured Peggy.

Martin smiled at her. 'Actually, they were miraculously low considering the bombardment the island has had to withstand. The soft rock it's built on is ideal for underground shelters, and out of a population of a quarter of a million, there were fewer than three thousand killed or seriously injured.'

'To be sure, that is a miracle,' sighed Ron. 'Especially when you think we lost so many just a few weeks ago after the hotel and boarding houses were hit down on the seafront.'

'I heard all about that.' Martin slipped his last crust of bread to Harvey. 'And I understand you and Harvey have been nominated by the press for some sort of bravery awards?'

'A lot of fuss over nothing if you ask me,' grumbled Ron.

'Not at all. What you did was very courageous, and you should be justly rewarded.' Martin stroked Harvey's head and patted his back. 'If this one gets recognition for all the times he's gone in to rescue people, then it's well deserved.'

'Well, if he does, I'll frame it and put it up on the mantelpiece in place of honour alongside all my photographs,' said Peggy as she slipped Harvey her own hard crust – she still hadn't got used to the gritty taste of the National Loaf and the crusts hurt her teeth. Harvey had no such discernment, and the crust disappeared without touching the sides.

'Ah, that reminds me. Here's something else you can put up there,' said Martin as he handed Peggy an envelope. 'Don't worry, I have copies back at Cliffe.'

Peggy drew out some small black-and-white pictures and studied the sweet face of her dark-eyed daughter Anne as she sat with Emily Jane in her arms and Rose Margaret at her knee. It had been taken in Vi's Somerset farmhouse as the light streamed in through the large window of the sitting room onto the comfortable old rocking chair.

'Emily Jane has lots of dark hair,' she said admiringly, 'and she looks just like Anne at that age. And how tall Rose is now, and how well and happy she looks. She's gorgeous, Martin – they both are. You must be very proud.'

Martin blinked rapidly, cleared his throat and made a great play of filling his pipe. 'I am, but I'd have felt much happier if I could have been down there with Anne when Emily arrived. I know she had the magnificent Vi looking after her, but it was hard for her, poor darling.'

'Harder for you being so far from them all, and living under such a strain,' said Peggy softly as she passed the photographs to Ron. 'Will you be able to get some leave soon, so you can visit them all?'

Martin passed the roll of tobacco to Ron and puffed on his pipe before he replied. 'All leave is cancelled for a while. There are many more raids planned, and we're losing aircraft and men at an alarming rate, so I'm afraid it's all hands to the wheel.'

Peggy stared at him. 'But that doesn't mean you, surely? You've done more than your bit already – and even the RAF have recognised that, which is why you've been flying a desk...' She tailed off as she saw his expression, and her spirits plummeted. 'Oh, Martin, no.'

He examined the bowl of his pipe for a moment. 'I'm afraid it does mean me leaving my desk again, Peggy,' he said solemnly, 'which is why I was so determined to come over today.' His expression was very serious as he finally looked back at her. 'I'll be on ops for the foreseeable future, as long as Air Marshal Harris continues his campaign of blanket bombing – and I totally agree with him that it's imperative to keep up the bombardment. The Germans have to be stopped; especially now they're developing some sort of new weapon.'

'What sort of weapon?' asked Peggy sharply.

'I think you'd better forget I mentioned that,' he said rather shamefacedly. 'A bit of a breach of secrets, don't you know.'

'How can I forget such a thing?' she breathed. 'What is this weapon supposed to do? Will we be safe in our beds if they fire it?'

'Peggy, please don't worry about it. The Germans are still at the very earliest stages of experimentation, and we have no intention of letting them develop the thing any further – which is why it's so important we continue with our bombing raids. But this is to go no further, do you understand?'

'Of course we understand.' Peggy gathered Daisy into her arms to be comforted by her warmth and weight. 'Oh, Martin, you will be careful, won't you?'

'I have every intention of coming back in one piece, Peggy, and as I'll be surrounded by some of the world's most skilled airmen, there really is no need to worry.'

Peggy looked unconvinced, so Martin continued, 'Young Randolph Stevens is flying his Lancaster alongside mine, and both Freddy Pargeter and Roger Makepeace will be accompanying Matthew in their Spitfires to provide us with fighter defence. We've been doing similar runs for some time now, so really, there's no need to fret over any of us.'

The thought of Cissy's Randolph and Rita's Matthew being up there with Kitty's Roger and Freddy gave her no peace of mind at all. But there was a war on, lives were being put at risk every day – and she simply had to accept that and not make Martin's job even harder by making a fuss.

'Will you be able to come to the wedding?' she asked, determined to change the subject.

'I sincerely hope so,' he replied, clearly relieved to be moving to an easier topic. 'But I might be a bit late arriving,' he warned. 'I'm hoping to dash up and see the parents for a couple of hours that day because I'll be on duty over Christmas and it will be the only chance I'll get. If the traffic's bad, or there's a raid, I could be delayed.'

Peggy had very little time for Martin's parents. They'd treated Anne very badly when she and Martin had been courting, for they'd disapproved of her lowly background and simply refused to accept that their son wanted to marry such a girl. They'd actually bothered to turn up for the wedding after a great deal of shilly-shallying which had hurt Martin dreadfully. But their cool disdain and stiff politeness had set them apart from the other guests, and they'd made their excuses within minutes of the speeches at the reception and left without even saying goodbye.

'Are they well?' she asked, to be polite.

'They seem to be coping all right,' said Martin. 'Unfortunately I don't get to see them much, and they don't write often.' He gave a sigh. 'I'm rather hoping that the birth of their second granddaughter might alter their attitude to Anne – which is why I want to take the photographs up to show them instead of just sending them in the post.'

Peggy didn't say so, but she doubted either of them would change their snooty opinion of her beautiful daughter – and as far as she was concerned, they could stick their money and position right up their expensive jumpers.

'Oh, Peggy,' Martin chuckled, 'your face is a picture. Please, never try and play poker.'

Peggy giggled, and Martin placed his large, warm hand over hers. 'I know they're trying, and their attitude hurts me as much as it does you and Anne. But when all's said and done, they are my parents, so I can't just ignore them.'

'I realise that,' said Peggy.

'Then let's not spoil our time together by being gloomy. You go and make a pot of your famous tea while Daisy and I find some toys to play with.'

There were tears in Peggy's eyes as she put the kettle on the hob. Martin was such a very nice man – one of nature's gentlemen – and she hated the thought that his visits to his parents were made out of duty and not love. It was all terribly sad, for how could any parent not be proud of such a brave son, and of such beautiful grandchildren?

As she hurried off into the bedroom to fetch Cordelia's tin of chocolate biscuits, which she'd hidden away in her wardrobe, she sent up a silent prayer of thanks that her children loved her, and if it was only possible, they would all be at home now, sitting round her kitchen table and chattering like sparrows.

The next hour was spent very pleasantly. Martin played on the floor with Daisy and her toys until she fell asleep. Ron regaled him with a very colourful account of the nights in the pub, which reminded him of similar occasions during his boyhood in Ireland. Cordelia passed the delicious biscuits round and told him she was having a lovely suit made out of the tweed her family had sent from Canada, and Harvey sat licking his lips in anticipation of getting his teeth into one of those biscuits.

Peggy finished writing her note to the lovely couple who'd lent her the cake decorations, then sat and watched them all. Her heart was full, for Martin was one of their own and every precious moment he could spend with them was a gift.

He finally looked at the clock and got to his feet. 'I must go,' he said regretfully, fastening the buttons on his uniform jacket.

He swept a tearful Cordelia into his arms and gave her a hearty kiss, tickling her cheeks with his moustache to bring back her smile.

Then he hugged Peggy, who was battling with her own tears. 'I'll be back before you know it,' he murmured before turning away to pat Harvey and shake Ron's hand. 'Look after them all for me, won't you, Ron?'

'To be sure, don't I always?' Ron grasped his hand firmly as his blue eyes became suspiciously bright. 'You watch what you're doing up there, boy,' he rumbled. 'My great-granddaughters are relying on you to come back in one piece – and so am I.' He cleared his throat. 'Honest to God, Martin, you've no idea how difficult it is for a poor solitary man to survive in this house full of bossy women.'

Martin grinned and softly punched his shoulder. 'You love it really, you old fraud,' he teased. Then he put on his cap, shot everyone a smile and was running down the steps and walking towards the back gate.

Peggy and Ron followed and stood in the door-way, Harvey between them as Martin turned and waved. And then he was gone.

'I'm sick of saying goodbye to everyone I love,' said Peggy tearfully. 'When is this awful war going to end, Ron?'

He put a strong arm round her shoulders and drew her close. 'When we've beaten the ruddy Germans,' he muttered. 'And that won't be long now, to be sure, for I'm betting they don't have chocolate biscuits.' He smiled down at her. 'I seem to remember there are still a couple in the tin, so 'twould be a terrible waste to leave them there to go stale.'

Peggy dug him affectionately in the ribs. 'Those are Cordelia's and you've already had six.'

He looked down at her in feigned disbelief. 'Ach,

to be sure, Peggy girl, you'll be exaggerating.'

She smiled through her tears. 'Not at all, you old rogue. I counted every single one, including the half you shared with Harvey.'

Chapter Four

Mary had received numerous letters from Barbara and Jack Boniface and her best friend Pat over the past weeks, and she'd read them all so many times that she knew them almost by heart.

Barbara had written long, rambling letters full of love and news and gentle gossip of the goings-on in the Sussex village of Harebridge Green. The young, rather simple-minded Gladys, who'd lost her mother on the same night as the rectory had taken a direct hit, was still happily living with her fearsome aunt, who was encouraging her to help with the WVS. All was well at Black Briar Farm, but two of the land girls had left, so they were a bit short-handed while they waited for their replacements. Her husband, Joseph, was still working long hours and doing his fire-watch and warden duties, but he was well and keeping very fit.

There hadn't been any raids or tip-and-runs since Mary had left the village, but the school had mysteriously burned down one night and it was suspected a couple of the local boys had made a camp in there and set it alight by accident. Its loss was felt by everyone, for the hall had become a popular meeting place for dances, parties and jumble sales.

Pat's letters were quite short, but she was still working at the rope factory and enjoying a hectic social life, and was now courting a young French Canadian soldier. She bemoaned the fact that the clothing ration was stricter than ever, and that the dowdy grey, black or navy utility clothing in the shops did absolutely nothing to flatter even the prettiest and most shapely girl.

Jack's letters had become more hastily written and were much shorter as he'd been immersed in his qualification course for the commandos, which he was finding far tougher than he'd expected but was enjoying immensely. He was still hoping to get some leave, but if he made the grade and got into this elite regiment he wasn't at all sure if it would be possible. He thought about her often and missed her horribly, and hoped she hadn't forgotten about him in all the excitement of her new life in Cliffehaven.

Mary had written back to them, describing her job and her billet, the rehearsals for the charity concert, and the new friends she'd made here in Cliffehaven. She made no mention of Findlay but had told them about playing the piano in the pub, the delightful surprise at discovering how talented Fran was on the violin, and the invitation to play the organ at the wedding.

She'd assured Barbara that although Doris was a bit of a tricky customer, her sister Peggy was lovely, and had gently taken her through the rather distressing news that Cyril Fielding was not the sort of father to pursue – and that her mother's identity and whereabouts were still unknown, and would probably stay that way.

Nothing had been resolved really, but she realised her search was at an end. Barbara had tried to persuade her to return to Black Briar Farm, but she had tactfully declined. She was enjoying her new freedom in Cliffehaven, and revelling in the chance to grow and mature and find her own path until it was time to take up her place at Lewes teacher training college.

She also assured Jack that of course she loved him still and thought of him constantly throughout the day as she sifted through the airgraphs – and at night, just before she went to sleep and dreamt of their future together. She didn't go into any details about her search for Cyril to him, but merely mentioned the fact she'd decided to accept the way things were and move on. The precious locket was always kept close to her heart, and if he could get leave over Christmas, she would try her hardest to get back to Harebridge Green to see him.

There had been no more news of any leave, and now it was the 18th of December and the wedding was the following afternoon. Peggy had been working non-stop to get the house ready in time, and tonight would be hosting a dinner for Suzy's parents as well as Doris, Anthony and Edward.

Doris was in a complete lather over all the arrangements for the reception she was holding in her home. She had bullied and bossed Mary and Ivy about to help clean, dust and polish the house until it shone, before commanding them to iron acres of white linen tablecloths and napkins and clean the silver. It had reached the point where they'd had more than enough.

They'd had a scratch supper of spam fritters and baked beans in the kitchen – the dining room had been off limits for two days as Doris had fussed over the table plan and decorations – and were about to escape for the evening when Anthony and his father came through the front door loaded down with boxes, cases and morning suits on hangers.

'We're just off,' said Ivy firmly. 'Mary's got to do a last rehearsal on the church organ and I'm meeting me mates at the pictures. We done what we can, but she ain't never satisfied with nothing, so we've given up.'

Mary smiled up at the two men as she greeted them. Edward Williams was a very ordinary-looking man in comfortable middle age, with a gentle outlook on life and a benign smile. He'd always been gracious to her and Ivy on his few visits home, and Mary liked him very much.

Anthony was tall and rather thin, his dark brown hair flopping over his brow, the horn-rimmed spectacles constantly slipping down his long nose. Dressed in his usual tweed jacket, corduroy trousers, shirt and sleeveless sweater, and with a shy, sweet smile, Mary could see why Suzy had fallen for him.

'I think you'll find your mother's in a bit of a flap,' she said quietly.

'I suspected as much,' muttered Edward dolefully as he hung the morning suits on the rack in the hall.

'That's why we've come,' said Anthony, pushing his glasses up his nose. 'Mother has clearly run you two ragged over the past few days, and we thought it best to take some of the pressure off you. But at least you'll have a quiet evening, as we're all due to go to Aunt Peggy's for dinner at eight.'

'Well, good luck,' Mary replied as she pulled on her coat and reached for her gas-mask box.

'Anthony, darling!' Doris rushed out of the sitting room and threw her arms about her son, ignoring her husband completely. 'You have no idea how much there is still to do, and these girls have proved to be utterly useless when it comes to ironing napkins correctly.'

Mary and Ivy bridled at this, for they'd spent hours trying to please her, but before Ivy could respond sharply, Anthony steered his mother out of the hall while his father tipped them a wink.

'Take no notice,' he said softly. 'Doris loves making a drama out of everything and doesn't think before she speaks.'

'Edward? What are you doing out there? We have things to discuss.' The imperious call came from the sitting room.

'It seems my presence has been royally commanded,' he said with a gentle but wry smile. 'Enjoy your evening, girls. Tomorrow can only get worse.'

Mary and Ivy were giggling as they left the house. 'He's all right, ain't he?' said Ivy as they hurried through the wintry night to the end of Havelock Road. 'Though Gawd knows how the pair of them put up with 'er.'

'The same way we do,' said Mary. 'By not letting her ride rough-shod over us – but I can honestly see why Edward moved into his flat. Having to put up with her day after day over so many years must have been a terrible strain.'

'Yeah. Did you see the way she virtually shoved him out the way to get to Anthony? Blimey, my dad would never have stood for that, and no mistake.'

Edward reminded Mary of Gideon in so many ways – although he would never have gone as far as being unfaithful to Emmaline – but she made no comment as they turned left to walk up the High Street, past the forlorn remains of the old church and vicarage which still tugged at her heartstrings and brought all the sad memories back.

They reached the point where Ivy would turn off for the large hall that had now been turned into a cinema courtesy of the Americans. 'I'll see you back at the house,' said Mary.

'Aren't you going to dinner at Peggy's afterwards?'

Mary shook her head. 'She did ask me, but she has enough people to entertain tonight, and it's really a family thing, so I'd've felt a bit out of it.'

'Fair enough,' said Ivy. 'Just don't eat all them biscuits we managed to buy this afternoon. I might be peckish when I gets back.' She grinned and headed down the side street as Mary continued on up the hill.

It would have been quicker to go along Camden Road, but as it meant having to pass the Anchor she preferred to use the back streets to get to St Andrew's. Findlay still gave her the creeps, though she managed to ignore him when he was working behind the bar and only went to visit Rosie when she was certain he was out. Yet she still dreaded bumping into him when she was walking on her own at night.

St Andrew's was a rather ugly Victorian church of red brick. It stood on a corner in about an acre of land, with the equally unattractive vicarage standing in the next plot. There was a graveyard and garden of remembrance at the back which had a memorial to the fallen of the First World War, and as Mary headed for the vestry door she noted that the wreaths of red poppies at the foot of the memorial were faded and battered after all the rain they'd had since early November.

The vestry was icily cold and made even darker by the blackout curtains that had been hung over the two small windows that overlooked the churchyard. As she switched on the light and went through the door into the body of the church she was greeted by the familiar scents of damp stone, candle wax and incense, poignant reminders of home and her father's church.

Her footsteps echoed beneath the vaulted roof and into the dark corners of the vast edifice as she walked down the stone slabs of the broad aisle, past the lines of pews towards the altar steps. She looked at the pulpit and had to smile, for it was very imposing compared to the one her father had preached from. Set high above the steps, it was made of ornately decorated oak and had two silver candle sconces and a canopy embellished with small symbolic figures of a lamb, roses and a cross.

Dipping one knee and bowing her head to the large crucifix that stood on the altar, she said a silent prayer and then glanced across at the lectern which had been carved into the shape of an eagle whose open wings held the leather-bound bible. Suzy's father would be reading from it tomorrow, and the page was marked by an embroidered white ribbon with long, silken tassels.

The scents and sounds of this church might have reminded her of the ancient one back in Harebridge Green, but actually it was on a much grander scale and didn't really possess the same quiet and rather majestic atmosphere of age and history. Yet she had to admit that the Victorian artisans were certainly skilled and took pride in their work as they decorated their churches, for there were carved heads of saints at the top of every stone pillar and ornate barley twists at the end of every pew, and although the stained-glass windows were now heavily covered in board, the vicar had shown her photographs of how lovely they were.

She climbed the steps to make her way through the choir stalls to the organ. It was a beast of a thing which soared up to the high ceiling and had more knobs and pedals and layers of keys than you could shake a stick at. The wooden surround had been intricately carved with birds and cherubs peeking out of climbing vines, and the organ pipes gleamed richly behind the delicate and rather dusty fretwork.

Mary lit the candles set in brackets on either side of the keyboards, found the music she needed and then settled onto the broad stool. The cold of the church was beginning to seep through her warm overcoat, and if she didn't start practising soon, her fingers would stiffen up.

She pulled out various stops and then touched the keys, her feet lightly dancing over the pedals as she played Handel's lilting and peaceful *Water Music*, which she would play as the congregation came in to wait for the bridal party to arrive. Then she went through the traditional 'Here Comes the Bride', and followed this up with the two hymns Suzy and Anthony had chosen.

As she played 'I Vow to Thee, My Country', and the music soared to the great high rafters and filled the church with its beauty, she heard the accompanying strains of a violin and turned to smile with surprise and delight at Fran, who was walking towards her.

'How lovely to see you, but what on earth are you doing here?' she said after they'd come to the end of the hymn.

'To be sure, I needed to escape for a wee while,' Fran replied as she plucked at one of the violin strings and adjusted a tuning peg. 'I've done all I can to help Peggy, and now Suzy's parents have arrived I thought I'd make myself scarce.'

'What are they like?'

'He's tall and rather handsome with wings of silver in his hair and grey, friendly eyes. She's elegant, blonde and beautifully turned out – just like Suzy really. They're obviously very rich and well connected and used to the very best of things, but there were no airs and graces and they put Peggy and everyone at ease immediately.'

She grinned wickedly, her lovely eyes glittering with fun. 'You can always tell real class,' she giggled, 'and poor Doris doesn't stand a chance of pulling it off. She'll no doubt be busting her corsets to try and impress them, but end up looking very silly.'

'I'm sure Edward and Anthony will rein her in if it looks likely,' said Mary with a smile. She blew on her cold hands and rubbed them. 'Look, I'd better get on before my fingers seize up. This place is as cold as a morgue and I still have to practise my piece for when they're signing the register.'

'Well, 'tis that I was going to ask you about,' said Fran rather hesitantly.

Mary frowned. 'Why's that?'

'I thought that as I had the violin it would be a chance to do something really special for Suzy,' she said in a rush. 'I wondered if you'd mind if I played while they were signing the register?'

'Of course I don't mind, and I'm sure Suzy would be delighted. But what about your duties as chief bridesmaid? Won't you be needed in the registry?'

Fran shook her head. 'I've already had a word with Sarah, and she'll look after everything while I'm playing.' Her expression was pleading. 'Please let me do it, Mary. I so want to.'

Mary laughed. 'You don't have to ask my permission, Fran. What are you planning on playing?'

'Bach's "Air on the G string",' she replied breathlessly, 'so I'll need you to accompany me. Do you know it?'

Mary was rather startled that Fran was familiar with such a piece. 'I have played it a few times, but I'm terribly rusty,' she said in a mild panic. 'Let me see if they have the sheet music in here, but it's unlikely because it's hardly church music.'

She got off the large stool and opened the lid. There were sheets and sheets of music which they hurriedly sifted through, and Mary was beginning to despair when she found an old book of classic Bach.

'Whew,' she said as she placed it on the music rest. 'You nearly had to play solo there and it wouldn't have done it any justice at all.' She adjusted the stops, looked at the music, then quickly began to play through the first few bars. 'Ah, I remember it now,' she sighed in relief.

Fran grinned and nestled the violin into her neck. 'I knew I could rely on you, Mary. Are you ready?' At Mary's nod she counted them in and drew her bow delicately over the strings.

Mary accompanied her on the organ, keeping it soft and light so the wonderful violin strains could sing out into the silent church. The music made the hairs stand up at the back of her neck and down her arms, and swelled her heart until she could barely see through her tears.

As the final note slowly faded and died, she sat back in awe, and had to dry her eyes. 'Well,' she said with a shaky laugh, 'that's guaranteed to get everyone emotional even if they aren't already.'

Fran grinned and tossed back her fiery hair. 'Ach, to be sure, Peggy and Cordelia always cry at weddings. They'd feel they were missing out if they didn't use at least three hankies.'

Mary smiled as she turned back to the beginning of the piece. Barbara was just the same, and liked nothing better than a good cry during a soppy film. 'Shall we run through it a couple of times more? Only I'm still a bit unsure in places, and you played it so beautifully I don't want to let the side down.'

They played it through until they were both satisfied, and then Mary went on to practise the final triumphal march that she'd play as the bride and groom left the church.

'There, I think that's enough for tonight,' she said as the last note drifted away. She gathered up the sheets of music and made sure they were in the correct order before placing them on the rest. 'You know, Fran, you'd be a real asset in our concert orchestra. Why don't you come along to one of the rehearsals?'

'It's not really something I've ever considered.' Mary blew out the candles and they hurried through the echoing darkness into the well-lit vestry. 'I'm happy enough to just play in the pub and leave that sort of thing to someone like you.'

'But you're very talented, Fran. Much better than the violinist Doris has managed to find.'

'Ach, well, 'tis better I stick to what I know,' she replied with a shrug. ''Tis not for me, Mary.'

Mary had to accept her refusal, but it was a terrible shame, for Fran would have lit up the concert and no mistake. 'The vicar said I could make tea or coffee,' she said as she pulled her gloves back on. 'And I could certainly do with something to warm me up. How about you?'

'I'd love a cup of coffee if there's any milk,' said Fran as she carefully cleaned the gleaming violin and tucked it back in its case.

Mary found some dried milk in the cupboard along with a bottle of Camp coffee. She spooned a small amount of the treacle-like liquid into the cups and added the milk once the kettle had boiled. There was no sugar, but then they hadn't expected to find any in these days of tight rationing.

'I wonder what sort of reaction you'll get from Doris when she sees you playing her violin,' she murmured as they perched on a table and wrapped their hands around the warm cups. 'I still haven't told her it was you I'd lent it to, you know.'

Fran shrugged. 'I hope she sees that I'm taking good care of it and can actually play it properly,' she said with a hint of asperity, 'I'd like to think she might change her opinion of me – but I doubt it. She once told me that I was a worthless Irish flibbertigibbet with half a brain and few morals.'

'That's a terrible thing to say to anyone,' protested a horrified Mary. 'It just goes to prove that she's a terrible judge of character as well as an awful snob. Frankly, if I was you, I wouldn't care less what she thought.'

'I wish I didn't, but it's not nice knowing someone has taken an unjust and undeserved dislike to you, is it?'

Mary heard the wistfulness underlying her words and had a painful memory of Emmaline's spiteful face and harsh accusations. 'No, it isn't,' she replied softly. 'But sometimes, no matter how hard you try to get them to approve of you, it makes no difference, and you have to accept it's a lost cause.'

Fran looked at her keenly. 'That sounds as if it came from the heart.'

'It did rather.' Mary blew on the coffee. 'But it

doesn't hurt quite so much now I know the reason behind it.' She saw Fran's questioning glance and smiled. 'It would take all night to explain, and there's little point in wasting time on things I can't change.'

She sipped her coffee and turned to another topic before the memories of Emmaline's coldness became too hard to bear. 'I know you said you learned to play the violin as a young girl, but where on earth did you learn the classics?'

'I had a wonderful music teacher at St Catherine's School. She was a nun, and I suspect that if she hadn't had the calling into the Church she'd have been a successful concert soloist. Her music made me cry it was so beautiful, and when she heard me play she insisted that I learned more than just the Irish tunes.' Her eyes went misty as she fell silent.

'She wanted me to go to music college and make a career out of it,' she continued. 'But we had no money for such things, even though I did win a part scholarship. Dear Sister Anne even tried to persuade the Reverend Mother to fund me, but of course she couldn't. There were lots of wee girls and boys in that school with talent, and if she did it for me, she'd have been inundated with requests from all the other parents.'

Mary thought it was desperately sad that this very talented girl had been denied a promising career in music because her parents weren't rich enough to pay for her tuition. Life could be terribly unfair. 'So, what made you take up nursing?'

Fran grinned. 'Well, me best friend took it up and I liked the look of it, so we both came to

England, found part-time jobs to pay our way and went to nursing school. To be sure, I was terrible homesick and it was a tough few years. There was never enough money for anything, and probationary nurses are given the longest shifts and the toughest, dirtiest jobs, so we were always exhausted. But I discovered it was something I was good at and enjoyed, so I stuck with it.'

She sipped her coffee, her face animated. 'Then me and June moved into Beach View once we'd qualified, and things got better. Suzy arrived shortly after war was declared, I got promoted to Theatre Staff Nurse, and I've never looked back.'

'I haven't met June, and Peggy hasn't mentioned her. Is she still at Beach View?'

Fran pulled a face. 'Me mam always warned me she was a flighty piece, and she was right – just as all mams are,' she added ruefully. 'Peggy threw her out when she caught her and some corporal rolling about half-naked in her bed.'

Mary almost choked on her coffee. 'In Peggy's bed?' At Fran's nod, she couldn't help but giggle. 'Goodness. That must have caused a ruckus.'

'I believe it did, but June never went into details and left to go back to Ireland shortly after that.' She drained the last of her coffee and rinsed the cup under the tap. 'Me mam said she was only home for a couple of months before she disappeared again, and there was a rumour that she was sent to the convent for unmarried mothers. The poor wee girl didn't deserve to be punished like that. Those nuns are evil by all accounts.'

Mary had heard about the convents that took in such girls, for her mother had constantly told her that was where she'd end up if she didn't mend her sinful ways. 'Are you still in touch with her?' she asked as she washed out her own cup.

'I wrote a couple of times, but never got a reply. Mam said she'd gone to live further west and her parents have all but disowned her.'

'That's so sad,' murmured Mary. 'The poor girl needs her parents most at a time like that. Will they ever forgive her, do you think?'

Fran followed Mary outside and waited as she closed the door. 'I hope so, but the Irish have long memories when it comes to sins – and June brought terrible disgrace to her family, so she did.' She eyed the door. 'Are ye not going to lock that?'

Mary shook her head. 'The vicar will come across to do it later.'

They walked into the street and Mary grinned as she squeezed her friend's hand. 'Suzy is going to be thrilled with your surprise, Fran. I'll see you back here tomorrow.'

'I'll be here, don't you worry.' Fran grinned back at her, then headed for Beach View with a backward wave.

Mary turned in the opposite direction and walked quickly through the narrow side streets until she came to the busy High Street where couples were strolling and groups of servicemen clustered on corners. She hoped the house in Havelock Road was quieter and that Doris and the two men had already left for Beach View. With Ivy out for the evening, it would be lovely to have a soak in the bath and read through her letters again.

Peggy had been feeling quite sick with anxiety as she'd waited for the arrival of Suzy's parents, and this had not been helped by Doris, who'd poked and pried and made snide comments about the mismatched glasses and cheap cutlery as she'd run a speculative finger along windowsills and furniture looking for dust. In the end, Peggy had told her in no uncertain terms to either keep her mouth shut or leave. Doris had flounced off in high dudgeon to sit in the dining room and smoke furiously on a cigarette.

Suzy came into the kitchen shortly after, looking lovely in a plain navy dress and creamy cardigan, her blonde hair freshly set and gleaming in the dim electric light, her eyes shining in her radiant face. 'Please don't worry, Auntie Peg,' she said, putting her arm round her shoulders. 'Mummy and Daddy are perfectly ordinary people, and I just know you'll get along with them.'

'But they're used to much better things,' fretted Peggy as she looked with fresh eyes at her shabby kitchen. 'Perhaps it would have been better if they'd gone to Doris's after all.'

'Don't be silly. They'd hate it there, and will feel right at home with you and the others.' She softly kissed Peggy's cheek. 'I've told them so much about you and Ron and Cordelia over the years that Mummy says she feels as if she already knows you. So please stop worrying and try to relax.'

Peggy drew her into a close embrace. 'I'm going to miss you so much, Suzy,' she murmured. 'You've become like a daughter to me, and this house won't feel the same without you.'

Suzy's eyes were suspiciously bright as they

broke the embrace and stood hand in hand. 'And I'm going to miss you all too,' she admitted. 'It's going to feel very strange to not wake up here each morning to the sound of Jane going downstairs, or Rita crashing about in her room – and not to have you to talk to when things are getting on top of me.' She sniffed back her tears. 'You've been a mother to me, Aunt Peg, and I really can't express how much that has meant to me over the past few years.'

Peggy's soft heart melted at this sweet sentiment and she had to take a moment to compose herself before she could speak again. 'Promise you'll visit us often?'

'Of course I will. I shall still be working at the hospital, so I'll never be that far away from you all. This is my home and you've been my family for so long that I'm not going to just walk away and forget about you.'

Peggy nodded, unable to speak for the lump in her throat.

Suzy squeezed her fingers. 'Just promise me you won't get too tense about things, Auntie Peg. Everything is organised to the last folded napkin, and Anthony and I want you to be at ease and enjoy tonight – and our wedding.'

Peggy tried her best to shrug off her misgivings, but as soon as Suzy went back upstairs, she started to dust and polish again. Once there was nothing else to tidy away or scrub clean she checked on Daisy, who'd been put to bed early, and then began to restlessly pace the hall floor, waiting to hear the sound of a car pulling up, for Suzy's parents were driving down from their London flat.

Fran had forced Ron into a chair and trimmed his wayward hair and eyebrows – much to his disgust – and he was decently dressed and shaved for once. Harvey had had a bath and a liberal dusting of flea powder, and the pair of them had been banished to the kitchen, where Edward and Anthony were in charge of the drinks.

Rita was on duty, but the rest of the girls were upstairs giggling and chattering, and Cordelia was regally ensconced with her knitting in one of the armchairs in the dining room. She had deliberately switched off her hearing aid, for she didn't like Doris and had made it absolutely clear she had no wish to hear anything she had to say.

The soft purr of an expensive engine alerted Peggy to the Jameses' arrival and her heart began to thud as she switched off the hall light and opened the front door. The Rolls-Royce gleamed in the pale moonlight as it pulled to a halt, and Peggy swallowed the lump of panic in her throat and plastered on a welcoming smile as the elegant and rather sleek couple climbed out.

'Mummy, Daddy,' cried Suzy as she raced past Peggy and ran down the steps to greet them. 'Oh, it's so lovely to see you both.' She kissed and hugged them both rapturously and then turned to introduce Peggy.

Mrs James was all smiles as she climbed the steps. 'My dear Peggy, what a delight to meet you at last – and on such a happy occasion too.'

The fair-haired woman looked far too young to be Suzy's mother and as Peggy shook her pale, soft hand, she noted the delicious fur coat and expensive handbag and shoes. 'It's lovely to meet you too,' she stammered. 'I do hope you'll be comfortable here, Mrs James, only–'

'Please, call me Evelyn, Peggy. After all, you've mothered my daughter for years, and I feel that, although we haven't met until today, we are already friends.'

Peggy caught Suzy's eye and saw the 'I told you so' expression on her face and began to feel a little easier, her smile becoming a fraction less stiff at this lovely greeting.

Evelyn hooked her hand into Suzy's arm and glanced across at her husband, who was busy delving into the boot of the Rolls with Ted and Anthony. 'Julian and I can't thank you enough for looking after our little girl so well, and actually we're rather glad we're not staying in some dreary hotel. We've heard so much about the warmth and lovely atmosphere of your home from Suzy that we're both looking forward to experiencing it for ourselves.'

Peggy led the way up the steps and into the hall, suddenly seeing how shabby it looked and how worn the stair carpet had become. But Evelyn didn't seem to notice as she shrugged off the beautiful fur and hung it over the newel post while Suzy introduced the girls, Cordelia, and Doris – who'd emerged from the dining room and just about managed not to curtsy.

'Hello, Peggy,' said Julian as he dumped a huge hamper on the floor and took her hand. 'Thank you so much for everything you've done for our girl, and for the enormous effort and upheaval this wedding must have caused you and your family.'

Taking in the handsome face with wings of silver

at the temples, Peggy looked into his darkly lashed grey eyes and could easily have melted. His smile, his warm, firm hand and melodious voice sent a thrill right through her that she hadn't experienced since she first clapped eyes on her Jim. 'It's no bother, really,' she stammered. 'Suzy's one of us, and of course we wanted to do all we could on her and Anthony's special day.'

'And this must be Ron,' said Julian. His smile was broad as he shook Ron's hand enthusiastic- ally. 'I've heard a great deal about you, and this fine fellow.' He bent to pat a delirious Harvey who was almost turning himself inside out at all the attention. 'A little bird in Westminster tells me you and Harvey are up for awards.' He tapped the side of his nose. 'But you didn't hear that from me.'

Ron went rather pink and tried not to look too irritated by this bit of news. 'Thanks for tipping me the wink,' he said gruffly. 'But it's all a lot of fuss over nothing if you ask me.'

Julian ignored this grumpiness and smiled. 'Now I understand you have a couple of ferrets,' he continued. 'I used to have one when I was a boy. I called him Archie, and I used to go rabbit- ing with him on the estate. Would it be possible to see them, do you think?'

Ron beamed and his blue eyes twinkled. 'To be sure, they're a little lively this evening, but I don't see why not.'

'Just don't let them out,' said Peggy in a panic.

Her words fell on deaf ears as they walked away and Anthony and Ted carried boxes and the hamper into the kitchen. Peggy shot a nervous glance at Evelyn. 'Those ferrets are a menace,' she explained. 'Once they get out, they take ages to catch.'

Evelyn giggled. 'So I've heard from Suzy,' she said. 'But that's what makes a house a home, isn't it, a bit of chaos now and again, and I'm sure you laughed about it afterwards.'

Peggy began to feel even more relaxed. Evelyn wasn't at all stuck-up, and Julian seemed to feel quite at home. As long as Doris didn't stick her oar in, it would all be all right.

Once the suitcases had been taken upstairs, the boxes and hampers were unpacked to reveal wine, whisky, gin, brandy and champagne. There was a whole cooked and dressed salmon, a cooked ham joint, packets of tea and coffee, sugar, butter, rashers of bacon, and a huge bag of precious white flour.

Peggy looked at it all in astonishment. 'But you didn't have to–'

'Of course we did,' said Evelyn firmly. 'Suzy told me how you've been scrimping and saving all your rations to make the wedding cake, and with so many people to cater for, we wanted to do our share. After all, it is our daughter's wedding and you've been so generous to all of us. The ham and salmon are for the reception, but please accept these gifts in the spirit they've been given.'

Peggy didn't know what to say, for she was overwhelmed not only by their generosity, but by their genuine warmth.

Evelyn's eyes were suspiciously bright too, and she squeezed Peggy's hand in tacit understanding before she turned to Anthony. 'Be a dear and open one of those bottles of champagne while

Peggy shows me the cake. It's time to celebrate and I've worked up quite a thirst on that awful journey down from London.'

As the girls crowded into the kitchen with Cordelia and Doris, Peggy went to the larder and opened the door. The cake had now been iced and decorated with the little figures, and the blue ribbon was tied round it so the bells hung just so. She was very proud of it and just hoped that the sophisticated Evelyn wouldn't think it too amateurish.

'Oh, Peggy, it's quite magnificent,' breathed Evelyn. 'You are clever.'

Peggy blushed and closed the larder door as the champagne cork popped very satisfactorily and the mismatched glasses were filled with the frothing golden liquid. There was still no sign of Julian or Ron, and Peggy hoped fervently that they hadn't already lost the fleeing ferrets and were trying to find them before anyone noticed.

Anthony pushed his glasses up his nose, went rather red in the face, and then put his arm round Suzy's narrow waist as the glasses were raised in a toast to the happy couple. After that, all of Peggy's careful plans for a structured evening went out of the window.

Julian came up from the cellar, the ferrets in his arms. 'Look, Evelyn,' he said with a beaming smile. 'This is Flora, and this is Dora. Aren't they marvellous?'

Before she could reply, the ferrets wriggled and squirmed, bit his finger and made a bid for escape.

Jane quickly slammed the kitchen door before they could get in the hall – Ron shut the door to the cellar – Peggy made a grab for Dora and missed – and Anthony narrowly escaped getting entangled in Flora as she shot like a bullet between his feet and joined Dora beneath the large kitchen dresser.

Harvey thought this was all great fun and tried to squeeze into the narrow gap, thereby making the heavy dresser rock so alarmingly that everything fell off the shelves.

Everyone had their opinion about how to get the ferrets out, and Peggy could barely speak for embarrassment and fury. As Ted and Anthony held the cupboard steady, and Harvey barked in excitement, Julian and Ron got down on the floor and reached beneath it.

'I've got one,' shouted Julian as he slid his arm back and raised a screeching, furiously wriggling Dora in triumph.

'So have I,' said Ron with equal jubilance. He glanced warily at Peggy. 'We'd better lock them away, I'm thinking. The look on Peggy's face doesn't bode well.'

Peggy was mortified, for Julian's beautiful suit was now covered in dust, fluff and dog hairs from when he'd been crawling on her kitchen floor, and his bitten finger was bleeding profusely. The whole evening was turning into a disaster.

'No harm done,' said Evelyn as she handed her a glass of champagne. 'I must say, you'd never get such good entertainment in a stuffy hotel.'

'But Julian's suit,' stammered Peggy.

Evelyn shrugged. 'It'll all brush off – and it's his own fault he got bitten. He shouldn't have brought the ferrets up here in the first place.'

'Well, it's clear this house hasn't been cleaned properly,' interjected Doris, who was fighting off Harvey's nose which had gone up her skirt. 'I think it's disgusting having such unwholesome creatures in the house. It's bad enough having to put up with this revolting dog.' She gave Harvey's nose a sharp slap, which made him yelp.

Evelyn regarded her coolly as Harvey whimpered and came to her for sympathy. 'Really? Well, I think it's marvellous to have pets in the house. And this fine dog looks clean and very healthy to me.' She gave Harvey a pat and a salted biscuit to assuage his hurt feelings. 'As for fretting over a bit of dust under cupboards, I think it shows signs of a wasted life, don't you, Peggy?'

Doris bristled and went puce, and Peggy defused the situation by raising her glass. 'Cheers,' she said to no one in particular, and took a large, restorative drink.

As Ted rounded up Doris and everyone chattered and drank their champagne, Peggy thought woefully about how the evening should have gone. She had rather hoped Fran would play for them, but she'd left on some secret mission shortly before the fracas with the ferrets, carrying the violin case, which, thankfully, Doris hadn't spotted. Drinks were supposed to be taken in the dining room and then she'd planned that they would all sit down for supper at seven-thirty – posh people didn't eat until late, she knew that much. It was now nearly eight, she noticed in despair, yet no one seemed at all inclined to leave the kitchen.

She looked round at the gathering. Cordelia sat

in queenly splendour by the fire, getting ever more flushed and giggly with each sip of champagne as Ted mildly flirted with her. Ron and Julian had returned from locking away the ferrets and were now making a ham-fisted effort to clean the wound on Julian's finger and stick a plaster on it. His Savile Row suit was still covered in dust and dog hair, and there were spots of blood on his once pristine shirt cuff – yet to Peggy's amazement, he seemed totally unfazed by everything.

Harvey rushed about trying to encourage people to give him more of the lovely little salted biscuits Evelyn had brought, and Doris sat rather primly on the hard kitchen chair, eyeing up Evelyn's silk suit, dainty shoes and triple string of pearls, clearly adding up the cost of such splendour and wondering if she had anything in her vast wardrobe that might outshine them.

The party carried on in the kitchen for almost another hour before they trooped into the dining room to eat cold baked ham, dried-up jacket potatoes and a winter salad fresh from Ron's garden. Fran had finally returned, and after disappearing upstairs with the violin case, had happily joined in the rather boisterous celebrations.

The conversations ebbed and flowed as they sat at the table long after the meal was over, and there was a great deal of laughter at Ron's outrageous stories – which were enthusiastically matched by Julian's own.

As the clock struck eleven, Ted and Julian loaded the cases of champagne, the ham and the salmon into the back of Ted's car. Having rounded up Doris, he said goodnight and thanked everyone for a wonderful evening, while Anthony drew Suzy into his arms for a lingering farewell kiss.

'I'll see you tomorrow,' he murmured into her shining fair hair. 'Please don't be too late, or I'll start to panic that you've changed your mind.'

'As if I would,' she replied fondly before she kissed him again and then shooed him off the doorstep. She stood there until they'd driven out of sight, then went back indoors to help Peggy clear the mess in the dining room.

The table was cleared and everyone helped – or, in Ron and Harvey's case, hindered with the washing-up and tidying away. Then it was time for a glass of Julian's brandy to round off the evening before they all went to bed.

As the house finally fell silent, Peggy lay listening to Daisy's soft breathing and smiled. There had been no need to worry that Suzy's parents would look down their noses – and she should have known that after having had the girl living here for so many years. As Jim would say, she was a worry-wart, and should learn to trust her instincts.

Doris, of course, had put on airs and graces all evening, her strangled vowels making it almost impossible to understand her lengthy descriptions of the important role she and her closest friend, Lady Chumley, played in Cliffehaven society. Thankfully Evelyn and James had true class and didn't turn a hair, but then Suzy had warned them of how she could be.

Peggy turned over in the large, empty bed and, in the soft candle-glow of the nightlight, could just make out the clothes she'd hung on the wardrobe door for tomorrow. Her one-time London evacuee, Sally, had spent days making the beautiful ice-blue silk suit from one of Doris's cast-offs, and Peggy had managed to track down just the right colour to dye the satin shoes she'd found at the WVS used-clothing store.

The old, rather battered blue straw hat had been freshened with a good dollop of starch, a ribbon of silk from the same material as the suit and three rather jaunty pheasant feathers which Ron had brought back from one of his poaching forays up in the hills. She'd known they'd come in use one day.

Peggy smiled again as her eyelids fluttered and sleep beckoned. She hadn't missed her sister's envious glances at Evelyn's outfit, and she wondered just how far Doris was prepared to go to try and outdo it tomorrow.

Chapter Five

Mary had been asleep by the time Ivy returned from her night out, and as the alarm clock shrilled, and Ivy carried on snoring, she realised she'd have to wake her. She gently shook her shoulder. 'Come on, Ivy, or you'll be late for work.'

Ivy burrowed further beneath the covers. 'Gerroff. I don't wanna go to work.'

Mary had heard this protest every morning and knew that Ivy would soon wake up properly and be as chipper and bright as always, so she pulled back the blackout and chintz curtains and the sun poured in. Ignoring her friend's deep groan of annoyance, she lifted the nets and opened the window to let the crisp, fresh air of a winter's morning flood into the stuffy room.

Leaning on the windowsill, she admired the sparkle of the sun on the silky water and the way the seagulls so effortlessly swooped and hovered over the beach. The sky was a pale blue and everything looked dewy fresh after the rain in the night. It was the perfect day for a wedding.

Ivy staggered out of bed, grumbling as she picked up her wash things. 'It's all right for some,' she muttered as she hauled on her dressing gown and peered at her reflection in the dressing-table mirror. She grimaced and hurriedly turned away. 'I gotta splitting headache,' she moaned. 'Can't you ring the factory and tell 'em I'm sick?'

Mary giggled. 'You have a headache every morning, Ivy. Go and get washed and dressed. It'll make you feel better, I promise.'

Ivy returned only a moment later, clearly still not in the best of moods. 'Someone's in there, so it'll be a lick and a promise in the cloakroom sink this morning,' she said grumpily. She dragged on her clothes, tied the laces on her boots and tried to brush the tangles out of her curly hair. Giving up on this task, she wrapped the headscarf over it and tied it firmly above her forehead. 'That'll have t'do,' she sighed.

While all this was going on, Mary quickly dressed in slacks and a sweater, mindful that both Anthony and Ted were in the other bedroom, so it wouldn't be appropriate to wander about in her dressing gown. Doris obviously hadn't forgiven

99

her husband enough to let him share her bed, and Mary had heard the two men talking and laughing quietly together through the wall, and had come to the conclusion that Ted hadn't objected to this arrangement at all.

The bathroom was still engaged, so she and Ivy took their toothbrushes, towels and flannels down to the hall cloakroom. Once Ivy was ready, she pulled on her coat and reached for her gas-mask box. 'I'll have me breakfast in the canteen,' she said. 'Me 'ead's in too bad a state to put up with an over-excited Doris this morning.'

'Thanks for your support, today of all days,' retorted Mary.

'Aw, yer know I don't mean ter drop yer in it, mate, but you'll be fine.' Ivy shot her a cheeky, dimpled grin as she slung the strap of the gas-mask box over her shoulder. 'Enjoy the wedding and keep some of that fancy food for me.' Before Mary could respond, she'd closed the front door behind her with a bang.

Mary quickly went into the kitchen to heat up the large pot of porridge that had been left on the stove. It would probably be wise to have her breakfast and then disappear as well. The thought of Doris having hysterics and causing a huge fuss wasn't her idea of a fun-filled morning either.

As she ate the porridge and toast she could hear movement upstairs and the sound of men's voices. Finishing off the last of her breakfast, she washed the dishes and went into the hall to collect her coat, bag and gas-mask box.

'Good morning, Mary,' said Edward cheerfully as he came down the stairs in twill slacks, shirt

100

and sweater, followed closely by Anthony, who was similarly attired but looked terribly pale.

Mary smiled at them. 'It looks as if someone needs a good breakfast inside them to fight off the collywobbles.'

'I doubt I could keep anything down,' said Anthony as his glasses slipped along his nose. 'I do hope I'm not ailing with something.'

'It's just last-minute nerves, and they'll disappear the moment you see your beautiful bride coming down the aisle,' said Mary, who'd heard her father say this umpteen times to nervous, sickly grooms. 'Now, I'm going out for a walk so you can get ready for the day. I'll be back about half-eleven to get changed, because it's a bit of a walk to the church and I have to be there by one-thirty in case there are early arrivals.'

'I'll give you a lift,' said Edward. 'There'll be plenty of time to get you there before I have to take Doris, Robert and Anthony.'

'We can't possibly spare the car,' said Doris bossily from the top of the stairs. 'I have to be at the hairdresser's at eleven, and then I have an appointment for a manicure – and I wanted to have a quick look in Plummer Roddis to see if they've got in their new stock of hats.'

'Then I'll drop you off first,' Ted replied placidly. 'Once you're ready to come home you can give me a ring and I'll fetch you.'

'But I have to be back here in time to instruct the girls I've hired to do the waitressing,' she protested. 'Really, Edward, it's all very inconvenient.'

'I'm perfectly capable of giving instructions to waitresses,' said Edward, 'and why do you need to look at hats when you have dozens of the things upstairs?'

'You're a man. You wouldn't understand,' she said dismissively. 'As for the girls, I have specific instructions which you're bound to either get muddled or forget entirely.'

Mary could see this might go on for a while, so she pulled on her coat. 'Don't worry about me,' she said to him. 'I can easily walk. Goodness knows, I've done it enough times.'

Doris sniffed, and having decided she'd won the tussle, disappeared into the bathroom.

'I really don't see why you should walk,' said Edward. 'After all, you're as much a part of this wedding as the rest of us. I'll make sure the car is available, don't you worry.'

'I don't want to cause trouble,' she said fretfully.

He smiled his gentle smile. 'Let me deal with Doris. Just be ready in time for me to take you to the church before the fun really starts. Now go and enjoy your walk, and I'll see you at lunchtime.'

Mary enjoyed her walk. She spent some time on the seafront, managed to get a cup of very nice coffee in the tiny tearoom at the end of the promenade, and found a lovely bar of Pears soap as a gift for Doris, who had yet to learn that Fran had borrowed her violin.

Returning to Havelock Road, she found Anthony and Edward in their shirtsleeves, studiously polishing a car that was so like her father's she had to swallow the sudden wave of grief. Avoiding the kerfuffle in the drawing room as Doris gave orders to the two poor girls who would be helping to serve drinks and food at the reception, she went into the kitchen to see what she could make for her lunch.

There were several cases of champagne stacked in one corner, and trays of glasses had been set out on the table beside a splendidly dressed salmon and a thinly sliced cooked ham which had been laid on silver platters. These were accompanied by endless dishes of winter salads, canapés, delicate sandwiches and little bowls of salted biscuits.

Her mouth watered at the sight, but she knew that if she took even one of those biscuits she wouldn't hear the last of it, so she made a spam sandwich, which would have to see her through until after the service.

'Make sure you clean up after yourself,' said Doris as she bustled into the room, resplendent in full make-up, pearls, an outrageously extravagant hat – and, most oddly, a floral overall over her underwear and pink fluffy slippers on her feet.

Mary had to bite her lip so she didn't giggle as she swept up the crumbs and Doris chivvied the two girls in to show them where everything was. It was a marvel that she even owned such things as a pinny and slippers, let alone allowed anyone to see her in them. Shooting the girls a look of sympathy, Mary left them to it and took her sandwich upstairs.

Once she'd eaten her lunch, she washed and began to get dressed. She didn't really have anything at all suitable for a wedding, and the only decent frock she possessed was the black velvet which she and Barbara had made out of a discarded ball-gown – and the last time she'd worn it was for her parents' funeral, which merely made her feel sad.

She was about to slip it on over her dowdy cami-knickers and vest when there was a brief rap on the door and Doris strode in carrying a clothes bag on a hanger and a large hatbox.

'Anthony has asked me to give you these. It's a gift from him and Susan – though why they should think it necessary, I have no idea.' She hung the bag from the wardrobe handle, put the hatbox on the bed and marched out again.

Mary stood there in her underwear and stared in amazement for some moments after the door had closed behind Doris. The blessed woman was the absolute limit, coming in here like that without a by-your-leave. Then she shrugged off the little barb of irritation and turned her attention to the bag.

With trembling fingers, she eased it up and over the hanger and gasped in delight as the lovely dress and jacket were revealed. Made of the finest, softest pale pink cashmere and lined with silk, it was as light as thistledown. With a scooped neck and short sleeves, it was the perfect length, and the little collarless jacket had piped edging in silk and discreet silver buttons down the front and at the ends of the sleeves. The label inside showed it had been bought from a French fashion house in London, and therefore had to have been incredibly expensive.

She was literally trembling with awe as she opened the hatbox to find not only a darling little cream hat which had pink silk ribbons and a bunch of tiny roses to match the dress and coat,

104

but a pair of low-heeled glossy cream pumps. As she lifted them out of the tissue paper she saw the small white envelope, and because her legs threatened to give way in all the excitement, she sank onto the bed to read it.

Dear Mary,
Please accept these gifts, for we cannot thank you enough for agreeing to play at our wedding. We do apologise that everything isn't as new as we would have liked, but my mother was also eager to thank you, and this was the only way we could think of being able to show our appreciation. We do hope you enjoy our special day, and that everything fits – we could only guess at sizes!
With many, many thanks,
Suzy, Anthony, and Evelyn

Mary sat on the bed in a daze until she realised that time was ticking away and she was now in danger of being late. She quickly left the bed and went to sit at the dressing table to use some of the make-up Ivy had persuaded her to buy. She was inexperienced and a bit clumsy, for she'd never been allowed to wear more than a dusting of powder before, and it took a bit of time to get it just right.

Having washed her hair the night before, she decided that only a sophisticated style would do and so brushed it out and twisted it into an elegant chignon which she tethered with hairpins. She then carefully stepped into the gorgeous dress, which slithered like swansdown over her skin and fitted perfectly. There was a bit of a struggle to fasten the tiny silver buttons at the nape, but once she'd stopped panicking this was soon achieved.

Slipping the jacket over it, she caught the faint reminder of some delicate, flowery perfume Mrs James must have worn, and when she looked at her reflection in the mirror, she almost didn't recognise the elegant, pretty young woman who stared back at her. Mary Jones from the rectory at Harebridge Green had never looked so grown-up, and for a fleeting moment she wished Jack could be here to see her in all her finery.

Turning from the mirror, she tried on the shoes and gave a sigh of disappointment. They were about half a size too small and would kill her feet if she had to walk anywhere, but she was determined to wear them, for she only had brogues and sandals, and they would have spoilt the look of everything. She took a few faltering steps to get used to walking in heels, and then sat back down at the dressing table and carefully placed the little hat over her hair, tethering it with the fancy silver-tipped pin that had come with it.

A scrabble inside Ivy's jumbled box of cheap jewellery produced a pair of fake pearl earrings, and she clipped these on. They were the finishing touch.

'Are you ready, Mary?' called Ted on the other side of the door.

'Coming!' She smoothed back a stray wisp of hair, took one last look in the mirror and went to open the door.

Edward was freshly shaved and looked very handsome in his morning suit. 'My word,' he said appreciatively as he looked her up and down. 'You do scrub up nicely, young lady. I'm so glad everything fits and looks so well; Anthony was so worried they might have got the colour and sizing wrong.'

'It's all wonderful,' she breathed. 'They've been terribly kind and very generous.'

He looked at his watch and pulled a face. 'We'd better get going or I'll get it in the neck from Doris.'

There was no sign of Anthony or Doris as they went downstairs and out to the car, and as Edward drove her to the church, Mary couldn't help but remember sitting beside her father in his car on that fateful last night. Determined not to spoil this happy day with sad reminiscences, she waved Edward a cheerful goodbye and hurried inside the church to have one more practice before people started arriving.

Beach View was in chaos, with girls dashing back and forth, calling to each other and arguing over whose turn it was to use the bathroom. Ron and Julian were miraculously dressed and ready, but they'd sought refuge from the female uproar in the kitchen with Harvey and a whisky bottle – which Peggy found very worrying.

Evelyn was cloistered with Suzy in the large front bedroom, and Cordelia was so beside herself with excitement, she couldn't stand still long enough for Peggy to pin on her hat.

'Cordelia, if you keep moving about I'll end up stabbing you with this hatpin.'

'Oh, I do so love weddings, don't you?' she

trilled as she plumped down on her dressing-table stool. 'What do you think her dress is like? I just know she's going to look an absolute picture, because Suzy's a beautiful girl to start with and brides are always radiant, aren't they?'

Peggy knew she didn't really expect an answer so she nodded and finally managed to get the pin into the hat. 'Do you want me to fasten your pearls and help with your earrings?'

'Yes, dear, if you would. They're far too fiddly for my old fingers.'

Peggy took the double string of pearls and fastened the silver catch at the back, and then carefully screwed on the matching earrings. 'There you are. Now stand up and let me look at you.'

Cordelia leaned heavily on her walking stick and heaved herself off the stool to turn this way and that to show off her new suit.

Peggy felt quite tearful, for the soft heather of the tweed enhanced Cordelia's lovely clear skin and white hair, and the way Sally had cut it was quite superb, for it fitted perfectly.

'Sally's done a wonderful job, hasn't she?' said Cordelia in delight as she admired her reflection in the long mirror behind the door. 'I haven't looked this smart in ages.' She turned back to the dressing table, opened her jewellery box and handed Peggy a lovely brooch of twisted gold encircling an amethyst of the deepest purple. 'Could you pin this on for me, dear?'

Peggy fastened the brooch to the jacket lapel and stood back to admire the effect. 'You look wonderful,' she said as she kissed her soft cheek. 'Now let's make sure you have everything you'll

108

need in your handbag then I'll help you down-stairs. I think Ron and Julian are about to open a bottle of champagne so we can drink a toast to a happy day.'

'Ooh, how lovely.' Cordelia's little face lit up and she grabbed her handbag, checked she had at least three handkerchiefs and then headed for the door. 'Champagne is supposed to be good for you, you know. My doctor said so.'

'I think he meant in small doses,' laughed Peggy as they made their slow descent to the hall. 'You'd better pace yourself, Cordelia, or you'll fall asleep during the ceremony and miss everything.'

'Stuff and nonsense,' she retorted as she headed eagerly for the kitchen. 'How could you possibly think I'd do a thing like that?'

Peggy smiled, for Cordelia could fall asleep at the drop of a hat. 'I'll leave you to the tender mercies of Ron and Julian,' she said. 'I still have to sort out Daisy and get dressed myself.'

'Well, don't be too long, or you might find we've drunk all that lovely champagne,' Cordelia replied with a giggle.

Peggy closed her bedroom door and let her breath out on a sigh. It had been a long, busy mor-ning and the day wasn't even half through. She returned Daisy's smile and quickly changed her nappy before seeing to herself. Having put on her make-up and tidied her hair, she pulled on fresh underwear and her one decent pair of stockings before slipping on the lace-edged slip that was made from the same material as the suit lining.

Once dressed, she stood and admired herself in the mirror, for the pale blue silk suit looked gorgeous and showed off her slender figure to perfection. The straight skirt reached to just below the knee, and the raglan-sleeved jacket had a deep collar which revealed a hint of the lacy slip where the front of the jacket was crossed over to be fastened at the side. With the matching sash tied round her waist, she grinned with satisfaction before she slipped on her shoes, pinned on the hat and hurried to get Daisy dressed in the lovely dress and coat Evelyn had bought in London.

Peggy emerged from the bedroom with Daisy in her arms to find that Evelyn was waiting for her in the kitchen with Cordelia, Ron and Harvey – and a glass of champagne. 'Julian's gone up to have a few quiet words with Suzy before everything gets going,' Evelyn said as she patted Daisy's cheek and admired her in her new outfit. 'I don't need to tell you that she looks utterly beautiful and that I've had to put at least four handkerchiefs in my bag.'

'Me too,' admitted Peggy, who thought Evelyn looked like a fashion plate in her gorgeous grey shantung dress and coat, and matching hat. Her shoes and handbag matched the cream band that ran round the hat, and pearls glowed discreetly in her ears and at her throat. 'You look lovely,' she breathed.

'And so do you. Where *did* you find that gorgeous suit?'

Peggy was in the midst of explaining about Sally when there was a knock on the front door. 'That must be our taxi,' she said and quickly drained her glass. 'Cordelia, Ron, it's time we were leaving.'

'Surely you aren't going to carry Daisy about all day?' Evelyn frowned with concern.

'Ron took the pram round to the church this morning and left it in the vestry,' Peggy explained as she chivvied Ron and Cordelia out of the kitchen to the anguished howls of Harvey, who'd been quickly shut in the cellar. 'She's far too heavy, and wriggles worse than an eel now she's finding her feet.'

Peggy opened the front door and looked back up the stairs to the lovely, excited faces of her girls as they leaned over the landing railings and waved. 'See you all in church,' she called up to them.

As the taxi pulled up outside the church and they climbed out, they could already hear the beautiful organ music drifting from inside. Other people were arriving and Peggy recognised them as Suzy's nursing friends from the hospital, so she said hello, introduced them to Evelyn, and then hurried in to greet the rather elderly vicar and put Daisy in her pram.

Having strapped her in firmly, she pushed the pram down the aisle, nodding and smiling to everyone before she kissed poor, nervous Anthony and shook hands with his very calm and rather dull-looking best man, who introduced himself as Robert Goodyear and explained that he worked with Anthony at the MOD. Peggy parked the pram by the front pew against the wall, gave Daisy her bottle of juice, then sat down and looked round at the gathering.

There was no sign of Martin yet, but then he had said he might be late. Cordelia and Evelyn were now coming down the aisle, and Ron slipped into a pew towards the back next to Rosie, who looked very glamorous in a black hat and pink suit. Peggy hoped she hadn't left Tommy in charge of the pub for the rest of the lunchtime session, for she could say goodbye to any profit if she had.

Just as Evelyn took her place on the bride's side of the church, Doris made a grand entrance on Edward's arm, her honey-coloured silk dress perfectly matching the long mink coat and hugely extravagant hat. The whole outfit looked new – Doris had obviously been shopping this morning. 'You can say a lot of things about my sister,' she muttered to Cordelia, 'but you can't deny she knows how to dress for the occasion.'

Cordelia eyed Doris up and down as she and Ted came to sit next to her, and then sniffed with disapproval. 'If you think so, Peggy,' she said acidly. 'Mutton dressed as lamb, if you ask me.'

Peggy wasn't at all offended by this, for she knew there was no love lost between Cordelia and Doris. She settled back to listen to the wonderful music, while Daisy waved her rag book about and beamed an almost toothless smile at everyone. Mary looked so different in Evelyn's lovely dress and jacket, and her hair really suited her that way. My goodness, she was growing up fast, and how beautifully she could play that ugly great brute of an organ.

The music came to an end and she saw Mary look towards the main door. Her heart began to thud and she could already feel the tears beginning to prick in anticipation. Then Mary played the opening phrase of the bridal march and everyone was on their feet.

A radiant Suzy virtually floated down the aisle

on her father's arm in a confection of white taffeta and lace, the bouquet of exquisite white lilies, dark green ivy and copper leaves trailing almost to her toes, the cobweb of veil drifting over her beautiful face.

And there were Peggy's girls following her in the dresses that Evelyn had brought down from her dressmaker in London. They were in soft shades of gold, silver and russet, except for the chief bridesmaid, Fran, who wore a deep shade of copper which enhanced her magnificent hair and made her look like a sprite that might just have momentarily ventured out of her forest glade.

Peggy could barely see as she shot a glance at Anthony, and the tears were already threatening to ruin her make-up when she saw how his eyes shone with love and his face lit up as Suzy came slowly towards him. How wonderful. How simply perfect it all was. Oh, she did so love weddings.

The service began as the young couple stood by the altar steps and the aged vicar welcomed them all and gave the usual preamble about marriage being a serious business in his quavering voice. Then they all stood again for the first hymn, 'Love Divine', and Peggy found she was too emotional to be able to sing, so just enjoyed listening.

The service continued and then Julian's wonderfully rich, deep voice rang out as he read the passage from the bible that told the story of the wedding at Canaan. This was followed by the heart-stirring 'I Vow to Thee, My Country', which left everyone reaching for their handkerchiefs.

The vicar led the couple to the altar, where they knelt in prayer before they exchanged their vows and Anthony slipped the wedding ring on Suzy's finger. Then he tenderly lifted the veil and shyly kissed his beautiful bride before they turned towards the congregation and, with beaming smiles, headed for the vestry to sign the register.

As Julian and Edward left their pews to join them so they could witness the register, Peggy's heart skipped a beat. Fran hadn't followed the rest of the bridal party but was standing on the altar steps, the violin nestled under her chin, her glorious hair and dress making her look almost of another world.

She shot a glance at Doris, who was staring at the girl with deep suspicion, and she could only pray that, for once, her sister would keep her mouth shut and not cause ructions.

And then the haunting strains of the violin soared to the high rafters and everything else was forgotten as the music captured and ensnared them and they were unable to tear their gazes from the glorious girl with the autumnal hair and shimmering, copper-coloured dress.

There was a stunned silence as the final note gently drifted away, then people forgot where they were and rose as one to applaud. Peggy was crying, and so was Cordelia – even Doris looked tearful, and as Peggy glanced round the church she could see an awful lot of handkerchiefs being put to good use.

Then Mary struck the first chord for the triumphal entrance of the newly married couple from the vestry, and Fran slipped in beside the

114

rather stunned-looking Robert Goodyear to join the procession down the aisle. She grinned at Doris and gave a naughty wink to Peggy as she walked past.

'Did you know about that?' rasped Doris.

'I certainly didn't,' Peggy replied truthfully. 'But wasn't she magnificent?'

Doris cleared her throat and delicately dabbed her eyes with a lace-edged handkerchief. 'You should have warned me it was Fran I was lending my very expensive violin to.'

'Oh, Doris,' Peggy sighed as everyone gathered their things and prepared to follow the bridal party out of the church. 'Just give the girl some credit for once. She'll do that violin no harm – you only have to see how lovingly she plays it to know that.'

'I grant you, she does play extremely well, which came as a real shock. One would never have imagined...' She noted Peggy's glare and quickly changed tack. 'But subterfuge is something I cannot forgive. It's clear that Mary was in on it, and I shall be having a few words with her once all this is over, I can tell you.'

'Oh, give it a rest,' snapped Peggy. 'They played at your son's wedding because they wanted to make their day special. Don't spoil it, Doris. Or I'm warning you, you'll have me to deal with.'

'Well, if you're going to be vulgar like that,' Doris retorted with a sniff, 'then there is obviously no point in carrying on this conversation.'

'Put a ruddy sock in it,' Peggy muttered crossly, 'and let us all enjoy the day without you carping on about things that don't matter.'

There were no church bells to ring out the joyous news of the wedding, for they'd been silenced for the duration of the war to be used only if there was an invasion, but no one seemed to notice as they rushed to be the first to congratulate not only the bride and groom, but also a triumphant Fran.

Peggy bumped the pram down the shallow steps and pulled up the hood. Despite the bright sun the wind was cold, and she didn't want Daisy to get a chill. She'd been marvellous during the ceremony, and when Fran had played, she'd sat wide-eyed and silent, as if mesmerised.

'Fran, that was truly wonderful,' Peggy said when she finally managed to get anywhere near her. 'I don't think I've ever seen people react like that in a church.'

Fran grinned impishly. 'Doris was po-faced, but she did compliment me on my playing and said I could borrow the violin for the foreseeable future as long as I promised to accompany Mary when she does the charity concert on New Year's Day.'

Peggy rolled her eyes. 'I might have known she'd want something in return.' She glanced across at the best man, who seemed to be completely transfixed as he stood at a distance and admired Fran with undisguised longing. 'I see you've got an admirer,' she softly teased.

'Lord help me,' whispered Fran. 'Robert's not my sort at all, but there's nothing I can do about it. Is he still staring at me like a lovesick puppy?'

Peggy nodded as she regarded the rather earnest, awkward young man. 'Give him a chance, Fran,' she coaxed softly. 'You can't always tell a book by its cover, you know, and he could turn out to be extremely nice.'

Fran chuckled. 'You'll not be match-making, now would you, Aunt Peg? To be sure, I'm happy the way I am.' She gave her a quick hug and moved away to talk to the other nurses while the young man's gaze followed her every move.

If only Robert had the gumption to approach her and actually talk to her, then he might get somewhere, thought Peggy in frustration. But then Fran was a lively spirit, and she probably terrified him with her beauty and her bright personality. The poor boy's admiration was doomed to failure unless he turned out to have some sort of saving grace.

Peggy turned her attention away from Fran and the lovesick best man and saw Mary being hugged and thanked by Suzy and Anthony before she was captured by Evelyn. She'd give her own thanks later, she decided. She looked round at the gathering to see if Martin had made it yet, but there was no sign of him, and she could only suppose that the traffic had held him up.

Peggy wandered from group to group, and although she chatted and laughed and gave the impression that she was quite happy to be on her own, there was a deep yearning to have Jim by her side, and his arm to lean on – not separated from him by the many miles between here and the Far East. And yet she wasn't the only woman on her own, and as time went on, she began to really enjoy herself.

Mary was feeling shy and rather embarrassed by

all the praise that had been heaped on her, and although she knew she looked as smart and sophisticated as everyone else, her feet were killing her in the tight shoes.

Once the photographs had been taken and the confetti had been thrown, Edward drove the bride and groom back to Havelock Road. Julian then crammed Doris, Evelyn, Cordelia, Rita, Jane, Sarah, Fran and Mary into his enormous Rolls-Royce, and they purred along feeling terribly grand as they giggled and gave regal waves to those who stopped to watch them pass.

As the bridal party formed a welcoming line in the hall, two of Anthony's work colleagues from the MOD drove back and forth to ferry the remaining guests from the church to the reception. The house was soon filled with laughing, chattering people who drank the champagne, ate the delicious food and admired the magnificent sea views from the drawing-room window.

Mary sipped the lovely champagne and saw that Doris was in her element as she graciously greeted everyone and made sure they had something to drink, and someone to talk to. Mrs James and her handsome husband were equally good hosts, and Anthony and Suzy held hands as they drifted from group to group in a haze of happiness.

As darkness fell and the blackout curtains were pulled, Suzy slipped away to change out of her lovely dress into a smart navy suit and hat. Everyone gathered on the doorstep to wish them well, and Anthony drove them away in the little car he'd borrowed from his office pool, the tin cans, balloons and old shoes rattling along behind them.

'Where are they spending their honeymoon?' Mary asked Peggy.

Peggy shot a glance at a rather tearful Doris to make sure she was out of earshot. 'Anthony bought a dear little house just to the north of Cliffehaven and they'll spend their honeymoon there settling in. But don't mention it to Doris, or she'll be on their doorstep before you can say knife.'

Mary smiled. 'My lips are sealed,' she promised.

Peggy sighed. 'I'm going to miss her dreadfully, you know,' she said wistfully. 'She's become so much a part of the family, and as she packed her things and slowly emptied her room, it was like saying goodbye to a daughter.'

'I can understand that,' murmured Mary. 'But knowing Suzy, she'll visit regularly, and you still have the other girls. I'm sure it won't be long before you have someone else to fill that empty room.'

Peggy dabbed her eyes with her rather soggy hanky. 'I'll leave it until the New Year now,' she said. 'Unless you and Ivy want to move in with me?' she asked hopefully.

Mary put her arm round her shoulders. 'I do appreciate the offer, Peggy, but we're settled here now. And I promise to visit often.'

'That would be lovely,' she murmured. 'I'd hate to think we might lose touch.'

Mary laughed as they headed back indoors. 'There's no fear of that,' she declared. 'You've done so much for me and been so kind, I look upon you as my most favourite auntie.'

'But you're all right with you-know-who now?'

Mary nodded. 'I keep out of his way and ignore him. He hasn't tried approaching me again.'

'Good. Now let's make a cup of tea before I have to get Ron and Cordelia home. All that rich food and champagne has left me with a terrible thirst, and Ron has had enough whisky to sink a battleship. He'll start singing next – and that would be too awful.'

Rosie had known it was risky to leave her brother in charge of the pub for the remaining half-hour of the lunchtime session, and she certainly wasn't prepared to let him loose with her takings during the busy evening. So she'd spent only an hour at the reception and hurried home expecting to find an empty till and no sign of Tommy.

But he'd surprised her, for the day's takings had been added up and noted down along with the amount of float he'd left for tonight. There was no sign of him, but as Monty was also missing, she had to assume he'd taken the pup for his walk, which again was a huge surprise. Tommy didn't do dog-walking – in fact he didn't do much at all except make a mess and get in her way – but for once he seemed to be on his best behaviour.

She breathed a sigh of relief, slipped off her high heels and went upstairs to make a cup of tea and get changed for opening time. Perhaps he really was trying to change his life around, though it would be a first – and she was always deeply suspicious when Tommy was on his best behaviour, for it usually meant he was plotting something.

She put her wedding finery away and was now in her usual black skirt and white blouse, her bare feet padding on the cold kitchen lino as she made a pot of tea and hunted out an aspirin. The champagne had flowed and she'd probably had too much of it to keep a clear head tonight.

The sound of scampering paws and the heavy tread of feet on the bare wooden stairs heralded their arrival. Monty leapt up and tried to lick her face, then wriggled and squirmed, his plumed tail thudding against the kitchen cupboard as she praised and patted him. 'Thanks for taking him out, Tommy,' she said. 'I've just made a pot of tea. Would you like some?'

He nodded and shed his coat and hat onto a nearby chair, then took the loaded tray into the sitting room and set it down on a low table by the couch. 'How did the wedding go?'

'Wonderfully well.' Rosie sank into the couch, and Monty immediately jumped up to sprawl across her lap. As she'd been absent for most of the day, she decided to ignore the dog hair on her black skirt and let him stay. She caressed his floppy ears as she went on to describe the bride, the bridesmaids and the ceremony, and how everyone had been so stunned by Fran's violin playing. 'She looked like a will-o'-the-wisp who'd strayed from her fairy kingdom,' she finished dreamily.

'Is she and that other girl coming in tonight to play?' he asked almost nonchalantly as he poured out the tea.

Rosie glanced across at him as she lit a cigarette. 'They're all still at the reception and won't play again until Christmas Eve.' She regarded him steadily. 'You know the rules, Tommy. You're to stay away from all the girls who come in here, especially Peggy's girls.'

He passed her a cup and saucer, lit his own cigarette and sat back in the armchair. 'I have no intention of going anywhere near any of them,' he said. 'I prefer my women mature and experienced. I just wondered when they'd be in next, that's all. A lot of the customers were asking after them this lunchtime.'

'I'll pin a notice up on the door about Christmas Eve.' She sipped her tea.

'That Mary isn't one of Peggy's girls, is she?' he asked casually.

Rosie looked at him through the cigarette smoke. 'What's it to you, Tommy?'

He shrugged as his gaze slid away and he tapped ash into the ashtray. 'Nothing. Only I heard she's new in the town, and I wondered how Peggy got to know her. They seem very pally.'

Rosie weighed her words carefully before she answered him. 'I have no idea,' she said, 'but she's a lovely girl, and Peggy and I have come to like her very much.' She eyed him speculatively. 'I don't know why you should be interested in Mary, but it stops now. If I find you've been pestering her again, then you're out on your ear. Is that understood?'

He heaved a great sigh. 'It comes to something when I can't have a friendly conversation with my sister about the people who come into her pub.'

'As long as that was all it was,' she replied sternly.

'Give me some credit, Rose,' he muttered.

His credit had run out a long time ago as far as

Rosie was concerned, but she'd made her point clear and as there seemed no profit in taking this conversation any further, she changed the subject. 'I'm expecting a delivery from the brewery tomorrow morning, so I'll need you to help me check the order and change those two empty barrels. I just hope they'll bring everything I asked for this time. We're already getting busy, and with Christmas and New Year looming I can't afford to run out.'

'I'm sure the brewery is aware of that,' he said with a shrug. 'But they can only bring what they have as long as the rationing makes everything scarce.'

Rosie nodded. 'Either way, I'll just have to manage.' She gave a sigh as she stroked Monty's silky coat. 'I'm rather hoping we can welcome in 1943 with some style, and that Fran and Mary will be off duty and able to play.'

'Surely they won't be expected to go to work on such a night?'

Rosie shrugged. 'Fran's a theatre nurse at the hospital and Mary works up at the Kodak factory. Their shifts are long and fairly irregular, so there's no guarantee they'll have any time off over Christmas. But I'll certainly ask and just hope they haven't made any other plans.'

Tommy didn't reply. He sat smoking thoughtfully for a while, then stubbed out his cigarette and drained his cup of tea. 'I have to go out for a bit. But I'm not on fire-watch tonight, so I'll be back in plenty of time to help when you open up at six.' He gave Rosie his most charming smile.

She watched as he pulled on his smart coat and hat then went whistling down the stair, slamming the side door behind him. Tommy was definitely up to something, but she was blowed if she knew what it might be. She stroked Monty as she sat there deep in thought. Tommy would have to be closely watched, for the last thing she needed now was any trouble.

Once all the wedding guests had drifted off to their homes, Peggy and the others from Beach View said their goodbyes to Doris and Edward, praising and thanking them for a marvellous day. They'd had to wake Cordelia, who'd fallen asleep in a chair overwhelmed with too much champagne and excitement, and Julian had driven everyone back home to a joyous welcome from Harvey.

Evelyn and Julian hadn't stayed long after that, for they needed to get back to London and it was a long, rather dangerous drive in the blackout. They'd arrived as strangers but left as friends, with an open, genuine invitation on both sides to visit when they could.

Peggy now sat in her kitchen wrapped in her warm dressing gown as the girls stopped chattering and moving about upstairs and the house slowly fell silent. She was tired, but her racing mind wouldn't allow for sleep yet, so she sipped her tea and lit a cigarette as she sat there and tried to relax after the lovely day.

It had taken her quite a while to calm Cordelia down and get her settled for the night after rather overdoing it on the champagne and rich food, but once the old lady's head had hit the pillow she was soon snoring. Ron had taken Harvey out for a long run after his day of imprisonment in the cellar, and Daisy had been a bit grizzly and overtired after all the fuss and praise, and it had been a while before she too had settled.

Peggy puffed on her cigarette. Martin hadn't put in an appearance at all today, and now she was getting worried. There had been no telephone call either, which was unusual, for Martin was a thoughtful man and would have known she'd become fretful at his no-show. There had been no point in even trying to get hold of anyone at the airfield, for such private calls were now frowned upon – and if anything had happened to him, she would have heard by now. All she could really do was wait until morning and hope he would get in touch.

Her thoughts meandered over the otherwise happy day and she felt a swell of pride for all her girls. Suzy had made the most beautiful bride; Fran had been quite magnificent; Rita, Jane and Sarah had looked wonderful in their dresses – and Mary had shone at the organ. All in all they had come up trumps and proved to Doris that she had no cause to look down her nose at any of them. At least she'd had the honesty to acknowledge Fran's talent – even if it did mean the girl had been blackmailed into performing at the charity concert she'd organised for New Year's Day.

How Jim would have loved it all, she thought as she sat there in the flickering glow of the range fire. He and Julian would have got on like a house on fire, and although he'd have had to have been watched closely in case he drank too much and started flirting with every woman in the place, he'd have been the life and soul of the party.

She'd missed him terribly all through the day, for a family wedding simply wasn't the same without him at her side.

Deciding that she would write to him tomorrow and tell him all about it, her thoughts strayed to Christmas. She and Jim had only spent two other Christmases apart, and that had been when he was fighting in the last war – now she would have to face another one without him, knowing that he was on the other side of the world.

She threw the butt of her cigarette into the fire and closed the range door. The weariness was making her morbid, and she needed to go to bed. The house was dreadfully untidy and it would take most of tomorrow to get it straight again. Then there was the washing, the queuing at the shops, her stint at the WVS... It was all getting on top of her and if she didn't let it go, she'd just collapse beneath the weight of it.

Chapter Six

It was Christmas Eve and the factories were still in twenty-four-hour production and would continue to be so right through what had once been the holiday season. Mary sat next to Jenny, sifting through the thousands of airgraphs that seemed to pour in every day.

Despite the strict no-talking rule set by the fiercely bossy Sergeant Norris, all the girls had learned how to hold short conversations without moving their lips as they kept their heads down and swiftly sorted the airgraphs into piles, which were then taken to another desk to be checked and sent to the service sensors. At least Mary no longer suffered from neck ache, but sitting down all day made her lethargic, and she was beginning to wonder if she'd end up with a bottom the width of a battleship.

The hooter went at six and she slowly got to her feet and stretched. There wouldn't be time to go back to Havelock Road and eat supper before she had to be at the Anchor, so she'd told Doris she'd eat at the canteen and stay at Peggy's as she always did after such a night, so she didn't have to walk home alone.

Ivy was on late shift, so would be working through the night, but at least she had Christmas Day off – whereas Mary had to work through it so she could have New Year's Day off for Doris's concert. Not that Mary really minded missing Christmas lunch with Doris and Edward, for it was sure to be dull, and Doris would probably go on endlessly about the wedding and the concert while poor Edward was ignored.

'It seems odd having to work on Christmas Day,' said Jenny as they pulled on their coats and grabbed their gas-mask boxes and bags from the locker. 'But then being so far from home and family doesn't really make it feel like Christmas, does it? I'd rather work than spend it at the hostel, to be honest. At least we get double pay, and a slap-up lunch, which should be quite jolly with all the other girls.'

'I feel the same,' said Mary as they went out

into the wintry night. 'Will they really give us a proper Christmas dinner, do you think?'

'They do it every year, apparently. And I've heard it's quite something, so we're in for a treat.'

Mary unfurled her umbrella and pulled up her coat collar against the bitter wind that was driving the rain across the factory estate. 'Are you coming to the pub tonight?'

'I'll say. Wouldn't miss it for the world.' Jenny smiled and opened her own umbrella. 'You and Fran have really livened up the place. It's a great pity the other pubs don't follow suit.' She grimaced at the lashing rain which had formed deep puddles on the tarmac and was gushing from all the gutters. 'I'll see you later then, if I don't drown on the way home.'

As Jenny hurried off towards the gate, Mary ran across the yard and went into the warm fug of the canteen. She waited in the queue for a plate of stew and mashed potato, a bowl of jelly and a cup of tea, and, not really in the mood for chatter, found a place at an empty table.

The canteen wasn't very busy, for most people went straight home at the end of their shift, and those coming on would have already eaten. But a few lingered during their break as their shifts over-lapped. Mary tucked into the hot food, for she was hungry after the long day and she'd only eaten a sandwich for lunch. As she finished her meal and drank her tea, her thoughts returned to Jack and to Christmas.

Jack was still on his course, and his last short note had told her that there would be no leave for at least the next week or so. He was exhausted most of the time, but doing well and passing all the torturous tests the training officers put them through, though he was getting a bit tired of being shouted at from the moment he woke up to lights-out. He signed off with love and hoped that, despite everything, she had a good Christmas.

Mary had been bitterly disappointed that she wouldn't see him, or be able to stay with Barbara and Joseph over the two days – and yet now she was rather glad things had turned out the way they had. Being at work would focus her mind on other things, and because she hadn't been able to return to Harebridge Green, she wouldn't be haunted by all the memories of past Christmases. And yet, even here, those memories still had the power to hurt and they returned with full force as she sat alone in the factory canteen.

Each year they had decorated the church with wreaths of holly, ivy and mistletoe, and dozens of candles that were lit for the midnight service. The Nativity crib, which looked a little more battered every time it came out of storage, had always been placed by the font, and each year she'd watched in awe as Gideon lovingly mended the wooden figures and repainted Mary's blue robes and the golden halo above the baby Jesus' head.

Gideon had always let her help decorate the sweet-scented tree in the sitting room with tinsel and silver baubles, and when she'd been very young, he'd lifted her up so she could put the rather scruffy angel right on the top. Then there was the stocking hanging by the fire, the plate of mince pies and carrots left for Father Christmas and his reindeer – and Christmas mornings, and the magic of presents followed by the morning service around the crib. And then home to turkey and silly parlour games with their visitors before a tea of iced fruit cake and turkey sandwiches. Once the evening had drawn in, Gideon would tuck her into her snug bed and read the story of that first Christmas in his melodic Welsh tones that soon sent her happily to sleep.

Every memory was redolent with Gideon, and Christmas could never be the same now he was gone. The knowledge that she would never hear his lilting voice again or feel his comforting arms around her made her heart ache, and she was blinded with sudden tears.

'Are you all right, dearie?' The plump woman in the white overall looked at her in concern as she cleared the dishes onto a tray.

Mary hastily blinked back her tears and gave a tremulous smile. 'Just feeling a bit homesick,' she replied.

'Yes, it's tough on you young ones at Christmas,' the woman said in sympathy. Then she smiled. 'Never you mind, dear. We'll soon have that blooming Hitler on the run and then we'll all get to go home.' She picked up the tray and waddled off.

Mary was strangely cheered by this, and she pushed back from the table and headed for the door. There would be other Christmases and the pain of her loss would gradually fade as Jack came home and life returned to normal – but for now she had to keep her chin up and get on with things as best she could.

Looking out, she realised that at least it had

stopped raining, even though the wind was still blustering. She pulled up her coat collar, tucked her umbrella under her arm, hitched her hand-bag and gas-mask box straps over her shoulder and hurried towards the gate.

She saw the woman pacing back and forth on the other side of the high fence, her chin tucked into her coat collar, her dark hair covered in a headscarf, and recognised her as the same one she and Ivy had seen several times before. Who she was and what she was doing there was a bit of a puzzle, but they'd come to the conclusion that she must have been waiting for someone to come off their shift.

Mary was about to head down the hill when the woman called out, 'Excuse me! Are you Mary Jones?' She stopped walking and looked at the woman, who was probably in her late thirties, maybe early forties. She was of medium height and very slender, her dark hair glinting from drop-lets of rain, and now she was closer to her, she looked rather familiar, though Mary couldn't think why. 'Yes, I'm Mary,' she said with a frown.

'Look, I'm sorry if I startled you,' the woman said. 'But I've been trying to catch you alone so we could talk in private.'

Mary's frown deepened. 'Do I know you?'

The woman shook her head. 'It doesn't matter who I am.' She put her hand on Mary's arm and drew her further from the curious guard at the gate. 'But if you're the girl who's been asking about Cyril Fielding, then I need to have a serious talk with you.'

Mary's pulse began to race. 'You know Cyril?'

'In a manner of speaking,' she replied dryly. 'Can I ask why you're trying to find him?'

Mary looked into the carefully made-up face and thought swiftly. This woman could be Cyril's wife, or some woman he'd abandoned or cheated out of money. She would have to tread carefully. 'I really don't think that is any of your business,' she said politely. 'And anyway, how did you know I was looking for him?'

'You were asking about him in the Lilac Tea-rooms.'

'But that was weeks ago. Why didn't you say something then?'

'I have my reasons,' the woman said cryptically. 'But I should warn you, Cyril Fielding is not a man to be trusted, and it would be wise to stop asking after him.'

Mary regarded her thoughtfully. 'I've already heard a great deal about Cyril – none of which gives me the slightest desire to have anything to do with him. How do you know him?'

'I met him many years ago, and got to know him too well,' the woman replied bitterly.

Mary thought she understood now: this must be one of his numerous discarded women. 'I'm sorry if he did you wrong,' she sympathised. 'And it was very kind of you to warn me about him, but I can assure you, I really am not interested in finding him any more.'

The woman's tense shoulders relaxed and she pulled her coat collar more firmly round her neck. 'Good, because whatever reason you had for try-ing to find him would only have ended in trouble.'

Mary regarded her steadily as they were

buffeted by the wind. 'You speak as if he's still here in Cliffehaven – but I was told that he'd left long ago, and no one has seen him since.'

Something sparked fleetingly in the woman's eyes before she looked away. 'Cyril certainly left, but there are some round here who have long memories, so talking about him would just stir things up.'

This was just what Peggy had said. But Mary was intrigued by this woman who clearly hated Cyril enough to come and stand outside the factory gate waiting until she was alone to warn her off. 'Well, I'm very grateful to you for making the effort to talk to me about all this, but why won't you at least tell me your name, and how you got involved with Cyril?'

'As I said before, it doesn't matter who I am. I'm just wondering what business a young girl like you would have with a man like Cyril.'

Mary realised then that the woman would tell her nothing. 'Private business,' she said mildly so as not to give offence. 'Now, I really do have to go because I have to be somewhere.'

'Yes, I know. You play at the Anchor, don't you?'

'Yes. Are you one of the regulars? I don't remember seeing you there.'

The woman shook her head. 'I'm not welcome at the Anchor,' she said flatly. She suddenly gripped Mary's arm, her expression intense. 'Watch out for Tommy Findlay. He might appear to be charming, but he's a snake.'

Mary was startled and immediately wary. The woman was too intense, too persistent – and far too secretive. A shiver of apprehension ran down

133

her spine as she eased her arm from the stranger's grip. 'I already know all about Tommy, and believe me, I keep well away from him.'

The woman nodded and stepped back. 'Good. Make sure you keep it that way.' She turned abruptly and headed quickly down the hill.

Mary watched until she was lost in the darkness, then she shivered again before she slowly followed her. It had been an extraordinary and unsettling conversation, and although it had confirmed that she'd done the right thing by bringing her search for Cyril to an end, Mary had the feeling that there had been far more to that woman than she'd first thought.

Her footsteps faltered and she came to a sudden halt as she remembered where she'd seen her before. Yes, it had been outside the factory gates – but before that she'd seen her outside the Anchor, with Findlay, and he'd called her Eileen.

It had been a worrying few days for Peggy, but a telephone call three nights ago had finally put her mind at ease over Martin. He'd been held up on his journey from visiting his parents and had then been ordered back to immediate duty. He hadn't had the time to telephone but had sent a message through one of his admin staff, which obviously hadn't reached her. He apologised profusely for worrying her, and promised to try and visit over the Christmas period if his duties allowed.

Peggy hoped he could make it, for she didn't like the thought of him stuck at the airfield without any of his family to share the day with. Yet the same applied to Cissy, for she'd telephoned in tears and said she had to remain on duty at least until New Year's Eve – and even that wasn't set in stone. Peggy had tried to soothe her, but it had been awfully difficult over a telephone, and once the heartbreaking call was over she too had burst into tears.

Now it was Christmas Eve and Peggy had decided not to go to the Anchor tonight. The weather was foul, Daisy was teething and Cordelia had a nasty cold. Having given Daisy her nightly dose of cod-liver oil and sung her to sleep, she then went up to settle Cordelia with a fresh hot-water bottle, a cup of hot cocoa and some Vicks VapoRub to ease her congestion.

'Thank you, dear,' she said as she blew her poor reddened nose. 'What a nuisance I'm being when you're so busy. I do hope I'm feeling better in the morning.'

'I'm sure you'll be fine after a good night's sleep,' soothed Peggy as she tucked in the blankets and pulled up the eiderdown. 'And you're never a nuisance, Cordelia,' she added softly. 'So please, just snuggle down and stop worrying.'

Peggy turned off the main light so the room was lit only by the bedside lamp. Leaving the door ajar so she could hear if Cordelia called out in the night, she went to check the bedrooms. Jane and Sarah were at the pub with Fran, who unfortunately was on duty tomorrow night. Rita was also out, but she was on fire-watch until the early hours of the morning. Mary would be sleeping here after the pub closed, and she would go into what had once been Cissy's bedroom, which was on the top floor.

Peggy noted that, as usual, Jane, Sarah and Fran had left their rooms neat and tidy, but that Rita's looked as if a whirlwind had gone through it. With a weary sigh, she picked the discarded clothing from the floor, pulled the bed-covers straight and plumped up the pillows. The furniture could have done with a dust, the floor needed sweeping, and there were biscuit crumbs in the upholstered chair that stood by the gas fire.

Peggy had to smile, for Rita was such a darling girl, and she knew she rather spoiled her. The poor child had lost her mother when she was still at junior school, and she and her father had struggled on until he'd been called up. His letters home had been few and far between, and Peggy knew how Rita depended upon her for the mothering she so sorely missed – but she really should try and keep her room tidy and clean. The other girls managed it, even though they worked the same long hours, so there was no excuse really.

She looked at the three framed photographs that stood on the narrow mantelpiece above the gas fire. Rita had inherited the dark hair and eyes of her mother's Irish ancestry, and the firm chin and steady gaze of her father. The third picture was of Rita and Cissy in their school uniform, arm in arm, grinning like imps at the end of a summer term long before war was declared.

Peggy closed the door and went upstairs to the large double bedroom where daylight would give a view over the rooftops to a glimpse of the sea. Suzy and Fran had lived in this room for three years, and it still felt strange not to see their things scattered about. Fran had moved to the smaller room which had once been Anne's, and although she'd settled in happily and assured everyone she was delighted to have her own room for a change, Peggy knew she was missing her best friend.

Suzy's quiet presence had become such an intrinsic part of her family that its absence was keenly felt by them all – especially Fran. Perhaps she should seriously think about asking Fran if there were any other nurses she might like to share with. She gave a sigh and closed the door. Her chicks were slowly flying from the nest to make new lives for themselves, and that was the way it should be. But that didn't mean she couldn't feel sad about it.

Peggy went downstairs and checked that the dining room was all ready for tomorrow's lunch. She didn't really need to, for she'd been in and out of here all day as the girls had helped her clean and sweep and set the table, but it wouldn't hurt just to take one more look.

Ron had carried the small tree home yesterday, having chopped it down from the tangled copse in the hills, and everyone had helped to decorate it with the old and rather tatty bits of tinsel and the few surviving glass balls. Faded paper chains hung from the ceiling – a poignant reminder of her young sons' last Christmas at home – and she'd hung one of the lovely boot-shaped felt stockings from the mantelpiece for Daisy.

Sally had made the Christmas stockings back in 1939 when she and her little crippled brother, Ernie, had been evacuated here from London. The family had all still been together then, but now Sally was married to the local Fire Chief,

John Hicks, Ernie was in Somerset with Anne, her children and Peggy's two boys – and that little, rather solitary stocking was yet another reminder of how scattered they all were now. But Daisy deserved to enjoy her first Christmas, even if she didn't understand what it was all about.

Peggy determinedly dismissed these thoughts and gave the table a final check. It was covered in a white linen, lace-edged cloth, with candles in jars placed down its length, and Sarah and Jane had made a lovely centrepiece with holly and ivy and green ribbon. The cheap cutlery had been polished, the mismatched glasses gleamed, and her mother's lovely linen napkins had been starched and folded into the shape of miniature mitres by a skilful Sarah.

There would be ten of them, including Daisy, sitting down for lunch, for she'd issued an invitation to Cissy's American, Randolph Stevens as well as – and rather reluctantly – to Captain Hammond, who was also an American and Sarah's friend up on the Cliffe estate. Peggy didn't know exactly what sort of friendship it was between the two of them, and fretted that the girl had had her head turned whilst there was still no news of her fiancé Philip in Singapore.

Yet she'd sent out the invitation when the call had gone out from the American commands to share Christmas with their boys who were so far from home at this special time, and she'd since heard that for every GI and airman there had been fifty such invitations. No doubt the promise of extra rations was a huge incentive, but on the whole the British had finally accepted the

Americans into their lives, and with so many of their own men away at war, their presence would fill the all-too-visible gaps at the festive tables.

Doris had decided she and Ted would eat at home and if the weather wasn't too atrocious or something more interesting didn't crop up, then they might come over for afternoon tea. Mary would be at work, and as Rosie knew Tommy would not be welcome, she'd felt she couldn't really leave him on his own, but might pop in later as the pub would be shut until Boxing Day.

Peggy's sister-in-law, Pauline, wouldn't be with them this year, for she'd travelled up to London today to be with her only remaining son who'd been reposted by the RNR to the Tilbury Docks. With her husband, Frank, Jim's older brother, still away with the army, and her other two sons lying somewhere beneath the Atlantic, Peggy could fully understand that Pauline needed to escape the sad memories of the empty house in Tamarisk Bay and be with her boy.

Peggy switched off the light, closed the door and stopped for a moment by the telephone. She'd managed to get through to Somerset earlier in the day and had spoken to everyone, which had upset her terribly. Anne had been quite tearful – probably suffering from the baby-blues – but her boys hadn't seemed at all bothered at having yet another Christmas far from home, and had bombarded her with all their plans for the holiday, which included a huge party for every schoolchild in the area which the Americans were planning in the village hall.

Her parcels had arrived, Vi was stuffing a turkey

that had been killed that morning, and there was a real Christmas pudding for afterwards. Vi had made two dozen at the beginning of the war when there had been no rationing and dried fruit was easily found, and her forethought meant that each year they had a proper plum pudding.

With a tremulous sigh, Peggy accepted that at least they were safe and well fed down there, and that Vi would make sure they had a wonderful time. She went into the kitchen. The shops were shut and Christmas was now only a few hours away. There was nothing left to do, and if she'd forgotten anything, then they'd have to go without.

The large chicken Alf the butcher had put aside for her had been gutted, plucked and stuffed with her homemade mixture of breadcrumbs, onions and dried herbs. There was a string of sausages, the tin of ham Cordelia had received from her family in Canada, and fresh sprouts, potatoes and parsnips from Ron's garden.

She hadn't been as forward thinking as Vi and didn't have a store of puddings, so she'd followed the latest recipe she'd found in the *Radio Times*. The enormous pudding was sitting in a china bowl in her larder covered with greased paper, but she did wonder what on earth it would taste like. With so little fruit left over from making the wedding cake, she'd had to use grated carrot and potato to moisten the mixture. A bit of real butter, two eggs from her chickens, and a little sugar along with cloves, nutmeg, cinnamon and a drop or two of brandy gave it the smell and texture of a proper pudding – but it would take three hours to steam it until it was cooked through, and there was no guarantee that anyone would like it.

She turned on the wireless for company and settled down to listen to the carol concert as she reached for the airgraphs which had arrived this morning. She'd only had time to skim through them and was looking forward to reading them properly.

Jim still seemed to spend a lot of time reading now that Colonel Grafton was down with a fever in the medical room, but he'd managed to get a dinner from the officers' mess of roast pork, courtesy of a steward he'd befriended. There had been great excitement at the first sighting of land, and as they'd docked he'd been quite overawed by the beauty of the brick-red earth and the lush green of the palm trees and surrounding jungle.

The name of the port they'd docked in had been blacked out, but Peggy guessed that it was probably somewhere in Africa. Jim went on to describe how the natives had come out in canoes to unload the ship, and as there were no restrictions on lights, the night scene of the clustered buildings that surrounded the port was quite stunning.

He'd packed for the Brigadier, who was leaving the ship to take command of his new regiment, and received a ten bob tip just before he'd disembarked. Stuck on board, he'd got bored with nothing much to do, and it was clear that he hadn't bothered to take up the offer of learning a new language. They were due to set sail the following day, but in the meantime, rain was heavy and the heat and humidity were almost unbearable.

And yet there had been lighter moments, for during a session of spud-bashing the natives had come alongside in their canoes to yell up to the men on deck, and some of them had started pelting them with potatoes. The natives had retaliated with lumps of coal, and the ship's officers had to break up the fight. It had turned out all right, because the natives then sold them bananas, which had been a real treat.

Jim had written eloquently about the jungle that covered the hills right down to the shoreline, and how the mist seemed to be caught like clouds in the jungle canopy which was alive with the sound of chattering insects and howling monkeys. He loved and missed her, sent a kiss and cuddle to Daisy, and hoped that everything was all right at home, and that they enjoyed Christmas. He'd signed it as always 'SWALK' – sealed with a loving kiss.

She put the airgraphs back into their envelopes and sat for a while trying to imagine the scenes he'd witnessed, and all the new experiences he must be going through. It seemed he was being well fed and that life on board was proving rather idle, if not very comfortable due to the heat and the mosquitoes. But all in all, she suspected he was having the time of his life, though he would find spending Christmas in the tropics very strange.

The click of the front door and a blast of cold air heralded the girls' return, and she quickly went to heat up some more milk for their cocoa. She grinned as they came into the kitchen chattering away like starlings. 'I don't need to ask if you've had a good evening,' she said. 'One look at your faces tells me it went well.'

As they took off their coats and scarves and left

their umbrellas to dry off on the cellar steps, they told her how full the pub had been, and how they could barely speak because they'd been singing all night.

Peggy smiled and nodded and served out the cocoa. 'Take that upstairs and get to bed quietly. Cordelia's asleep and I need you bright-eyed and bushy-tailed in the morning with so much to do.'

Fran, Jane and Sarah kissed her and hurried off, but Mary lingered.

Peggy was immediately concerned. 'What's the matter, dear?'

'I had the strangest conversation with someone earlier this evening, and I'd like to talk about it, if you wouldn't mind,' she said hesitantly.

Peggy sat down and cradled the warm mug of cocoa in her hands. 'It wasn't Tommy again, was it?'

Mary shook her head. 'It was a woman. I thought she looked familiar, but it wasn't until she'd gone that I remembered who she was. It was that Eileen I'd seen Findlay talking to the other week.'

As Mary went on to describe the encounter and the conversation that followed, Peggy's uneasiness grew. When the girl had come to the end of her story, she asked, 'Are you absolutely positive it was the same woman? Can you describe her to me?'

'She was probably in her late thirties, maybe a bit older. Thin and about average height, but smartly dressed and made up as if she'd just been to the beauty parlour. She had dark hair, and I think her eyes were brown, although it was difficult to tell in the dark. She had a funny accent too, and it reminded me a bit of Ivy's – but Ivy's with the rough edges smoothed, if you know what I mean.'

Peggy hesitated for just a moment, but it was long enough for Mary to become suspicious. 'You know who Eileen is, don't you?'

'I was just thinking that your description could fit any number of women,' Peggy hedged. 'Without seeing her myself, I couldn't possibly be sure.' She patted Mary's knee. 'I shouldn't worry yourself over it, Mary,' she soothed. 'Whoever this Eileen is, she obviously had your welfare at heart. I should just accept that and forget about it.'

Mary finished the last of her cocoa. If she's local then I might see her again, but you're right. She was only trying to help, and I think I rather over-reacted, if the truth be told, because she caught me on the hop.' She smiled and kissed Peggy's cheek. 'Thank you, Peggy. Now I really must get to bed. I have an early start in the morning.'

Peggy stared into the fire after Mary had gone upstairs. The fact that Eileen Harris had made a point of speaking to her meant that Tommy Findlay had heard about the girl's search for Cyril, and was still capable of manipulating Eileen into doing his bidding. Thankfully, Mary hadn't revealed the reason behind her search, but Peggy knew that now Tommy's curiosity had been aroused, he wouldn't just let it go. The net was tightening.

Chapter Seven

Christmas morning dawned bright and crisp, and Peggy was up early to bath and dress Daisy before the hullabaloo began. Ron had already left the house to walk Harvey and Monty; Rita had returned from her night shift at the fire station to snatch a couple of hours' sleep, and Cordelia and the rest of the girls were still upstairs, so at least she had the kitchen to herself for a while. There was a lot to do this morning, and if she didn't get on with it they wouldn't eat until late afternoon.

'Happy Christmas, Peggy,' said Mary as she came into the kitchen and held out a small parcel wrapped in newspaper. 'It isn't much,' she said hurriedly. 'But I hope you like it.'

Peggy was touched that the girl had spent her hard-earned money on a gift for her when it really wasn't at all expected or necessary. She unwrapped the parcel and beamed in delight at the lovely box of scented talc. 'Oh, my dear, that's a real treat, but you shouldn't have, honestly.' She gave her a hug and reached for the small parcel she'd placed on the table. 'Thank you, Mary, and here's a little something for you too.'

'But I didn't expect anything, Peggy.' Mary unfolded the wrapping of white butcher's paper and drew out a hand-knitted blue woollen scarf. 'Oh, Peggy, it's lovely, and just what I need, and it will go with my favourite sweater perfectly!

Thank you so much.'

She kissed Peggy's cheek and sat down with a happy sigh. 'I've done very well this Christmas,' she said as Peggy bustled about the kitchen. 'Barbara and Joseph sent me a lovely pair of almost new grey slacks, and Pat sent me a pair of earrings.' She giggled. 'I know I shouldn't have, but I opened them yesterday, knowing I'd be out all day today.'

Peggy had managed to keep her soppy emotions under control, and now she dished out the porridge and started browning the toast. 'I suppose your Jack hasn't had the time to go shopping, what with trying to get into the commandos. Still, I expect he'll send something when he can.'

Mary nodded and looked rather down-hearted, which made Peggy wish she hadn't mentioned the boy. 'You're welcome to join us after work, and stay another night,' she said quickly. 'Doris and Ted said they might pop in for tea, and if Ivy's at work too, I don't like the thought of you going back to an empty house.'

Mary's smile was a little wan. 'Ivy's actually off today, but she's planning on going to friends. Perhaps I should have moved in here. It's becoming a second home.'

'Well, you think about it. You know you're always welcome.' Peggy put the toast on a plate, stopped Daisy from splattering her porridge everywhere and started preparing the mountain of vegetables.

The dilemma of what to do about Mary still made her fretful, and she certainly would have been happier if the girl moved in here so she

146

could keep a closer eye on her. But even then it would prove difficult, for she still had to go to work, still played the piano in the pub and could still be accosted by Tommy or Eileen at any time.

'Thanks for everything, Peggy,' said Mary a while later as she quickly washed her crockery and prepared to leave. 'I'm sorry I can't stay and help, but I certainly might come back tonight – perhaps with Ivy, if that's all right?'

'Of course it is,' she replied warmly. 'It'll be quite a party, I suspect.'

Mary left for the factory just as Daisy decided to throw her bowl on the floor, which resulted in great spatters of slippery porridge across the lino. 'Oh, Daisy, did you *have* to do that today of all days?' Peggy groaned and reached for a cloth, wondering what other mishaps the day had in store for her.

Harvey arrived with Ron in tow and shot up the steps to enthusiastically lick the linoleum clean before trying to snaffle the last of Daisy's toast.

'Get down, ye heathen beast,' rumbled Ron as he grabbed his collar. 'Sit and stay or go and eat your own breakfast downstairs.'

As Harvey shot off to inspect his bowl, Ron put his arm round Peggy's shoulders. 'A happy Christmas to you, Peggy, girl.' His bristled chin rasped her cheek as he gave her a smacking kiss. 'And look what I found up there this morning.'

Peggy eyed the spray of mistletoe and laughed. 'You'd better hang it up in the hall, though goodness knows we don't want to be giving our American guests the wrong ideas.'

'Ach, to be sure, every girl likes a kiss at Christmas,' he said with a naughty grin. 'My Rosie was very accommodating earlier.'

Peggy chuckled. 'I just bet she was, you old rogue.'

'Talking of old rogues,' he said as he fished about in his disreputable trouser pocket, 'Jim asked me to give you this on Christmas morning.'

Peggy's eyes widened as she undid the ribbon and wrapping paper to find a square jeweller's box. As she opened it, she gasped in surprise and delight, for it was the most perfect garnet ring set in gold. 'Oh, Ron, it's beautiful,' she breathed as she slipped it on her finger.

'Aye, my boy has always had good taste,' he replied proudly. 'Takes after his da, of course.'

Peggy smiled. 'Of course he does,' she murmured with great affection as she patted his grizzled cheek. She gazed down at the lovely ring, wishing Jim was here so she could thank him properly and share this special day with him the way they always had. Yet how lovely that he'd thought to do such a thing when he'd had so many other worries before he'd set sail for India. She'd treasure it always, but for now it would be safer in its box until she'd finished preparing the lunch.

She slipped it off her finger. 'I'll put it away and wear it later,' she said as she blinked back her tears.

The morning passed quickly as the girls and a much more cheerful Cordelia came downstairs to have breakfast and help prepare the vegetables. Ron very carefully carried the wireless into the dining room so they could listen to the morning carol service from Westminster Abbey, and the King's speech in the afternoon, and they all trooped in after him to give Daisy her stocking and to open the presents they'd put under the tree.

Peggy had found a doll amongst the toys at the WVS, and once she'd given it a good wash and made a new outfit for it, it looked almost new, and Daisy spent the rest of the morning cuddling it. She'd also received a rattle which Ron had made out of a piece of hollowed-out wood filled with dried beans, an orange, some soft sweets and a rag book.

The girls had clubbed their clothing coupons together and bought Peggy a lovely pair of fur-trimmed gloves which looked very glamorous. For Ron, they'd secretly unravelled two of his most disreputable old jumpers and used the wool to knit a sleeveless pullover, socks and gloves, which they insisted he kept for best. Ron had asked Rosie's advice and bought Peggy and Cordelia some lovely scented soap.

Cordelia had knitted what purported to be scarves for everyone – it was difficult to tell what they were because they were inches wider at one end than the other, were full of holes where she'd dropped stitches, and had several kinks in the middle. But Peggy knew they would all wear them for, despite the terrible knitting, they'd been made with love.

Peggy watched Cordelia with great affection. She was obviously feeling much better today, for she was twittering and giggling as she cooed over the cheap little brooch, the second-hand silk scarf, the hand-knitted woollen mittens and hot-water-bottle cover that the girls had given her. They had done well too, for Peggy had knitted each of them a pair of socks as well as gloves, and they'd bought each other books, hair-slides, sweets and bath salts.

Ron had brought a bottle of sherry from the Anchor, courtesy of Rosie, and they all sat admiring and showing off their gifts as they sipped it and got into the spirit of Christmas while the carol service came over the wireless. Daisy crawled about the floor and became more interested in the discarded newspaper than her new toys, while Harvey chewed on the bone Alf the butcher had put aside for him.

Peggy left them to it and went into the kitchen to check on the chicken and the steaming pudding. There was condensation streaming down the windows and walls, so she risked freezing to death by opening the window and the back door to try and dry everything off. She could feel the damp of it on her face and in her hair, and hoped it hadn't spoilt her set or made her make-up run. Deciding that her hair and face repairs would have to wait until later, she drained the potatoes and parsnips and dropped them in the roasting tin of hot lard.

The front door slammed and she glanced up at the clock in panic. If that was the Yanks, they were early. She quickly shoved the tin into the oven, ripped off her apron and patted her hair in the hope it didn't look too straggling and limp. But she hadn't reached the door when a beloved little figure raced in and threw herself into her arms.

'Cissy,' she squeaked as she held her tightly. 'Oh, Cissy, I didn't think you could come.'

'Super, isn't it?' Cissy said breathlessly. 'The Air Vice-Marshal changed his mind about me having to be on duty when he heard Randy had been invited.' Her face was alight with happiness. 'And I don't have to be back until midnight. Isn't that just too brilliant for words?'

Peggy laughed and hugged her again. Her daughter had picked up the lingo of the upper-class men and women she worked amongst, and she sounded very posh and grown-up. 'So where is he then? You haven't left him stranded in the hall, have you?'

Cissy took off the neat uniform cap, unpinned her blonde hair from the regulation victory roll and shook it out so it fell over her shoulders. 'He and Matt are just bringing in stuff from the car they managed to borrow. You won't believe the special ration pack Randy's been given.'

'Matt's here too? How lovely. Rita will be thrilled.'

Cissy grinned. 'She's already in seventh heaven because she saw him out of the window and dashed down to greet him.' She leaned closer. 'I think they're having a bit of a canoodle on the doorstep. I do hope the neighbours won't be too shocked.'

Peggy giggled. 'My neighbours have witnessed far worse than canoodling, believe me. Do you remember when your father and I came back from the pub one night and he carried me in over his shoulder? I swear they must all have seen my underwear that night.'

'Happy Christmas, ma'am,' said Randolph as he came in laden with a box, which he placed on

151

the table. 'It's sure nice of you to invite me into your home on this special day.'

Peggy was horribly flustered and could only hope he hadn't overheard her talking about her knickers. 'It's lovely to see you too, but I won't invite you again unless you start calling me Peggy,' she teased. 'Come and give me a hug, and then show me what you've brought.'

He was tall and sturdy and his hug almost squeezed the breath out of her. Once she'd gained her equilibrium she turned to Matt, who'd appeared similarly loaded with a box, with Rita following close behind him. 'Goodness,' Peggy managed after he too had kissed and hugged her. 'What a lovely surprise, Matt. Rita thought you couldn't make it.'

'I hope it's all right,' he said with a frown. 'But it was a last-minute thing and I didn't have a chance to warn you.'

Peggy waved away any concern she might have had about stretching the chicken even further than it already had to be. 'The more the merrier,' she said gaily.

'Well, that's jolly good, because I'm afraid you're going to have to put up with me too,' said another voice.

'Martin! Oh, how lovely.' She hugged him tightly, her mascara in danger of smudging as her eyes filled with tears. 'But why didn't you tell me you were coming?'

'Like Matt, it was all a bit last minute.' He twirled his moustache and his eyes twinkled. 'And don't worry about stretching the food too thinly. The Americans have been incredibly generous to

152

the families who've invited their boys for the day, and I think you'll find there's more than enough in there to keep us all well and truly fed.'

Randy opened his box to reveal fruit juice, evaporated milk, a huge pack of bacon rashers, powdered coffee, sugar, rice, peas and lard. Matt's box contained bottles of the American drink Coca-Cola, along with tins of spam, several bars of lovely chocolate, two cartons of cigarettes, a bottle of gin and another of whisky.

Peggy had to sit down to get over the shock. 'Gosh,' she breathed.

'The gin and whisky are from me,' said Martin. 'Couldn't let our American cousins have it all their own way,' he said heartily as he patted Randy's shoulder. 'Now, where are Daisy and Cordelia? I have a little something for each of them.'

'They're in the dining room,' Peggy managed, her gaze still fixed to the bounty that now covered her kitchen table.

'Peggy,' said Sarah rather nervously from the doorway. 'This is Captain Delaney Hammond.'

The tall, broad-shouldered American soldier held a box in one arm as he gave a smart salute to everyone in the room and advanced on Peggy with his hand stretched out. 'Delighted to meet you at last, ma'am,' he drawled.

Peggy's hand was clasped in his strong, warm fingers and she looked up into startlingly blue eyes, and the rugged, very attractive face of a man who looked as if he was more at home riding the range than standing beside one in her kitchen.

'It's very nice to meet you, I'm sure,' she stammered. If she'd known how handsome he was she'd have had even more misgivings about this friendship and no mistake.

'Thank you for inviting me,' he said, 'and I hope you'll accept this special ration pack on behalf of the United States Army.'

As he drew out yet more tins of spam, ham and fruit, packets of sugar, flour, real butter, rice and more peas, Peggy wondered if she was dreaming.

'I knew that Flight Lieutenant Stevens would also bring one of these, so I added a few bits and pieces which I hope you and the other womenfolk might appreciate as more personal gifts,' he said quietly. He placed a dozen pairs of nylons on the table, along with yet more cigarettes, twelve gold-coloured powder compacts and matching tubes of lipstick.

'I hope I have the numbers right,' he said with a frown. 'But if I haven't there's plenty more at the PX, which I'll give to Sarah to bring back.'

'It's more than enough,' Peggy said as she tried to take in all this largesse. 'I'm overwhelmed to see so much food and lovely luxuries all in one place – and to think you've been so kind...' She was almost in tears.

'Ma'am, please don't cry,' said Captain Hammond softly. 'I think I speak for all of us when I say we are most honoured by your invitation. Being so far from home and family, we really do appreciate you sharing your Christmas with us, and this is really only a very small token of our thanks.'

Peggy could no longer hold back the tears, and she gave him a tremulous smile in an attempt to ease his concern. 'I always cry when I'm happy,' she said distractedly. 'Please don't worry.' She

154

dabbed her eyes, wondering if she looked like a panda, for her mascara must be smudged by now.

'Take those lovely compacts, nylons and lipsticks into the other room and make yourselves comfortable while Sarah and I put everything away. I'm sure Ron would be delighted to share out that whisky.'

As Rita and Cissy led them out of the room, Peggy set aside one of the packets of bacon and a tin of ham before handing Sarah the tins of spam and packets of rice. She had no fear now that she might run out of food for everyone.

'Captain Hammond's very handsome,' she said casually as she carried the rest of the goodies to the larder. 'How old did you say he was?'

'I don't think I did,' said Sarah, her eyes twinkling. 'But seeing as how interested you are, he's thirty-eight, very married, has two children and a ranch in Wyoming. His passions are horses and cattle, and in his younger days he used to ride the bucking broncos at the rodeos. He likes country folk music, is a prolific reader and enjoys walking in our English countryside and going to the cinema and theatre.'

Peggy's smile was wry. 'It seems you know him very well,' she replied. 'Just be careful, Sarah. He's very attractive and you're both far from home and–'

'He's a friend, Auntie Peggy, and that is as far as it goes,' Sarah interrupted firmly. 'He knows all about Philip, and because he's such a gentleman, I've never had to say anything else. He gives me a lift home sometimes, or comes into the office for a chat – but please don't see more into

155

this than there is. I'm still in love with Philip and prepared to wait for as long as it takes until I can be with him again.'

There was no mistaking the truth in the girl's expression and Peggy was able to relax a bit – yet she knew from experience that friendships between men and women rarely worked, for sooner or later the spark that had attracted them in the first place could turn into something far more complicated.

'You finish putting all this away while I add more water to that saucepan under the pudding before it boils dry. Then we can go and join the others. The meal won't be ready for another hour, and I could do with a drop of whisky and perhaps try some of that fizzy dark drink with it.'

'It's a bit of an acquired taste,' said Sarah, 'and gives me the hiccups. But we get a lot of it up at Cliffe, so I'm getting used to it, and it's delicious with whisky.'

Peggy made no comment, for she hadn't known Sarah even drank whisky, but she did wonder if she and the very attractive Delaney Hammond shared the odd glass or two before he drove her home.

The Christmas dinner in the canteen had certainly lived up to its reputation and Mary had been so full after it that she'd almost fallen asleep during the afternoon. The repetitive work didn't help, and her eyelids had grown heavier as the day had progressed.

'Thank goodness that's over,' sighed Jenny as the hooter went and there was a mad scramble to clock off and get home. 'I thought I was going to drop off and start snoring.'

Mary laughed. 'So did I, but with old gimlet eyes Norris watching every movement, I didn't dare.' She fetched her things from her locker and Jenny pulled on her overcoat.

'I'll walk down the hill with you tonight,' said Jenny, linking arms as they passed through the guarded gate. 'There's a party on at a friend's house, and I'm in the mood for a good knees-up.'

Mary was glad of her company, for she still found it a bit of a trial walking in the darkness on her own. 'Where do your friends live?' she asked as they headed towards the humped-back bridge which would take them into town.

'In the big house next to the hospital in Camden Road. There are eight of them sharing the house, which they rent from the owners who've gone to Wiltshire. Some are nurses, a couple work at the factory and the rest are girls I used to share with at the hostel.'

'How are you getting on living up there? Is it still very noisy?'

Jenny nodded. 'Worse than ever, really, now another woman and three small ones have moved in, but I'm hoping to move into the house in the New Year, because one of the nurses is getting married and leaving Cliffehaven.' She laughed. 'I can't tell you how marvellous it'll be to have a bit of space with no screaming children running about.'

They came to Camden Road. 'Well, enjoy the party, and I'll see you tomorrow,' said Mary.

'You're welcome to come and join in the fun,' said Jenny. 'They're a lovely bunch of girls and

157

won't mind at all.'

'That's really kind, but I sort of promised I might go to Peggy's tonight. Besides, I need a bath and to get changed. I've been wearing these clothes for two days now.'

'Well, the offer's there. TTFN.'

'Ta-ta for now,' she called back. She was still smiling as she hurried along Havelock Road. And then, in the deep shadows of the overhanging trees, she saw the figure of a man detach itself from the darkness.

Her smile froze as her heart began to pound and she came to an abrupt halt. Poised to flee back towards Camden Road, she peered into the ever-shifting shadows of the wind-blown trees. 'Who's that?'

'Mary? Mary it's me, Jack.'

'Jack? Oh, Jack,' she yelled as they ran towards each other. And then she was in his arms, lifted off her feet and being swung round, her bag and gas-mask box abandoned on the pavement.

He smothered her face in kisses and held her tightly until she was breathless. 'I'm sorry if I frightened you, Mary,' he said after they'd shared a lingering kiss. 'But the old girl in there wouldn't let me in, and I didn't want to go back to the YMCA in case I missed you.'

'Trust Doris to be awkward,' she replied as she traced the lines of his face with her hands. 'You're frozen,' she exclaimed. 'Just how long have you been waiting for me?'

'About an hour or so,' he replied dismissively, 'but that's no hardship now I've found you.'

Mary kissed him again, so glad to feel his arms

about her and to know that nothing had changed between them despite the long separation. 'How long can you stay?' she asked tentatively.

'Until the twenty-seventh. I came home yesterday and spent some time with Mum and Dad, and then caught the first train down this morning. They gave me five days' leave in all, but I have to return to my regiment at the end of it, and that's a whole day's journey.'

She leaned back in his embrace, her emotions a mixture of hope and dread. 'Does that mean you failed the commando course?'

He grinned down at her and kissed the tip of her nose. 'Of course not, silly. Passed with flying colours, didn't I?' He rammed on his beret, stood to attention and snapped off a salute. 'You're looking at Lance Corporal J. Boniface of Number Six Commando. At your service.'

Mary giggled nervously, for a sudden, awful fear had swept through her and she didn't want him to see how badly his news had affected her. 'Seeing as how you passed the course, I'm sure you're brave enough to face Doris again while I get washed and changed.'

'I've braved many things these past weeks, but your landlady is enough to terrify even the most hardened of men.' He broke into a smile. 'But I'm sure I'll manage somehow with you at my side.'

Mary's giggle was genuine as she retrieved her overnight bag, gas-mask box and handbag from the pavement before tugging at his arm and drawing him towards the front door. 'We won't stay long,' she promised.

'Before we go in, there's something I want to

159

give you,' he said quickly.

She suddenly remembered the pot of brilliantine she'd sent him for Christmas. 'Did you get my parcel? I know it wasn't much, but I couldn't think of what to send.'

He smiled down at her and ruefully ruffled his very short hair. 'I certainly did, and although most of my hair has been butchered by the army barber, it helps to smooth down what I've got left.'

He drew a small square parcel from his uniform jacket pocket. 'I didn't have much time to buy anything, but I managed to get away into the nearest town the other afternoon to find you this.' He handed it over. 'I do hope you like it.'

Mary once again dropped her overnight bag so she could fumble with the string and paper and open the box. There, nestled in cotton wool, was a lovely bangle of twisted silver. 'Oh, Jack,' she breathed as she slipped it onto her wrist. 'It's the loveliest thing.' She put her arms round his neck and kissed him passionately.

'Goodness,' he spluttered. 'I must remember to give you a present every time I come on leave if that's the thanks I'll get.'

'Don't go getting any ideas, Jack Boniface,' she teased. 'Just because we're far from home, doesn't mean you can take liberties.'

He kept his arms around her, his voice soft. 'Are you still wearing my locket?'

'Oh, yes. It's always right next to my heart.' Realising things were getting a bit heated, she gave him a peck on the cheek, picked up her bag and slotted her key into the door. 'Let's get inside before we both freeze to death.'

160

Doris came out of the drawing room, her expression radiating disapproval. 'I do not allow my boarders to have male visitors,' she said imperiously.

'This is Jack,' said Mary, feeling the glow of her happiness warm her face. 'He's a friend from home and is only on leave for a couple of days. Would it be all right if he came in while I got washed and changed?'

'He'll have to wait in the dining room,' said Doris. 'I have guests in for drinks.' She eyed Jack's highly polished, spotlessly clean boots. 'Take those off,' she ordered. 'I don't want mud tramped into my carpets.'

Mary and Jack exchanged looks of amusement, and as he obediently unlaced his boots, Mary raced up the stairs.

She decided to forego the bath and have a thorough strip-wash instead, and having done so, she changed into her good skirt and blue sweater and brushed out her hair, which thankfully she'd washed that morning. Her mind whirled as she tried to think of somewhere they could go so they could be together and have the chance to talk in private. He clearly wasn't welcome here and all the pubs were shut. Peggy's house was full of visitors, the one remaining hotel had been requisitioned by the Canadian Army, and the YMCA was completely out of the question because women weren't allowed over the doorstep.

She gave a sigh of frustration as she finished brushing her hair. If only Doris had been more approachable, they could have spent the evening in her dining room – but even if she had given permission, they would both have been uncomfortable. Doris was the sort to listen at the door and come in and out to make sure they weren't up to anything – not that they would be. How different she was to Peggy, who would have welcomed him inside to wait for her, fed him and made him feel instantly at home.

Mary regarded her reflection in the mirror, noting how her eyes sparkled and her face shone with happiness. There was only one place to go, really, she decided as she draped Peggy's blue scarf round her neck, checked that her locket hung straight, and pulled on her overcoat.

She hurried downstairs to where she could hear the clink of glasses and the chatter and laughter of a small gathering coming from the drawing room. She found Jack looking horribly miserable in his stocking-feet, sitting on the edge of a dining-room chair with his green beret clasped in his hands. Her heart went out to him and she could have slapped Doris for her thoughtlessness.

'Get your boots on, Jack,' she said. 'We're going somewhere we'll both be welcome.'

'I simply cannot have this room occupied any longer,' said Doris from the doorway. 'I need to set out the supper for my guests.'

Jack sprung to his feet as if on a parade ground.

'That's all right,' said Mary flatly. 'We're just leaving.'

'But I need you to help serve the buffet supper,' said Doris. 'Ivy has deserted me to go to some party, and Edward has returned to his apartment pleading indigestion and a headache. It's most unreasonable of you to disappear and refuse to help after all I have done for you.'

Quite what she'd done for Mary was a bit of a mystery, but she didn't pursue it. 'As you've made it plain that Jack isn't welcome here then I'm afraid you'll just have to manage on your own.'

Doris went off to the kitchen in a huff and Mary chivvied Jack out into the hall and waited impatiently while he got his boots back on. 'Tie the laces outside,' she hissed. 'If we hang about she might find something for both of us to do, and believe me, Jack, you won't want to get stuck with that lot.'

They made their escape and once they were out of sight of the house, Jack tied the laces on his boots and then gave Mary a hearty kiss. 'So, now you've slayed a dragon, where are you taking me?'

'To Peggy Reilly's house. You'll get a warm welcome there, I can promise you that – and you'll be allowed to keep your boots on,' she added with a giggle.

'Well, it can't be a frostier welcome than her sister's,' he said with a grin as he adjusted the beret so it sloped towards one eye. 'How come they're so different? From all you've said in your letters, Peggy sounds the exact opposite of that haddock-faced, snooty old cow.'

'Jack,' Mary spluttered as she playfully slapped his arm. 'You're not in the barracks now, you know.'

'Sorry,' he said bashfully. 'But she really did get my goat, Mary.'

'I know, and I'll forgive you anything now I've got you to myself for a while.' She slid her hand into the crook of his arm, admiring her bracelet

163

as they began to walk along Havelock Road. 'By the way,' she said, 'I forgot to tell you how handsome you look in that uniform.'

He swaggered a bit and chuckled. 'Glad you think so,' he replied. 'It took a great deal of effort to earn the right to wear it, I can tell you.' He looked down at her and winked. 'You don't scrub up too badly either. This sea air and new life is obviously doing you good.'

She blushed as he gave her a peck on the cheek. 'I'd like to hear about the course, and the men you've been training with. Is it really as tough as you make out, or is that just all talk to impress us girls?'

'It's the toughest thing I've ever had to do,' he said as they crossed the High Street and strolled along Camden Road.

As he talked about the barracks, the other young recruits who'd volunteered to try for the commandos and the torturous obstacle courses and tough training they'd gone through, Mary realised just how much he had actually enjoyed the comradeship of other men, and being challenged both physically and mentally to be his very best.

'Out of the thirty of us who were in our troop we lost nineteen. There were some injuries, but mostly it was a matter of lack of stamina or determination. You had to really want it, Mary, to be utterly focused and determined to get through, or you simply couldn't make it.' He grinned down at her. 'There were a couple of times I was tempted to pack it all in, but you know me – once I start a thing I like to see it through.'

'Where will they send you, do you think?'

'I really don't know, and even if I did, I wouldn't be allowed to tell you. My guess is it will probably be North Africa – but actually, it could be anywhere.'

Mary thought about the commandos that had been killed or captured during the disastrous Dieppe Raid, and her heart beat just that little bit faster. She gripped Jack's arm, never wanting to let him go.

'Hey,' he said softly as he came to a halt. 'Don't worry about me, Mary. I'm part of an elite force, trained to the hilt and ready to do my bit. I'll be fine, really I will.'

She closed her eyes on her tears as he kissed her lightly on the lips. She had to believe he would come through – for if she didn't then she would be lost. She snuggled into his side as he kept his arm round her shoulders and they began to walk again.

As they headed towards the shops she saw two people on the opposite pavement and recognised them immediately. It was Findlay and Eileen – and they were deep in conversation.

Mary kept her chin dipped into her coat collar and, shielded by Jack's sturdy figure, managed to pass by without them even noticing. What was it with those two? Eileen had been so scathing about him, and yet here she was, on Christmas night, once more deep in some intimate conversation with him.

She decided to stop puzzling over something she would probably never solve, for every moment of Jack's leave was precious and she'd be foolish to waste even a second on either of them.

Rosie had been stuck indoors with Tommy, and although she'd cooked a large lunch of roast chicken for them both which they'd washed down with a good bottle of wine, the atmosphere had been far from festive.

It had soon become clear that his mind was on other things, for he said very little, seemed to be always on edge, and smoked far too many cigarettes. In the end, she was relieved when he said he was going out – though where that might be was anyone's guess. Everything was shut, and there were very few people in Cliffehaven who would welcome him into their homes. Yet she didn't really care, for it was just good to have the place to herself for a while.

She took her time to get changed into something more appropriate for Peggy's party, and as she clipped on her sparkling earrings she checked her appearance in the mirror. Satisfied with her hair and make-up, she adjusted the square neckline of her navy dress and smoothed it over her hips before checking that her legs didn't look too horribly streaky.

Her last decent pair of nylons had been ripped to shreds on a nail sticking out of one of the crates in the cellar, so she'd dyed her legs with gravy browning, which was tricky enough – but trying to get the pencil-line straight at the back had been a real struggle. 'There are times,' she muttered, 'when I wish I had a sister – or at least another girl in the house.'

Monty yapped and wagged his tail, his bright-button eyes eagerly watching her every move from the doorway to her bedroom. He knew they were going out and was becoming impatient.

'You're no help at all,' she told him fondly.

He barked again and nudged his leash towards her.

Rosie chuckled. 'Yes, you're coming too. But first I have to find my navy shoes.' With Monty following her closely, she padded along the short passage between the two bedrooms and pushed open Tommy's door.

She gave a cluck of annoyance, for it was in a mess again, and stank of beer and cigarettes. She opened the dormer window to let some fresh air in, but then had to shut it quickly against the wind that was tearing up from the sea.

'He'll just have to put up with the smell,' she said crossly. 'But once he's left for good, I'm probably going to have to fumigate the place.'

Monty sniffed at the dirty clothes strewn across the floor and then sat down to gnaw on an abandoned brown brogue.

Rosie left him to it – if Tommy left his things lying about, then he only had himself to blame if Monty chewed them. She went to the large mahogany wardrobe and opened both doors. Tommy's suits, jackets, shirts and trousers hung from the hangers, sweaters were folded on the top shelf, and his shoes were lined up on the bottom. For a man who'd spent the last few months in prison, and who insisted he had very little money, Tommy had a lot of very expensive clothes.

She rummaged about, trying to find the shoebox she was certain she'd left in here, and as she swept back all the clothes that dangled in her way, she delved right to the back of the deep wardrobe.

167

The shoebox was there as she'd known it would be – but it wasn't the only one, and she stared in amazement at the great stack of them lined along the back. 'How many shoes does one man need?' she muttered. 'No wonder he never has any damned money.'

She lifted the first one out and frowned at its weight. Intrigued, she opened the box and stared in horrified disbelief at what lay inside. A cold fury surged through her as she took out the two half-bottles of whisky and set them on the floor. Then she lifted out the rest of the boxes, only to discover more whisky, gin, rum and numerous packets of cigarettes and rolls of pipe tobacco. Tommy was up to his old tricks again.

'You bastard,' she breathed. 'How *dare* you?'

Trembling with rage and sick at his betrayal, she sank onto the unmade bed and wondered what to do. She couldn't tell Ron, because he'd be round here like a shot to punch Tommy's lights out – and although her brother fully deserved it, violence never solved anything.

She certainly couldn't put the bottles in her bar, for they were all marked with the insignia of the American Army, and she didn't want to hide them anywhere in case there was a sudden raid by the police. They knew where he was and what he was, and she was certain they were just waiting for an excuse to put him back in prison and throw away the key.

'And I'd be the first one to congratulate them,' she rasped. 'But if I tell the police what I've found they'll think I had something to do with it and arrest me too. God, what a mess. How could you *do* this to me, Tommy? How *could* you?'

As Monty put his muzzle on her knee and looked up at her sorrowfully, she stroked his head and gave a tremulous sigh. The cigarettes and tobacco weren't marked, so she could give them away, but the booze would have to be poured down the drain. It was a terrible waste, but she had no other option.

With her mind made up, she quickly filled her handbag and a shopping bag with the cigarettes and tobacco pouches, which she'd take to Peggy's as Christmas gifts. The cigarettes were Craven A, which was a luxurious brand, so they'd be a real treat, and Ron would appreciate the tobacco.

With a puzzled Monty trailing her footsteps, she carried armfuls of bottles into the kitchen, tracking back and forth between the rooms many times before all the boxes were empty. Opening two bottles at a time, she watched the alcohol glug down the sink.

By the time all the bottles were empty, her kitchen smelled like the bar downstairs, so she sloshed bleach down the sink and put the window on the latch whilst she ran down to get a crate from the cellar. Stacking the bottles into it, she now had the dilemma of how to dispose of them. She couldn't just put them with the other empties for the brewery to collect, for they'd be spotted immediately. Nor could she put them in the dustbin. That many bottles would arouse the suspicions of even the slowest-witted dustman.

'What to do, Monty?' she asked frantically.

Monty whined and wagged his tail.

Rosie looked at the pup and then back to the

crate of bottles. The council tip would have been the sensible answer, but it was right on the northernmost corner of Cliffehaven, and she couldn't walk that far in the blackout carrying that loaded crate, for there were too many wardens and nosy parkers about.

Then she had a sudden brainwave. 'We'll bury them in the back garden,' she said to the pup, who looked back at her in puzzlement.

Quickly changing out of her good clothes, she pulled on an old pair of slacks, a sweater, head-scarf and flat shoes. Carrying the heavy crate downstairs, she locked the side door so Tommy couldn't get in while she was busy hiding his ill-gotten hoard, then went down to the cellar to find the spade.

She slid back the bolts on the back door and stepped out into the gloomy winter afternoon of her dank and neglected patch of garden. With a glance up at the neighbour's window, she was thankful to see that the blackouts had been drawn so there was little likelihood of the old trout seeing what she was up to.

Deciding that the best place to bury everything would be beneath the flagstone path, she put down the crate and began to prise the slabs up with the corner of the spade. It wasn't as tough as she'd expected, because all the rain they'd had recently had softened the ground, and she soon had a square cleared so she could begin to dig down.

Monty sat and watched her, head on one side, eyes questioning.

Rosie ignored him and dug deeper until she

was satisfied that the hole was big enough. She was tempted to smash the bottles so they were made smaller, but that sort of noise at this time of the evening would surely bring her nosy neighbour to the window.

She was perspiring now, despite the bitter, buffeting wind, but at last all the bottles lay in the hole. Covering them with the earth, she tamped it down hard and then winced in pain as she tore a nail whilst placing the flagstones on top. Seething with pain and fury, she stamped repeatedly on the flagstones until she was satisfied they were evenly balanced with the rest.

Out of breath and spurred on by her rage, she shovelled the remaining earth under the privet hedge, shoved a few bits of moss between the slabs and stood back to check that everything looked as it should. But the gathering darkness made it difficult to see anything, so at first light tomorrow morning, she'd have to come out and check that she'd left no evidence behind of her evening's work.

'Come on, Monty. Back indoors while I get washed and changed, then it's off to Peggy's. I don't want to be here when Tommy gets back, because if I see him, I'll ruddy well kill him.'

She bolted the back door, tossed the spade and the empty crate down into the cellar and went upstairs to wash her hands before she restacked the shoeboxes at the back of the wardrobe. He'd get a nasty shock the next time he opened them, and that was a fact. It would no doubt cause endless trouble too, but she was more than ready to fight her corner.

Chapter Eight

The wonderful meal was over and even Harvey was too full and lazy to move from his comfortable place beneath the table. Now their glasses had been filled so they could listen to the King's speech and give the loyal toast. As they waited for the announcer to introduce him, the men stood respectfully to attention, and Peggy watched everyone's faces, knowing how important this moment was for all of them.

And then the hesitant, rather solemn voice of King George came into the room.

'It is at Christmas more than at any other time that we are conscious of the dark shadow of war,' he began. 'Our Christmas festival today must lack many of the happy, familiar features that it has had from our childhood. We miss the actual presence of some of those nearest and dearest, without whom our family gatherings cannot be complete.'

The tears were already welling and Peggy reached for Cissy's hand to let her know that she shared in the sadness of missing Jim and the rest of their family.

'But though its outward observances may be limited,' the King continued, 'the message of Christmas remains eternal and unchanged. It is a message of thankfulness and of hope – of thankfulness to the Almighty for His great mercies, of hope for the return to this earth of peace and

172

goodwill. In this spirit I wish all of you a happy Christmas.'

'And to you, sir,' said Martin as he and everyone else raised their glasses.

'This year it adds to our happiness that we are sharing it with so many of our comrades-in-arms from the United States of America. We welcome them in our homes, and their sojourn here will not only be a happy memory for us, but, I hope, a basis of enduring understanding between our two peoples.'

'Here, here,' said Ron as the glasses rose again in a toast to Randy and Captain Hammond, who looked suddenly rather bashful.

There was utter silence as the King continued to speak of the victories that had been won that year, and of his confidence in the future now the British forces had been fortified by the massive armies of the United States. He spoke of the blows that had been struck by the armies of the Soviet Union against the German invasion, and of the counter-strikes of the Australian and American forces in the Pacific.

Peggy sat forward in her chair and gripped Cissy's hand as he continued, 'India, now still threatened with Japanese invasion, has found in her loyal fighting men more than a million strong champions to stand at the side of the British Army in defence of Indian soil.'

She looked down at Jim's garnet ring and blinked away her tears as the King talked of the tasks ahead, which might prove harder than those already accomplished – and was heartened by his confidence in the future, for they no longer stood

173

alone and ill-armed, and their resolve had not been shaken despite all they'd been through.

As he went on to talk to those listening from overseas, she was forcefully reminded of how vital it was to defend even the remotest part of the Empire, for its value was beyond price.

'Wherever you are serving in our wide, free Commonwealth of Nations you will always feel "at home". Though severed by the long sea miles of distance you are still in the family circle, whose ties, precious in peaceful years, have been knit even closer by danger. The Queen and I feel most deeply for all of you who have lost or been parted from your dear ones, and our hearts go out to you with sorrow, with comfort, but also with pride.'

Peggy's tears were running freely now as she thought of her two lost nephews, of Jim out at sea somewhere, and her children and grandchildren so far away in Somerset – and of the many friends that Cissy and Martin would never see again. The toll of this war was already too great, but Peggy knew that not one of them in this room today would ever contemplate surrendering.

As the King finished his address by asking them to welcome the future in a spirit of brotherhood so they may live together in justice and peace, Peggy helped a tearful Cordelia to her feet as they all stood and raised their glasses.

'To the King – and to peace,' they chorused.

There was a long moment of silent contemplation before Martin broke the spell by going across the room to the gramophone. Having wound it up, he placed a record on the turntable and carefully set the stylus down. The lively sound of one of the big bands filled the room and slowly but surely the youngsters took to the floor.

Peggy mopped away her tears, blew her nose and decided it was time to pull herself together and make a pot of tea for herself and Cordelia. The rich food and alcohol was beginning to take its toll on both of them, and now the youngsters had the gramophone going, she was in danger of getting a headache.

She was just warming the pot when she heard the back door slam, and she looked towards the cellar steps expecting to see Rosie and Monty. Her smile widened in welcome as she saw it was a bright-eyed, radiant Mary with a very pleasant-looking young commando in tow.

'Goodness me,' she said in delight. 'You must be Jack. What a lovely surprise for Mary – and congratulations on passing the course.'

He grinned back at her as he whipped off his beret, and his rough, strong fingers enveloped her hand. 'Thank you, Mrs Reilly,' he said, his voice soft with a Sussex burr. 'I hope you don't mind us turning up like this.'

'Well, of course I don't – as long as you stop being so formal, and call me Peggy. Come in, come in. Now I'll introduce you to everyone and then get you some food. I expect you're both hungry, aren't you?'

'I'm all right,' said Mary, 'but Jack's been hanging about waiting for me since he got off the train, so I suspect he's ravenous by now.'

'But didn't Doris give you anything while you waited?'

Jack's grin broadened. 'Only earache,' he said.

Peggy looked to Mary for an explanation, and once she'd heard it, she hid her fury with a tight smile. 'Well, you're in my home now, and we don't stand on ceremony here. Come on into the other room so you can meet everyone, then I suspect you'd like some time alone while you eat your supper.'

She saw the wistful look that shot between them and knew she'd been right. Leading the way into the chaos of the dining room, she had to shout over the sound of 'Chattanooga Choo Choo' to be heard as everyone turned to wave at them and she pointed out who was who to Jack.

Cordelia was leaning on her walking stick and wriggling her bottom in time to the music, the two American boys were jitter-bugging with Sarah and Cissy, Matt and Rita were in a world of their own as they slow-danced, while Martin and Ron danced their own version of the American craze with Jane and Fran. Daisy was sitting in her high chair banging out her own rhythm with a spoon, while Harvey stretched out beneath the table and snored.

Peggy looked up at Jack's stunned expression and laughed. 'As I said, we don't stand on cere-mony here.' She led the way back to the relatively quiet kitchen. 'Sit down and I'll get some food for you both. There's plenty left.'

She made the pot of tea, dished up a full plate of meat, potatoes, stuffing and vegetables for Jack, and a smaller plate for Mary despite her protesting that she was still full from lunch. Love gave the young good appetites, and Jack looked like a lad who enjoyed his food.

'Where are you staying, Jack?' she asked as she opened a bottle of beer for him.

'I'm at the YMCA. It's comfortable enough, and after living in barracks, it's a definite improvement.'

Peggy would have offered him a bed here, but she'd made a strict rule long ago that she wouldn't have young men staying overnight. It got the girls unsettled and could lead to all sorts of shenanigans. Not that Jack looked the sort to try his luck, for he was obviously very taken with Mary – but he was a young, fit lad who'd been living in a barracks full of men for weeks on end without sight or scent of female company. It would be foolish to put temptation in his way.

'They'll look after you there,' she said comfortably. 'Now you eat up and have some time together. You know where we are, should you want to join in later.' She gave them both a beaming smile, picked up her two cups of tea, and left them to it.

Returning to the dining room, she had barely placed the cups on the table when she was whisked into Martin's arms and twirled round until she was quite giddy. Martin had certainly not lost any of his energetic exuberance, that was for sure, and it was a while before her pleas for a rest were heard.

She finally managed to escape and sat down with a bump to catch her breath. It was wonderful to have the house ringing with noise and laughter again, but oh, how she missed Jim. His absence was felt even more strongly on days like this, and she wondered wistfully where he was and what he was doing. And then there was Anne and her two little ones, and Bob and Charlie, who were no doubt having a whale of a time at the Americans' party in the village hall.

It was unfair to be separated at such a time, and she realised suddenly this must be how millions of others were feeling right this minute, for as the King had said in his speech, war had divided families and torn loved ones apart, and of course there was always the fear that once it was over, things might not be the same ever again.

Determined to banish such dark thoughts on this special evening, she sipped her tea, lit a cigarette and sat back to watch the fun.

Captain Hammond was a terrific dancer, she noted, and young Randy wasn't bad either. Rita and Matt were still unaware of the music or their surroundings as they shuffled round in a tight circle and gazed into one another's eyes, and poor Jane was having terrible difficulty trying to follow Ron's own version of the quickstep which didn't at all go with the music. Sarah had gone to sit by Cordelia to have a cigarette, while Martin topped up everyone's glasses.

Peggy glanced across at the clock on the mantelpiece and realised with shock that it was way past Daisy's bed-time. She weaved through the dancers to the high chair and lifted her out.

Daisy was in no mood to leave the party, and she kicked her feet and began to bawl in protest as she waved her arms about. This brought Harvey from beneath the table to see what the matter was, and he only just missed being trampled by the dancers. He decided he didn't like what was happening and shot back into his refuge beneath the table to chew on the mangled ham bone he'd got for Christmas.

Peggy fetched Daisy's night bottle from her bedroom and carried the yelling, struggling baby upstairs to wash and change her into her nightclothes. She would normally have done this in the kitchen, but she didn't want to disturb the lovebirds, and as Doris had treated them so appallingly, she wanted them to feel right at home.

Once Daisy was prepared for bed, she warmed the quarter-bottle of milk formula in the bathroom sink with some hot water then went back downstairs to her bedroom. The noise from the dining room was making the old walls vibrate, but as Daisy usually slept through air raids, Peggy wasn't concerned that it might disturb her.

She held her in her arms as she gave her the bottle and watched as her eyelids fluttered and she finally fell asleep. Kissing the top of her downy head, she gently placed her in the cot and drew the blankets over her. It was the end of Daisy's first Christmas, and although she would probably never remember it, Peggy was certain that she'd thoroughly enjoyed it.

As she left her bedroom there was a knock on the front door, and she opened it to find Rosie and Monty on the doorstep. One look at Rosie's face told her that her friend was trying very hard not to show how upset she was. 'What's happened, Rosie?' she asked as they hugged.

'Nothing that I couldn't put right,' she replied briskly, unclipping Monty's leash. He hared off to find Harvey, and she stepped inside and handed Peggy the shopping bag. 'Happy Christmas, Peg.

I'm sure you'll enjoy these for a change from your usual brand.'

Peggy looked in astonishment at the several dozen packets of Craven A. They were a posh, expensive brand and hadn't been seen in the shops for ages. 'Good grief, Rosie. Where did this lot come from?'

'Let's just say Father Christmas delivered them and leave it at that.' She took off her coat and hung it over the banisters, then patted her hair and plastered on a smile. 'It sounds as if they're having fun. How many waifs and strays have you taken in tonight?'

'There are two in the kitchen and a couple of American boys in the dining room, as well as Cissy, her young man and Martin.'

Peggy regarded Rosie thoughtfully, noting the broken fingernail and chipped varnish and the smudge of mascara beneath one eye. Rosie always looked immaculate, but tonight she was clearly not quite herself. 'Do you need to talk about whatever's bothering you, Rosie?'

She shook her head. 'I need a large gin, if you've got one going – and I could do with a bit of a dance as well. Being stuck in the house with a moody Tommy for most of the day hasn't been the best of fun.'

'I don't know what he's got to be moody about,' retorted Peggy. 'He's got a roof over his head, thanks to you. And is probably living high on the hog with you running about after him and cooking him meals.'

'Well, something's got him on edge, and that's a fact,' Rosie replied. 'But whatever it is, he's keeping it to himself – as usual.'

Peggy wished there was somewhere in the house that wasn't occupied so they could have a proper talk. It was a bad sign for Tommy to be moody, and the only reason for it as far as she could see was his anxiety over Mary's search for Cyril Fielding. 'Tommy isn't up to his old tricks again, is he?' she asked, holding up the shopping bag.

Rosie gave a deep sigh. 'He'll never change, Peg, and I was stupid to even hope that he might.' She took Peggy's hand. 'Don't tell Ron, or it will just make everything ten times worse.'

Peggy was wise enough to realise this, for Ron was fiercely protective of his Rosie and if he caught even a whiff of trouble from the hated Tommy there would be serious trouble. 'I'd better hide all this away in my bedroom,' she murmured.

Rosie opened the catch on her large handbag and drew out several packets of pipe tobacco. 'You'd better put these in with them. Ron will get suspicious if I give him too many at once. Perhaps you could eke them out?'

Peggy didn't like the subterfuge, or the fact that she was being asked to hide what could only be stolen or black-market contraband. But Rosie was her friend, and it wouldn't be the first time she'd had illicit goods hidden about the house – Jim and his father had often come home from their fishing trips to France with things they shouldn't have.

'I'll see to them, don't you worry.'

'Thanks, Peg,' she said with a sigh of relief. 'I hate to get you involved, but if they're found in the pub I could not only lose my licence, but get thrown into gaol.'

Peggy opened her bedroom door and Rosie followed her in to head straight for the cot, where Daisy was spreadeagled and fast asleep in the flickering glow of the night-light. 'She's so lovely,' she murmured wistfully. 'You are lucky, Peg.'

'She's a good baby most of the time,' Peggy replied as she stood on the dressing-table stool and pulled down her overnight case from the top of the wardrobe. 'But when she's teething, or in one of her bad moods, her yelling can go right through your head and nothing will soothe her.'

She stuffed the overloaded shopping bag into the small case, snapped the clasps shut and shoved it back out of sight. 'There, that should do it.'

Rosie tenderly drew the blanket over Daisy's sprawled body, and ran a finger through the dark curls. 'It's at times like this that I... That are the hardest,' she managed, her voice unsteady. 'Just her baby smell is enough to bring it all back.'

Peggy thought her heart would break and she drew Rosie into her embrace and held her until she was more composed. 'I know, and I do understand,' she soothed as they sat on the end of the bed.

Rosie dried her tears with a handkerchief. 'I know you do – and I should have learned to put it all behind me after so long – but now and again it sweeps over me like a great tidal wave and I simply don't have the strength to fight it.'

Knowing what she did, Peggy really didn't have an answer to this – and anything she said now could open up a real can of worms. As she listened to the joyous shouts from the dining room, she decided it would be best to try and lighten the mood.

'Why don't you fix your make-up before we join the others? It sounds as if the party is really livening up in there.'

Rosie nodded, but she didn't move from the bed. 'He's been seeing Eileen again,' she murmured, her gaze still on the sleeping baby.

Peggy experienced a jolt of alarm, even though this statement had come as no surprise. 'Really?' she stuttered. 'But I thought they couldn't stand the sight of each other?'

'I saw them together just after he was released from prison, and again tonight. They're up to something, I just know it. Tommy's been too on edge lately, and I recognise the signs.'

Peggy squeezed her hand, took a deep breath and decided it was time to find out just how much Rosie knew about her brother. 'Could it have anything to do with Cyril Fielding?' she asked as casually as she could.

Rosie frowned as she looked back at her. 'Who the heck is Cyril Fielding?'

The relief was overwhelming. 'Oh, no one of any importance,' she replied lightly. 'He's another Tommy, really, and I heard a rumour that he was in the area again.'

'Perhaps I should ask Tommy about him and find out just what he's up to.'

'No, don't do that, Rosie,' she said hastily. 'The less you know about Tommy's business, the better. You really don't want to get dragged into any trouble if the police start asking questions.'

Rosie took a deep breath and let it out on a sigh. 'You're right, as always, Peg. I just wish I hadn't agreed to him coming to stay.'

She reached into her handbag for her powder compact and lipstick and began to repair her makeup. 'Let's forget about Tommy and enjoy what's left of the evening. I don't know about you, but I am in serious need of a gin and some cheering up.'

Peggy smiled back at her as they went out of the room, but she had a horrible feeling that she shouldn't have mentioned Cyril. Rosie was being pushed to the limit of her patience by her brother, and if they got into one of their usual heated arguments, it was quite possible that she would fire off questions about Fielding – and that could really stir things up.

As Jack tucked in to his plateful of food Mary discovered that she was hungry after all and had polished off her own plate. They were sitting in the kitchen with Harvey and Monty, who were drooling in anticipation by the table.

Jack mopped the last of the gravy up with a crust of bread, broke it into two and within seconds they'd disappeared down the dogs' gullets. He grinned and ruffled their shaggy heads. 'I miss having dogs about the place,' he said.

'Your mum keeps them out of the house, so I don't know how,' said Mary fondly.

'I know they're there, and every time you go outside, you're assured of a warm welcome.' He smiled at her as he reached for her hand. 'It's so lovely to be here with you at last, Mary. You can have no idea of how much I've missed you.'

'I've missed you too,' she murmured as they leaned towards one another and softly kissed.

Jack cocked his head as Bing Crosby crooned about a white Christmas from the other room. 'Do you realise we've never danced properly together?'

'You're forgetting all the times you stomped on my feet at the harvest barn dances,' she teased.

'No, I meant properly.' His expression was very serious as he stood up and held out his hand. 'Will you dance with me, Mary?'

She went into his arms and rested her head against his shoulder as he held her close and they swayed and shuffled in time to the song. It didn't matter that it was Peggy's kitchen, or that they were being watched by two puzzled dogs – or even that their dance floor was faded linoleum – for they were together, and that was all that counted.

As the music came to an end they kissed and drew apart. 'I have to leave soon,' he said, glancing at the clock. 'It's almost eleven and they lock the hostel doors at midnight.'

'Then let's join the party for one more dance before you walk me back. It would be rude not to show our faces after Peggy's been so very kind.'

He grinned down at her and they hurried into the dining room, where they were met with knowing smiles and cheers. Blushing furiously, they joined in the long, snaking line of the conga, which took them back out into the hall, up to the first landing, down again and round the kitchen before returning to the dining room, where Cordelia waved her stick at them in excitement and beckoned them over.

'I like the look of your young man, Mary,' she said, all of a twitter. 'What's that uniform?'

'It's the Special Service Brigade of the Commandos,' shouted Jack over the surrounding noise. He proudly showed her the badge on his cap and the insignia on his arm.

She eyed both with a deep frown. 'Spectacles Service for the brocade of commodes? What a very odd thing to belong to. But I suppose you must know what you're doing.'

Jack looked utterly confused and Mary laughed. 'She's very deaf, and although she's wearing her hearing aid, she's probably finding it difficult to hear anything with all this racket going on around her.' She leaned closer to Cordelia and loudly explained exactly what Jack had said.

Cordelia giggled. 'Silly me.' She gripped Mary's hand and pulled her closer. 'He looks very nice, dear, and I'm glad he's come home for Christmas.'

'So am I,' Mary replied, giving Jack a quick grin. 'But we've got to go now, Cordelia.'

'Already? But you've only just arrived and I haven't had a dance with him yet.'

Mary glanced frantically at the clock. At this rate they'd have to run all the way back to Havelock Road. 'Perhaps next time, Grandma Finch,' she said as she kissed her cheek and wished her a happy Christmas.

Grabbing Jack's hand, she pulled him across the room. 'We'll say a quick goodbye to Peggy then we must rush, or you'll be locked out.'

Peggy made Jack promise to visit again when he was next on leave, then she shooed them out before they were held up any further.

Mary grabbed her bag, coat and gas-mask box as they hurried through the kitchen, and Jack grinned fondly at the dogs which were now sleeping peacefully in front of the fire. Hand in hand they ran down the twitten and crossed over to Camden Road.

'Where is the YMCA? I don't remember seeing it.'

'It's in a big house close to the station in the High Street,' he said as he loped along at a steady jogging pace. 'The chap at the station told me where it was, and said the original place had been flattened during a fire-bomb attack.'

Mary tugged on his arm. 'Can you slow down? I'm not as fit as you, and I'm getting a stitch in my side.'

His grin was mischievous as he came to a halt. 'Sorry. I forgot you were just a feeble female.'

She dug him in the ribs. 'I'll give you feeble, you rotter,' she panted.

He tipped back his head and laughed, then grabbed hold of her, slung her over his shoulder and began to run.

'Put me down,' she squealed, half in fright, half in amusement, pummelling his back with her fists.

But he paid no attention and carried on running, to the great entertainment of those walking past.

As his boots thudded on the pavement and she was jolted up and down, her handbag and gas-mask box swung from her wrist and she found she had to cling on to his jacket. She was roaring with laughter now and could only hope that her underwear wasn't on show to all and sundry as shouts of encouragement and whistles of approval followed them down Camden Road.

He continued on over the High Street and

along Havelock Road until he came to a skidding halt outside Doris's gate. 'Uh-oh, we've been rumbled,' he groaned.

Mary twisted round and saw Doris on her doorstep saying goodbye to four of her guests. 'Put me down, quick.'

'What *do* you think you're doing?' snapped Doris as the gathering on the doorstep turned to stare. 'Put that girl down immediately.'

'He was just giving me a lift home,' giggled Mary as he carefully deposited her onto the driveway.

There were a couple of titters from the onlookers, but Doris was clearly not amused. 'I expected rather more decorum from you, Mary Jones,' she said flatly. 'Get indoors.'

Jack kept his arm about her. 'We haven't said goodnight yet,' he said, and promptly swept Mary into his arms and gave her a passionate kiss.

Mary was giggling so hard she had to cling to him. 'Stop it,' she hissed against his lips. 'You'll get me thrown out.'

'Stop that disgusting behaviour immediately,' stormed Doris. 'It's an utter disgrace, and I don't know what the world's coming to.'

'Well, there is a war on, Doris,' tittered one of the women. 'And they probably only have a few hours together.'

'Yes, I wouldn't be too hard on them, dear,' said another. 'They are very young.'

'Young or not, war or not, I will *not* abide this sort of behaviour on my doorstep, and I'm amazed that you should both condone it,' she said stiffly.

'I've got to go,' murmured Jack as he continued to hold Mary to him. 'Will you be all right with that old battleaxe?'

'I'll be fine.' She kissed him quickly and stepped away. 'I'm not working until lunchtime tomorrow, so I'll meet you by the pier at nine.'

'Make it eight,' he pleaded. 'We have so little time together.'

'Eight it is. Now go, before they lock that blessed door.' She stood and watched as he ran down the road, then turned back with some trepidation towards the house.

'Good luck, dear,' said one of the women as she patted her arm. 'And don't fret about Doris. Her bark is often worse than her bite.'

As Doris's friends walked away, Mary realised that whatever Doris said couldn't take away the sheer magic of the time she'd spent with Jack. 'I'm sorry you don't approve,' she said as she stepped into the hall. 'But Jack and I are almost engaged, and he's only here for such a short time. We were having a bit of fun, that's all,' she finished lamely.

'Bits of fun lead to other things,' said Doris waspishly. 'I'm sure your parents wouldn't have approved of what I witnessed tonight.'

'I don't think my father would have really minded,' she said as she thought of Gideon. 'He knew how I feel about Jack.'

Doris glared at her. 'That is no excuse, and if I catch you behaving in that manner again I will have no other option but to throw you out.'

Mary had borne years of listening to the same sort of threat from Emmaline, and she felt quite calm as she took off her coat and slung it over her arm. 'I do hope it won't come to that, Mrs Williams, because it really wouldn't be at all fair.

Goodnight.' She turned on her heel and ran up the stairs.

The party at Peggy's broke up soon after Mary and Jack had left. Martin, Cissy and the boys had to be back at Cliffe aerodrome by midnight, and Captain Hammond had to report in to the Cliffe Estate at the same time. Fran had already reluctantly gone to her night shift at the hospital, and Ron was walking Rosie back to the Anchor.

Peggy hugged them all and told them to go carefully before she pulled Cissy into her arms. 'You take care of yourself, darling,' she murmured into her hair. 'And try to come and see me more often. I miss you so much.'

'I miss you too, Mum, but with such a busy rota, I'm never certain of when I can get enough time off to borrow a car and make the journey down here.' Her blue eyes were misty with tears. 'Thanks for a wonderful Christmas – and for asking Randy to join in. He and the other boys don't say much, but I know how very grateful they all are.'

Peggy was too emotional to be able to reply, so she hugged and kissed her again and reluctantly let her go. As the last service truck left Beach View Close, she waved goodbye, closed the door and let her tears finally flow. They were all such lovely young people, and she'd been glad to give them a few hours of fun and laughter in these dark and very uncertain times.

'Let's make a pot of tea, shall we?' Rita put her arm about her waist and gently steered her towards the kitchen where Jane was already putting the kettle on the hob. 'We've all had such a wonderful time today, Auntie Peggy, so why are you crying?'

'I hate saying goodbyes,' she said as she made a tremendous effort to dry her eyes and get composed. 'And those boys are all so brave – risking their lives so we can sleep safely in our beds.'

'I think you're just overtired and that it's the gin doing the talking,' teased Rita as she pressed her down into the chair by the rather feeble fire. 'You know it always makes you maudlin.'

Peggy suddenly realised someone was missing. 'Where's Cordelia?' she asked sharply. 'Surely we haven't left her asleep in the dining room?'

Jane grinned as she warmed the teapot. 'Sarah took her up when everyone was leaving. She's probably already tucked up in bed and snoring.'

Peggy sighed contentedly and lit a cigarette. She was a very lucky woman to be surrounded by such lovely, caring girls, and although she missed Jim, Anne and Cissy and her two boys dreadfully, their companionship and sweetness went a good way towards easing the pain of separation.

The dread grew with every step as Rosie leaned on Ron's arm and they approached the Anchor. If Tommy had discovered his booty was missing there would be the most frightful row, and she was too tired and too full of gin to be able to stand up to him. She'd probably acted rather foolishly by getting rid of everything, but there really hadn't been any alternative if she stood any chance of keeping her licence as well as the roof over her head.

'Rosie, darlin', is something bothering you?'

Ron came to a halt and took her hands as he looked deeply into her eyes.

'No, of course not,' she said firmly. 'I've just had a very long day, and probably too many gins.' She kissed him and smiled as a sudden thought came to her. 'Why don't you come up for a nightcap?'

He was clearly tempted. 'Won't Tommy be about? I don't fancy him playing gooseberry.'

Rosie knew she had to persuade him, for if Tommy was at home, she'd know immediately if he'd discovered what she'd done, but he wouldn't dare cause trouble in front of Ron. If that indeed was the case, then she'd have to play it by ear and make other arrangements. 'He went out earlier, and if he's where I think he is then he probably won't be back before morning.'

Ron waggled his eyebrows and there was a glint of naughtiness in his eyes. 'Then what are we waiting for?' He whistled to the dogs, which were watering a nearby lamp-post, and then followed Rosie down the alleyway to the side door.

Rosie's heart was pounding as she stepped into the narrow hall and the dogs dashed up the stairs. 'Tommy?' she called. 'Tommy, are you home?'

'Shh, don't wake him up,' hissed Ron as he slid his arm round her waist.

Rosie tried to giggle and flirt as she would normally have done, but her heart was drumming and she was too worried about having to face Tommy to do it properly.

'What's the matter?' Ron asked with a frown. 'And don't tell me it's nothing. You've not been yourself all evening.'

'Maybe that's because I'm tired of sharing my

home with my brother.' She drew back from his embrace and started to climb the stairs. 'I'm used to having my own clean, tidy space, and I'm getting sick of having to clear up after him and getting him out of bed to be on time for where he should be.'

'Then tell him to leave,' said Ron as he reached the snug sitting room.

'You know I can't.' She kicked off her shoes and glanced down the narrow hall to Tommy's bedroom. The door was shut and it was silent.

'Why not?' persisted Ron as he poured out two fingers of brandy into glasses.

'Because I made him a promise, and unlike my brother, I keep my promises.' She eyed the brandy she didn't really want. 'I'll just go and see if he's asleep, then we can settle down to a bit of a cuddle without fear of being disturbed.'

'Don't for the love of God wake him up,' he whispered hoarsely.

Rosie tiptoed down the hall and, after a moment of hesitation, carefully opened the bedroom door. The room was empty and just as she'd left it. Tommy had yet to come home. A great wave of relief swept through her and she closed the door.

Returning to the sitting room, she found Ron was sitting rather disconsolately on the couch sandwiched in by both dogs. She ordered them down and snuggled up next to him, at last able to relax. Taking the glass of brandy from him, she raised it in a toast. 'He's out, so here's to you and me and some time on our own.'

Ron sipped the brandy and gathered her close

to kiss her. 'Happy Christmas, Rosie. I don't suppose...?'

'You suppose right,' she giggled.

Chapter Nine

Mary was fast asleep and dreaming of Jack, so she didn't hear Ivy creeping in at two in the morning, until she tripped over a shoe she'd left on the floor and fell against Mary's bed.

Mary woke with a start. 'What on earth?'

'Shh, or the old cow will 'ear.' Ivy giggled and collapsed across Mary's feet. 'I've had a blindin' Christmas, Mary. Them Yanks certainly know how to party.'

Mary peered at her alarm clock. 'It's two in the morning,' she hissed. 'For goodness sake, Ivy, stop messing about and go to your own bed.'

Ivy made a sterling effort to sit up, but failed miserably. 'I can't,' she giggled. 'I'm sorta stuck.'

The giggles were catching, and as Mary tried to get her friend to her feet, she was somehow put off balance, and they both fell with a thud to the floor. They lay there in the darkness, trying hard to stifle their laughter, knowing that Doris was only feet away at the other end of the landing.

Mary finally managed to take control. 'You've got to get out of those clothes and into bed before she wakes up and storms in here,' she said in a hoarse whisper. 'She's already torn me off a strip, and if she sees you like that, we'll both be out on

194

our ear.'

Ivy rolled onto her stomach and, with a great deal of help from Mary, managed to get to her feet. She swayed a little and then stumbled over to her bed. Flinging back the covers, she kicked off her shoes, wrestled with her overcoat, which she let drop to the floor, and climbed in.

'You can't go to bed in your clothes,' Mary protested.

'Why not?' Ivy pulled the covers over her head and within seconds was fast asleep.

Mary gave a sigh which was a mixture of relief and amused exasperation. At least she was in bed, and Doris hadn't caught them. She climbed back into her own bed. There were less than five hours before she had to be up to eat breakfast before she met Jack. She curled beneath the covers and tried to ignore the awful racket that Ivy was making. Unable to settle, she swung back out of bed, went across to Ivy and rather roughly rolled her from her back onto her side in the hope that this would stop her from snoring. Thoroughly out of sorts and now wide awake, she snuggled back under her covers and imagined she was at work sorting through the airgraphs in the hope that this repetitive and tedious occupation might encourage the return of sleep.

It must have done eventually, for Mary opened her eyes as her alarm clock rang out and saw that it was almost seven o'clock. She threw back the covers and pulled on her dressing gown. Ivy's snoring was softer now, and all Mary could see of her was the top of her tousled head.

She pulled back the two rows of curtains and breathed a sigh of relief. Boxing Day had dawned brightly and the sky was a clear blue which was reflected in the calm sea. It was going to be a beautiful day. 'Ivy, it's time to get up. The sun is shining, the wind has dropped and it's getting late.'

There was no reply and no change in the rhythm of her breathing.

Mary put her hand on the hump of her shoulder and gently rolled her back and forth. 'Ivy, wake up, for goodness' sake, or you won't have time to eat breakfast before you have to be at work.'

Ivy emerged from the covers bleary-eyed, her make-up streaking her face, her fair hair tangled. 'I've gotta blindin' headache,' she groaned.

'That's hardly surprising,' Mary said fondly. She handed her a glass of water and two aspirins. 'Here, take these, and then sort yourself out while I use the bathroom.'

When she returned to the bedroom she was relieved to see that Ivy had shed her best clothes and was struggling to get into her dungarees. 'That must have been quite a party yesterday,' she said with a smile in her voice.

Ivy yawned expansively as she fumbled to fasten the shoulder straps. 'Yeah, it were. The Yanks took over the big hall where we usually go to the pictures. They 'ad a band and tons of food as well as booze, and I was danced off me feet all night.'

She shot Mary a rather weary but cheeky grin. 'It were ever so good, and Chuck walked me home an' all.' She grimaced. 'He got a bit fresh and I had a bit of a job to fight 'im off, but all in all, it were a smashing do.' She pulled on a sweater

196

and then tried to get the tangles out of her hair. 'Wot about you?'

'My Jack turned up and we went to Peggy's. It was quite a party there, too.' Mary went on to describe how Jack had carried her home – and how Doris had reacted.

Ivy burst out laughing. 'Blimey, Mary, you ain't 'alf a caution. And here's me thinking you was ever so quiet and ladylike. Her ladyship must've had a blue fit.'

Mary could feel the blush spread across her face as she thought how it must have looked to everyone. 'It was embarrassing, and she's certainly not best pleased with me at the moment, that's for sure. But if she does tell me to leave, you and I can always go to Peggy. She keeps asking us to, and I know she's got an empty room.'

'That sounds blinding,' said Ivy as she gave up on her hair and tied a scarf over it. 'I've about had it with her ladyship and that's a fact.'

She looked back at Mary her expression suddenly thoughtful. 'But, funny enough, I quite like it with just us two after living all squashed up in one room with the rest of me family – and this place is a regular palace. Perhaps the old bat ain't that bad if you can steer clear of 'er. And let's face it, Mary, she ain't 'ere most of the time anyways.' She grabbed her washbag and headed for the bathroom.

Mary stared after her in amazement. She'd never for a moment imagined that Ivy would prefer living here with Doris when she could have had the warmth and homeliness of Peggy's Beach View. But then she shrugged and accepted that

197

she too had turned down the chance to live at Peggy's for the very same reason. It was easy and rather pleasant just having Ivy to share with, and together they could deal with Doris and enjoy the comforts of Havelock Road, knowing that Peggy would always be there if they needed her.

She finished dressing and quickly applied some powder and lipstick before brushing out her long hair and leaving it to hang sleekly down her back. The thought of seeing Jack in less than an hour had made her eyes sparkle and her pulse race – but then the knowledge that it could only be until midday when she would have to spend the rest of his leave at the Kodak factory dampened her spirits.

As Ivy came back in and began to throw her discarded clothes onto the bed, Mary came to a decision. 'Ivy, I'd like you to do me a really big favour.'

Ivy's blue eyes twinkled as she looked back at her. 'You want me to call you in sick so you can spend the day with your Jack.' She shrugged. 'Why not? You ain't done it before, and I might need you to return the favour one day.'

Mary gave her a hug. 'Thanks, Ivy. You're a real pal.'

The dimples appeared. 'Yeah, and so are you. Sorry about last night. I were a bit worse fer wear, as me mum would've said.'

They hurried downstairs to the kitchen and made toast. There was still a lot of sliced ham in the fridge, and as Doris had yet to put in an appearance, they sandwiched the ham between the toast with tomato relish. As they munched this delicious breakfast and drank copious amounts of tea, they chattered about the parties they'd been to and their plans for that evening. Not that Mary had any real plan, she was just happy to be with Jack wherever they ended up.

It was a quarter to eight by the time they'd washed their plates and put everything neatly away. They left the house, and as they reached the end of Havelock Road, Ivy ran up the hill towards the factory estate and Mary headed for the sea-front.

The gulls were mewling as they hovered in the chilly breeze, and squabbled and shrieked from the rooftops and lamp-posts. The sea sparkled as waves broke against the shingle and the white cliffs at the other end of the bay looked majestic between sky and sea. If it wasn't for the coils of ugly barbed wire, the gun emplacements and the stench of oil which lay in thick clumps on the shingle, it would have made a perfect seaside postcard.

Mary hurried along the deserted promenade, her gaze fixed on the skeletal remains of the pier, which had the shattered remnants of a German fighter plane rusting within its embrace. And there was Jack, unmistakeable in his khaki trousers and shirt, green sweater, dark brown leather jerkin and the green beret that was drawn down to his right eyebrow.

Her heart was thudding as they ran towards one another. He swept her into his arms and she forgot about everything as she was lost in his sweet kiss.

Rosie was feeling rather woolly-headed this morning, due to the brandies she'd shared with Ron and the lack of proper sleep. He had left at two in the morning and she'd thought she'd be able to drop off – but with every creak and groan of the ancient building she'd tensed, wondering if it was Tommy.

She'd finally managed an hour or two, but was still so on edge that she was finding it almost impossible to concentrate on anything. She pulled on slacks and a sweater and quickly checked that Tommy hadn't slipped home without her noticing, then she hurried downstairs in her flat shoes and into the bar with Monty dancing about her legs.

Sliding back the bolt on the back door, she stepped out into the scrap of neglected garden, her gaze falling immediately on the slabs. They weren't quite in line with the others and were still standing a bit proud, so she stamped down on them until she was satisfied. There was still a bit too much earth piled on either side, so she quickly kicked some of it over the slabs and the rest into the long, weed-infested grass.

Monty thought this was a good game and began to dig furiously round the slabs, sending dirt, moss and weeds flying.

'Stop it, Monty,' she snapped as she made a grab for his collar. 'For goodness' sake, you'll get me shot,' she hissed. She had to drag him back into the bar and close the door firmly on his howls of protest before she went back to repair the damage. Then, seeing a few dead branches which had been blown off the surrounding trees, she gathered them up with an armful of rather soggy leaves and twigs, and dropped them haphazardly over everything.

She added a few more bits she'd found by the hedge and studiously regarded her handiwork. That would have to do, and as she'd never seen Tommy venture out here over the years, she could only pray that old habits died hard and he remained uninterested in anything beyond the back wall of the bar.

'I see you're doing something about your garden at last.'

Rosie was so tense that she nearly jumped out of her skin. She looked up at the scrawny middle-aged woman who was leaning out of her side window. It was Mrs Flynn, one of the nosiest women in Cliffehaven.

'I thought I should try and tidy it up a bit,' she stammered.

'Not before time, if you ask me,' Mrs Flynn replied with a sniff.

'I don't remember asking you anything,' muttered Rosie as she nudged the twigs and leaves with the toe of her shoe.

'Well, you don't want to be piling all that dead wood so close to the house,' the woman said bossily. 'Start a bonfire there, and you'll set everything alight.'

'I was just clearing it,' said a tight-lipped Rosie.

'You won't get far doing it like that. You need a rake to get all the leaves and twigs up properly – and it wouldn't hurt to cut that grass either. My Derek gets the most terrible hay fever every spring because of all the seeds and pollen you've got growing in there.'

Derek was her overweight, idle husband who was always professing to be ill with something, and Rosie couldn't have cared less about him. She'd certainly had enough of this unwarranted interference. 'Yes, you're right, Mrs Flynn. I'll go and find a rake now.' With that, she turned away, opened the back door and slammed it hard behind her. 'Nosy old crow,' she muttered as she shot the bolt home.

She pushed past a dancing Monty, who now had his leash dangling from his mouth in anticipation of a walk, and quickly washed her hands in the sink beneath the bar, then went to fetch her coat and scarf. She still felt as if her head was full of cotton wool, and her mood was definitely not sunny after that little run-in – but hopefully that would improve after some fresh air and exercise.

The knowledge that she would have to be back, dressed and ready to open the bar at eleven, didn't excite her. If she ever needed a proper day off, this was it. The bar would no doubt become crowded with people escaping their families after being closeted with them all the previous day, or with others who were drinking the 'hair of the dog' after having had too much the night before. Then there were the servicemen and women and factory workers who hadn't had Christmas day off and those who were simply bored with their own company.

She gave a deep sigh as she fastened the lead to Monty's collar. 'Come on, little man,' she said fondly. 'Let's see if some fresh air and exercise will blow the nasty old cobwebs away.'

It was bright and sunny, the breeze quite crisp,

and as she went up the hill and took the short cut through the twitten that ran between the terraced houses, she looked to see if Peggy or Ron were about. But there was no sign of anyone and all she could hear was Daisy yelling at the top of her lungs. Poor Peggy. There was little chance of a lie-in with that racket going on.

Dragging Monty away from the gate, she continued to tramp along the twitten until she came to the steep slope that would take her up onto the great, sweeping headland that protected Cliffehaven from the sea. Judging she'd gone far enough for Monty not to race back to Beach View in search of Harvey, she let him off the lead.

Freed at last, Monty shot off with the speed and grace of a young greyhound, bounding up the steep incline and disappearing into the trees.

Rose followed at a slower pace, her calf muscles tightening rather painfully as she ploughed on up the hill. This was where Ron took him and Harvey most mornings, and on rare occasions she joined them. She didn't usually come up here on her own, or even do this sort of walking, for she soon got out of breath and unpleasantly hot – but today she was content with her own company, for the tranquillity of the silent hills was a balm to her troubled thoughts.

She reached the brow and watched Monty dashing back and forth with his nose to the ground in search of who knew what, and then turned to look out to sea. It looked lovely beneath the clear blue sky, the sun-diamonds twinkling on the silky ripples as the terns and gulls glided and swooped.

She breathed in the scent of salt and damp

earth, of lush grass and the musk of decaying foliage. Despite the gun emplacements that had been erected in a ragged line along the cliff-top, it was difficult to believe there was a war on up here, for the ravaged town was out of sight and all was peaceful.

Monty came to sit beside her, his tongue lolling as he panted like a steam train. Rosie stroked his head, glad of his quiet companionship. She hadn't wanted a dog, for they could be a terrible tie, and with the pub to run, there were few opportunities to give him the exercise he needed. And yet she'd fallen in love with him the moment Ron had carried him into the pub, and now couldn't imagine life without him.

How uncomplicated animals are, she thought as she threw a stick for Monty to chase and resumed her walk. They need only love, food and shelter and give so much loyalty and affection in return. Whereas humans – like her brother – were unreliable and capable of betrayal, their loyalties dependent on what they could gain from their relationships. She knew this wasn't totally fair, for there were others like Peg and Ron whose love and loyalty had never been in doubt – but then, thankfully, not everyone was like Tommy.

Having walked as far as the ruined farmhouse, Rosie sat for a while as Monty continued his endless hunt for things in the grass. Finally, aware that time was getting short, she reluctantly began the long walk back, Monty now firmly restrained by his leash as he was inclined to do a disappearing act, and no amount of calling would bring him back until he was good and ready.

There was still no sign of movement at Beach View and Daisy was still yelling fit to bust, which must be giving Peggy a terrible headache by now. Rosie would have called in to offer a hand, but as she'd stayed out too long already, she was in danger of being late to open up the pub, so she carried on walking.

She had almost reached the Anchor when she saw something that made her steps falter. Mrs Flynn was on her doorstep, arms folded, talking to Tommy. A chill of foreboding swept away her sense of wellbeing and she had to square her shoulders and steel herself to approach them. 'Good morning again, Mrs Flynn,' she said with a tight smile.

'I was just telling your brother that he should have rolled up his sleeves and helped you clear the garden.' Mrs Flynn's rat-like features looked sharper than ever as she eyed him disdainfully. 'It's man's work, and while you're at it, those trees need pruning. They're scraping at my roof tiles.'

'If I'd known my sister was in the mood for gardening, of course I would have only been too glad to help, Mrs Flynn,' said Tommy with his most charming of smiles. 'Now, if you'll excuse us, we have to get ready to open the bar.'

'You need to keep the noise down,' she shouted after them. 'My Derek can't sleep at night for all the racket, what with the piano and such and all that singing.'

'There's a war on, Mrs F.,' said Tommy over his shoulder. 'And it's better to hear singing and music than it is to hear bombs dropping.' He pushed open the side door. 'And may one drop on you, you nosy, interfering old witch,' he muttered.

Despite her anxiety, Rosie couldn't help but smile. 'Tommy, that's unkind.'

'Well, she asked for it.' He unwound his scarf and took off his overcoat. 'And what's all this about you tidying up the garden first thing this morning? You've neglected it for years, so why start now?'

Rosie's pulse was racing and the pleasantly warm glow she'd acquired from her walk became an icy chill as she turned away to unclip Monty's leash and slip off her shoes and coat. 'I woke early and went out there for some fresh air, saw the state of it and decided to make a start on clearing it up,' she said before she ran up the stairs.

He gave a chuckle as he followed her into the kitchen. 'Are you sure you haven't been burying a body out there?' he joked. 'Ron proved a bit of a nuisance at last, has he?'

Her heart seemed to miss a beat, but she managed to keep her hands steady enough as she put the kettle on the hob and hunted out clean cups. 'Don't be daft,' she said lightly. 'Now, do you want tea or coffee?'

'Coffee, please. I've got a bit of a hangover.'

This was much safer ground and Rosie was able to relax a little. 'So, where did you get to yesterday?'

'I went to the party the Yanks put on in the big hall that's now used as a cinema. It was quite a do, and I met a lovely lady who very kindly gave me a bed for the night.'

'Spare me the details,' she said with a shudder. She made the coffee and handed it over, at last daring to look him in the eye. 'Don't forget you have to be on fire-watch tonight.'

He heaved a sigh. 'You never stop nagging me, do you?'

'It's important, Tommy,' she said firmly.

'Well, I've got things to do this afternoon, so I'll have to leave before we close at two.' He shot her a smile that she noticed didn't quite reach his eyes. 'I'm sure the ever-loyal Ron will be on hand to help in my absence.'

'What things?' she asked sharply.

'None of your business,' he snapped as he put down the cup so hard it spilled the untouched coffee everywhere. Turning on his heel, he headed down the hall. 'I need a bath and shave and to get changed. Hopefully, by that time you'll be too busy to carry on giving me the third degree.'

Rosie flinched as he slammed the bathroom door. 'Oh, God,' she whispered tremulously to a whining Monty. 'I can't stand much more of this.'

Peggy wasn't feeling quite the ticket this morning, and Daisy wasn't helping because she'd woken in a foul temper and had screamed and shrieked her way through her morning bath and most of breakfast.

Sarah and Rita had made an early escape to work, but Jane and Fran were still trying to catch up on their sleep upstairs, and Peggy doubted they were having much success.

'Oh dear,' said Cordelia as she finished her toast and home-made jam. 'Isn't there anything you can do to stop her making that noise?'

Peggy tried spooning another helping of porridge into her daughter's open mouth, but Daisy spat it straight out and went stiff with fury. 'She's overtired after her late night,' Peggy shouted over the racket. 'I'm sorry, Cordelia, but you'd find it far more comfortable if you turned off your hearing aid.'

'It's already off,' she replied with a grim expression. 'Goodness me, I think I'll take my cup of tea and book into the other room.'

Peggy gave a deep sigh and tried once again to coax some porridge into Daisy, but the spoon was swept away by her small fist and the porridge ended up splattered all over Peggy's clean apron. 'Right, that's it,' she said in defeat. 'You can jolly well go without.'

She left the table and started on the washing-up, trying her best to ignore Daisy's constant, ear-splitting yelling. But she was clumsy this morning and a plate slipped through her soapy fingers, caught the edge of the draining board and smashed to smithereens on the floor. It was the final straw.

Drying her hands, she wrestled to get the furious Daisy out of her high chair and carry her into the hall. Strapping her firmly in her pram, she almost threw the covers over her before wheeling it into the dining room.

Cordelia looked up from her book in horror. 'What *are* you doing? I've come in here for some peace and quiet.'

'I'm going to shut the door on her in here, so you'd better come back to the kitchen. I can't stand this any longer, and a bit of solitude might calm her down and bring her to her senses.'

Cordelia didn't look totally convinced, but she regarded the screaming baby, rolled her eyes and made her way out of the room. 'I can't think what's got into her today,' she muttered. 'She's usually such a good little thing.'

'She's overtired – just as we all are,' Peggy replied as she dumped the bottle of juice in the pram along with some toys, and closed the door firmly behind her. She wouldn't leave her for long, but she and Cordelia would go mad if they had to listen to that all morning – and it wouldn't hurt Daisy to learn that such behaviour would not be tolerated.

She returned to the kitchen to find Cordelia already happily ensconced in her favourite chair by the fire, with Harvey lying sprawled at her feet whilst Ron slurped his tea at the table. 'Are you going to help Rosie in the pub this lunchtime?'

'Aye, I'll be doing that, so I will. So you can put your list of things to do back in that apron pocket.' He drank some tea and clattered the cup in the saucer. 'I'm on Home Guard duty this morning, by the way. We've got some new recruits that are barely out of school and still too young to enlist. It's down to me to teach them how to shoot straight and lay mines without blowing themselves up.'

'Isn't that rather dangerous?'

'It is if they don't do it properly,' he rumbled. 'But it's not live ammo, so they'll survive.'

Peggy lit a well-earned cigarette and sat down at the table. She could still hear Daisy yelling, but it was much fainter now, and not quite so furious. 'Was Tommy at home when you took Rosie back last night?' she asked casually.

Ron shook his head and then waggled his eyebrows. 'To be sure, he was nowhere to be seen, so Rosie and I had a bit of time to ourselves for a change.'

'That's good,' she said distractedly.

He eyed her sharply. 'Has Rosie said something to you that I should know about?'

Peggy thought about the cigarettes and tobacco hidden in her bedroom and quickly busied herself by stirring her tea. 'Of course she hasn't,' she fibbed. 'Although I think she's getting tired of having Tommy hanging about all the time. By all accounts, he's not the easiest or tidiest person to live with.' She shot him an affectionate smile. 'A bit like you really.'

'I'm not in the least like that weasel,' he protested, his eyebrows drawing fiercely together. 'And if she's sick of him being there, she only has to give me the nod and he'll be out on his ear quicker than you can blink.'

'She doesn't want any trouble, Ron. Just let things be, if only for her sake. He knows what will happen if he blots his copybook.'

'Aye.' Ron finished his tea and began to fill his pipe with tobacco, his expression grim. 'And he'd better keep looking over his shoulder, because I'm watching his every move.'

Tommy had disappeared out of the door the moment Ron had arrived fresh from his Home Guard duties, so Rosie had felt instantly more at ease and was able to serve her customers with genuine smiles and cheerful banter.

210

It was busy, as she'd suspected it would be, and with the two barmaids off for the day, it could have been quite stressful. Yet she and Ron were used to working together and as they got into the rhythm of dealing with the clamour of customers, time passed quickly and rather pleasantly.

It was half an hour before closing when she looked up from pulling a pint to see Mary and her young man come into the bar. They were immediately surrounded by people asking her to play the piano, but she firmly refused all requests and determinedly led Jack to the counter.

'Hello, love,' Rosie said in delight. 'I didn't expect to see you in here today.'

'We've been walking round the town for most of the morning and got a bit cold out there.' Mary took off the scarf Peggy had given her for Christmas and stuffed it into her coat pocket.

Rosie poured a pint for Jack and a lemonade for Mary. 'No, keep your money,' she said as Jack fished out his wallet. 'This one's on me.' She checked no one else needed serving and leaned on the bar. 'I'd have thought you two would have found somewhere cosy to spend your last few hours together, rather than come into this noisy old place.'

'Well, we did have coffee and a scone at the tea rooms,' said Jack, once he'd sipped the pint and nodded his approval. 'But there's only so long you can sit in there before you start getting dirty looks from the waitress.'

Rosie regarded him with some puzzlement. 'But what about Doris's place? Surely she wouldn't mind if you used her sitting room for the day?'

She saw the youngsters exchange glances and felt a stab of pity. 'Oh, I see. Well, that's too bad of her.' She stood back from the bar and folded her arms, determined not to show how furious she was with Doris. 'Why don't you take those drinks upstairs? There's only Monty and Harvey up there to keep you company, so you won't be disturbed until Ron and I've finished here.'

'What about your brother?' asked Mary.

Rosie heard the nervousness in the girl's voice and caught the young man's sudden frown of concern as he looked questioningly at Mary. 'He's out,' she said quickly, 'and not due back until much later tonight.'

Mary visibly relaxed her tense shoulders. 'Then that would be lovely, Rosie. Are you sure you don't mind?'

Rosie laughed. 'Of course I don't mind. Good heavens, I'd be a pretty poor friend if I made you walk round the town all day when I have a lovely cosy room upstairs. There's some chicken left over from yesterday, so make yourselves a bit of lunch while you're at it. I expect you're hungry now after being out in the cold for so long.'

Mary shot her a shy smile. 'Thank you, Rosie. We were wondering where we could go, and neither of us felt right about descending on Peggy after she gave that marvellous party last night.'

'It was fun, wasn't it?' She noticed that there were three people waiting to be served and that Ron was busy at the other end of the bar. 'Now get yourselves upstairs, and don't mind the mess. I just haven't had the time to clear up today.'

'Is it wise to let them loose up there on their

own?' muttered Ron as they stood side by side drawing pints.

'About as wise as letting you stay until two in the morning,' she countered fondly. 'Don't worry about it, Ron. They're young and in love and have so little time together – it's the least I can do.'

'You really like Mary, don't you?'

Rosie smiled as she realised just how protective she'd become towards the girl. 'Yes, she's a lovely, sweet girl – the sort that any mother would be proud of. I suppose, having heard some of her story from Peg, I want to make things all right for her.'

Ron grinned back at her. 'You and Peggy are a couple of old softies. You know that, don't you?'

'There's nothing wrong with a bit of love and warmth when it's needed, Ronan Reilly,' she retorted with a cheeky wink. 'Now get on with serving that beer before it goes flat.'

'Rosie is lovely, isn't she?' Mary took off her coat and patted the two dogs, who were delighted to see them after being shut in the upstairs rooms since opening time.

'It's really kind of her to let us stay, but why were you so hesitant about her brother?'

Mary knew he'd ask, and had prepared herself. 'He's all right, really,' she fibbed. 'But he's a bit old to be playing gooseberry and it would have been embarrassing, that's all.'

He seemed to accept this, and sat down beside her on the sagging couch. He looked round the room which was cosy with comfortable, chintz-covered chairs and thick rugs. The two dogs were now sprawled in front of the hearth despite the fact no fire had been lit. 'It's nice up here, isn't it? I've always had a bit of a hankering to have my own pub.'

She looked at him in amazement. 'You never said anything before about this secret hankering – and from what I've seen these past few weeks, it isn't an easy life. Poor Rosie never gets much time to herself, and she's always worn out.'

He grinned as he put his arm round her shoulders and pulled her close. 'It's a dream most men have, but I am aware of the realities. Now come here and let me kiss you.'

The time sped past and soon Ron and Rosie came up the stairs to join them for a meal of cold chicken and bubble and squeak which Mary had put together. They left shortly afterwards to take the two dogs for a walk, promising to return with fish and chips if any of the fishmongers were frying tonight.

Mary and Jack settled down on the couch with the radio turned down low and spent a lovely afternoon talking, cuddling and making plans for the future – and when things got a bit intense, Mary ordered him to sweep the hearth and light the fire while she washed the dishes and tidied up the kitchen. It was fun to play house, with Jack busy in the sitting room while she pottered in the kitchen, but goodness only knew what her mother would have said about it, for she definitely wouldn't have approved.

It was almost five o'clock when Ron and Rosie returned triumphantly with lovely fish and chips, which they ate straight out of the paper. 'That was delicious,' said Mary as she finished the last chip and licked her fingers to savour the salt and grease.

'Well, I'll be off to me Home Guard duties,' said Ron, feeding the dogs with the scraps of batter from his fish. 'It's an all-nighter, so you'll not see me until tomorrow.' He gave Rosie a hearty kiss, clicked his fingers at Harvey, and they both clattered down the stairs.

'And I have to open up,' said Rosie. She stood in front of the mirror above the fireplace to freshen her make-up. 'I'm on my own tonight, so it's bound to be hectic.'

'Could I help at all?' asked Jack eagerly.

Rosie chuckled. 'Have you had any experience other than from the other side of the bar?'

He shook his head, his expression rueful. 'But I'm a quick learner, Rosie, and you need a hand.'

'All right then. We'll give it a try, but it will mean Mary being on her own all evening.'

'No, it won't,' said Mary as she gathered up the greasy newspapers and folded them into the wood box by the hearth. 'I'm coming down too, and because it's the only way to repay you for giving us such a lovely day, I'll be more than happy to play the piano.'

'Oh, but you don't want to be doing that on your last night together,' gasped Rosie.

Mary took her hand and gave her a kiss on her soft, freshly powdered cheek. 'We can't think of anything we'd like more, so please let us do it.'

Rosie relented gracefully, and they trooped downstairs. She ordered Monty to stay by the inglenook, before giving Jack a swift course in how to pull a pint correctly, and the mechanics of working the till, then sent him down to the cellar to fetch a couple of crates. As the clock struck the hour, she pulled back the bolts on the door and the first few customers strolled in to the sound of Mary playing the piano.

It was now just past eleven and Rosie had locked the door after her last customer. Mary and Jack quickly helped to finish washing the glasses and clearing up the bar, for they could see how tired she was. Once everything was neat again, they went upstairs and Mary made her a cup of tea before reluctantly gathering up her things.

'Thank you again, Rosie,' she said as she gave her a hug. 'You've given me and Jack a wonderful day, and we're so very grateful.'

'I was glad to do it,' she replied, returning the hug. 'And if you ever need to talk, or feel like a bit of respite from Doris, you know where I am.'

Mary blinked back her tears, unable to voice her gratitude and affection for this lovely woman who'd become such an important part of her new life here in Cliffehaven.

Rosie held her arms open to Jack. 'Now, you take care of yourself and come back to this lovely girl,' she said, giving, him an enthusiastic hug. 'And the next time you come on leave, there'll be a spare bedroom, so you can stay with me instead of that soulless hostel.'

Jack blushed to the roots of his cropped hair. 'Thanks, Rosie. You've been a true friend to both of us.' He clasped Mary's hand. 'Look after my girl, won't you?'

Rosie's smile was soft. 'Of course I will – and so will Peggy. Now get out of here before I start getting tearful.'

Mary's hand was warm in his as they left the Anchor and walked down the street, and she could feel the strength in his fingers, and the sturdiness of him as she leaned into him. The day had been perfect, but now it was almost over and they would have to say goodbye, not knowing what the future held, or how long they would be apart. She blinked back her tears, determined not to make a fuss, but her heart was aching as every step took them closer to that parting.

'You've fallen on your feet here,' he said. 'Rosie and Peggy remind me of my mum, and I do feel easier about leaving now I know there's someone to look out for you.'

Mary roused herself from her dark thoughts and forced a smile into her voice. 'I don't want you worrying about me,' she replied with a lightness that belied the heaviness in her heart. 'Just take care of yourself and come home safe and sound.'

He pulled her into his side as they walked silently towards Havelock Road, their true thoughts unspoken, their fears hidden deep inside. As they reached the house he drew her into the deep shadows of the overhanging trees. Taking her in his arms, he kissed her and then held her for a long moment, his chin resting on her head. They had no need for words, for each knew what was in the other's heart.

With a deep sigh he finally stepped back. 'I have to go, Mary,' he said brokenly.

Mary clung to his hands. She wanted to beg him to be careful, to not forget her – to come home safe and unharmed and not put himself to any unnecessary risk by being a hero. But she said nothing, knowing that he would return if he could, and that their future was now in the hands of Fate.

'I love you,' she said, her voice soft and unsteady as she battled with her tears.

'I love you too, my own, sweet, precious Mary.' His eyes glistened and the muscles in his face moved beneath the tanned flesh as he struggled to hold in his own raw emotions. He released his grip on her fingers, took a step back and then turned and ran down the road.

Mary stood there until she could no longer see him or hear his boots thudding on the pavement. 'God go with you, Jack,' she managed through her tears. 'And keep you safe so you can come home to me.'

Chapter Ten

Mary was waiting outside the ramshackle drill hall which overlooked the allotments, her Christmas scarf pulled up to her chin, her gloved hands deep in her coat pocket. It was the day after Jack had left and she felt empty inside and rather lonely, but she had other concerns to keep her mind occupied at this moment, for the orchestra were already tuning up, and Fran was late.

This would be the first rehearsal that Fran could

attend, for she'd been on duty at the hospital on the other occasions, and if she missed this one, there were only two more before the concert. The conductor, Algernon Beamish, was a stickler about attendance and he hadn't taken kindly to Doris's insistence that Fran join the orchestra, which he considered to be his creation – he certainly wouldn't be pleased if she didn't even show up.

Mary heard the sound of running footsteps and turned with a smile as Fran came haring up the road still in her nurse's uniform and cape. 'You're cutting it fine. I didn't think you'd make it.'

'I very nearly didn't,' puffed Fran. 'To be sure, Matron was in a terrible mood today and I had to stay on to watch over one of the probationers.' She finally got her breath back and grinned. 'It was lucky I took the violin to work with me. I'd never have made it at all if I'd had to go back home to fetch it.'

'Well, you're here now, so we'd better go in and introduce you to the others before they get started on the first piece. You'll know some of the orchestra, because they're servicemen who play along with us at the pub.'

Fran suddenly hung back as Mary went to push open the door. 'I'm not too sure about this, Mary. What if they say I'm not good enough and tell me to leave?'

Mary laughed. 'That isn't going to happen in a million years, Fran. You really must start believing in yourself, you know, because you're so talented you'll probably put the rest of us to shame.'

She took Fran's hand and firmly led the way

into the hall with its bare wooden floor and dusty rafters lining the tin roof. The main body of the small building was crammed with chairs, music stands and people, the grand piano that had been lent by the Mayor had been tucked away in a corner by shelves laden with scout and guide equipment; and the rather large harpist had to squeeze behind her instrument because it was jammed in the other corner.

Everyone stopped tuning their instruments as Mary introduced Fran, who went as red as a beetroot and looked ready to run for the hills when she spied Robert Goodyear amongst the musicians. Mary knew her friend had managed to avoid him since he'd been best man at Suzy's wedding, but he'd taken to hanging about outside the hospital, which was rather disturbing, for he never approached her, or tried to speak, just stood gazing at her as she hurried away.

'You didn't warn me he'd be here,' she hissed to Mary.

'I didn't think you'd come if I did.' She shot her a rueful smile. 'Sorry, Fran.'

Their whispered conversation was interrupted by the elderly conductor, who was portly and balding and rather pleased with himself, as he'd once been well known in music circles until he'd been caught by the entire string section in flagrante with a married lady cellist. 'You're late,' he said. 'Sit over there and let me hear what you can do before I agree to you joining us.'

Mary squeezed Fran's hand and then hurried over to the piano and took off her gloves. It was wise to keep her coat on like everyone else, for

220

the place was freezing, with a draught whistling beneath the door and through the two badly fitting windows.

She watched as Fran greeted the servicemen she knew from the music nights at the Anchor, then sat down and took her time to tune up her violin. Mary started to fret, for she'd forgotten to warn Fran not to play an Irish jig as her introductory piece. It wouldn't go down well with Mr Beamish, who was clearly already prepared to dislike her inclusion into what he thought of as *his* orchestra. But it was too late now, and everyone was waiting.

It was then that she noticed Robert Goodyear. His brown eyes were liquid with longing as he clasped his gleaming clarinet in his large hands and watched Fran's every move, and she could understand now how disconcerting Fran must find this silent adoration Perhaps she'd been wrong to keep his presence secret.

Fran finished tuning the violin and, after taking a deep, steadying breath, began to play the first movement of a Bach sonata. As the beautiful notes rang clearly and sweetly through the hushed room, Mary relaxed and felt an enormous pride in her friend's undoubted talent. And when she came to the end there was rapturous applause from everyone – even the middle-aged violinist, who was already aware that she fell far short of Mr Beamish's high standard.

The conductor was harder to please. 'Not bad,' he said snootily. 'But this is light music for the masses, not a formal recital of the classics. Having had to wait for you to grace us with your presence, we shall now get on with our programme. We will begin with Grieg's "In the Hall of the 'Mountain King.'" He raised the baton, waited for the rustling of sheet music to cease, and then brought it down for the first beat.

Mary loved this piece and was thrilled at the sound the small orchestra was making considering how few rehearsals they'd managed to have. Following the Grieg, there was a piece from Tchaikovsky's ballet, *Sleeping Beauty,* and then they played through several popular tunes from films such as *Top Hat, For Me and My Gal* and *Holiday Inn.*

'Thank you,' said the conductor. 'That was almost up to the standard I was hoping for. Let us get on now with *Rhapsody in Blue.*' He looked from Mary to Robert, who was still gazing at Fran. 'Mr Goodyear, if you could tear yourself away from ogling our new violinist. We are waiting.'

Robert went scarlet as the others stifled their laughter. He fumbled with his sheet music and blew a couple of nervous notes on his clarinet. Then, with one last desperate glance at Fran, he nodded to Mary, who was waiting patiently at the piano, and began to play the most mesmerising opening glissando. Mary's scalp tingled. She'd never heard him play with such intensity or passion before, and by the look on Fran's face, she too was completely swept away in the music, to the point where she almost missed her cue.

As the orchestra joined in and played through Gershwin's masterfully haunting piece, Mary noted with a smile how often Fran kept glancing across at Robert. It seemed the poor man had finally caught her attention and she could only hope that his awkward shyness wouldn't let him down when the rehearsal was over.

The Town Hall clock struck ten and everyone gathered up their sheet music and stowed away their instruments, in a hurry to get home or back to their barracks. Mary covered the grand piano in blankets to keep out the cold and damp, and the lady on the harp used thick old curtains to do the same for her instrument. They would be moved over the following days to the larger hall nearer town where the concert was to take place, so they could rehearse there and get used to the acoustics.

Mary glanced across and saw that Fran was deep in conversation with Robert, who no longer looked quite so shy – although his colour was a bit high and he kept clutching his clarinet case to his chest as if his life depended upon it.

Fran's face was animated, her graceful hands emphasising her words as she shook back her hair and looked up into his face. Whatever she was saying had him ensnared, but he was clearly not struck dumb with awkwardness for he was actually holding a proper conversation with her.

Deciding it would be tactless to interrupt this budding friendship of mutual admiration, Mary pulled on her gloves and followed the others outside. Perhaps Peggy was right after all, for it was surprising what one could discover about a person when they were given the opportunity to shine. And Robert had certainly shone tonight.

It was the first day of 1943, and with news of Russia's slow but steady victories in recapturing territory from the Germans, and the great advances being made by the Combined Forces in North Africa, there was finally hope in the air that this New Year would prove to be a turning point in the war.

Rosie skimmed through the newspapers she hadn't had time to read over the Christmas period, and then set them aside as she realised she hadn't really taken in any of the news at all. She would have liked to go to the charity concert this afternoon to show her support for Mary and Fran, but the timing was all wrong and she was exhausted. It had been an incredibly busy night in the bar, and because she'd managed to get an extended licence for once, the party had gone on until midnight. It had been almost three in the morning before she'd finished clearing up and could fall into bed.

She eyed her reflection in the bathroom mirror and grimaced. She needed a long session at the hairdresser's to refresh her set and get rid of the dark roots that were showing through the platinum. Her skin looked washed out, and there were shadows beneath her eyes and the tracery of more fine lines. The late nights and the stress of waiting for Tommy to discover what she'd done were really starting to tell.

She plastered on her make-up and tried to hide the ravages of the past six days with a thick dusting of powder and a swipe of lipstick. The light coming in through the window wasn't kind, for it merely emphasised the faint lines that had appeared suddenly at the corners of her eyes and along her top lip. Perhaps she should just tell him what she'd done, and get it over with. She couldn't go on like this for much longer.

She pulled on her skirt and tucked in her blouse, then brushed out her hair and tried to find the energy to smile as she clipped on her earrings. Ron would be back soon from taking the dogs for their walk, and there was the vaguest of chances that people had had their fill of drink the night before and would stay at home to nurse their hangovers. She could do with a quiet lunchtime, for her supplies had run very low over the Christmas period and the drayman wasn't due for another two days.

As she left the bathroom and headed for the kitchen, she could hear Tommy thudding up the stairs and along the hallway to his bedroom. He'd gone out very early to make his daily report to the police station and had disappeared for almost three hours – now he was in danger of being late for his stint with the Home Guard. Yet she said nothing, for it would only have been a waste of breath and he would accuse her of nagging, so she set about making herself a cup of coffee to try and boost her low energy.

'What the hell have you done with my booze and fags?' roared Tommy as he came storming into the kitchen, his face flushed and his eyes glittering with fury.

Rosie's heart hammered as she pressed back against the draining board and blinked up at him in fear. 'I poured it away,' she managed in a whisper.

Tommy went even redder and his blue eyes were like shards of ice. 'You did *what?*' he roared. His hands were fists as he advanced on her. 'You stupid, brainless *bitch*. Do you know how much money that lot was worth?'

Rosie felt the warmth of his spittle on her face and her hand trembled as she wiped it away. 'Of course I do,' she rasped.

'Then why? *Why?*' he stormed.

Her pulse was racing and she was finding it hard to even breathe. 'Because it was illegal,' she stammered as she tried to edge away from him. 'If the police found it I'd lose everything – and I couldn't risk that.'

'Selfish, *stupid* bitch,' he snarled, his fists rising as he trapped her in the corner. 'You only think of yourself, don't you?'

'I have to,' she said, with rather more defiance than she actually felt. 'There's no one else to look out for me.'

'I'm your brother, and of course I'll look out for you,' he shouted. 'In fact I was going to move it all today, so you and your precious *fucking* pub wouldn't get involved.'

Rosie flinched at his language but somehow found the courage to face up to him. 'Don't swear at me in that filthy way,' she shouted back at him. 'I'm not one of your common tarts.'

'I'll bloody well swear at you as much as I fuck-ing want,' he yelled, his fist hovering within inches of her face. 'What did you do with the fags?'

'I burned them,' she replied as she kept a wary eye on that fist and managed to wriggle out of the corner. He was perfectly capable of hitting her, for he'd done it before, a long time ago. 'You should be grateful I didn't go straight to the police. Because I had every right to, you *rat!* How *dare* you use my place for your black-market carrying on after you promised to stay on the right side of the law?'

Tommy was white with rage. 'Grateful? *Grateful?*' He moved to cut off her escape through the door. 'Do you realise that those fags and bottles of booze would have set me up so I didn't have to rely on you for everything? Do you realise,' he continued as he jabbed a tobacco-stained finger at her face, 'that they were my insurance to pay off my bastard debts and get straight again?'

Rosie was no longer cowering, for her temper was up and she refused to be browbeaten any longer by her bullying, foul-mouthed brother. She slapped away the jabbing finger and gave him a hard shove in the chest that sent him stumbling back.

'And do you realise that you've put my home and business at risk?' she stormed. 'I don't *care* what you planned to do with the money. It wouldn't have changed anything. You still would have been up to all your old tricks – lying and cheating and making everyone's lives a misery.'

'I had people waiting for that consignment,' he shouted. 'What am I supposed to do now? Eh? Eh?' The jabbing finger once again pointed at her chest.

Rosie grasped his wrist and gave it a sharp twist. She was strong from years of pulling pints, lifting barrels and sorting out drunks, and she felt a modicum of victory as he yelped in pain. 'It's your mess, you clean it up.'

He cradled his injured wrist. 'But they paid a deposit, and I don't have the money any more,' he whined.

'Tough,' said Rosie. 'And don't think you can come to me to bail you out, because I've had enough, Tommy. You're on your own this time.'

He was ashen now, the anger replaced by something far deeper and more dangerous. 'But they're not the sort to cross. And I could be in serious trouble, you stupid cow. And it's all your fault, you stupid, *stupid* bitch. You owe me, Rosie, and I won't take no for an answer.'

Rosie eyed him coldly, aware that the mood had changed and if she wasn't careful she'd find herself giving in to him once again to protect herself from the violence she knew he was more than capable of meting out. But her fury was all-encompassing and she was incapable of keeping her mouth shout. 'Who are these people you owe money to? More low-lifes? Other spivs?'

'Blokes I do business with – and they won't take this lightly, believe you me.'

Rosie glared at him and didn't feel one ounce of sympathy. 'Well, you can tell Cyril Fielding that there's no money and no more deals. And if you get beaten up, then it's your own...'

She fell silent as the colour drained from his face and he had to grip the narrow table to keep his balance. 'God Almighty Tommy,' she breathed. 'What have you got yourself into this time? Who is this Fielding?'

He shook his head as if trying to clear away the shock and sank down into a kitchen chair. 'How do you know about Fielding?' he rasped.

Rosie felt a pang of alarm. Tommy was clearly shaken to the core, and she'd never seen him so distraught. 'It doesn't matter how I know about him,' she said dismissively as her thoughts whirled. 'Who is he and what sort of trouble have you got us both into?'

His smile was sickly and didn't reach his eyes. 'No one,' he replied. 'No one you need to be scared of, anyway.' His hands trembled as he lit a cigarette. 'Who told you about Fielding?' he asked as he sucked in smoke.

Rosie frowned, wary that Tommy might be laying some kind of trap which could embroil other people in his shenanigans. 'Does it matter?'

He seemed to have regained his equilibrium, for his hand no longer shook and his expression was unreadable. 'I don't like it when other people pry into my private business,' he muttered darkly. 'And Fielding is part of that business which I need to keep quiet.' His arctic glare pierced right through her. 'Who was it?'

Rosie knew then she would never tell him, for Peggy wasn't a part of this and needed to be protected. 'I can't remember,' she said flatly. 'And even if I could, I doubt I'd tell you, because you've caused enough trouble, and there's no knowing where it might lead.'

She regarded him evenly as she folded her arms. 'Who is this man? And why does he have to be such a secret?'

He smoked his cigarette in silence, his gaze narrowed and fixed on a distant point over her shoulder as he thought how to answer her.

The tense silence was so great she could actually hear the blood coursing through her veins and feel it reverberate in her skull. 'Don't even think about lying to me this time,' she warned. 'Because if you do, and I find out, then you can pack your bags and take your chances out there on your own.'

He seemed to consider this for a moment and then gave a deep sigh. 'He was someone I invented a long, long time ago,' he admitted.

This was not what she'd expected to hear and she stared at him as she slowly sank onto the other chair. 'Invented? But why?'

'I had an insurance scam going, and because it was conducted by post and in advertisements in the paper with a Post Office box number, no one knew that Cyril was really me.' He looked at her speculatively. 'Was it Ron who told you?'

'Why should it be Ron?' she asked defensively.

'Because he somehow found out about Cyril just as the scam was starting to bring in a good wedge of money, and we had a set-to.' He flicked cigarette ash carelessly onto the scrubbed linoleum floor. 'He threatened to tell the cops, so I had to leave town for a long while after that – which lost me a lot of money.'

Rosie quickly tried to work out how long ago that could have been, but it was almost impossible, for Tommy often disappeared for months, even years, on end – sometimes at his own volition, but more often to serve time in prison. 'When was this?'

He regarded her coldly. 'I told you. A long time ago – eighteen years – maybe more.' He took a breath. 'So, was it Ron?'

'No, absolutely not,' she said truthfully.

He nodded. 'I believe you, because you never could tell a lie, even as a kid.' He smoked and flicked more ash onto the floor. 'If it wasn't Ron, then it must have been Mary Jones,' he said eventually.

'Mary?' she gasped in horror. 'What on *earth* could Mary have to do with all this?'

'She's been asking around about Cyril.'

Rosie couldn't believe what she was hearing, and it took a moment to get her thoughts together. 'But why? She's new to the town and far too young to have ever heard of Cyril – who, in fact, never really existed.'

'I don't know,' he said grimly. 'But she's definitely been asking about him, because Eileen overheard her in the tea rooms. I even got Eileen to approach her to try and find out why, but the girl clammed up and wouldn't say.'

'You got Eileen involved?' She felt a deep chill and had to wrap her arms tightly about her waist to keep herself from trembling.

He looked at her then. 'I had no other choice,' he said flatly. 'You, Peggy and Ron were following my every move and I knew I didn't dare approach the girl to ask her myself. It's obvious she doesn't know that Cyril and I are the same person, and if I'd said anything to her, it could have opened up a whole can of worms.'

A prickle of dread ran up her spine. 'How? Why?'

'There's the possibility that one of her family was someone I sold those dodgy insurances to, and I couldn't risk her going to the law once she discovered the truth.'

Rosie shivered as she remembered his strange, persistent interest in Mary, his questions about her and the way he watched her as he worked behind the bar. It all made sense now – but that was the least of her worries, for Tommy was like a terrier when he was after something, and she knew he wouldn't just let this go.

She saw that he was watching her closely, expecting some reaction from her. 'You and the truth have been strangers for many years, Tommy. It would serve you right if all your past sins came home to roost.'

Tommy rolled his eyes. 'So says the woman who's carrying on with another man while her husband rots in a mental asylum,' he said sarcastically. 'How does it feel up there on your sanctimonious mountain, Rosie?'

'Don't you *dare* use my private life to justify your filthy carrying-on,' she snapped. 'And stop putting ash on my clean floor.'

Tommy meekly reached across for a saucer. 'Sorry,' he muttered. 'That was unfair after all you've done for me.'

Rosie nodded acceptance, but she was immediately wary, for Tommy rarely apologised for anything unless he wanted something. She watched him as he stubbed the butt out in the saucer. Her main priority now was to protect Mary, and to try to persuade him to leave her alone.

He looked back at her speculatively. 'I don't suppose you could ask Mary why she's looking for Cyril?' he said. 'Only you seem to have taken her under your wing and she trusts you.'

'It's because she trusts me that I'll say nothing to her whatsoever. She hasn't mentioned a word of any of this to me, and I've heard absolutely no gossip about it at all. It seems she's either forgotten all about it, or decided not to continue her search for Cyril. Either way, it's best to let sleeping dogs lie.'

He glowered at her and she took a deep breath. 'Frankly, Tommy, I've done you enough favours, and you should be worrying more about the man you owe money to than young Mary.'

'Then I've no alternative but to ask her myself,' he said grimly. 'I'll get the truth out of her and make sure she keeps her trap shut in future.'

'No,' she snapped in alarm. 'You leave Mary alone. She's just an innocent girl, and I won't have you frightening her.'

They sat and stared at one another and the silence became heavier, the tension growing between them.

As it grew unbearable, Rosie was forced to accept that she really had no choice in the matter if Mary was to be kept safe. 'All right,' she sighed. 'But I'll do it in my own way and in my own time. You'll just have to be patient.'

His scowl lifted immediately into a beaming smile. 'That's my girl. Now, there's the small matter of the money you owe me for the fags and booze.' He glanced at his watch. 'My buyer's expecting me at one, so you've just got time to run down to the bank before we open.'

Rosie pushed back the chair and smoothed her skirt over her hips. 'Hell will freeze over before I give you another penny,' she said flatly. 'And don't even think about trying to find my bank book or my savings, I've given them to Peggy to look after.'

The smile faded and the scowl returned. 'I need the money, and if I don't get it, they won't just stop at giving me a hiding. They'll come here, and you'll be sorry, Rosie. Very sorry indeed.'

But Rosie was not to be cowed – not this time – never again. 'If one single thing in this place is damaged then you'll never find out why Mary was looking for Cyril – and the police will get to hear about your latest scam. Lie down with dogs, Tommy, and all you'll get is fleas.'

She walked out of the kitchen with her head high despite the hammering of her heart, and went downstairs to the bar. It was almost eleven and she had a pub to run.

Mary had stayed the night at Beach View after the long session in the Anchor, and as she had the day off, she was luxuriating in the all-too-rare chance of a lie-in. Unlike Fran and the others, she hadn't drunk more than a few sips of beer at midnight to welcome in the New Year, so she wasn't suffering from a hangover. But she rather hoped that Fran wasn't feeling the effect of all those gins Robert had bought her last night, for they were due to play at Doris's charity concert this afternoon.

Mary smiled to herself as she thought about Robert and Fran, and how the shy, awkward young man had begun to blossom now Fran had finally taken notice of him, and they'd discovered just how much they had in common.

She eventually washed and dressed and went downstairs with her overnight bag, to find both Fran and Rita nursing cups of tea and looking very wan. 'Oh, dear,' she sighed in sympathy. 'Is it very bad?'

'Ach, to be sure, me head's splitting, so it is,'

moaned Fran.

'Mine isn't much better,' grumbled Rita, 'and I'll get it in the neck if my boss sees me like this.' She glanced up at the clock on the mantelpiece and groaned. 'Only another hour to go and I have to be on duty. I'm never drinking again, I swear.'

'You should have a constitution like mine,' chirped Cordelia, who was preparing vegetables for tonight's supper. 'I had five sherries and a glass of champagne, and feel as chipper and bright as a sparrow.'

'Lucky you,' sighed Fran. 'I feel like death warmed up.'

Mary helped herself to the last of the porridge, poured a cup of tea and sat down. 'Where're all the others?'

'Peggy's gone next door to help old Mrs Black pack the last of her things. She's moving down to Devon to live with her daughter now she's finding it hard to cope on her own,' said Rita. 'Ron went out before we came down, and I suspect he's gone to the Anchor. Jane and Sarah are both at work, though how they managed it after last night, I'll never know.'

'They have the same constitution as me,' said Cordelia with pride. 'It's in the family blood, you know.'

'The only thing running through my veins this morning is gin,' said Fran as she dragged herself to her feet. 'I'm going for a bath, and will meet you at the hall at half one.'

Mary gave her a gentle hug. 'Just don't be late,' she warned softly. 'You know what our illustrious conductor is like about time-keeping.'

'To be sure, I'll be there in body, if not in spirit. Will ye not fret, Mary?'

Mary smiled as Fran drifted out of the kitchen and slowly climbed the stairs. She had no worries about her not turning up, for she was reliable to a fault, and would no doubt be as animated and bright as always once she'd had time to recover. It never failed to astonish her how quickly the other girls could revive after downing so much alcohol – but as the taste and smell repelled her, she wasn't at all tempted to follow suit despite all the teasing she had to take about her endless glasses of lemonade and cups of tea.

'I'd better get washed and ready for work,' said Rita with great reluctance. 'Good luck this afternoon, Mary, although I'm sure you don't need it.' She pushed back her chair and ran her fingers through her untidy mop of dark curls. 'Matthew's coming over tonight if he's back in time from his latest raid on Jerry, so I really do have to sort myself out.' She gave Mary a wan smile and headed for her bedroom.

'Will you be all right, Grandma Finch?' Mary asked with some concern as the sharp, flashing knife cut through the vegetables and missed the tiny fingers by a gnat's whisker.

'Oh, I shan't be all night, dear. Not after the late one I had yesterday.'

'Would you like some help preparing the parsnips? They look a bit tough, and that knife is very sharp.'

'Help with the parson?' Cordelia frowned. 'What parson are you talking about, dear? I'm sure he might have a few rough edges, but if he can play the harp, then he can't be all bad.' She smiled beatifically. 'I do so like to hear the harp when it's well played, don't you?'

Mary laughed. 'I certainly do.' She gently took the knife and, ignoring Cordelia's mild protest, quickly finished off the vegetables before there was a nasty accident. 'There, that's all done, now I'd better get back to Havelock Road and do a bit of practice before the concert.'

'Yes, it was fun, wasn't it? But it didn't look to me as if you needed any practice, dear. That was all most efficient.' Cordelia settled happily into her chair and picked up her knitting. 'You'd better run along, or you'll be late for the concert. I am looking forward to it, you know, and so is Bertram.'

Mary had yet to meet Bertram Grantley-Adams, but she'd heard all about him from Peggy, and thought it rather sweet that two elderly people had found such a lovely companionship so late in life. 'Thank you,' she replied, and, before she could get into any more convoluted conversations, took her leave.

She arrived back at Havelock Road and obediently took off her shoes and hung her coat on the rack before going upstairs. As she reached the landing she heard noises coming from her bedroom and was surprised that Ivy was at home, for she was supposed to be at work until five. Yet, as she opened the door, it was not Ivy who was digging about in the wardrobe.

'Mrs Williams, what are you doing in here?' she asked sharply.

Doris didn't seem at all fazed at being caught

poking about in other people's intimate belongings. 'I needed to find out if you had anything suitable to wear for the concert,' she said as she continued to rummage through the wardrobe. 'With so many very important people attending, it's vital you don't let the side down.'

Mary crossed the room, noting the open drawers which had clearly been rifled through. She reached past Doris and pulled out her black dress. 'I think you'll find this is perfect for the occasion,' she said coolly. She closed the wardrobe doors firmly and hooked the hanger over the handle.

'I have asked Fran to wear something respectable for a change,' said Doris. 'If she turns up looking like a ragamuffin, that black skirt and white blouse in the wardrobe will have to do.'

'Those are Ivy's and would be far too short and tight for Fran,' she replied with some asperity. 'Was there anything else you wanted to look at? Or have you seen enough?'

Doris stood tall, her chin lifted in defiance. 'There is no need to use that tone with me, girl,' she said stiffly. 'I have every right to come in here. This is my home and you are only here under sufferance. If there was any justice in the billeting rules you'd be elsewhere, and I must say I'm appalled at the state of untidiness in here, and the lack of decent underwear between you.'

Mary had accepted long ago that she and Ivy were unwelcome guests, but she was coldly furious that this woman thought she had a right to poke and pry. Yet she knew better than to tell her what she really thought about her, and kept her tone level.

'I'm sorry you feel that way about us living here, and if it's such a burden, then I'm sure the billeting office could find us somewhere else to lodge.'

Something sparked in Doris's eyes. 'There's no need to take that attitude,' she said frostily. 'The billeting people have enough to do without shifting people from place to place.'

Mary realised that although Doris didn't like the idea of having lodgers, there was nothing she could do about it, and if she and Ivy left, she'd have to take in two others. It was a tiny victory, but she wasn't finished with Doris yet. 'As for the underwear, it's expensive and takes a lot of clothing coupons to buy new, even if it is only the utility stuff on offer. Ivy and I don't have a lot of spare cash to spend on luxuries, so we have to make do and mend.'

'Very commendable, I'm sure,' said Doris with a sniff as her gimlet gaze took in Ivy's tumbled bedding and the discarded clothes on the floor. 'But it's a pity that neither of you are appreciative enough of my hospitality to keep my room clean and tidy. I expect it to be straightened before we go to the concert, Mary. I will not have such disorderliness.'

Mary didn't bother to reply as Doris swept out of the room and closed the door behind her. She looked at the mess surrounding Ivy's bed and began to pick up the clothes. She really was the limit, but Doris was worse, and she began to wonder if the woman made a habit of coming in here to poke about in things that didn't concern her. Did she go as far as reading letters and diaries? She wouldn't have put it past her.

239

She glanced across at the bedroom door. There was no key, and to ask for one now would only put Doris's back up further. Yet Ivy would have to be warned of what had happened today, and their precious letters would have to be hidden somewhere the nosy old trout wouldn't think of looking.

As she cleared the detritus of Ivy's clothing from the floor and stowed it away, her thoughts raced. The only safe place would be in their gas-mask boxes, for they had to be carried at all times, and were only left in the bedroom when they were in the house. Tugging the bedclothes up and smoothing down the counterpane, Mary retrieved her letters from her underwear drawer and tucked them away with her diary in her gas-mask box. If Doris had read what she'd written about her, then it served her right – at least it would save Mary the effort of actually telling her to her face what a horrid, snobbish piece of work she was.

She realised it was getting late, so she quickly changed into her black velvet dress and tied back her hair with a matching ribbon. She decided to borrow Ivy's pearl earrings, then carefully put on some light make-up. Slipping on the rather tight shoes she'd been given for Suzy's wedding, she grabbed her gas-mask box and went downstairs.

'I'd like to practise for a while, if that's all right,' she said to Doris, who was eating a lunch of soup and sliced wheatmeal bread in the dining room.

'I'm glad to note that you at least appreciate some of the advantages of living here,' she replied sourly. 'I shall be driving to the hall in exactly one hour so I can greet my friends and make sure everything is in order so the concert runs without any unfortunate hitches.'

Five minutes before the hour was up, Doris came downstairs resplendent in a smart tweed suit and nifty felt hat which sported two pheasant feathers. Her matching leather handbag and gloves gleamed, and her make-up was immaculate. 'I hope you've had something to eat,' she said. 'I don't want you fainting in the middle of everything.'

Mary nodded and went to fetch her coat from the hall. She'd had the last of the soup and two slices of bread and marge, which should see her through until supper.

The car sparkled in the sunlight that shafted through the clouds, and Mary climbed in beside Doris with some misgivings. The mixed scents of leather seats and of oil and petrol were so familiar after all the years she'd sat beside her father that the memories of those times were almost too painful to bear.

As Doris drove out of the driveway and into the road, all the memories faded, for unlike Gideon, Doris was not a careful driver. She raced along, careless and impatient of pedestrians and other vehicles, her hand constantly hitting the horn if either dared to get in her way.

Mary clung to the seat, certain they'd crash into something at any minute.

Doris finally brought the car to a screeching halt outside the large hall and yanked on the hand-brake. 'I shall be giving a lift to my friends after the concert,' she said as she reached for her handbag.

'So you'll have to walk home.'

Mary glanced ruefully down at the tight shoes and wished she'd known about this arrangement earlier so she could have brought a more comfortable pair to change into. Still, she thought, as she followed Doris down to the side entrance, it would mean not risking life and limb in that car again, even if she did have to resort to walking barefoot all the way back.

As she stepped into the back-stage area of the hall she saw Fran and Robert deep in conversation and smiled. Their friendship was blossoming and Robert looked very handsome and perfectly at ease in his black dinner suit and white tie. It seemed his admiration was no longer unrequited and he'd discovered a previously hidden faith in himself, for the awkwardness had been banished and there was a confident air about him now.

As for Fran, she looked quite stunning in the navy blue dress she'd borrowed from Sarah. She'd left her hair to fall loosely down her back and over her shoulders, but had swept it off her face with a blue velvet Alice band. Her make-up was light, and all sign of any hangover had vanished.

She rushed over to Mary and gave her a hug. 'Isn't this fun? I can't wait to get started, can you?'

'I'm glad you're not nervous,' laughed Mary. 'I'm shaking like a leaf.'

'Don't be ridiculous, the pair of you,' snapped Doris as she grabbed Fran's arm. 'Stand still, girl, and let me look at you.' She eyed Fran up and down. 'I suppose you'll do,' she said gracelessly. 'But it's a shame you didn't have something black to wear. Navy's not really suitable and that hem is far too short.'

Fran pulled a face at her back as Doris went off to say hello to Robert. 'Poor Bob, he hates it when she corners him like that,' she said anxiously. 'Do you think I ought to go and rescue him?'

Mary shook her head. 'He's capable of dealing with Doris, by the look of it. You've given him the courage to face just about anything now you've finally taken notice of him.'

Fran blushed and dipped her chin so her hair fell about her face. 'To be sure, Mary, he's a shy wee man, but I'm thinking he has hidden depths.' She tossed back her hair almost defiantly. 'I could never have imagined he would play the clarinet so wonderfully well – and with such passion too.' She gave a soft chuckle as she glanced across at him to find he was watching her. 'There's definitely more to Robert Goodyear than meets the eye,' she murmured.

'I'm glad to hear it,' replied Mary. 'But it's time we got to our places and stopped thinking about other things, or we'll have the wrath of the conductor on us.'

'It'll be very different to playing at the Anchor, won't it?' said Fran as they followed the others through the wings and onto the curtained-off stage. 'What if I play a wrong note, or lose the timing?'

Mary gave her an affectionate smile. 'Don't worry, Fran. We've practised all the pieces until our fingers are numb, and there are twenty other people around us giving their support – including the faithful Robert. We'll get through this, you'll see.'

With Fran playing at the concert and the other girls at work, Peggy had had no option but to leave Daisy with Ron. It was on the firm understanding that he was not to take her up into the hills on one of his poaching forays.

The last time he'd taken her up there to the private estate by the Memorial hospital, he'd returned with a pocketful of disgusting eels which he'd then boiled until they were a horrid, jellied mess in her best baking bowl. She'd torn a strip off him and no mistake, and she rather hoped it had been stern enough to make him think twice about doing it again and risk getting himself arrested into the bargain.

She had dressed carefully in her best skirt and sweater, her smart overcoat and her new fur-trimmed gloves. It was important to show her support for her girls and not to let the side down, and she certainly didn't want Doris to have anything to moan about – although she was bound to find something.

'Bertram double-barrelled', as they now called him, had come to Beach View in his little car, and she'd squeezed in behind Cordelia, who was looking very smart in the suit she'd worn to Suzy's wedding. Bertram, ever the gentleman, had given each of them an early rosebud plucked from his greenhouse as buttonholes, while he sported a tweed jacket and twill trousers with a rather dashing yellow waistcoat to match the rose in his lapel.

You could say what you liked about Bertram – and there was some talk about him being a bit of a lady's man – but he could certainly cut a fine figure, and Cordelia seemed quite happy to ignore the gossip and enjoy his company.

They'd arrived at the hall in plenty of time, and after buying raffle tickets and checking out what the prizes were, they found their seats in the second row. Peggy had wanted to sit in the front so the girls could see her, but Doris had commandeered all the best seats for her snooty friends who were now hobnobbing and making disparaging remarks about the other members of the audience.

'Have you turned on your hearing aid?' she asked Cordelia as they all sat down.

'Well, of course I have, dear,' she replied. 'I'll turn it up when the film starts.'

Peggy frowned. 'It's Fran and Mary's concert, Cordelia. Surely you haven't forgotten?'

'Oh dear,' she twittered. 'I am a silly old thing, aren't I? Of course it is. I don't know where my mind goes sometimes, I really don't.' She turned to Bertram with a broad smile as he handed her a box of Lyons chocolates. 'Oh, how lovely,' she sighed as she plucked one from the box. 'What a thoughtful man you are, Bertie. And they're my favourite peppermint creams, too.'

Peggy tried not to show her concern, but there had been several occasions recently when Cordelia forgot things quite quickly – not things from the past, but everyday things. Perhaps it was time to take her for a check-up at the surgery.

Her thoughts were interrupted by the smattering of applause as the curtains opened to reveal the musicians and the portly conductor, who looked frightfully important in his white tie and black tailcoat as he took a bow. Peggy had known

245

from Fran that there would be an orchestra but she hadn't realised just how large it was, and she began to fret that it would prove too much for Fran and Mary to cope. After all, they'd only played at the Anchor, and the music there was hardly of concert standard.

Everyone looked terribly smart – the men either in black tie or dress uniform, the four women in their best frocks – although the second violinist faded into the background in that grey, and the voluminous red velvet was a bit much on the rather plump harpist. It clashed with her ruddy face and scarlet lipstick. But Fran looked lovely in Sarah's blue dress, and Mary was elegant in black velvet – and even Robert looked quite the thing in his black tuxedo.

She glanced from Robert to Fran and didn't miss the secret smile they gave one another, which made her feel very contented. It was good that they had found each other. He was a steadying influence, and her liveliness would gee him up a bit. Her own instincts were rarely wrong, and she'd known the minute she'd met him that beneath that shy, rather awkward exterior beat the heart of a man capable of anything if given half a chance. As far as Peggy was concerned, it was a perfect match.

She took a surreptitious glance around the large hall and recognised the reporter from the local paper sitting at the back. Doris was greeting the Mayor and the members of the Town Council, looking very much in charge as she escorted them to the front row with an obsequious smile. There was no sign of Ted, but then he was probably busy managing his staff at the Home and Colonial store, which was rather surprisingly open today.

Peggy saw that nearly every seat was taken, and there were still a few latecomers arriving. Doris was certainly a whizz at organising things, and the charity for injured servicemen and -women would assuredly have a large boost to their funds after today. She crossed her fingers and prayed that her girls would not be fazed by such a large and important audience.

The lights dimmed in the hall and there was an expectant hush as the spotlight hit centre stage to reveal Doris standing at a microphone. 'Lady Chumley; Your Worship, Mayor Hammond; Archbishop Grey; Reverend Philips; ladies and gentlemen,' she began in her best upper-class voice. 'I have had the great honour of being asked to raise money for a most worthy cause, and I hope that you will not only enjoy our little concert, but dig deep when it comes to purchasing raffle tickets, which will be on sale all afternoon. There are–'

Her speech was interrupted by the warning pips, and there was a breathless hush as everyone waited to see if the air-raid sirens would follow. Doris glared furiously and the sirens remained silent. It seemed that not even the Luftwaffe dared to ruin her moment of glory.

'As I was saying,' she continued grandly, 'there are some magnificent prizes to be won, and these have most generously been donated by our well-wishers. All proceeds will go to help our brave men and women who have been injured during their heroic fight against the tyranny of Adolf Hitler and Emperor Hirohito.'

As Doris went on and on, Peggy stopped listening. She'd seen the prizes and had set her sights on either the joint of pork or the large chicken. She took one of Cordelia's chocolates and let it melt slowly in her mouth, relishing the almost-forgotten taste of peppermint cream and rich, dark cocoa.

Doris was clearly enjoying her moment in the limelight as she kept waffling on, but Peggy could hear rustling and the shifting of bottoms on seats and knew the audience was getting restless. If this had been the music hall, they'd have been throwing things at her by now and booing her off the stage.

It was only when Doris introduced the conductor and the members of the orchestra that Peggy took notice again, and she sat up straight, hoping the girls would spot her in the audience and take comfort from knowing she was willing them to do well. They both looked very serious and rather sombre in their black and navy, and Peggy could tell they were having trouble with last-minute nerves, for their little faces were quite pale.

She held her breath as the conductor raised his baton, but let it out on a sigh of pleasure as the first perfect notes rang through the silent hall and sent a shiver of delight right through her. It was going to be all right.

The audience sat entranced as the wonderful music filled the auditorium, and their applause could surely be heard from the street outside as they showed their appreciation. It was after the interval, when Robert played the opening glissando to *Rhapsody in Blue,* that you could have heard a

248

pin drop, and Peggy felt a shiver of pleasure run right to her core as the sensuous, intoxicating music filled the hall. She'd had no idea he could play like that – but didn't doubt for a minute that this talent had brought him and Fran closer.

When Gershwin's glorious music came to an end the hall erupted. People were on their feet calling for more, their faces alight with the joy that the music and the artistry of the players had brought them.

Peggy was in tears, and so, she noticed, was Cordelia, who'd forgotten to bring a handkerchief. Scrabbling in her bag, she handed her spare one over and then settled down eagerly for whatever was to come next.

The concert ended with the rousing 'Rule, Britannia', and this was followed after an absolute barrage of requests for an encore by 'Land of Hope and Glory', which brought everyone to their feet to sing along. The effort the orchestra had put into the show was clear in their shining faces as they took their bows and mopped their foreheads.

Peggy was on her feet and applauding as Mary, Fran and Robert came to the front of the stage and, holding hands, took their bows.

Doris bustled onto the stage with the Mayor and Lady C., who gave each girl a small bouquet of flowers and Robert a rosebud buttonhole. Then it was time to announce the winners of the raffle, and Peggy squeaked in delight as she discovered she had a winning ticket. Her disappointment was huge when she discovered she'd just missed out on the joint of pork, and had won a washing-up mop, a tea towel and a very small

249

bar of Sunlight soap.

They left their seats and shuffled towards the main doors, along with the rest of the audience. It was already dark, and Peggy was looking forward to getting home to take her corset off and have a nice cup of tea. But first she wanted to congratulate the girls and Robert on a wonderful concert.

As they went down the steps towards Bertram's car she saw them emerge from the stage door. 'You get Cordelia settled,' she said to him. 'I won't be a minute.'

She hurried over and grasped the girls' hands. 'That was truly wonderful,' she breathed. 'And as for you, Robert Goodyear, you're a dark horse, aren't you? I never had an inkling that you could play the clarinet, let alone so wonderfully well.'

He blushed to the roots of his hair. 'I'm not that good,' he protested with soft modesty.

'Oh yes, you are. It made me get goose-bumps.' She looked at the three of them. 'Now, are you coming back to me for tea? Or are you off to celebrate?'

'I'm on night shift, Peggy,' said Mary, 'so I can't, I'm afraid. Perhaps another day?'

'Bless you, dear, you're always welcome, but it seems a pity you have to work after such a splendid afternoon.'

'Robert and I are going out for our supper tonight,' said Fran, 'so I'll not be back until late.'

Peggy beamed with pleasure. 'I'm glad to hear it. See you later.' She turned and headed back to the car. Things were going swimmingly between the two of them, and she couldn't help but hope that perhaps in a few months there might be another engagement, or at least some sort of declaration. She knew she was an old romantic at heart, but she did so love it when things worked out well.

Chapter Eleven

Peggy arrived back at Beach View to discover that the house next door had already been requisitioned by the billeting people, for now Mrs Black had left town, there were several women busy moving their few belongings in. Having had a short chat to welcome them to Beach View Close, she made them all a pot of tea and left them to it. Mrs Black had always been a nice quiet neighbour, but she was very elderly, and Peggy was rather looking forward to having women of her own age living next door.

She returned to her own kitchen to find that the girls were still at work, Bertram had already left for his home on the other side of town, and Cordelia was trying, without much success, to make another pot of tea. There was no sign of Ron, Harvey or Daisy, and she could only hope that they were with Rosie at the pub, and not trekking across the hills in search of illicit game.

'Let me do that, Cordelia,' she said as she quickly took charge of the heavy kettle. 'I don't want you scalding yourself.'

'Oh dear, I feel so useless,' she replied sadly as she regarded her gnarled hands. 'But this cold is making my arthritis very painful.'

Peggy could see how swollen her knuckles had become after sitting in that cold, draughty hall, and felt a pang of deep sympathy. 'While the tea's brewing, we'll get changed out of our finery and bundle up in front of the fire. And I think it might be an idea if you put your gloves back on,' she added as they headed for the stairs. 'They'll keep your hands much warmer.'

Having changed into less formal clothes and wrapped themselves in extra sweaters and cardigans, and with thick socks and slippers to keep their feet warm, Peggy settled Cordelia by the meagre fire and tried to stoke some life into it.

But the anthracite and coal dust just smoked and looked sullen, and the few bits of wood she'd placed on top took an age to catch. It was a good thing they'd put the stew in the oven this morning, otherwise it would never have got cooked in time for tea.

She checked the stew, poured Cordelia a cup of tea and went out into the freezing gloom to retrieve her washing, which was now as stiff as a board. Leaving it to drip from the wooden airer that was strung by pulleys from the scullery ceiling, Peggy shivered and shut the back door. It was getting colder by the minute, and she wouldn't be at all surprised if they didn't have snow by morning.

'I hope Ron wraps Daisy up warmly when he brings her home,' she said fretfully as she reached for the latest airgraphs which she hadn't had time to read. 'It's bitter out there.'

'It's not much warmer in here,' muttered Cordelia.

Peggy set the letters aside. 'I'll make you a hot water bottle.'

She had just filled the stone bottle when she heard the warning pips. She stilled, waiting for the sirens, praying they wouldn't sound out on this bitter night. But her prayers weren't answered, and as the sirens began to whine, she quickly wrapped the stone bottle in a cloth and tucked it into the emergency box she always kept for when they had to go into the shelter. As the sirens shrieked to full-pitch she ran into the hall to fetch their coats and outdoor shoes.

'Can't we just sit it out in here?' pleaded Cordelia. 'We'll freeze to death in that shelter.'

'I'm not risking that again,' Peggy replied firmly. 'Remember what happened last time we got caught indoors? You ended up with a broken arm and bruised ribs and I almost bled to death.' The sirens were going full-blast all over the town now and she wrestled to get an overcoat over all Cordelia's cardigans and button it up. Adding a scarf and a woollen hat that looked like a tea-cosy, Cordelia was finally bundled up like an Eskimo.

Dragging on her own overcoat, Peggy helped Cordelia down the cellar steps and then out into the garden. Cordelia leaned heavily on Peggy's arm as they carefully negotiated the path, which was as slippery and lethal as an ice-rink. The air was like a knife cutting through to their lungs; the stars were coldly bright against the black sky and the moon was glowing. It was a perfect night for an enemy raid.

The Anderson shelter stank of damp and mould, the floor littered with leaves that had blown in from the nearby trees, and every corner was strung with thick spiders' webs. It was as cold as a morgue. Peggy quickly settled Cordelia into her deckchair, which was jammed into a corner, and then added pillows to ensure she didn't slip out of it if she fell asleep – which she usually did within minutes of taking out her hearing aid.

The sirens were louder and more demanding now and Peggy knew she didn't have much time before some officious warden came along and shouted at her to turn off her kitchen light. 'I'll be back in a minute,' she said once she'd lit the tilly lamp.

Dashing back to the house, she kicked off her slippers and rammed her feet into her outdoor shoes. She grabbed her scarf, gloves and hat and shoved the airgraphs into her pocket. With the door closed on the range fire, she turned off the light and reached for the heavy box.

She fumbled her way down the stairs, slammed the back door behind her and skidded and slipped down the treacherous path, guided by the bright moon and the phosphorescent beams of the searchlights that swayed back and forth across the dark sky. She was shivering by the time she'd closed the shelter door and her nose and fingers were tingling with the biting cold.

'I do hope it's a short raid,' whimpered Cordelia. 'I don't think I can survive a whole night of this terrible damp cold.'

Peggy quickly placed a blanket over her knees and another round her shoulders before tucking the hot water bottle under her hands. 'I'll light the kerosene stove and that will chase away the chill,' she soothed. But as she lit the stove and turned it so Cordelia could get full benefit of it, she was worried. Cordelia rarely complained, and this bitter cold was dangerous for elderly constitutions already weakened through arthritis.

Cordelia snuggled into the blankets and pillows as the first squadron of Spitfires, Hurricanes and Typhoons took off from Cliffe aerodrome and screamed overhead. But the thunder of the enemy bombers was ominously close, and the metal walls of the shelter began to vibrate from the noise.

Peggy kept a wary eye on Cordelia as she pulled on her gloves and hat and then wound the scarf round her neck. She could already feel the damp chilling her bones and see the hazy clouds of her breath, and could only thank goodness that Daisy would be in Rosie's dry and much warmer cellar during the raid. Then she suddenly remembered that Sarah had to walk across the hills from the Cliffe estate to get home, and for the first time, prayed that Captain Hammond was at hand to drive her to safety. She was still suspicious about that friendship, but at least he had his uses, and he was charming – she couldn't deny that.

Having ensured they were both wrapped up against the cold, Peggy lit the small primus stove, poured fresh water from the thermos into the tin kettle and put it on to boil. There was a jar of Bovril in the emergency box, and a nice hot beefy drink would go some way to making their situation more comfortable.

Once Cordelia had her gloved hands wrapped round her tin mug, Peggy sat down on the bench and listened to the thud of the Bofors guns, the rattle of the flak and the roar of planes. It was going to be a noisy night.

As the corrugated iron walls streamed with condensation and the noise overhead grew steadily worse, Cordelia carefully sipped her Bovril while Peggy retrieved Jim's airgraphs from her skirt pocket. Under normal circumstances, she would have read out the interesting bits to Cordelia, but with the racket going on overhead, it would have been impossible, so she settled down to try and read them in the faint, flickering light of the tilly lamp.

The convoy Jim was on had crossed the equator, and they'd marked this with a ceremony which involved an officer dressed as Neptune, and several marines done up as mermaids, which caused a great deal of hilarity. The captain presented Neptune with a drink of beer, so he would bless the ship and give it a safe passage. This was followed by a sort of playful mutiny in which officers were captured, smothered in tar and custard, and then thrown overboard. Once everyone had had their ducking there was dinner of goose and marrow, and they got paid their wages. It was the most fun Jim had had since they'd set out on this voyage.

In the following letter, Jim wrote how the weather was changeable, hot one minute, and surprisingly cold the next. One of the convoy ships broke down and they'd left her with a destroyer as an escort while they steamed round waiting for her to be mended, which had taken all day. Time passed with quizzes, boxing matches, concerts and deck sports, and because the weather had turned very cold, they'd changed back into battledress, which felt very odd after so long in the lightweight tropical kit. The sighting of whales, seals and a large flock of albatross had lightened his spirits, but he was missing her terribly and beginning to hate the restrictions of life on board. They were due to disembark within the next few days, and from there they would be sent to their various postings. He loved her more than ever, sent kisses to everyone and signed it, as usual, SWALK.

Peggy had tears in her eyes as she carefully put the airgraphs back in their brown envelopes. She missed him too, every single moment of the day and night. She looked up as the noise of the bombers and fighters increased and shook her fist. 'Damn you, Hitler,' she hissed. 'Damn you to hell and back.'

The Anchor had only been open for five minutes when the sirens started. The bitter weather had kept people at home, and Rosie's barmaids had the night off, so she'd bolted the front door and gone down into the cellar with Ron and Daisy, the dogs running eagerly in front of them. Harvey still hated the sound of the sirens, and he sat in a corner howling piteously until they were replaced by the shriek of fighters and the drone of bombers, and then he slumped down beside an unfazed Monty to happily doze.

Rosie sat close to Ron on the sagging couch with Daisy in her lap. Harvey and Monty had commandeered the other couch and were stretched out like emperors, contentedly snoring as the dogfights went on overhead. 'Daisy's such a good

257

baby,' she said as she cuddled her. 'She doesn't seem to mind the noise at all.'

'Aye, well, she's been born to the sound of it, so she has,' said Ron proudly. 'She's a bonny wee girl, and has her mother's spirit.'

Rosie held the tiny girl close, revelling in the scent and feel of her against her heart. If only things had been different – if only... But they were the saddest of all wishful words, for there was no changing the past and she'd had many years to learn to live with the consequences.

'Are you all right, acushla?'

Rosie barely heard Ron as she looked down at the baby in her arms and marvelled at the long eyelashes that were fluttering in sleep against the sweet, soft cheeks, and the tiny fingers that were laced beneath her chin. How darling she was, how very precious. Oh, how deep were her regrets and how much she envied Peggy and all other mothers, for she had so much love to give and had been denied the chance to ever know what it was like to hold and care for her own child.

'Rosie?'

She hastily pulled her thoughts together. 'I'm just tired,' she replied. 'The long days and busy nights have started catching up on me, that's all.'

He put his arm round her and gently drew her into his side so her head could rest on his sturdy shoulder as she cradled the sleeping Daisy. 'You should get that brother of yours to do more,' he rumbled. 'Where was he all day – and why isn't he here now?'

Rosie shrugged. 'I don't know and I don't really care,' she confessed. 'I've had enough of looking out for him.'

Ron drew back so he could look down into her face. 'Is there something you'll be wanting to tell me, Rosie?'

Rosie couldn't lie to him, but she'd have to be careful not to rouse Ron's temper – it would only make things worse if he and Tommy got into a fight. 'He seems to have got himself into debt, yet again, but he's chosen the wrong people to owe money to. I've told him straight I'm not giving him a penny, and that he'll have to wriggle out of it the best he can.'

'To be sure, he's capable of wriggling out of most things,' Ron said flatly, 'but at least you had the sense not to give him any more money.' He regarded her for a moment. 'But how did he get into debt in the first place? Who are these people?'

'I honestly don't know who they are. He refused to tell me.'

'Which means they're a bunch of crooks.' He removed his comforting arm and sat forward on the couch so he could look her in the eye. 'He's up to his old tricks again, isn't he?'

Rosie's gaze flicked away and she gave a shrug.

Ron was silent for a long moment as he reached in his pocket for his roll of tobacco. As he opened it and began to fill his pipe, his hands stilled. 'This is good tobacco, Rosie. Where did you manage to find it, because I haven't seen this brand in the shop for months?'

Rosie licked her lips and couldn't think clearly enough to answer him.

He reached for her hand. 'Rosie darlin', you've got to stop protecting him. Especially if he's dealing on the black market. You have too much to lose if the police come calling. And they will, Rose. As sure as eggs is eggs.'

'I know,' she sighed in defeat. 'That's why I gave the tobacco away and put the drink down the sink.'

Ron gave a low whistle. 'That was a dangerous thing to do, Rosie girl. How did he take that?'

Rosie finally managed to look him in the eye. 'Not well. But that's an end to it, Ron,' she said firmly. 'I don't want you getting all steamed up about it. Tommy's in enough trouble over the money he owes – he'll get what's coming to him without you becoming involved.'

'Aye, I can see you're right about that,' he said solemnly. He concentrated on filling his pipe with the illicit tobacco. 'But there's more to your worries than just Tommy, isn't there?'

'I think Tommy's enough to be going on with, don't you?' she said lightly as she got up from the couch and placed the sleeping Daisy in her pram. She took her time to pull the covers over her, for she was trying desperately to think of a way to distract him from this dangerous line of questioning.

'I hope this raid doesn't last too long,' she said as she headed for the primus stove to boil a kettle. 'It's not good for a baby to be in such a cold place.'

Ron crossed the floor and gently stilled her hand. 'Rosie,' he said softly, 'stop that and look at me.'

She reluctantly turned to face him, knowing that her thoughts and fears were showing in her expression.

'I got back with the dogs and overheard some of your conversation with Tommy this morning,' he said quietly. 'You're worried about young Mary, aren't you?'

She nodded, and that acknowledgement eased the great weight she'd been carrying on her shoulders ever since morning. 'So, you know about Cyril?'

'I know it was an alias Tommy used many years ago. But how does young Mary fit into all this?'

She shrugged and gave a deep sigh. 'That's the strangest part of it. I can't see how she could be, but Eileen overheard her asking about Cyril, and now Tommy's got it into his head that she'll cause trouble if she finds out the truth.'

Ron frowned. 'Eileen? But why should Eileen Harris be dragged into it?'

Rosie shook her head and gave a wry smile. 'Tommy can still wrap her round his little finger – more fool her.' She folded her arms tightly round her waist, her dislike for Eileen coming through in the flat tone of her voice. 'I don't think she actually cares much what happens to him as long as it doesn't affect her comfortable little life – but she was willing enough to approach Mary to ask why she was looking for Cyril.'

Ron regarded her steadily. 'And what did the girl say?'

'Absolutely nothing, according to Tommy – which of course is like a red rag to a bull. Now he wants me to question her.'

Ron nodded. 'Yes, I heard that part. Do you think it's wise, Rosie? After all, it might lead to all sorts of complications, not only for Tommy, but for you as well.'

She frowned as she looked back at him. 'It might be awkward, certainly, and I shall have to be very careful not to upset her in any way. But I can't see that there could be anything the girl might say that could affect me. Tommy's past was always going to catch up with him sooner or later – and I've never played any part in his dirty dealings.'

She smiled then and kissed his cheek. 'Don't worry about me, Ron. I'm tougher than I look.'

She turned away to make them both a cup of tea so she didn't see the anxiety etched into his face or the trembling in his hand as he tried to light his pipe.

As the enemy bombers thundered overhead and the dogfights between the fighter planes continued, Tommy Findlay crawled into the profound darkness of the alleyway and slumped onto the ground amid the stinking litter that had spewed out of the dustbins. The pain in his broken leg was all-encompassing, spreading like fire through his body and roaring in his head. His eyelids were so swollen he could barely see, and as he struggled to breathe through his broken nose, the agony in his battered chest made him whimper.

The beating had been thorough and dealt with brutal efficiency by the four thugs, and Tommy barely heard the battle going on above him, for only the torment of his agony existed. Yet, deeply buried beneath that unbearable pain lay the knowledge that if he remained here, he would die.

He tried to move, but he no longer had the strength to even lift his head. Defeated, he drew up his knees, curling into the throbbing, gnawing pain, and almost welcomed the release from his torture that only death could bring.

It was Jenny's night off, but Mary and Ivy had spent a good deal of their night shift sitting in the vast underground shelter with the other factory girls. It had all been rather jolly as they'd swapped knitting patterns and gossip, tried each other's nail varnishes and lipsticks, and made plans for the following weekend as the bombers and fighters roared overhead.'

And then the world erupted in an ear-shattering blast of sharp masonry and choking dust that threw them into a vicious maelstrom, then blessed oblivion.

Mary eventually opened her eyes and for a moment wondered where she was, and what had happened. There seemed to be a dead quality to the sounds she could hear, and the darkness, although inky black, was filled with suffocating, acrid dust.

As her senses slowly returned, she realised she was lying amidst broken shards of brick and concrete, and, through the ringing in her ears, she could hear screams and groans echoing eerily through a numb silence. The shelter had been hit, people were injured, she had to try and help. However, as she attempted to move she found that the lower half of her body seemed to be weighted down.

Fighting to breathe and tamp down on the surge of terror which threatened to overwhelm her, she gingerly wriggled her toes and fingers

263

and flexed her limbs. Nothing seemed to be broken, but she felt bruised and battered from head to foot and there was something sticky on her forehead. She ran her finger carefully over the large lump and winced as she found the deep cut just beyond her hair line. It was all right, just a nasty cut that would probably stop bleeding before long. Now she had to find some way of removing whatever was pinning her down without bringing the whole lot on top of her.

She reached behind her, and, after a quick exploration, realised she was covered in rubble. There didn't seem to be any rafters or supporting beams across her, so she slowly and carefully began to pick away at the rubble until she could wriggle free. She sat up, coughing and spluttering from the cloying dust that seemed to have filled her mouth and nose, and blinking rapidly in an attempt to get the stinging grit out of her eyes.

'Ivy,' she called into the confusing darkness. 'Ivy, where are you?'

'I'm over here,' she called back through a hacking cough. 'Are you all right?'

'Yes,' she replied as she hawked the filthy muck from her lungs and fought to breathe without inhaling yet more dust. 'Are you?'

'Everything seems to be working, but I got a bleeding great lump outta me flaming knee, I'm bruised from head to blooming toe, and me new dungarees 'ave 'ad it.'

Mary scrambled carefully over the debris towards her voice, and as they found one another they tearfully clung together, thankful that they were alive. Others were now moving about too, and the girls could hear some calling for help with the more seriously injured. It was still pitch black and the enemy bombers droned above them as they finally headed for the Channel.

Mary gripped her friend's hand as another part of the shelter wall collapsed and they were once more covered in a cloud of acrid dust. 'It's all right, Ivy, we'll be out of here soon,' she muttered with rather more certainty than she felt.

'I 'ope so,' Ivy replied dolefully. 'I've left me spam sandwiches on me work bench, and some other bugger will get them if I ain't quick off the mark.'

Mary chuckled and gave her a hug. Ivy was always thinking about her stomach, but at least it meant she was feeling her usual cheeky self.

The all-clear sounded just before eleven and, with a deep sigh of relief, Peggy turned off the heater and the lamp before gently waking Cordelia. They were both stiff from sitting so long in the cramped shelter, and it took a while to get Cordelia mobile.

They emerged from the Anderson shelter to an empty sky. The air was heavy with the stench of cordite and smoke, but thankfully all the bomb-blasts had been some distance away, so there was hope that Cliffehaven had escaped any serious damage.

Peggy took Cordelia's arm and helped her along the icy path and up the steps to the kitchen, where the fire in the range had finally decided to come to life. Settling her in the chair with her blankets, Peggy hurried to boil the kettle and check on the stew. It had gone a bit dry, but everyone would be glad of it by the time they got home.

Once she'd retrieved the rest of the bedding and the box of supplies from the shelter, she poured fresh hot water into the stone bottle and quickly placed it in Cordelia's bed so that it would warm the sheets. Then, as the old lady dozed by the fire, she laid the table for their very late tea and settled down rather anxiously with a cuppa to wait for the others.

Sarah came in first, having been driven home by Captain Hammond, who quickly popped in to say hello before he rushed back to the estate.

'It's chaos up there,' she said as she took off her thick coat. 'An unexploded bomb was found very close to the Timber Corps accommodation and everyone had to sit about in the manor house while the Americans' bomb disposal team went in to defuse it.' She shot Peggy a weary smile. 'Needless to say, the GIs used this as an excuse to throw a party.'

Fran turned up minutes later with Jane, who immediately raced upstairs to the bathroom. Fran held her hands out to the fire. 'Poor Jane hates those buckets behind the hessian screens and refuses to use them, hence the dash upstairs,' she explained.

Peggy didn't blame Jane for holding on, for those buckets stank and there was a distinct lack of privacy despite the screens. 'Where's Robert?' she asked. 'Didn't he bring you back?'

'He has to be back in his office, so he dropped us off and apologises for not coming in.' She shook back her hair and gave a deep sigh. 'We've spent most of what should have been a lovely evening in a cold, damp, smelly shelter trying to keep warm – but at least we're all still in one piece, so I suppose I shouldn't be complaining.'

Peggy looked anxiously at the clock. Ron should be home by now with Daisy – and where was Rita?

Then the back door slammed and Harvey came racing up the stairs to be followed by Rita, who was looking very dishevelled. 'Goodness me, Rita,' breathed Peggy. 'What's happened to you?'

'A bomb went off up on the factory estate, and we had to dig a few people out.' She must have seen Peggy's look of horror, for she added quickly, 'No one was too badly hurt and Mary's fine. Most of the damage was minor and as soon as the all-clear sounded it was back to work. She said she'd call in tomorrow afternoon to see you and put your mind to rest.'

Peggy hadn't realised she'd been holding her breath, and she let it out on a thankful sigh. 'I'm due to have a cup of tea with Rosie tomorrow afternoon, so I'll leave a message with Doris so Mary can meet me at the Anchor.' She noted the dirt on Rita's little face and the weary set of her shoulders. 'Why don't you have a quick wash and get out of those filthy clothes before tea? You'll feel more ready to eat if you're clean.'

Rita nodded and plodded upstairs just as Ron stomped up the cellar steps with a drowsy Daisy in his arms. 'She's been as good as gold,' he said as he handed her to Peggy. 'Rosie gave her something to eat and a bit of her bottle to help her settle – but I think she needs changing again.'

'Sarah, could you help Cordelia to the table and then finish dishing out the stew while I see to

267

Daisy? There's bread in the larder if anyone wants it.'

Peggy hurried to her bedroom, where she changed Daisy's nappy and quickly relieved her of the thick layer of cardigans which had kept her warm on her journey home. Once she'd given her a cuddle and rocked her back to sleep, she put her in the cot and wrapped her snugly in her blankets.

She was blessed, really, for most babies would have been screaming by now after such a disturbed night – but then Daisy possessed a pair of very strong lungs and a furious temper when she was thwarted, so she wasn't absolutely perfect – just as near perfect as she could be. She kissed the sweet, slumbering face, stroked her dark curls and left the room, more than ready for her share of stew.

It didn't take long to scrape the bowls clean and mop up the last vestiges of the stew with the gritty bread, and because it was now almost midnight and everyone was exhausted, it was time for bed. 'The washing-up can wait until morning,' said Peggy. 'Sleep well, girls.'

They kissed her goodnight and Peggy helped Cordelia out of her chair and up the stairs. Having made sure she was settled and warm, she went back to the kitchen to dampen down the fire and turn off the lights.

Harvey was snoring on the rug, his paws scrabbling as he dreamed of catching rabbits, and Peggy envied the ease with which he managed to drop off. She still found it difficult to come to terms with sleeping alone and would often lie awake for hours despite being exhausted.

She was about to turn out the light and go to her own bedroom when Ron came back into the kitchen. 'Peggy,' he said solemnly, 'I know you must be tired, but there's something we need to discuss, and I'm sorry, but it won't wait until morning.'

Immediately alarmed, she sat down at the table. 'What is it, Ron? What's happened?'

'Nothing – as yet. But I overheard something today, and I think it's important you should know about it before you go and see Rosie tomorrow afternoon.'

Peggy felt the colour drain from her face and she clasped her hands tightly on the table so they wouldn't tremble. 'Go on.'

As Ron recounted what he'd learned, and the conversation he'd had with Rosie, Peggy's dread grew heavier. 'I knew about the contraband – I've got a suitcase full of cigarettes and tobacco on top of my wardrobe,' she said almost dismissively as she tried desperately to think how to say what she needed without giving too much away. 'But it's vital Rosie doesn't broach the subject of Cyril with Mary.' She reached across the table and gripped his hand. 'It could destroy her, Ron.'

Ron's blue eyes sharpened beneath his lowering brows. 'If this is going to hurt my Rosie, then I'm thinking it's time you told me the secrets you've been keeping, Peggy Reilly.' His gaze never wavered. 'And don't deny it, girl. I know you too well.'

Peggy regarded him in silence for a moment, and then came to the only sensible conclusion

269

open to her. It was indeed time to tell Ron, for Rosie would need support from them both to help her through the dreadful inevitability of what was about to come.

Her tears were not for herself, but for Rosie, as she revealed the truth of what had happened all those years ago. And yet, by the time she'd reached the end of the tragic story, she felt unburdened finally, for she'd carried that secret for too long.

Ron took her hands and grasped them tightly, his face etched with pain, his eyes suspiciously bright. 'Mother of God, Peggy,' he rasped. 'She's been carrying that inside for all these years?' He paused a moment to get his emotions under control. 'But she has to know, Peggy. You realise that, don't you?'

Peggy nodded.

'And so does Mary,' he added softly.

'No, Ron,' she moaned. 'It would be too unkind after everything she's been through.' She clutched at his hands. 'Couldn't we just persuade Rosie to say nothing to her – to leave things as they are?'

He gave a deep sigh and then came round the table to draw Peggy into his arms. 'You know that would be impossible once Rosie knows the truth, Peg.' He held her close, his chin resting on the top of her head as his rough old hands gently stroked her hair.

'But it would be so cruel – not only to Mary, but to Rosie too,' she sobbed. 'Oh, Ron, I just don't know what to do for the best.'

His voice was a deep rumble in his chest as he continued to hold her. 'You know, Peggy darlin', cruelty often lies in the well-meaning silence, not in the barbs of truth, and there have been enough lies and secrets. It's time to cauterise this wound that has been festering over the years, and to make a fresh start.'

Chapter Twelve

Their rescue from the bomb-blasted shelter had come even before the all-clear had sounded, and as the men and women from the fire brigade and rescue services had dug away the debris, Mary and Ivy had closed their eyes against the bright lights of their lamps. They'd emerged into the night to discover it was snowing, and they'd lifted their faces to it, revelling in its cool, soft touch as they'd breathed in the cold, clean air that burned its way through their raw throats and into aching lungs.

After Rita had checked to see that both of them were all right, she'd sent them over to a girl from the ambulance service, who'd inspected their cuts and bruises, declared them to be minor and dabbed them with iodine.

'Perhaps this'll mean we don't 'ave to finish our shift,' said Ivy as she'd woefully inspected her ripped dungarees and bloody knee.

They hadn't noticed the doughty figure of Sergeant Norris, and her booming voice had made them both jump. 'Production does not come to a halt because you've got a grazed knee.' She was sporting a bandaged wrist and a black eye, and her usually pristine army uniform was torn and dirty –

but her parade-ground manner remained intact. 'Wash your hands and faces and get back to your posts immediately.'

Mary and Ivy had rolled their eyes at one another and then hurried through the swirling snow to their separate factories. Any hopes of a cup of tea or a proper wash had been dashed.

Billy Watson might only have been seventeen, but he knew when he was on to a good thing. He'd spent the past three hours chatting up Marlene as they'd sat in the public air-raid shelter, and she'd proved to be a right little smasher who could be easily persuaded to partake in a bit of slap and tickle. Now he was leading her down the quiet alleyway which just happened to be on the way to her billet.

She complained a bit about the cold, for there was snow on the ground and it was still coming down quite heavily. But he promised he'd soon warm her up as he kissed her and shuffled her back into the deeper darkness, his hand already exploring the delicious flesh between stocking top and knicker-leg. It was a curse not to be able to take girls back to his room, but his mum would blow a fuse if she caught them and he was in too much of a hurry to try and find somewhere else.

He was about to press her up against the wall when she stumbled over something and gave a cry of fright. 'What's that? Oh, Billy, I don't like it 'ere. Can't we go somewhere else?'

'You're safe with me, darling,' he said as he urgently pressed himself against her and scrabbled to get into her knickers. 'It's only a pile of rubbish.'

She twisted away from him. 'I don't like it, Billy. It pongs, and I'm freezing me tits off.'

Frustration made him sharp with her. 'Then shut up and let me warm them,' he rasped as he made a grab for her.

The soft groan stilled them.

'What were that?'

He prickled with unease as his desire fled. 'I dunno,' he whispered as he dug in his pocket for the small torch he always carried.

'Let's get outta here, Billy,' she whimpered. 'I don't like it.'

There was another groan, and Billy was rigid with fear as he fumbled to switch on the torch. He didn't like it either, but he wasn't about to make a fool of himself in front of Marlene.

The pale beam swept across the scattered litter and overflowing dustbins in the narrow alley, catching the tail of a swiftly disappearing rat.

Marlene squealed and grabbed his arm, making the beam flash back and forth over something sticking out of the snow-covered rubbish. 'What was that?' she demanded, her voice high-pitched with fear.

Billy's hand was shaking so much the beam danced over the exposed leg and foot. 'Christ Almighty,' he breathed as the full import of what he was seeing sank in.

Marlene began to scream, and Billy clamped his hand over her mouth. 'Shut up or we'll have the coppers on us,' he hissed as his terrified gaze remained on the snow-covered body.

Billy had never seen a dead person before, and although in some macabre way he found it fascinating, he was loath to approach it. He stood transfixed, his hand pressed against Marlene's mouth as she tried to fight him off and scream her lungs out.

It was only when the body moved with a groan that Billy released his hold on Marlene. As her piercing screams echoed into the night, his courage failed, and he took flight.

Ron hadn't slept well, for he was a man who knew too much – and yet he had no possible way of putting things right for either Rosie or Mary. He'd tossed and turned as he'd thumped his pillow and tried to force himself into sleep, but his overactive mind refused to be still. So many pieces of the puzzle had finally slotted into place, but there were many more which simply didn't fit, no matter how hard he tried – and it was those pieces that made him dread the coming day.

He'd eventually become impatient with his thoughts and the inability to sleep, so he'd climbed out of bed and quietly left Beach View with Harvey to go to the Anchor. There had been no sign of life upstairs, for it was only just light and Rosie was probably still asleep, so he'd taken Monty with him and had spent the past two hours tramping the hills with the dogs.

He could think up there in the settled silence of those ancient hills, which were now dusted with a thick coating of snow that glittered in the rising sun, making everything as pretty as a frosted Christmas card. The temperature was slightly warmer now the snow had come, and as the dogs had raced about in delight, he'd let his mind wander until he'd found a way through the labyrinth of knowledge he'd acquired over the past twenty-four hours. The solution, he realised, was ridiculously simple – but he would have to apply it with great care.

The Town Hall clock struck seven as Ron headed towards Camden Road and the Anchor. He usually stopped in to have a cup of tea with Rosie after he'd walked the dogs, but since Tommy had moved in that pleasant ritual had sadly come to an end. It was hard enough to stomach Tommy any time of the day, but first thing in the morning was too much to ask, and he deeply resented the loss of those precious quiet times with his Rosie.

As Harvey and Monty watered the lamp-posts and walls and dashed back and forth, Ron strolled along with his hands in his pockets, his mind going over his plan, testing it for flaws until he was absolutely certain that nothing could go wrong.

'Hello, Ron. Long time no see.'

Ron was so deeply engrossed in his thoughts that he hadn't seen his old friend and fellow Somme survivor, Sergeant Albert Williams, walking towards him. Bert was in his sixties and should have retired from the police years ago, but the war had meant he'd stayed on. He was an imposing figure in his uniform, and was an expert at sniffing out trouble. But he'd never risen any higher in the ranks, for he wasn't an ambitious man and preferred being in the thick of it on the streets rather than behind a desk.

'Hello, Bert,' he replied as they shook hands. 'It's a bit early for you, isn't it?'

Bert nodded solemnly. 'I'm sorry, Ron, but I've

had a bit of bad news for your Rosie.'

Ron felt a stab of fear that was mingled with a selfish hope that Rosie's insane husband had finally died. 'What news?'

'Her brother was found just before midnight in an alleyway. He'd been well and truly beaten, and if he'd stayed there much longer in the snow he'd have frozen to death.' Bert knew Tommy of old and there was very little sympathy in his ruddy face.

Ron glanced up to the window above the pub sign. 'How did Rosie take the news?'

'She was a bit shocked to begin with – well, it's not the sort of thing one expects to hear first thing in the morning, is it? But she made me a cup of tea, and seemed perfectly all right by the time I left. In fact, she told me she wouldn't be visiting him in hospital, and that as far as she was concerned they could keep him in for as long as they wanted.'

'Prison would be the best place for him,' muttered Ron. 'But we can't always get what we wish for, can we?'

Bert smiled in agreement before he regarded Ron thoughtfully. 'I know you and he have had your run-ins, and I can't say I blame you – he's a toerag of the first water. But you wouldn't happen to know anything about this beating, would you, Ron?'

He shook his head. 'Regretfully not, Bert. Though I've been tempted many a time, believe you me.' He looked back at his reliable old friend, who'd turned a blind eye on many occasions in return for a nice bit of salmon or a bottle of French brandy. This was an auspicious meeting, for it meant his plan could now be put into place immediately. 'But Rosie's all right, is she? Not too upset?'

Bert grinned. 'As right as rain, and as lovely as always. I envy you, mate. She's quite a sight in that silky dressing gown, isn't she?'

Ron chuckled. 'To be sure, she is, but I'm thinking your Betsy would not be pleased to hear you saying that.' He pulled his pipe out of his pocket, remembered he had only the illicit tobacco to fill it with, and stuffed it away again. 'Tell me, Bert. How long is Tommy expected to stay in hospital?'

'He should probably be in there for a week or so. The beating was very severe and left him as swollen and split as an old football, with three cracked ribs, a broken nose and leg, and at least two missing teeth. But they're stretched to breaking point as it is, and the ward sister told me he'll be given a series of out-patient appointments and be discharged later today.'

'Did you manage to get a statement from him?'

Bert shook his head. 'And I don't expect to. He might be as crooked as a nine-bob note, but he's not stupid. That beating was enough to keep his mouth well and truly shut.'

Ron nodded as he looked thoughtfully at the two dogs which were now drinking noisily out of the old horse trough that had stood on this site for over a century. 'Would you be having a wee moment for a cup of coffee, Bert? Only all this talking has given me a terrible thirst, so it has.'

Bert's ruddy face glowed with a beaming smile. 'I reckon I can do better than coffee,' he said.

'There's a bottle of good malt whisky in my desk drawer if you're not disinclined to drinking it in my office at the station.'

Ron grinned as he slapped his old friend's arm. 'To be sure, Bert, that's the best offer I've had all morning.'

It was almost nine o'clock by the time Ivy and Mary reached Havelock Road, for they'd had to work an extra three hours to make up for the time they'd lost whilst trapped in the shelter. They were still shaken up by the experience, but at least they'd had a tea break and some breakfast in the canteen, so they weren't still finding grit between their teeth.

They let themselves into the house and wearily shed their filthy coats and boots, aching for a long, hot bath and their beds. 'Oh, look,' said Mary with a squeak of delight. 'We've both got post.' She quickly retrieved the letters from the hall table and handed Ivy her two before shoving her own into her gas-mask box.

'Good grief,' exclaimed Doris as she came down the stairs resplendent in dressing gown, curlers and full make-up. 'You look like a couple of chimney sweeps.' She bustled over to them and eyed their filthy clothes. 'Get those off immediately and take them – and your coats – out to the scullery. I can't possibly have all that dirt traipsed into the house.'

'Yeah, we're fine, thanks fer askin',' snapped Ivy as she undid the straps and let her tattered dungarees drop to the doormat to reveal her bruised body, much-mended knickers and a greying brassiere. 'A bomb hit the bleedin' factory shelter and the firemen 'ad to dig us out,' she continued furiously as she peeled off her socks. 'Only four people were taken to the hospital – not that you're interested, of course – but Gawd save us if we get a bit of muck on yer bleedin' floor.'

Doris went pale beneath the carefully applied make-up. 'You will not use that gutter language in my home,' she snapped. 'Mary, take off those clothes before you go a step further.'

Mary was too tired to argue, so she stripped off her torn slacks and dirty shirt and sweater, whipped off her socks and bundled everything up with her coat to carry them out to the freezing cold lean-to where Doris kept the rather terrifying washing machine.

'And give them a good shake outside before you put them in my machine,' ordered Doris. 'It's expensive to repair, and I will not have it clogged up with dust and debris and goodness knows what else.'

'But it's brass monkeys out there,' protested a still-seething Ivy.

'You don't seriously expect us to go out there in our underwear, do you?' asked Mary in disbelief. 'Don't you realise it's snowing?'

Doris peered through the window and clucked. 'Leave them on some newspaper and do it later then,' she said waspishly. 'And don't use all my hot water having baths. A proper strip wash will be quite adequate.'

'But if we don't have baths we'll get your sheets all mucky,' said Ivy, who was holding onto her dignity by folding her arms and glaring with defiance. 'And believe me, Mrs Williams, I got rubble and dust in places a strip wash ain't never gunna reach.'

Doris reddened. 'Just get upstairs and stop being a nuisance,' she snapped. 'I have visitors coming for morning coffee later on, and I don't want them catching sight of either of you.'

They were about to hurry off when Doris's voice stopped them. 'By the way, Mary. There's a message for you from my sister. She will meet you upstairs in the Anchor at three o'clock this afternoon.'

'Oh, all right. Thank you.'

Doris sniffed. 'I can't think what you find so attractive about that ghastly place or indeed that Braithwaite hussy – but then I have standards which you are clearly lacking. Go to bed, the pair of you.'

They ran upstairs to their bedroom and tossed a coin to see who would be first in the bath. Ivy won, so Mary stripped off her underwear and wrapped herself in her warm dressing gown to watch the snow come down before she read her letters.

It looked lovely, lying thick and white along the branches of the trees, the rooftops and lamp-posts, masking the ugly barbed wire along the seafront and turning the poor old ruined pier into something quite festive. She watched from her high vantage point as a solitary dog-walker strolled down the promenade, leaving traces of their passage behind them in the pristine whiteness, and then she smiled as she saw a group of young soldiers having a snowball fight, while two little girls and their mother made a snowman in their garden. It seemed that snow brought the child out in everyone.

She turned away from the scene and eagerly opened the first of her letters. It was from Jack, but distressingly short, for he was about to leave on his first posting that very day. He was forbidden to tell her where he was heading, but promised to send her the address and write when he could. His letters would be airgraphs from now on, so that told her he was being sent abroad, which made her feel very uneasy.

He continued on to tell her that the memory of their short time together over Christmas would stay with him always, and that he could never in a million years imagine life without her. He ended by signing his name with a flourish and adding SWALK at the bottom.

Mary held the letter close to her heart before reading it again, and then reluctantly folded it back into the envelope.

The second letter was much longer and full of detail and gossip from Barbara. There had been several tip-and-runs across the county, but luckily they were all still in one piece. She'd bumped into Mary's friend Pat and her young man as they came out of the village shop, and she'd passed on her best wishes and a promise to write again soon.

Joseph was beginning to feel his age as he had to take on more of the work now the promised extra land girls had not materialised, and his elderly farmhands could no longer put in a full day. Gideon's car was regularly oiled and polished and his trunk was now stored up in the farmhouse attic.

The church would not be rebuilt, but there was talk of putting up emergency housing where the rectory had once been, for more and more people were escaping the bombing in the cities and seeking refuge in the countryside. The rubble had already been cleared, and it was rumoured that the prefabricated houses would be arriving within the next few weeks.

Barbara felt no resentment about not having Jack home on Christmas Day, for it had been lovely just to see him once more before he was sent away again. She did fear for his safety, but then the commandos had made a man out of him, and she was so proud that she often wondered if she'd bored everyone to death by talking endlessly about him. She signed off with much love and the hope that Mary would soon come home, for they missed her.

It was a lovely letter and Mary's eyes misted over as she tucked it away in her gas-mask box. She would write back tomorrow on her day off when she'd have more time. Now, all she wanted was to bathe away her aches and pains, and get a good few hours of sleep so she could enjoy her afternoon with Rosie and Peggy.

Peggy had spent a restless night worrying about the planned afternoon tea with Rosie and Mary. Rising at dawn, she'd watched the clock impatiently until it was a decent hour to make the out-of-town telephone call which she knew now was so vital. It was a difficult conversation, but once it had been achieved, she felt much better about things.

She waited until ten to telephone Rosie, because she knew her friend liked to have a lie-in each morning to counteract the late nights she put in behind the bar, and it would have been unfair to disturb her. The news about Tommy hadn't come as too much of a surprise, for it was inevitable that he'd get his comeuppance sooner or later, but she had been concerned for Rosie.

Rosie had actually been quite philosophical about it all, and was far more interested in organising their little tea party that afternoon. She wouldn't be visiting Tommy in hospital, had no real desire to give him houseroom any more, and certainly wasn't planning on acting as his nurse and general dogs-body until he recovered.

Peggy put down the receiver at the end of the call and stood there deep in thought as she watched Daisy crawl about the hall floor. She was dreading this afternoon, and bitterly regretted telling Ron the whole story, yet she knew the truth could no longer be avoided. Whatever the outcome, it wouldn't make for the pleasant afternoon's tea party Rosie was looking forward to, and she wished with all her heart that she could turn back the clock eighteen years, and undo what had been done back then. Yet she'd been as powerless then as she was now, and there was nothing she could do to halt the gathering pace of inevitable Fate.

With a deep sigh, she picked up Daisy, ignored her protests and put her in the playpen with her toys and a digestive biscuit. She had a lot to do this morning, and Daisy was far too mobile now for her to be able to keep an eye on her all the time.

To keep her hands busy and her mind on other

things, Peggy scoured out the bathroom before she gathered up the laundry and carried it down to the scullery where the old boiler and wringer awaited her. What she wouldn't have given for a machine like Doris's didn't bear telling, but there was no way on earth she could have found the money for something so grand.

Cordelia was reading Daisy a story, doing all the voices and using her hands to illustrate the tale and keep her amused. The girls were at work except for Rita, who was still asleep, and Ron had disappeared before breakfast, so the house was pleasantly quiet for a change.

The copper boiler gurgled and rumbled, and the scullery was soon full of steam as she prodded the washing about in the hot soapy water and then dragged it out piece by piece into the stone sink. Rinsing each item thoroughly, she vented her spleen on Tommy Findlay by yanking hard on the wringer's handle to squeeze out the water as if it was his neck.

By the time everything was washed to her satisfaction, she was out of breath and sweating, and her hair was sticking to her head under the scarf. There was a tin tub and a basket full of clean washing now, and she hoisted the heavy basket onto her hip and stepped outside. There was still some snow lying in the shadows, but most of it had turned into treacherous ice, some of which hung in long needles from the gutters and windowsills and shone like glass on the paving slabs.

Treading very carefully, she carried the basket to the line, her heated hands and face already stinging from the cold wind that was coming off the sea. If this weather continued, she thought as she pegged out the sheets, there would be more snow tonight. The man on the wireless had said this was the coldest snap to be recorded for several years, and she could absolutely believe it.

She was about to hang up a towel when she heard the telephone ringing, so she left it in the basket and slipped and slithered her way back indoors to answer the call. 'Hello?'

'It's me – Doris.'

Peggy's spirits plummeted and she sank down onto the hall chair. 'Is it important, Doris? Only I've got a busy morning's work to get through.'

'Busy or not, I do think you might actually give some of your precious time to your sister when she is in need,' replied Doris, who didn't at all sound needy.

'Oh dear,' sighed Peggy. 'What's happened now?'

'It's Ted,' she replied. 'He's decided he prefers living in his flat above the Home and Colonial, and has turned down my offer to return home.'

Peggy honestly couldn't blame him. Doris had been a nightmare all through the arrangements for the wedding, and things hadn't improved much since. 'I'm sorry to hear that,' she said tactfully. 'But you seemed to be getting on all right these past few months What's changed?'

As Doris went on and on to catalogue all of Ted's perceived faults, Peggy lit a cigarette and tried to concentrate. It was suspiciously quiet in the kitchen, and that usually didn't bode well.

'Are you listening, Margaret?'

Her imperious voice brought Peggy back to the one-sided conversation. 'It strikes me, Doris, that

285

if he's such a failure in everything, you'd be better off without him. As it's clear he has no wish to move back in, then perhaps you should just call it a day and get a divorce.'

'I couldn't possibly,' she snapped. 'It would cause the most ghastly scandal.'

Peggy was about to reply when there was an almighty crash which echoed up from the cellar and almost drowned out the sharp cry of pain. 'I've got to go.' She slammed the telephone receiver down and raced past a grizzling Daisy to the cellar steps.

Cordelia was lying across the threshold, her leg twisted beneath her, her head jammed against the back door. The old tin bath Peggy had been using as an extra laundry basket was on its side, spilling the last of the washing across the concrete floor, and the ironing board had been knocked from its hook on the wall to land within inches of Cordelia's head.

'Cordelia! Oh, God, Cordelia,' she gasped as she flew down the steps and fell to her knees beside the tiny, still figure. With trembling hands she touched her face, noting how pale it was, and then she saw the blood darkening her hair.

'Rita!' she yelled. 'Rita, I need help.'

Rita was at her side in an instant. 'It's all right, I heard the crash. I'll ring for an ambulance. Don't move her, Auntie Peg, she could have damaged her neck or spine.'

As the girl raced back into the house in her pyjamas, Peggy took Cordelia's hand and tried to rub some warmth into it. The wind was tearing across the garden, making the washing snap on the line, and blasting its arctic breath through the open doorway and over the inert form on the floor. 'Cordelia,' she urged. 'Cordelia, you have to wake up. Please, please, love. Open your eyes.'

'I told them to come round the back, and they should be here in less than five minutes,' said Rita as she ran down the steps armed with the blankets from the emergency box. 'Better not to move her head, but at least these will keep her a bit warmer.'

'She won't wake up, Rita,' said Peggy hoarsely. 'And there's blood, look.'

'Head wounds always bleed a lot,' Rita replied gruffly as she tucked both blankets around Cordelia and tried to blink away her tears. 'Don't worry, Auntie Peg,' she said tremulously. 'She'll be fine. I'm sure she will.'

The clanging of the ambulance bell grew nearer and Rita ran outside in her bare feet to meet them.

Cordelia didn't stir, but the bright red blood was blossoming like a poppy through her white hair, and there was a blue tinge to her skin. Peggy grasped her hand. 'Hold on, Cordelia,' she said urgently. 'Help's on its way.'

The two men came sliding down the garden path and quickly examined Cordelia. 'She needs to go to hospital,' one of them said grimly. 'That ankle looks as if it might be broken, and I don't like the look of that head wound, or her colour. Has she gained consciousness at all?'

Peggy shook her head, too numbed by shock to talk.

Whilst Rita kept Cordelia's head steady, they gently lifted her onto a stretcher. One of the men put a brace round Cordelia's neck to protect it from any jarring, and as Rita and Peggy anxiously held their breath, they carried her precariously down the glassy path and along the twitten to the waiting ambulance.

'I'll go with her,' said Peggy. 'Can you stay and look after Daisy?' At Rita's nod, she grabbed one of Ron's disreputable old coats and dragged it on as she slithered down the path in her slippers and hurried to catch up with the ambulance before it drove off.

Within seconds of her climbing into the back, the doors were slammed, and to the urgent clanging of the bell, they were screeching into a tight turn and heading down Camden Road to the hospital.

She was too concerned about Cordelia to notice Ron, who was walking with some determination towards Beach View with a grim smile of satisfaction on his face.

Chapter Thirteen

Rosie was only dimly aware of the ambulance clanging its way down the street, for the pub was busy, the noise rising as the beer flowed. She could have done with some help today, but one of her barmaids was down with influenza, and the other was visiting her sister whose husband had been recently killed in the Atlantic.

There was no sign of Ron, which was unusual,

but he had taken Monty out this morning, and she'd spotted him and Bert strolling down the street deep in conversation, so she supposed he'd been sidetracked by the promise of a glass or two of the malt whisky Bert always kept in his desk drawer. Yet Monty had been delivered home at some point during the morning, for he was now asleep in front of the inglenook fire, his long, skinny legs sticking out as he snored. It was odd that Ron hadn't popped in to say hello, especially as he must have known from Bert about Tommy.

As she pulled pints and exchanged lively banter with her customers, Rosie had soon discovered that her brother's plight was now common news that elicited very little sympathy, but a great deal of speculation. She listened to the gossip and fended off the endless questions by saying she didn't know who'd done it or why. She didn't really want to think about her brother, and how close he'd come to dying from the cold, and supposed she should have felt at least some pity for him However, her well of loyalty had long since run dry, and Tommy was a survivor – he'd pull through this as he'd pulled through everything else, and would, no doubt, be back to his old ways the moment he was up and about again.

But it was worrying that there were such brutal thugs in Cliffehaven who were out for revenge, and although they'd beaten up Tommy, was that enough? What if they decided to come here and smash things up – or take her stock to make up for what Tommy hadn't delivered? She'd have to take more precautions from now on, she decided, like keeping the side door locked at all times, and arming herself with a cricket bat or something.

She grasped the pump handle to pull a pint, angry with herself for being so stupid, for acting on impulse and getting rid of the drink and cigarettes. She should just have telephoned Bert Williams and told him what she'd found, then none of this would have happened. Tommy would have been sent back to prison, she would have got her life back, and things could have returned to normal.

As she rang the bell for last orders and the crowd began to thin out, she set her mind firmly onto this afternoon's tea. She'd managed to get a sponge cake from the bakery and a lovely packet of biscuits from the Home and Colonial before she'd opened up this morning, and she'd washed her best tea set which she'd laid out on the low table in her sitting room. There was a fresh packet of tea, and even some sugar, so it would be a real treat for Peggy and dear little Mary.

She quickly served the final few drinks, keeping a close eye on the clock. As she collected the empty glasses and encouraged the slow to finish their drinks and leave, she wondered if Ron would come this afternoon as he'd promised. It wouldn't be easy to question Mary about why she'd been searching for Cyril Fielding, and although she'd been very unwilling to carry out Tommy's order to do so, her own curiosity had been piqued. Peggy had told her snippets of Mary's background, but not enough to explain things fully, which was rather frustrating to say the least. But the whole thing was just so odd, and she couldn't help but wonder what Mary's story really was.

She bolted the door behind Fred Smith, who was always the last to leave, and then turned to Monty, still sprawled in front of the fire. 'Come on, you lazy thing,' she said fondly as she stroked his ears. 'Upstairs for a saucer of tea and a biscuit while I get out of these clothes and have a nice bath.'

As Monty stretched and yawned, Rosie saw the discarded newspaper on the table. She glanced at it and discovered it was folded back to the daily horoscopes, so she took a moment to read what the day had in store for those born under the sign of Pisces, and then thoughtfully tucked it under her arm. She didn't hold much store with all that nonsense, but she knew Peggy might like to read it – and it could come in handy later on as a way of getting Mary to open up about herself.

Monty's claws clicked on the uneven brick floor as he followed her out of the bar and then raced up the stairs, eager for his daily saucer of milky tea. Rosie didn't immediately follow him, for the side door was unbolted as usual. She then decided she was getting paranoid. If the thugs were determined enough, all it would take was a broken window to gain access – and besides, she didn't want to be running up and down the stairs to let her visitors in. But it might be wise to find something heavy to defend herself with.

A short rummage in the cellar unearthed a baseball bat that one of the American GIs had left behind some months ago. She felt the weight of it and gave it a practice swing. It was perfect.

A fretful Peggy had been sitting in the crowded

and rather noisy accident and emergency waiting area for almost an hour. She was vaguely aware of the curious stares of those around her, and realised she must look very silly in her slippers, wrap-round apron and Ron's tatty, smelly jacket. But actually she didn't care. What was happening to Cordelia was all that really mattered.

Rita finally came in a while later carrying not only Daisy, but a large, rather bulky bag. 'Uncle Ron came home, so I told him what had happened, and he said he had something to do first, but he'd be here as soon as he could.'

'What could possibly be more important than Cordelia?' Peggy was overwrought, and her tone was a little sharp.

Rita seemed to understand, for she just shrugged and sat down. 'I don't know, but he was certainly acting mysteriously.' She divested Daisy of some of her sweaters and tucked the knitted mittens in her coat pocket. 'I'm sorry I've been so long, but Daisy took a while to soothe after that crash woke her up, and I had to get dressed. I thought you might need these,' she murmured as she handed over the bag. 'Is there any news yet?'

Peggy regretted her sharpness. 'No, nothing really,' she said wearily. 'She's had to go off for X-rays, despite the fact she has yet to come round.'

She looked inside the bag and felt even more guilty at having snapped at the girl. 'Thanks for my things, darling,' she said as she pulled her coat, scarf, shoes and purse out of the bag. 'Ron's jacket smells horrid, and goodness only knows what he's been keeping in the pockets,' she said with a grimace as she wriggled out of it and stuffed it in the bag alongside her apron and ruined slippers. 'And I've been gasping for a cup of tea, but of course without my purse…'

She was in the middle of pulling on her overcoat when Rita's words suddenly sank in, and she frowned. 'What do you mean about Ron acting mysteriously? What was he up to?'

Rita was having trouble keeping Daisy on her lap, for she was wriggling like an eel in her attempt to get down to the floor. 'The last I saw of him, he was dithering about in the kitchen in his poacher's coat looking furtive. I went upstairs to get dressed, heard the back door slam a short while later, and by the time I'd come back down, he was gone.'

Peggy really couldn't concentrate on Ron's strange behaviour, not with Cordelia being so poorly. 'I do wish someone would come and tell us what's happening,' she said anxiously. 'Cordelia's head wound isn't serious, thank goodness, but she still hasn't come round, and although he hasn't said anything, I can tell that the doctor is getting rather concerned.'

She fidgeted with the strap on her handbag as her deepest dread surfaced. 'I'm worried, Rita. She should have woken up by now. You don't think we're going to lose her, do you?'

Rita gave up the struggle with Daisy and sat her on the floor before taking Peggy's hand. 'They wouldn't be wasting time on X-rays if they thought that. Please don't fret, Auntie Peg. Grandma Finch is much tougher than we all realise. She'll come through this, you'll see.'

Peggy realised Rita was trying to look on the

bright side of things, but it didn't help ease her very real fears. She glanced at the clock and then snatched up her purse. She had to do something to pass this endless wait, or she'd go mad. 'I'm going to get a cuppa,' she said. 'Do you want one?'

At Rita's nod she went off to get two cups of tea from the café that had been opened by the WVS in what had once been a small treatment room. On her return, she discovered that Daisy was crawling happily between the feet and chair legs, looking up occasionally with a beaming smile to those who cooed at her before continuing her exploration.

Rita rounded her up, and as she squirmed and protested on her lap, she was placated with some watery juice from her bottle and one of the rather stale biscuits Peggy had just bought. Once she'd had her fill she demanded to be put down again and Peggy advised Rita to let her. 'She'll only start yelling, and the people here are poorly enough without her noise going through their heads. Besides, your tea's getting cold.'

As Daisy sat happily on the floor, and gnawed on her second biscuit, Peggy could see that she'd become fascinated by the life of the busy hospital department which swirled around her. Doctors, nurses, orderlies and porters dashed back and forth between the cubicles; patients came and went, and those still waiting to be seen were doing their best to appear stoic during the long delays. When Daisy saw Ron coming towards her, she lifted up her arms and beamed in delight. 'Dadda, dad, dad, dad.'

Peggy closed her eyes in despair at this, for her

baby should know by now that this wasn't her daddy. Damn this bloody, bloody war.

Rita told Ron there was very little news and he sat down to start filling his pipe. 'What the hell was she doing down there in the first place?' he asked once he'd got it going satisfactorily.

'I can only guess she was attempting to help put the washing out,' said Peggy. 'And if Doris hadn't chosen to telephone at that precise moment, none of this would have happened.' She glared at him. 'What have you been up to, Ron? Rita says you've been acting oddly.'

'Ach, to be sure, 'tis only me usual way of doing things,' he replied with a twinkle in his eyes as he stretched out his sturdy legs so Daisy could clamber onto them. 'I'm thinking young Rita has an overactive imagination, so I do.'

'Well, whatever it is that you're up to, it can stop,' she said crossly. 'Now. Right this minute. There's enough trouble to be going on with, without you acting up.'

'Ach, Peggy girl, you're overwrought about Cordelia.' His great rough hand caught hold of her fingers. 'She'll be fine. Tough as nails, that one.'

'So everyone keeps telling me,' she muttered as the tears came. 'But she's old and frail, Ron, and that fall... That fall could...' She leaned against his broad shoulder as she sobbed, and the lack of any reply from him told her that he too was deeply concerned.

Rosie had cleaned the apartment and shut the door on Tommy's untidy bedroom. The kettle was filled and ready to bring to the boil, she'd made spam sandwiches to go with the cake and biscuits, and everything was laid out on the low table between the couches and chairs. Monty had been sternly ordered to lie on the hearth rug and be good. She'd caught him sniffing the biscuits earlier and didn't want a repeat performance.

She had taken a leisurely bath and changed into her favourite blue woollen dress, which enhanced the colour of her eyes and didn't make her look quite so washed out, and her make-up had been freshly applied. She'd begun to relax and look forward to the afternoon, for she'd relented and telephoned the hospital to see how Tommy was. The ward sister had told her that the doctor insisted he be kept in overnight for observation, but he would probably be discharged tomorrow lunchtime if there was no sign of concussion. This news had come as a mixed blessing, for it meant she would have him home again tomorrow, but at least she wouldn't have to face him tonight, and for the first time in many weeks could enjoy her comforts.

'Hello? Rosie?'

Monty leapt to his feet and shot down the stairs as Rosie stood at the top and welcomed Mary. 'Hello, dear, it's lovely to see you. But don't let him jump all over you like that, he'll ruin your nice coat.'

Mary continued to make a fuss of Monty as she grinned back up at her. 'Oh, I don't mind,' she said cheerfully. 'It's just lovely to get such a warm welcome.'

'Monty, that's enough,' Rosie said sternly. 'Come on up, Mary. Peggy should be here soon, but we can have a cosy little chat while we wait for her.'

Mary managed to disentangle herself from Monty's rapturous welcome and came up into the sitting room to take off her coat and scarf. 'I heard about your brother,' she said awkwardly. 'That was a terrible thing to happen.'

Rosie gave a small shrug. 'He's his own worst enemy, and will get over it,' she said dismissively, her attention caught by the bruises and cuts on Mary's face. 'Good heavens,' she gasped with concern. 'What happened to you?'

Mary smiled ruefully as she touched the cut on her bruised forehead, and told her about being trapped in the shelter. 'It wasn't a very nice experience,' she said finally, 'but at least we all got out, and even those who were taken to hospital weren't that seriously injured.'

'Well, I'm glad you're safe. Now sit down and make yourself comfortable while I go and put the kettle on.' Rosie walked into the tiny kitchen and lit the gas under the kettle, watching Mary surreptitiously through the open doorway as she warmed the pot.

It was a shame about the cuts and bruises, but they would heal and leave no trace. She was such a pretty girl, with that long, dark hair and lovely blue eyes – and in a way she reminded her of someone, but she couldn't for the life of her think who.

As she carried in the teapot, she saw Mary was looking at the newspaper she'd left on the arm of the couch, and realised this was the perfect moment to find out more about the girl. 'I don't really believe in all that stuff, but I always find myself reading the horoscopes, don't you?'

'No, not really,' Mary said shyly. 'My parents were very religious, so this sort of thing was always frowned upon.'

'Oh, but it can be quite fun,' said Rosie enthusiastically as she put the teapot on the tray and reached for the paper. 'Let's have a look at what the Oracle has in store for you today – just for a giggle, mind. What's your star sign?'

Mary's returning smile was uncertain. 'I have no idea what you're talking about,' she confessed. 'What's a star sign?'

Rosie settled down on the couch beside her and pointed out the twelve separate paragraphs under their headings. 'I was born on March the second, so I come under the sign of Pisces, the fish. Each of these is the name of the star formations we can see in the sky at night, and according to the astrologers our lives are influenced by the sign we were born under.' She saw Mary's sceptical expression and grinned. 'I know it sounds daft, but it's only a bit of fun, so please humour me.'

'It all sounds gobbledygook to me,' Mary replied, 'but seeing as how neither of us takes it seriously, I suppose it won't do any harm. I was born on or around the tenth of October in 1924.'

Rosie felt a pang of something close to pain, then dismissed it firmly. She looked at Mary in confusion. 'Don't you know the date you were born?'

'Not really. You see, I've never managed to get hold of my birth certificate, but I've always celebrated the day on the tenth.' She leaned forward to examine the newspaper in Rosie's lap. 'That would mean my sign is Libra. So what does it say?'

Rosie gathered her scattered thoughts and

began to read aloud. 'You will have some difficult dilemmas to face today, but never fear, they can be easily solved. Be prepared to hear from some-one in your past, and open your heart to the person who loves you.'

Mary giggled. 'What a load of tosh. Honestly, Rosie, you can't really believe all that, do you?'

'Of course I don't,' she replied, folding the paper and setting it aside. 'The tea must be mashed by now, so let's have that cuppa.' She poured the tea into the bone-china cups which were rimmed in gold and decorated with roses. 'I don't know what's happened to Peggy,' she said anxiously as she glanced at the mantel clock. 'She's very late.'

'I expect she's held up at home,' said Mary as she accepted the cup and saucer. 'There's always someone needing her for something.'

Rosie suspected that if that was the case, Peggy would have telephoned her to warn her she'd be late – she was always good like that. But Peggy's whereabouts were secondary to her curiosity about Mary's lack of knowledge concerning her birth. She knew from Peggy that the girl had been adopted by a vicar and his wife, and that she'd lost them during a tip-and-run following an enemy bombing raid. Other than that, she actually knew very little about Mary. It was time to discover more, and even perhaps broach the thorny subject of Cyril Fielding.

'This is nice, isn't it?' she said, settling back into the cushions. 'We so rarely have the chance to talk properly, what with the pub and everything, and as we seem to have become good friends despite all that, I'd love to hear about your life before you came to Cliffehaven.'

Mary sipped her tea and then shot Rosie a wry smile. 'I suspect Peggy has told you most of it, so there's not much more I can add.'

'Peggy actually hasn't told me much at all, only that you came from a small village in Sussex, and that you lost your adoptive parents during an enemy raid and were taken in by your lovely Jack's parents,' said Rosie truthfully. 'But I must admit I do find it intriguing that you don't have a proper certificate with your date of birth on it.'

'Well, it has proved to be a bit of a nuisance now the war's on,' Mary admitted. 'Bits of paper seem to have taken on a huge significance suddenly. But because I'd lived in Harebridge Green all my life, and my father was the rector, it was easy to get a proper identity card, ration books and such, without having to produce a birth certificate.'

'But surely you'd have adoption papers? Or were they destroyed in the raid?'

Mary's hand was a little unsteady as she raised the cup to her lips and took a drink of tea.

Rosie noticed and was immediately contrite. 'Oh, Mary, me and my curiosity – I didn't mean to upset you, love. Let's forget about it,' she said quickly, 'and just have a natter about something else.'

Mary put the cup and saucer down and shook her head. 'I'm not upset, not really, and I'd like to tell you. But it's quite a long story, and it doesn't have a very nice ending, I'm afraid.'

'Only if you want to,' Rosie murmured as she took her hand. 'It won't make a jot of difference to our friendship however it ends, but if you'd rather not, then I'll quite understand.' Her genuine regret at having upset Mary made her cross with herself. She should stop prying and poking into the girl's life – for what did it really matter if she'd been looking for Cyril? It was none of her business.

'No, really, I'd like to tell you, because I know you aren't the sort of person to judge others just because things have happened to them which were completely out of their control.'

Rosie patted her hand and watched as the girl composed herself, wondering once again who she reminded her of – especially in profile, with those high cheekbones and the neat little nose.

'I never knew I'd been adopted,' Mary began. 'It was only after the rectory burned down and Jack's father found Daddy's old trunk that I learned the truth.' Her voice faltered, but she carried on relating how her life had been with the gentle, loving Gideon and the cold, self-possessed Emmaline.

As Rosie listened she began to feel even closer to this young girl, for it was clear she'd never known a mother's love. Rosie's soft heart went out to her and she had to determinedly resist taking her in her arms and giving her a cuddle, for Mary would probably have been embarrassed by such a show of affection.

'I found Daddy's diaries in the trunk,' Mary went on. 'And I was a bit reluctant to read them at first because they were his private thoughts and feelings and it didn't feel right to pry.' Her smile was soft and sweet as her eyes grew misty. 'But I'm glad I did, because it meant I got to really know him, and to understand how his marriage to Emmaline survived.'

She gave a sigh. 'She was never an easy woman, and what he did was done out of love for her, and in the belief that I was a gift from God which would ease her suffering after all the babies she'd lost.'

'He sounds a lovely man,' said Rosie softly. 'You were lucky in that respect.'

Mary looked down at her hands, which were tightly knotted on her lap. 'I know,' she replied, her voice unsteady with emotion, 'but it would have broken his heart if he knew how I found out the truth, for he'd never imagined for one minute that I would read that 1924 diary, or find the piece of paper he'd tucked inside it.'

She flicked the long hair from her face. 'It broke my heart too,' she admitted. 'But I suppose that was the price I had to pay for snooping.'

'It wasn't snooping, Mary,' Rosie reached for her hand again. 'You had a right to know, and if he'd lived, he would have told you eventually that you'd been adopted.'

Mary returned the pressure on Rosie's fingers. 'He wrote that he dreaded telling me, and that he'd planned to reveal the truth on my twenty-first birthday. But even if he'd lived, I doubt he would have told me the whole story, for the adoption was never legal.'

Rosie frowned. 'But how could that be? He was an honest man of the cloth.'

'He was a soft-hearted, gullible man who was thoroughly taken in by someone who could tell a good sob story' she replied with more than a hint of sadness. 'And that someone was my real father.'

Rosie felt a prickle of unease and tried to make light of it by joking that her erstwhile father sounded very like her brother.

Mary's smile was wan. 'He does rather, doesn't he? But unfortunately there's more than one man like Tommy in this world, and my father evidently shared the same disreputable traits.'

Rosie felt a great deal of sympathy for the poor girl. It couldn't have been at all easy to discover that not only were you adopted, but that your father was not the most honest of people. But she said nothing and let Mary gather her thoughts so she could tell her story in her own way.

Mary stared into the teacup. 'They drew up a private agreement that Gideon would raise me as his daughter, and that my father would have no further contact with me. There was no formal stamp on the agreement or witness signature – and nothing anywhere that gave a clue to my mother's identity.'

Rosie's pulse was beginning to race and she felt cold to the very bone. 'But how could a man give a child away without the mother's consent?' she asked, her voice raw with anger.

'According to the account in Gideon's diary, she'd gone shopping one day and simply never returned – and without a name or any clue as to who she was, I have to accept I'll never find her.'

Rosie was so outraged on Mary's behalf that she could barely speak. 'But your father must have signed that agreement with Gideon, so you must know who he was,' she managed. 'Did you come to Cliffehaven to find him?'

Mary nodded. 'Daddy mentioned in his diaries

that my father was a travelling salesman and had met my mother during his time here. I stupidly thought that someone might remember him, you see – and that would lead me to finding out who my mother was.'

She took a tremulous breath. 'But I've since learned he was nothing but a crook and a woman-iser who's spent time in prison and couldn't be trusted to tell the time, let alone any kind of truth. So you see it's all rather hopeless really.'

Rosie's thoughts were in chaos, putting things together, sifting through everything Mary had told her until she couldn't bear it any longer. 'How did you find all that out?' she asked.

'Peggy asked Ron about him after I'd confided in her, and he remembered him only too well. It was a terrible shock when Peggy told me what a crook he was, but as no one knows where he is, or even if he's still alive, I decided to give up my search and leave well alone. After all,' she added with a soft, sad smile, 'it's sometimes better not to know the truth when it can only be ugly and ultimately damaging, don't you think?'

Rosie stared at her as the words rang in her head and common sense warned her urgently not to take this any further – for she suddenly realised who it was that Mary reminded her of, and if her mind wasn't playing tricks on her, then she already knew the answer to the question she so desperately wanted to ask. But something deeper and more primal took over, for there had been too many years of silence – and she wanted to hear the girl's answer to all the questions that had haunted her for so long.

She battled to breathe as her pulse raced and her heart thudded. 'What was your father's name?'

Mary regarded her with a frown. 'Does it really matter?'

Rosie could only nod.

'You've gone very white, Rosie. Aren't you feeling well?'

Rosie waved away her concern. 'Tell me,' she rasped. 'Please, Mary, what is his name?'

'Cyril Fielding.'

Rosie felt as if her heart was in her throat. She couldn't breathe, and her head was spinning as a terrible darkness threatened to overwhelm her. She heard Mary's distant cry of alarm but was incapable of saying anything to reassure her – and then she did something she had never done before. She fainted.

Peggy had been all too aware of how swiftly time was passing, and of the impossibility of being in at least three places at once. It was with a huge sense of relief that they finally managed to speak to a doctor and learn that Cordelia had regained consciousness and was in no danger. The suspected fracture had turned out to be a painful wrench and tearing of her ankle ligaments and tendons, the head wound needed a couple of stitches and there were signs that she was slightly concussed. She would stay overnight under observation and if the doctor agreed, they could take her home at lunchtime the following day.

Peggy and Ron spoke to a very drowsy Cordelia and made sure she was comfortable in the hospital bed before they made a dash for the Anchor, leaving Daisy in Rita's capable hands. Ron had left Harvey at home, not wanting to bear the wrath of Matron, who hated dogs in her hospital, so they'd come through the side door of the Anchor quietly and listened at the bottom of the stairs to see how the land lay.

Peggy could barely breathe as she listened to the conversation going on upstairs, and she would have rushed up there and comforted both of them if Ron hadn't grabbed her arm and silently warned her to wait and not interfere.

They'd stood there and listened to the whole sorry tale, but as it slowly drew closer to its inevitable conclusion, they exchanged concerned looks and took a step nearer to the bottom stair.

When they heard the soft thud on the floor and Mary's cry of alarm, Ron bolted up the stairs calling for Rosie.

Peggy dithered, and then decided that Ron could deal with whatever was going on up there, for she had something far more urgent to do. She backed away and, with an anxious glance at her watch, headed once more for the side door.

Chapter Fourteen

Mary was still trying to come to terms with the shock of seeing Rosie crumple to the floor in a dead faint. She was on her knees beside her, reaching for her hand and trying to push a whining, fretful Monty out of the way, when Ron burst into the room.

'Get away,' he ordered the pup as he fell to his knees and gathered Rosie's limp body into his arms. 'Rosie, acushla. It's all right, I've got you, you're safe. Wake up, my love.'

Mary was rather embarrassed by this outpouring of raw emotion, so she got to her feet and ran into the kitchen to dampen a tea towel and pour a glass of cold water. Returning to the sitting room, she placed the folded towel over Rosie's forehead, gave Ron the glass, and knelt beside them unsure of what to do next.

It was a long, tense few minutes before Rosie's eyelids fluttered and the colour began to return to her face. Ron held her close to his heart and tried to persuade her to drink some water. Her blue eyes slowly focused on Mary and she reached out a trembling hand to touch her face. 'Flora?' she whispered. 'Flora, is it really you?'

Mary gasped, her gaze fixed on Rosie, her thoughts and emotions racing through her at such terrifying speed she couldn't voice any of it. She fought for calm as she reached for Rosie's hand and held it to her cheek. 'Mother?' she breathed.

Rosie closed her eyes and a tear seeped through her lashes as Ron continued to hold her. 'Oh, Flora,' she said tremulously. 'My darling, sweet little girl.'

Mary glanced at Ron, who was looking quite grey with concern, and then returned her gaze to Rosie as she battled with her mixed emotions. There was joy at finding her, thankfulness that she was a lovely, caring woman who'd already become a friend – and a deep sense of shock and anger that Rosie had abandoned her. 'Oh, Rosie,' she managed through her tears. 'Is it true? Are you *really* my mother?'

'This isn't all about you, Rosemary Braithwaite, so pull yourself together and stop behaving as if you're in some second-rate melodrama.'

They all turned sharply towards the neatly dressed, slender, dark-haired woman standing with a flustered Peggy in the doorway. Mary gaped at her in disbelief. 'What on earth are *you* doing here?'

The woman made no reply, but her intense gaze was fixed so firmly on Mary that she began to feel very uneasy.

'I know it must come as a bit of a shock, Mary,' said Peggy as she came into the room, 'but it was necessary to bring her.'

'But I don't understand.' Mary looked at Peggy in bewilderment. 'What has all this got to do with her?'

Peggy glanced from Mary to Rosie and Ron, clearly unsure of how to reply.

But Rosie seemed to have recovered fully from her faint, and she struggled out of Ron's embrace to reach for Mary's hand. 'It's all right, Mary. Really it is.' She then glared furiously at the other woman. 'What the hell *are* you doing here?' she snapped.

'I didn't want to come, believe you me,' replied Eileen Harris. 'But Peggy insisted, and once she'd told me what all this is about, I knew I had no choice.'

'I'm sorry, Rosie,' said a fretful Peggy as she and Ron helped her up from the floor so she could sit on the couch. 'But this has got to be resolved once and for all – and that can only happen if everyone involved is present.'

'But we aren't all present, are we?' said a tight-lipped Eileen as she perched on the very edge of the other couch. 'The cause of all this – as usual – is nowhere to be seen.'

Mary looked at them all in tearful frustration. She couldn't understand any of it. 'You're all talking in riddles,' she said in utter confusion. 'If, by that, you mean my father, then how could he possibly be here? No one's seen or heard from Cyril for years.'

Eileen tore her gaze from Mary and looked wide-eyed at Rosie. 'She still doesn't know, does she?'

Rosie shook her head and reached an unsteady hand for her cigarettes. 'I haven't had the chance to tell her anything,' she said, 'and I think you should leave it to me to explain.' She blew smoke. 'At least she'll get the truth from me – which is more than I can say for anything you might tell her,' she added bitterly.

'You never listened to anything I had to say,' retorted Eileen, the colour rising in her perfectly made-up face. 'And you clearly wouldn't admit the truth if it up and bit you.'

Rosie gave a grunt of disdain as she shrugged Ron's calming hand from her shoulder. 'There speaks the pot calling the kettle black,' she snapped. 'You're a liar, Eileen. Always were and always will be.'

Eileen got to her feet as the colour drained from her face. 'If that's what you want to believe, then I can't do much about it. But if you gave me the chance to tell my side of things, you might actually, for once, admit that what happened was not my fault.'

'You should try seeing things from my point of view,' Rosie snapped. 'But then you've always been a selfish, self-seeking bitch and couldn't care less about the damage you cause others.'

'Stop it,' begged Mary. 'Stop it, both of you. Whatever the truth is – however you see things – this isn't helping,' she said brokenly. 'If you don't call a truce and calm down, I'll leave and never come here again. It's hateful seeing you like this, Rosie.'

'Oh, Mary, I'm so sorry,' said Rosie, clasping her hand. 'I couldn't bear to lose you now I've finally found you after all these years.'

'I'm sorry too,' said Eileen gruffly as she sat down again. 'But what you have to understand, Mary, is that Rosie and I haven't seen eye to eye for years, and all this raking up of the past has opened old, very deep wounds.'

There was a long silence which Peggy eventually broke. 'Then I think it's time you stopped fighting and just told her – calmly and sensibly – what happened, and with as much thought for Mary's feelings as possible,' she said. 'From what I've heard, the actual truth is far from black and white, and you each have a very different story to tell.'

She went to squeeze in on the other side of Mary and put her arm about her shoulders. 'Mary, love, I know you've already told Rosie your story, but I think Eileen should hear it too so that there are no further misunderstandings.'

Mary was comforted by Peggy's sheltering embrace, but there were too many unanswered questions clamouring in her head. 'Before I do that, I would like some straight answers from both of you,' she said, looking from Rosie to Eileen. 'Firstly, what is it I don't know about Cyril Fielding? Secondly, are you my mother, Rosie – and if so, what has *any* of this got to do with Eileen?'

She didn't miss the surreptitious glances that flew between the two women, and wondered if this was simply a tacit agreement to say as little as possible. 'I'd appreciate the whole, unvarnished truth, no matter how awful it might be,' she said flatly.

There was a long, tense pause before Rosie spoke. 'Cyril Fielding never existed,' she said in a low, unsteady voice. 'It was just a name conjured up by ... by...' Rosie took a deep breath and gripped Mary's hand. 'By my brother Tommy,' she said in a rush

Mary couldn't breathe – couldn't think – couldn't articulate the horror and shock that was surging through her. She was aware of Rosie's grip on her fingers, of Peggy's arm about her shoulders and of the very real anguish in Rosie's face. 'Tommy?' she managed finally. 'Tommy's my father?'

Rosie nodded as tears brimmed and threatened to fall.

Mary's thoughts were whirling and a worm of horrifying suspicion began to make itself impossible to ignore. 'But... But he's your brother,' she gasped. 'Surely you aren't trying to tell me that you and he...?'

Rosie went ashen. 'No! Oh, God no, Mary, of course not.'

Mary experienced an overwhelming sense of relief that was laced with deep grief. 'So you aren't my mother, after all,' she said through her tears.

Rosie shook her head, her lovely blue eyes awash with sadness.

That small gesture shattered all hope, and brought such a deep, physical pain to Mary's heart that it took a long moment to recover from it. 'Then I don't understand,' she murmured into the heavy silence. 'Why keep Cyril's identity such a closely guarded secret? And as you aren't my mother, how did you know I'd once been called Flora?'

Rosie was clearly making a tremendous effort to control her own emotions as her grip tightened on Mary's hand. 'I swear to you, Mary, I didn't know anything about Cyril until the other day; and I certainly didn't know you'd been asking after him.'

Mary listened as Rosie told her how Tommy had confessed to using that alias, and how worried he'd been about the possibility that Mary's family had been victims of his insurance scam and she was out to cause trouble with the police.

Mary's hurt was all-encompassing as she slowly withdrew her hand from Rosie's grip. It was hard enough to accept that this was not her mother, but to realise she'd betrayed their friendship by spying for Tommy was unbearable.

'So that's what this tea party was all about?' she said brokenly. 'You were just trying to find out why I was looking for Cyril.'

'That was only a tiny part of it,' Rosie confessed as she mopped her tears and tried valiantly to keep calm. 'I've come to be very fond of you, Mary, and wanted to get to know you better. I had no real intention of doing Tommy's dirty work, but your search for Cyril intrigued me – it didn't make sense. You were too young, and the sort of background you had didn't fit the picture that Tommy had painted of his victims – they were usually wealthy, you see, not country vicars.'

Mary battled with her disappointment and pain as she thought about this and then came to realise that she should actually be grateful for Rosie's meddling – for without it, the truth would have stayed buried. And she'd asked for the truth, no matter how unpleasant it turned out to be.

She looked across the abandoned tea things at Eileen, understanding now that, for some reason, she too had been following Tommy's orders. Then she felt a deeper sense of betrayal as she turned sadly to Peggy, for she'd come to love and trust her and hadn't for one minute suspected that she'd been lying to her for all this time. 'You knew Cyril was Tommy all along, didn't you?'

'Not until very recently,' said Peggy as she flicked a glance at the silent, solemn Ron. 'It was only when I asked Ron about Cyril that I learned who he was – and once I knew, then it was vital to protect you from him. Ron didn't know about him being your father,' she added hastily. 'Not until last night, anyway, when it became clear that all this was going to come out.'

'But I'm not a child, Peggy. I trusted you to tell me the truth – so why didn't you?' Mary demanded.

'How could I?' said Peggy softly. 'He'd already

313

frightened you by trying to pick you up that night, and you'd started playing the piano here, and were in and out visiting Rosie who'd become a friend.'

Peggy gave a deep sigh. 'It was better you knew only that your father was a complete rotter and not worth the effort of trying to find him. You had to stop asking about Cyril, don't you see? Otherwise Tommy would have got to hear about it and...'

'He would have pestered me until he knew the whys and wherefores – and then once he realised who I was ... I dread to think what might have happened then,' Mary finished softly. Her head was throbbing, her heart was aching, and she was still finding it almost impossible to deal with what she'd learned, for within a few minutes she'd gone from joy to despair – from trust to doubt – and ultimately to a deep and painful sadness.

Yet, as the silence in the room continued, she realised Peggy was not to blame for any of this, and she loved and admired her too much to continue being cold with her. She took Peggy's hand. 'I do understand why you kept quiet,' she said softly, 'and I'm grateful you cared enough to protect me.' She held Peggy's gaze as she laced their fingers. 'How long have you known that Tommy had fathered a child?'

'Many years,' she replied as she dabbed away her tears. 'It was a confidence Rosie shared with me that I've kept ever since. Neither Ron nor my Jim ever knew about it.'

Mary gave a deep, wavering sigh as she gathered her scattered thoughts. 'My father, whatever he calls himself, is a crooked, womanising spiv, and that is something I've already managed to come

314

to terms with. It's just the fact that he's Tommy Findlay that I'm finding hard to accept.' She shot Rosie an apologetic, uncertain smile.

'I don't blame you,' said Rosie as she blew her nose on Ron's handkerchief. 'He's not exactly the sort of relative anyone would wish for,' she said with some asperity, 'and I'm just so sorry you ever had to find out about him.'

Mary nodded and managed to find a modicum of comfort from her words. The room had gone very quiet, she noticed. Ron was sitting on the arm of the couch next to Rosie, his unlit pipe clenched between his teeth, and Monty lying at their feet; Peggy was fidgeting in the tight squeeze on the sofa, while Eileen remained isolated on the other side of the low table. And yet, in that silence was a tangible sense of tension – of things unsaid – of emotions being tightly restrained.

Eileen's expression was apprehensive, her slender figure rigid with some unspoken anxiety as she fumbled to light a cigarette. Yet, as Mary met those unwavering brown eyes which had watched her throughout, she saw something flicker there momentarily before she looked away. Was it apprehension, or something much deeper? It had been too fleeting to tell.

'I'm going to make a pot of fresh tea,' said Peggy as she glanced fretfully at the clock and began to clear the cups and saucers onto the tray. 'It's the best medicine I know for calming people down and soothing hurts.'

Mary watched as she went into the kitchen, the leggy pup following her in anticipation of a treat. The silence in the room was profound and Mary

315

could almost feel the hostility between Rosie and Eileen as they momentarily caught each other's eye and swiftly looked away.

Peggy returned some minutes later with the tea tray, and once everyone had a cup, she perched on the very edge of the small couch next to Mary. 'Drink up, love,' she murmured. 'It'll make you feel better, I promise.'

As the tea was sipped and cigarettes were lit, the silence continued, and Mary felt a squirm of nervous apprehension in the pit of her stomach. The moment had come to bring this whole upsetting business to its conclusion.

She put down the empty cup, flicked back her hair and cleared her throat. 'I'm sure you all remember that I had several questions to ask,' she said, with a firmness that surprised her. 'Now I know that Tommy was my father – which probably explains why Rosie knew me as Flora – it's time to ask the most important question of all.'

She looked at each of them, noting how they were steeling themselves for what she was about to ask. 'Who was my mother?'

Tommy had had enough of being in hospital, even though he'd been here less than twenty-four hours and had spent most of that time unconscious with morphine. He hated the restrictions of being forced to lie in bed, the bustling, po-faced nurses who clearly didn't approve of him; Matron's hectoring manner; and the disgusting food they insisted upon serving up.

He wasn't actually hungry but he couldn't have eaten it even he'd wanted to, for his jaw was swollen, his lips were split, and the raw sockets where his two front teeth had once been were small pits of agony. The only advantage to all this was that he couldn't smell the antiseptic stench of the place, for his broken nose had been tightly plugged with lint.

He lay in the bed, his breathing as shallow as possible through his damaged mouth, for every movement sent sharp pains from his cracked ribs into his chest. He couldn't see very much through his bloodshot eyes and swollen lids, but at least the swelling had begun to go down, thanks to the ice-packs the nurses frequently replaced. His whole body felt as if it was on fire despite the pills the doctors had given him for the pain, but at least the plaster on his broken leg had eased the agony he'd gone through as he'd crawled into that alleyway.

Tommy was feeling very sorry for himself and wondered, resentfully, why Rosie hadn't rushed to his bedside the minute she'd heard what had happened to him – or at least put in an appearance during this afternoon's visiting hour. He could have died last night in that bitter cold, and if that girl hadn't started screaming blue murder, which had alerted the people in the flats nearby, he doubted he would have been found before morning – and then it would have been too late.

He wished he could ease the deep pains in his ribcage, but every movement was agony, so he just had to lie there simmering with rage. Didn't Rosie realise that he'd taken that beating to protect her and that precious bloody pub of hers? The Copeland brothers had been threatening to do the place over, to smash it up and clear the stock in

317

return for the money he owed them – perhaps even rough up his sister to underline their message – and he'd begged and pleaded and made promises he knew he had no hope of keeping so they punished him and left Rosie alone.

Yet, as he lay there plucking nervously at the sheet with his torn hands, a nasty cold trickle of doubt dowsed his self-righteous anger. There was no guarantee that the Copeland thugs would keep their word. Now they'd dealt with him and got him out of the way, they could very well be plotting to go to the Anchor to take what they considered was owing to them. And Rosie would now be there alone every night.

He gripped the sheet and began to tug at it, careless of his torn nails and bruised knuckles. He had to get out of this bed to warn her. But the sheet and blanket were tightly binding him, and each pull on his battered muscles made him hiss with pain.

And then he froze in terror as the swing doors clattered back and four large men appeared on the ward. Their double-breasted black pinstripe suits strained against their bulky chests and muscled arms, and the brims of their dark fedoras were tugged low over their hard, narrowed eyes as they surveyed the ward.

Brushing aside the nurse's protests, they headed straight for Tommy. It was the Copeland brothers and they were clearly not in a pleasant mood.

Tommy's mouth dried and his heart hammered so hard he could barely breathe. He couldn't even squirm up against his pillows, hampered as he was with the plaster cast and the heavy bandaging around his chest, so he waited, trapped in the hated bed as they advanced on him.

He blinked up at them through his swollen eyelids as they blocked out the light and loomed over him like black harbingers of death, and his cracked ribs protested sharply with each terrified breath. 'What do you want?' he managed to stutter.

'We've come to see how you are,' said the eldest brother in a tone that froze the blood in Tommy's veins.

Tommy knew better than to reply, for Alfie Copeland wasn't a man who had any time for two-way conversations.

'Let this be a warning to you, Findlay,' the man continued. 'Next time you try to cheat on us, we'll give you a proper hiding.'

Tommy shook his head vehemently, although it hurt like hell. 'There won't be a next time,' he lisped through his missing teeth. 'I promise.'

Copeland's cold glance travelled from Tommy's face to the plaster on his leg, and he reached down casually and grabbed the exposed toes in an iron grip. 'Let's hope you've learned to keep your promises, Findlay, or you won't be the only one to end up on a slab in the morgue.'

His humourless smile was vulpine and chilling. 'And that would be a shame. Your Rosie's a good-looking woman.'

Tommy's heart was pounding so hard he thought it would burst from his chest as the grip on his vulnerable toes increased and began to twist until he could feel the bones grind agonisingly against each another. He knew that to cry out and bring attention to what was happening would only make things worse, and he almost bit through his lip as the torture continued and the keening in his throat rose to a desperate, high-pitched whine.

And then suddenly the pressure was eased and he sank back into the pillows with a sob of relief.

'How dare you come into my hospital and ignore my nurses!'

Copeland moved back from the bed and all four brothers raised their hats to the furious Matron, who'd arrived like a marauding galleon under full sail. 'We were just visiting our friend,' said Alfie with all the charm of a cobra. 'I'm delighted to see how well you're looking after him. Good day to you, Matron.'

Before the astonished woman could reply they'd walked out of the ward, leaving the doors clattering back and forth behind them.

Matron glared down at Tommy. 'Who were those men?' she demanded.

Tommy closed his eyes and refused to answer.

'I do not allow visitors on my ward out of hours,' she continued as she forcefully straightened the bedding. 'And I certainly don't appreciate that sort of rough type coming in here disturbing my nurses and my patients.'

Tommy ignored her as he kept his eyes closed and tried to recover from Copeland's rough handling. But his ribs were shooting pains through his chest and his broken leg felt as if it was on fire. He had to get out of here – had to leave Cliffehaven and get as far as possible from the Copeland gang – and if at all possible, persuade Rosie to get out too, before they carried out their threats.

He lay there and let the woman take his temperature and pulse as his mind raced. There was always a nurse on the ward, and he wouldn't get very far on this broken leg without crutches or a wheelchair. But there had to be some way. There just had to.

Chapter Fifteen

The silence that met Mary's question was deeply uneasy. Ron fidgeted on the arm of the couch and all three women refused to look at one another.

And then a soft, unsteady voice broke the silence. 'I'm your mother, Flora.'

Mary stared at her, unable to believe that she was the one she'd been searching for, had foolishly dreamed about in the desperate hope that despite everything, she'd regretted abandoning her. And then she felt a cold rush of fury sweep through her. 'So why didn't you acknowledge that fact earlier? You certainly had plenty of chances.'

'I didn't know who you were until today,' she stammered.

Mary gave a snort of derision. 'Really? I find that very hard to believe.'

'If I'd known, then of course I would have said something,' she persisted.

'I doubt it,' retorted Mary. 'You'd already proved you were no sort of mother by abandoning me before I was less than ten days old, so I can hardly expect you to welcome me with open arms now.'

Eileen's brown eyes were huge in her ashen face. 'I didn't abandon you,' she rasped.

'Yes, you did,' Mary snapped. 'You walked out, never to be seen again, and left me to Tommy's tender mercies. I'm amazed you dared to ever show your face here again, let alone still be in cahoots with him – and don't deny it, Eileen. I've seen you with him on more than one occasion.'

'I'm not denying that Tommy can still get me to do his dirty work – he can be very persuasive. But as for walking out on you...' Eileen gulped as she fought back her tears. 'I never did that, Flora – in fact, if it had been at all possible, I would have kept you.'

Mary shook her head in disbelief. This woman was her mother – and even though she'd been faced with the living proof of what she'd done, she still couldn't be honest.

Eileen edged forward in her, chair, eager to re-assure her. 'I loved you, Flora – really I did – and giving you up for adoption was the hardest thing I've ever had to do.'

Rosie snorted. 'You're such a liar, Eileen. You were keen enough to give her away, even before she was born, so don't put on the martyr act to make yourself look good in front of the poor girl. Peggy and I know the truth,' she said coldly, 'so you're not impressing anyone.'

Eileen's gaze hardened and her lips thinned as she returned Rosie's glare. 'You didn't exactly cover yourself in glory either,' she snapped. 'None of this would have happened if you'd kept your word.'

'What do you mean?' barked Rosie as she shook off Ron's restraining hand and struggled to her feet. 'I keep my promises. Which is more than I can say for you. If you'd had a shred of decency...' She took a shallow, shuddering breath and clenched her fists. 'But you didn't, did you? You just went your own sweet way without a single thought for anyone else, and to hell with the consequences.'

'That's an out-and-out lie!' Eileen was now also on her feet with her hands clenched and her eyes stormy.

Mary looked at them both through her tears, stunned by the anger and bitterness that lay between them. It was horrible, and she wished with all her heart that she'd never started this.

'That's enough from both of you,' ordered Ron. 'Can't you see you're upsetting Mary with your poison?' He gently but firmly drew the furious Rosie back to the couch and glared at Eileen until she too was sitting down again.

'Right,' he said. 'I've heard a great many things this afternoon and it strikes me that we need to clear the air before we go any further – and we can only do that if you tell the truth.'

'But I have been telling the truth,' protested Eileen.

'Not from where I'm sitting, you haven't,' retorted Rosie.

'Ron's right,' said a tearful and very confused Mary, who couldn't stand this awful state of affairs any longer. 'We won't get anywhere like this. All I'm asking from both of you is honesty Surely you can grant me that one simple thing without fighting about it?'

'The truth is rarely simple,' said Peggy with a deep sigh. 'As I suggested before, I think each of you should tell us the way you see it.'

Mary regarded her with affection and relief. 'Thank you for being the voice of reason in all this, Peggy – I hate seeing everyone being so hurtful and angry. And as Rosie and Eileen can't agree on anything, I'll tell my side of the story first.'

She glanced at Rosie, who was still glaring at Eileen. Eileen fidgeted in her seat and looked at no one as she furiously smoked her cigarette. Peggy's sweet face was concerned and Ron was determinedly concentrating on lighting his pipe. Yet the atmosphere was still heavy and Mary had to take a series of deep breaths before she could get her emotions under control and her voice steady.

She told them how she hadn't known she was adopted until very recently, and gave them a short description of her life at the rectory with the Reverend Gideon Jones and his wife Emmaline before they had been killed in the tip-and-run.

There was absolute silence as she continued. 'Cyril – or rather, Tommy – had been an infrequent member of Gideon's congregation in Carmine Bay for some months before he turned up at the rectory one day with me in his arms.'

'Tommy? Going to church?' gasped Rosie.

'I don't believe it,' said an equally shocked Eileen.

Mary ignored their interruption and carried on with her story. 'Tommy had clearly done his homework thoroughly, for he must have heard the local gossip, seen the gravestones of their dead babies in the churchyard and known that Gideon and Emmaline were about to move to another parish so they could begin afresh. His timing was perfect,' she said bitterly.

'He told Gideon that he'd had a fling with some girl during his rounds as a travelling salesman, and that my mother had abandoned me shortly after he'd set her up in a flat here in Cliffehaven.'

'*What?*'

'Shut up, Eileen. You'll get your turn,' snapped Rosie.

Mary ignored the short, venomous exchange, knotted her hands in her lap and continued. 'Tommy told Gideon he was at his wits' end to know what to do, for although he professed to absolutely adore me, it was impossible for him to keep me as he'd wished. His wife had threatened to divorce him if he didn't have me sent to an orphanage, but that was something he could never contemplate, as he'd been raised in such a place and had suffered very badly at the hands of those who should have cared for him.'

Mary heard Rosie's sharp intake of breath; saw the puzzled look on Eileen's face and gave a sad smile. 'Gideon was a gentle, honest man who took people at face value, never suspecting that they might be lying to him. But when I read his diaries, even I began to suspect that the story was too deliberately put together so it would have maximum impact on Gideon's soft heart. And of course, with me in Tommy's arms, it was the perfect set-up. Now I know it was Findlay, that suspicion has been confirmed.'

She clasped her hands in her lap as the tense

silence deepened. 'Gideon saw this opportunity to take me in as a gift from God. His wife, Emmaline, had lost several babies which had sadly been still-born, and I would fulfil all her needs and give them both the little family they'd always longed for.'

Her lips twisted wryly at the memory of Emmaline and her cold, bitter heart. She dismissed the images which had been conjured up and ploughed on with her tale.

'Gideon and Tommy drew up a private agreement that very afternoon while I was wrapped in a blanket on a nearby armchair. Gideon would raise me as his and Emmaline's child, and take me with them to their new parish in Harebridge Green. Tommy would have no more contact with me.'

She gave Rosie a tremulous smile. 'It was probably the only time in his life that your brother actually kept a promise, because none of us ever saw or heard from him again.'

'I can't believe he went to such lengths,' fretted Eileen. 'Was the agreement ever made legal?'

'Were you happy with Gideon and Emmaline?' asked Rosie.

'I was never formally adopted,' replied Mary, 'and because I never knew who my mother was, it was impossible to find a birth certificate.' She regarded Eileen fleetingly before turning to Rosie with a smile. 'Gideon was a wonderful father, kind and gentle, if a little absent-minded. I miss him dreadfully.'

'And Emmaline?' asked Eileen sharply.

'She never could quite get over the fact that Gideon hadn't discussed this agreement with her before signing it – or that his affection for me had been immediate and unwavering. But having played the delicate, grieving and childless little woman for years, she could hardly refuse to keep me. However, the fact that I was illegitimate, and had come between her and Gideon, was something she couldn't forgive.'

Mary took a deep, trembling breath and blinked away her tears. 'She was a rather self-centred woman who enjoyed being pampered because she'd been unable to bear a live baby, and I spoiled things for her slightly. I tried very hard to make her love me, but nothing I did could make her warm to me – so in the end I was forced to accept that she never would.'

'Oh, Mary, I'm so sorry you weren't happy,' said Rosie as she reached for her hand.

'I don't see why you should be,' she replied softly as she returned the pressure on her fingers. 'I wasn't your child, and you aren't to blame for any of this.'

'Humph. She's as much to blame as her conniving, lying brother,' spat Eileen. 'So don't let her fool you with her tears and soft words.'

Rosie visibly bridled, her fists knotted on her knees as she glared back at the other woman. 'If you were honest for once,' she retorted, 'you'd realise we're all to blame for what happened to Mary.'

'Then tell her your side of the story and let us be the judge of who's the honest one around here,' snapped Eileen.

Rosie could see that Mary had been deeply upset by the recounting of her childhood and was still

327

utterly confused, so she pulled herself together, and after an encouraging nod from Peggy, began to speak.

'Tommy and I were both born to loving parents and raised in a leafy suburb of London where they owned a small hotel. He was a sunny, handsome little boy who our parents rather spoiled, and he learned very early on that he could get away with most things if he used his considerable charm – especially on women.'

Rosie mangled Ron's handkerchief in her restless fingers. 'Unfortunately for all of us, he also realised that this charm opened doors to making easy money. And to my parents' shame and despair, by the time he was twenty, he was well on his way to a life of crime and had already spent a short time in Borstal.'

Rosie remembered her mother's tears and the way she'd been shunned by those she'd once considered friends. Her poor father had shouted and threatened to no avail, and had finally been forced to throw Tommy out of the hotel once his son's reputation had started to affect the business. It had been terrible for her to witness their pain and confusion, for none of them could understand how he'd come to be so unscrupulous and devious when he'd had only love and care throughout his childhood.

She gathered her thoughts. 'He eventually married and had two children, but he rarely spent much time with them because he was always chasing a dodgy deal or another woman.'

She looked at Mary, her smile sad. 'As far as I know, he's never been a travelling salesman – it's just not his style. He preferred living the easy life, and would find himself some woman who could set him up nicely for a few weeks, and once he'd spent her money or got bored he'd leave for pastures new. The grass on the other side of the fence was always greener to Tommy.'

'So the story he told Gideon *was* all lies,' said Mary.

Rosie nodded. 'He's a convincing liar – that's why he's such a good conman.'

She glanced across at Eileen. 'But he was caught out when Eileen told him she was pregnant. He tried to deny he was the father until she stood up to him and told him straight that if he didn't support her she would make life very difficult for him.'

'But how could she do that?' Mary's expression was confused.

Rosie gave a soft grunt. 'Like Tommy, she'd done her homework. She knew about his wife and family who live along the coast, and had discovered the details of the scam he was running at the time – which I now know he conducted under the name of Cyril Fielding.'

'You were a part of that?' breathed Mary as she looked accusingly at Eileen.

'The whole thing disgusted me, and I would have nothing to do with it,' she said firmly. 'But I do admit that I used my knowledge of it to ensure that he took responsibility for my situation. I might have been young, but I was no fool.'

'So you blackmailed him,' stated Mary.

'He got me pregnant. I had no choice,' she retorted.

Mary frowned as she turned back to Rosie. 'How

did you know what went on between Eileen and Tommy? Surely they would have kept it secret?'

'Tommy confided in me,' she replied. 'He wouldn't usually, but he'd been drinking and was feeling rather sorry for himself; but he never mentioned Cyril, just the insurance scam and Eileen's condition. He was at his wits' end to know what to do, for he was between the devil and the deep.'

Rosie lit a cigarette and blew a stream of smoke to the ceiling. 'He was terrified his wife would find out, because she came from a family who'd never approved of the marriage and would do all they could to make sure a divorce left him with nothing.' Her lips twisted in disgust. 'But he was even more terrified that Eileen might use her knowledge of his insurance scam to inform the police. Either way he was in trouble, and for once he couldn't think of a way out.'

Mary frowned at Eileen, who was listening to all this very closely. 'So, why didn't you make arrangements for me to be legally adopted by someone as soon as I was born? That way you'd've both been rid of me,' she added bitterly.

'Well, it wasn't quite as simple as that,' said Rosie before Eileen could reply. 'You see, I persuaded them not to.'

'But why? Surely it was the only logical solution?'

Tears sparked in Rosie's eyes, and it was a moment before she could speak. 'There was a better solution, Mary – or at least, I thought it was at the time.'

She dipped her head and took a series of shallow, trembling breaths in an attempt to stay calm and focused. 'You should know something of my background first, because I'm hoping it will help you to understand why things happened the way they did.'

Mary nodded, her blue eyes fixed on Rosie in silent encouragement.

Rosie puffed on her cigarette and then stubbed it out in the ashtray. 'I met my husband, James, while I was helping to manage my parents' hotel. He'd come to live there while he was looking for a house or flat near his new job at the newspaper office. They were dark times back then, with the threat of war looming, but he was a glorious light in my rather dull existence, for he was always laughing and enjoyed parties and dancing and all the happy things in life. I loved him very much.'

Rosie's fingers trembled as she brushed a solitary tear from her cheek. 'My parents could see how things were going between me and James, so they gave me a generous amount of money as a wedding present to provide me with some security. James left his job as a junior reporter, and we took over his parents' pub in Chippenham on their retirement. We'd only been married a few months when war with Germany was declared and James enlisted into the army.'

Rosie looked down at her hands, twisting Ron's handkerchief in her lap. She remembered how tearful she'd been when she'd waved goodbye to him at the station, and how he'd smiled at her and kissed her so tenderly before he'd become lost in the great ocean of khaki. He'd looked so handsome in his uniform, his dark eyes and youthful face alight with excitement as he'd promised her the war would be over before Christmas, and that he'd bring back wine and cheese and chocolate to celebrate.

But there had been no joyful Christmas reunion that year – in fact she hadn't seen him again until four long years had passed – and when she'd met him off the train he'd been a very different man to the one she'd said goodbye to, and they'd never lived intimately together as husband and wife again.

Rosie determinedly drew strength from the happier times they'd shared before he'd gone through the horrors of trench warfare in the Somme. 'I had hoped that our few months of marriage might bring me the baby I so longed for, but it was not to be,' she continued. 'I carried on running the pub and lived quietly on my own, poring over his letters and longing for the day when he would return home.'

She dabbed her eyes. 'But when he did return, he was a very sick man, prone to terrible fluctuating moods. He'd be laughing almost hysterically one minute and then be deep in depression the next. Intimacy repelled him and he refused to even kiss or hold me, moving into the spare room down the landing and locking the door against me.'

She hated talking about this in front of Eileen, but Mary needed to know it all, and it was a very small sacrifice to make in the light of what had happened to the poor girl.

She took a deep breath and continued. 'James couldn't sleep without having nightmares; he hated the crowded, noisy bar, and would fly into the most frightening rages over the slightest of things. I began to fear for my life.'

Rosie hesitated as she remembered how he'd rampaged through their living quarters above the bar, smashing everything in sight and threatening to kill her if she got in the way or tried to stop him. She closed her eyes, the images of those awful months so clear in her memory that they could still cause her physical pain.

'He'd been such a kind, loving man before,' she went on softly, 'and now and again I still caught glimpses of the James I'd married, and hoped with all my heart that he would recover.' She sighed deeply. 'But the episodes of violence increased and he became a stranger – a terrifying and dangerous stranger that I didn't know how to control. I sought help from his family, but they dismissed my fears and refused to believe there was anything wrong with him, so I had no choice but to turn to our doctor.'

She felt Mary's hand creep into hers and took heart and strength from her touch. 'He was committed to a secure asylum within hours of the doctor's visit, and that is where he's been ever since. My dreams of having a family were shattered, for the law doesn't allow me to divorce him because of his madness, so I was left in a half-world, with no chance to start again.'

'Oh, Rosie, how awful. I can't begin to imagine the pain and fear you must have gone through,' said Mary.

'Don't be sad for me, Mary. I'm a survivor – and I'm at my best when things appear to be insurmountable.' She smiled at her and squeezed her fingers. 'I decided to sell the pub and move right away from all the bad memories – and from James's family, who never forgave me for having him committed.'

'But that's terrible,' gasped Mary. 'It was the only thing you could do.'

Rosie shrugged. 'They didn't quite see it that way, unfortunately.' She looked across at Eileen and was surprised to see something approaching concern in her expression. She looked away, for the last thing she needed from Eileen was any sort of pity.

'My parents had brought me and Tommy to Cliffehaven for wonderful childhood holidays,' she said into the silence, 'and because I remembered it as a tranquil place, I thought I might find the peace I needed here to make a new life for myself, even though I'd lost my chance of ever having a child to call my own.'

She smiled up at Ron, who was still uncomfortably perched on the arm of the couch beside her. 'I was lucky, because the Anchor was for sale, and this lovely, scruffy old Irishman was working behind the bar until a new owner could be found.' She momentarily rested her head against his sturdy arm. 'Needless to say, I bought the pub and have been here ever since.'

'To be sure, ye've brought a breath of fresh air to the auld place, Rosie girl,' he rumbled. 'I just hope that this life you've chosen has fulfilled you, despite being cheated out of the family you so wanted.'

'That hope dwindled and died the moment James was committed,' she replied softly before turning her gaze back to Mary, who was silent and still beside her.

'I'd been here for two years when Tommy told me about Eileen and I dared to hope again. I begged him to let me have the baby neither of them wanted, for it was already a part of our family through Tommy, and I was desperate to keep it, for it would be the answer to all my prayers. When he and Eileen voiced their doubts about this plan, I promised to pay the rent on Eileen's flat while she was away, and arranged for her to go to a very private refuge in a nearby town once she'd started to show. All the medical bills at the private hospital would be paid by me on the understanding that Eileen would sign the formal adoption papers and return to London after you were born, and Tommy would go back to his wife.'

She gave a tremulous sigh. 'They finally agreed and promised to do as I asked. I was so happy that I felt as if I was walking on air for weeks. I turned the other bedroom into a nursery and then went shopping in another town for a pram and a cot and all the delicious little things a baby would need. I needed to be discreet, you see, for Eileen's condition had to be kept secret if the plan was to work. Once the baby was born and I brought her home, then I would just say quite truthfully that I'd adopted her. The gossips could make up their own stories as far as I was concerned.'

She lit another cigarette, even though she didn't really want one, but the core of the story was close to being revealed and she needed something to keep her hands occupied.

'I borrowed a car to drive over to visit Eileen once a week, taking presents of chocolate and books and magazines to stop her from getting too bored during those final four months. We spent a lot of time together and I thought we'd become friends as we strolled round the lovely grounds of the refuge in that Indian summer of 1924.'

She shot a scathing glance at Eileen before she took Mary's hands and smiled. 'And then you were born on the tenth of October,' she said on a sigh. 'You were so perfect, so beautiful, and I fell in love with you from that very first moment, wanting to bundle you up and carry you straight home. But of course you had to stay in the hospital for ten days until the doctors were satisfied that you had no underlying health problems, and all the formal paperwork was completed for the adoption.'

Rosie's chuckle was sharp-edged. 'I came back here in a terrible state of frustration and anxiety. Ten days felt like a lifetime and the solicitor refused to be hurried to get the paperwork in order. I also had to run this place, so there was very little chance of being able to visit you everyday, but I moved heaven and earth to see you when I could.'

'What happened to change things?' asked Mary softly.

There was a hitch in Rosie's voice as the painful memories returned full-force. 'Tommy came to visit a week after you'd been born and told me Eileen had changed her mind about me adopting you, and had already spoken to the adoption people about giving you to someone else.'

She ignored Eileen's instant denial and talked over her, her voice sharp with anguish. 'He said she was adamant she didn't want the baby to stay in Cliffehaven because she was already settled here and didn't want you being a constant reminder of her shame every time she walked out of her front door.' She licked her lips and shot a venomous glare at Eileen. 'Her flat is just a few steps away from here in Camden Road,' she said.

'Tommy then said that he too was reluctant to have you living with me, as it was bound to cause gossip, and if his wife heard about it – which she would have – she'd have started questioning him and soon got to the truth.'

Rosie ran her fingers through her hair and swallowed the lump in her throat as she remembered that awful night. 'I begged and pleaded with him for hours, but he wouldn't budge – and he eventually just walked out of the door leaving me and my shattered dreams behind.' She blinked back her tears and took a shuddering breath. 'And when I went to the clinic the next day to try and persuade Eileen to change her mind, it was only to find that she had made some private arrangement over the adoption and discharged herself.'

'Lies,' barked Eileen. 'It's all lies.'

Rosie ignored her as she held Mary's hand and looked into her wan little face. 'I was in despair, Mary. So low that I just wanted to crawl away and die. But when I went to Eileen's flat, desperate for an explanation, there was no sign of her – or Tommy. I came back to the Anchor, bolted the doors and stood in the nursery as my hopes and dreams lay in tatters about me. Then I climbed into bed and stayed there, too heartsick even to care what happened to me or what day of the week it was. It wasn't until Peggy and Ron broke in to see what was happening that I started to recover. But I didn't see hide nor hair of Eileen or Tommy for months afterwards.'

She gripped Mary's hand, desperate for her to understand her pain and anguish at having lost her. 'They broke their promises to me and betrayed me to the point where I can't forgive either of them,' she said brokenly. 'But I want you to know, Mary, that I loved and wanted you so much that the pain of losing you still lives in me, and when October comes round every year, it's almost unbearable.'

Mary released her hand and put her arms about her. 'I do believe you, Rosie,' she murmured against her cheek 'Thank you for loving me so much, and I wish with all my heart that things had turned out differently.'

The sound of a slow handclap drew them apart. 'Oh, well done, Rosie,' said Eileen with heavy sarcasm. 'You certainly know how to cover yourself in glory, don't you? That was a masterful piece of story-telling. But you seem to have forgotten one rather important detail that I'm sure everyone would like to hear.'

Rosie frowned. 'What detail?'

'The fact that it wasn't me who broke their promises. It was you.'

Rosie immediately stiffened. 'You've got a brass neck, Eileen Harris,' she said coldly. 'You sit there and accuse me of such a thing when you know full well it was you who broke that promise and took my baby from me.'

'Flora wasn't your baby,' replied Eileen icily. 'She was mine and Tommy's, and once you'd gone back on your word, Tommy did the only thing he could. He took Flora to the adoption people, who had a nice couple lined up to have her.'

'But he didn't do that, did he?' broke in Mary before Rosie could retaliate. 'He took me to Carmine Bay where he made a private arrangement with Gideon, who he knew was moving away to Sussex and a new parish the following day.' She sat forward on the couch. 'And I have proof of that, Eileen. It's in the agreement, and in my father's diary.'

Eileen's aggression withered and died as she slumped back in the chair. She chewed her lip, her eyes suddenly bright with tears. 'But he told me,' she said plaintively. 'He swore blind you were with the adoption people.'

Mary regarded her with growing pity, for she was obviously as gullible as Gideon had been. 'Didn't you find it odd that you weren't asked to sign any formal papers? Or that the adoption people didn't get in touch with you?'

Eileen slowly shook her head. 'I didn't know what was going on,' she said in a voice barely above a whisper. 'But Tommy said... He swore that...' She fell silent, her expression confused and woeful.

Mary resisted her natural urge to comfort her, for although she felt sorry for her, there was something about her that she couldn't warm to. 'When I found out about the agreement between Tommy and Gideon, I went to the library and looked into the adoption process, Eileen,' she said softly. 'And believe me, there's a great deal of legal paperwork involved – unless you're Tommy Findlay.'

'I'd already signed one lot of papers just after you were born,' Eileen managed, the tears streaking her make-up. 'I didn't know there should have been more, because Tommy and Rosie dealt with all of that.'

'Without signing that last document you'd withdrawn your permission to let me be officially adopted,' said Mary flatly. 'Tommy lied to you, just as he lied to everyone else.'

'But why? I was happy for Rosie to have you, because after I'd got to know her better, I knew she'd be a good and loving mother. I was ready and very willing to go back to my family in London because I didn't want to watch you growing up with someone else – it'd have been much too hard.'

'I think my brother has a natural aversion to legal bits of paper,' said Rosie. 'He knew that if Flora was legally adopted there would be a trail which would lead to you and him. I know the laws are strict on adoptions and that it's incredibly rare for children to be able to trace their parents, but it has been known, and he certainly wouldn't have wanted to risk her turning up at some stage and making trouble for him.'

Mary nodded. 'I think you're right, Rosie,' she said thoughtfully. 'His agreement with Gideon was under a false name, with no mention of my mother – so he'd effectively cut off any search.' She glanced across at Eileen. 'And as it was highly doubtful that you would come looking for me, or even know where to begin to find me, he'd got it all wrapped up.'

Eileen sat forward on the couch, her face streaked with tears, her hands open in supplication. 'Whatever you might think of me, Mary, I did come to love you very much in those few days I had with you. I'd never imagined how strong that bond between mother and baby could be, and when Tommy came to take you away, it broke my heart – really it did. And even to this day I'll never forget the awful moment when he walked out of the door for the final time with you in his arms. It was the hardest, cruellest moment of my life.'

An awkward silence greeted this statement, broken only by the sound of Eileen's quiet weeping. Rosie's attitude towards her began to soften, and yet the hurt that had been caused was too deeply rooted, had had too many years to fester, to be entirely dismissed by sentiment and tears.

She watched as Peggy went across to Eileen and drew her tenderly into her embrace, murmuring that it would be all right and that they believed her. Peggy was soft-hearted and loving, and Rosie wished she could be so easily forgiving.

Mary shifted on the couch next to her, and Rosie reached for her hand. The poor child had been bombarded with it all and was still clearly struggling to come to terms with the fact that Eileen and Tommy were her parents. It was one heck of a thing to have to face, and she wondered how long it would take for her to really absorb it all.

Eileen eventually managed to stem her tears and get her ragged emotions in check. She looked at each of them as she used Peggy's clean handkerchief to mop her face, but when she spoke, her voice still held the fragments of her hurt and despair.

'I met Tommy in London when I was barely

seventeen,' she began. 'He was handsome and sophisticated and so much older than me that I was dazzled and flattered into thinking I was in love. I was a young, shy girl and left my family to come down here to be with him, thinking we'd get married.'

She fluttered her hands helplessly in her lap and forced a rueful smile. 'Then I found out he already had a wife and two children, and I would have gone back to London if I hadn't suddenly discovered that I was expecting a baby. I was frightened and didn't know what to do. I couldn't go home, my father would have thrown me out for disgracing the family – and I hadn't had the chance to make any friends here, so there was no one to turn to for help.'

She sniffed back her tears and lit a cigarette. 'When I told him I was pregnant he denied it could be his – then he offered to pay for an abortion.' She shot Mary an apologetic glance and quickly looked away. 'I refused to do that – I simply couldn't have gone through with such a terrible thing. So I blackmailed him to make him take responsibility, and he found me the flat above the bakery. I realised it would cause a terrible scandal if anyone found out about my condition, so when Rosie came up with the offer of taking the baby and setting me up in another town until she was born, I jumped at the chance.'

She paused to sniff back her tears. 'Rosie and I became close friends over those months, and I trusted her and Tommy to keep their promises. I knew it would be hard to give my precious baby away – but at least I knew she would be loved and wanted and given a wonderful home.'

She swallowed the hard lump in her throat as she remembered that awful morning when Tommy had come to see her in the hospital. 'When he told me you no longer wanted to keep Flora I was so shocked I couldn't think straight. I'd trusted you, grown to really like you, and now you had betrayed not only me, but my baby girl. So I let him take her, believing I was doing the best thing for her.' She blinked back her tears as she looked from Mary to Rosie. 'But in the end, it was Tommy who betrayed us all, wasn't it?'

'He certainly did,' said Rosie with a deep sigh. 'Oh, Eileen, I'm sorry I didn't give you the chance to explain years ago. I know you tried, but I was so hurt I couldn't bear to face you.'

Eileen nodded. 'I can understand that now, and I'm sorry too – for being such a fool to believe that you really had changed your mind when I knew how much you loved my little Flora.'

Rosie accepted her apology, but there were still things that niggled her. 'But where did you go? Why didn't you come back here and ask me why I'd changed my mind? I would have done if the shoe was on the other foot.'

Eileen's smile was sad. 'I wasn't as sure of myself back then as I am now, and I was too hurt and angry to face anyone for a while, so I used the money Tommy had been giving me to pay for a room in a boarding house in another seaside town and stayed there until I felt strong enough to come back here.'

'But why here? Why not go back to London?' asked Mary. 'Surely you must've realised it'd be awkward with Rosie just across the street?'

Eileen shrugged. 'I had the flat and the rent was paid for several more months. There was a good job going in the Council offices and when I applied for it I got accepted immediately. I couldn't face going home, not after what I'd done, so I decided to keep out of Rosie's way and just get on with things the best I could.'

'Well, you've got a nerve, I'll say that,' said Rosie with a touch of asperity. 'I don't suppose it ever occurred to you that I might not appreciate bumping into you again?'

'Don't let's fight any more,' said Eileen wearily. 'We both know we've been victims of Tommy's twisted mind, so let's leave it at that and try to start again – for Mary's sake, if nothing else.' She got to her feet, her gaze steady as she reached out a hand to Rosie. 'What do you say, Rosie?' she murmured.

Rosie saw the genuine appeal in the other woman's eyes and knew that to refuse this offer would be both churlish and unkind. She stood and went across to take her hand. 'I'll be glad to give it a try, Eileen,' she murmured. 'We were good friends once, and I'm sure, we can find some way to be so again.'

Eileen nodded. 'Thank you, Rosie.'

Rosie knew it would take time to heal those deeply seated wounds, and that perhaps the friendship wouldn't be as strong as it once had been. But they had taken that first, difficult step on the long road to recovery.

Mary watched this rather touching scene and tried to come to terms with everything she'd learned today. She was heartsore and weary from

344

it all, and not at all sure how she felt about any of it. There was little doubt that she'd been loved by both women when she'd been born, and although Eileen was her real mother, she felt more drawn to Rosie. There was a warmth to Rosie that was lacking in Eileen, a softness and genuine kindness which she suspected Eileen did not possess.

And yet as they both turned to look at her, she knew they expected something from her – a word, or a smile – or even an acknowledgement that would ease some of the pain that Tommy had caused all those years ago through his lies and machinations.

'I'm glad you're friends again,' she said as she moved from the couch to stand awkwardly by them. 'And of course I don't blame either of you for what happened. But this has all come as a bit of a shock, and it will take time for me to come to terms with it.'

'So you'll forgive us, Mary?' asked Rosie, once again on the brink of tears.

Something shifted in Mary's heart, and she realised it was up to her to repair the damage that had been caused, and to help all of them to start to heal. 'There's nothing to forgive,' she said softly as she took their hands. 'Eileen, it's clear to me now that you didn't abandon me and only wanted the best for me. And Rosie, I know you loved me very much and I wish with all my heart that things had worked out differently for you.'

Mary looked into their tear-streaked faces and gave them an uncertain smile. 'We all suffered because of one man's lies, but I want you to know that I will never regret the fact that I had Gideon for a father, so something good did come out of all this.' She squeezed their fingers and then stepped back, unable to offer more than kind words and perhaps a fledgling friendship.

'But you'll stay in Cliffehaven, won't you?' pleaded Eileen.

'We couldn't bear to lose you now we've found you again,' said Rosie tearfully.

Mary regarded them and realised with sudden, painful clarity that she couldn't give either of these women what they so clearly yearned for – and that there was really only one place she wanted to be right at this moment. 'I'm sorry,' she said softly, 'but I really can't stay – not now.'

'Then come home to those who've always loved you,' said Barbara Boniface as she stomped up the last few stairs and entered the room.

Mary flew into her open arms and felt the warmth and love of her familiar embrace enfold her. 'Oh, Auntie Barbara,' she sobbed in relief. 'How did you know I so longed to be with you right this minute?'

'Because you gave Peggy my number in case of emergencies and she telephoned me this morning. I've been standing on the stairs listening for the past ten minutes,' she replied as she kissed Mary's tear-stained cheek and lovingly smoothed back her hair. 'And because I have loved you since the first day I held you in my arms, and knew that this search of yours would inevitably lead to you needing me.'

Mary wrapped her arms around Barbara, realising now that she'd had no need to search for her mother – for she'd been there all the time.

And that knowledge brought her the deepest sense of peace. The circle was closed, the past set aside, and the unbreakable ties that bound her to Barbara were sealed with a loving kiss.

Chapter Sixteen

Tommy sat on the stairs and blearily tried to understand what on earth was going on in Rosie's sitting room. He could barely think at all, for his body was throbbing from the agonising pain that the effort to get here had caused – yet to see Eileen and Rosie in the same room and embracing tearfully was something he never thought he'd witness.

The fact that Mary and Peggy – and the fat woman he'd seen coming in earlier – seemed to be involved in this display of tears and overwrought emotion was really confusing, and his sluggish brain simply couldn't deal with it. He knew the reason behind the enmity between Rosie and Eileen – it was of his making, after all. But what the hell had happened to bring such a turnaround? And why were Peggy and Mary involved in this ridiculous carry-on?

He closed his eyes and tried to clear the fog in his head, but that only made him feel giddy, so he quickly opened them again and clung more tightly to the banister. The sheer effort of getting up those narrow stairs had almost killed him, and he was trembling from the effort of trying to hoist himself up onto his one serviceable leg, distressed to discover that his nose was bleeding again.

At least they hadn't heard him, and were too occupied with their tears and their talking to spot him lurking on the stairs. He battled to regain his strength in those few minutes, knowing he'd need every ounce of it if he was to see his plans through.

His escape from the hospital had been much easier than he'd expected, for once the doctor had agreed he could be discharged early the following morning, the nurses had let him move more freely about the ward. He'd managed to bundle up his ruined clothes from the bedside locker and hide them beneath the hospital dressing gown as he'd watched and waited until the staff nurse left the ward, so he could charm the probationer into finding him a pair of crutches so he could use the bathroom.

She'd followed him down the corridor to the bathroom and was planning to wait outside – but he'd scotched that idea by reminding her that the staff nurse had left her in charge of the ward and wouldn't be best pleased if she came back to find it deserted. Having assured her he could manage quite well, he'd breathed a tremulous sigh of relief when she finally went bustling away.

His struggle to get dressed had been painfully slow, and because his suit trousers were not only torn but stained with blood, mud and the filth from the alleyway, he'd shoved them in a waste bin and decided to risk going out in his pyjamas. On his journey to the bathroom he'd seen the abandoned wheelchair parked conveniently outside the next ward, so once he'd checked that the coast was clear, he'd hobbled towards it and sunk gratefully into it using the dressing gown as a blanket to camouflage his pyjama trousers.

But he'd soon discovered that a wheelchair is an unwieldy thing to manoeuvre when all the muscles in your body protested at every move, and his cracked ribs grated bone on bone with needle-sharp stabs. It had taken him many minutes to get the thing along the corridor and out onto the hospital forecourt, by which time he'd been sweating profusely and almost passing out with the pain.

The damned thing had proved to be murderously heavy to propel along the blasted pavement, and he'd been all too aware of the curious stares of those he passed along the way. The several hundred yards between the Anchor and the hospital felt like a million miles, but determination and fear of the Copeland brothers had kept him going.

He'd hesitated momentarily as a large woman bustled past him and disappeared down the alley to the side door. Wondering who on earth she could be and what her business was at the Anchor, he'd manipulated the wheelchair to the door that she'd left ajar so he could get some sense of what was going on upstairs. He couldn't actually hear what was being said, but it didn't take long to recognise the voices that drifted down to him, and he was shocked to the core that Eileen's was one of them.

As the large woman seemed to have joined the others, he'd gathered up the crutches, dragged himself out of the wheelchair and bumped up the stairs on his behind as quietly as possible, so he could listen in and find out what they were talking about. If Cyril Fielding was mentioned, then he'd have to just take his chances, for he was now on the point of collapse.

Thankfully, there had been no sign of the Copeland brothers during his journey, and the women still seemed to be fully occupied in some tearful exchange that made absolutely no sense to him. He dragged himself up onto his good leg, and once he'd got his balance on the crutches, he decided he'd recovered enough to put his plan of escape from Cliffehaven into action.

'Very touching, I'm sure,' he drawled with deep sarcasm. 'But when you've all finished blubbering, I could do with a hand.'

He saw Ron shoot to his feet with a glower as Monty growled deep in his throat and the five women silently stared at him in shock. There was obviously not going to be any offer of help. He gritted what was left of his teeth and hobbled into the room on the crutches. 'I don't know what the hell this is all about, and I don't want to,' he slurred through his split lips. 'But the Copeland brothers are likely to pay a visit, and it would be better if they don't find any of us here.'

'The Copeland brothers?' rasped Ron as he took in the battered face, missing teeth and the plaster-cast. 'Was it them who did that to you?'

Tommy didn't even glance at Ron as he headed slowly and painfully into the room on his way to the narrow hallway and his bedroom. 'Pack your bag, Rosie, we're on the next train out of Cliffehaven.'

'I'm not going anywhere,' she snapped.

He turned to glare at her. 'Don't be stupid.

Whatever's going on here is not important compared to what they'll do to you and this place.'

'They'll do nothing as long as it's light,' said Ron, 'and by the time it's dark I'll have the police here waiting for them.' He eyed Tommy with deep disgust. 'If you're involved with scum like the Copelands, then you deserve everything you got,' he rumbled. 'But you put my Rosie in danger, and I'll never forgive you for that, you heathen swine.'

'Sticks and stones, old man,' he said dismissively. 'You don't frighten me.'

Ron eyed him with loathing as he clenched his meaty fists and held onto his famous temper. 'There are plenty of ways to skin a cat, Findlay, so I wouldn't be too cocky if I were you.'

Tommy didn't like the sound of that, for he knew Ronan Reilly was perfectly capable of getting him banged up in prison again, and he wondered suddenly if the old bastard was up to something.

He saw him put a protective arm round Rosie as the other women edged back towards the couch in a huddle.

'What's going on here?' he demanded of Rosie. 'Since when have you and Eileen become best friends?'

'Since we all discovered what a lying, cheating, devious rat you are,' retorted Rosie.

'You're despicable,' rapped out Eileen, 'and worth less than the dirt on the bottom of my shoes.'

'You're a dishonest toerag who should be ashamed to even face us,' said Mary sharply, her face pale with distaste.

'You're not a man,' hissed a venomous Peggy,

351

'but a worm. A low, despicable worm. So why don't you crawl back under your rock and leave decent folk alone?'

He was feeling light-headed and unsteady, and couldn't understand what on earth had made them gang up on him like this when he was so obviously in pain and needing a bit of sympathy. Realising he wouldn't make it as far as the bedroom, he placed the crutches carefully against the arm of the chair, and eased himself into it.

'That's a bit strong for you, isn't it, Peggy?' he asked lightly.

'It's Mrs Reilly to you,' she spat. 'And if I was the sort of woman to use stronger language, believe me, Thomas Findlay, I'd throw the entire dictionary at you.' She looked down at him, arms folded tightly round her skinny waist, her face alight with fury. 'You have absolutely no idea what's been going on here this afternoon, have you?'

He shook his head and closed his swollen eyelids. 'I'm sure you're about to tell me,' he said wearily. 'But make it quick. I've got a splitting headache and your voice is making it worse.'

'Hello, Cyril. Remember me?'

He opened his eyes with a start and looked blearily at Mary as his heart began to pound against his cracked ribs. 'I'm Tommy,' he rasped.

'You are when it suits you,' she replied coldly. 'Well, I'm your daughter, Flora.'

Tommy froze and stared up at her, his addled brain working desperately to clear the fog of pain and think straight. 'I don't have a daughter,' was all he managed.

Mary looked at the other women who'd come to

stand protectively at her side, thereby surrounding him. 'He obviously needs a little reminder of the truth. Shall we tell him how we found out about the way he lied and betrayed us all?'

Tommy's blood ran cold in his veins and the icy sweat beaded on his battered face as he tried and failed to think of a way to wriggle out of this situation. 'I don't know what you're talking about,' he muttered as he glanced from one angry, set face to another.

'Remember Gideon Jones and his childless wife Emmaline?' Mary's voice was low and un-emotional as she and the other women closed in around him. 'Remember going to his church in Carmine Bay once you'd discovered the sad story of their lost children, and the fact they were about to move to another parish in another county? They were prime targets, weren't they?'

Tommy pressed back in the chair as Rosie leaned towards him. 'And remember how you lied and told me Eileen had changed her mind about me keeping Flora?'

'And how you tricked me into handing over my baby so you could give her away to strangers,' added Eileen.

Tommy grabbed one of the crutches and began to jab at the women to get them out of his way as he struggled out of the chair. 'I don't have to sit here and listen to this,' he hissed. 'If you won't heed my warning about the Copeland brothers then that's up to you, but I'm getting out of here.'

'You're not going anywhere, Findlay,' said Sergeant Williams as he and three hefty constables stormed up the stairs and into the room. 'At least not until we've searched this place thoroughly for illicit contraband.'

Monty began to growl and Ron quickly silenced him before he nodded to the women to move away from Tommy.

Tommy's sneer of contempt encompassed them all before he turned back to the sergeant. 'Help yourself,' he said dismissively. 'There's nothing of interest to you here.'

'Really?' Sergeant Williams rocked back and forth on his heels as two of his men began a perfunctory search behind the couches and under the cushions. 'That's an unusual state of affairs for you, Findlay. You've usually got something stashed away.'

'Not this time,' he replied smugly. 'I'm a law-abiding citizen now, and wouldn't dream of breaking the terms of my probation.'

Sergeant Williams surveyed Tommy from his bruised and battered face to the cast on his broken leg. 'Had an accident, have we?' he asked with more than a hint of sarcasm. 'Run into a couple of fists, and maybe a heavy boot or two?'

Tommy didn't reply, for Williams was a wily old bastard and probably already knew who'd given him a beating. He watched through his swollen eyelids as two of the policemen began to search through Rosie's kitchen cupboards, and felt a certain satisfaction that they were wasting their time.

'I understand you've discharged yourself from hospital,' the sergeant continued. 'Now why would you do that when it's clear you're still a very sick man?'

'I hate hospitals,' he muttered.

354

'Hmm.' He turned to his men, who were still opening and shutting drawers and cupboards in the kitchen. 'You two go and search the bedrooms while PC Carter minds the stairs and I have a chat with Mr Findlay here.'

Tommy's eyelids had puffed up again and it felt as if there were grains of sand scratching his eyeballs as an army of drummers marched through his head. Yet he managed a sickly smile as the two policemen headed down the hallway. 'Look where you want,' he called after them. 'You won't find anything more than my dirty underwear.'

'I see you haven't lost any of your bravado, Findlay,' said Williams, 'but then it's a rather necessary commodity when mixing with people like the Copeland brothers, isn't it?'

'I dunno what you mean,' he replied as he sank back into the chair and battled against the nauseous headache.

'Come, come, Findlay. The Copelands are your friends. Why, they even took time out of their busy, nefarious schedule of robbery, intimidation and violence to visit you in hospital this afternoon.'

Tommy was fighting not only the blinding headache but the gnawing pains that were shooting through his tortured body. 'How do you know that?' he rasped.

Sergeant Williams rocked on his heels as his stony-faced constable stood at the top of the stairs and kept an eye on Tommy. 'Matron became most concerned over your welfare once she'd discovered who your unsavoury visitors were. She telephoned me at the station, and I sent Carter here to go and keep an eye on their office at the abattoir and see if he could discover what they were up to. I also had a man watching you – which is how I knew you'd be here this afternoon.'

Despite the agony he was in, Tommy's curiosity had been piqued, and he looked through his swollen eyelids at the sergeant, noting he seemed to be very pleased with himself. This didn't bode well, and the sweat was cold as it ran down his back.

'The Copeland brothers are creatures of habit and never stray far from their office – it must be the stench of all that blood and raw meat that attracts them,' the sergeant added with a sneer. 'Carter didn't have long to wait until he saw them piling into their delivery van, armed to the teeth with clubs, knives and chains.'

Sergeant Williams beamed with pride as he glanced across at the beefy constable. 'Despite his size, Carter is fleet of foot and managed to get to a telephone box to warn me the Copelands were looking for trouble, and that he'd overheard them planning to do over this place.'

Tommy heard Rosie gasp in horror and ignored her. He was far more interested in hearing from Williams what had happened next.

'We were waiting for them, and let them get as far as the side door of the pub before we trapped them in the alley. It was like shooting fish in a bucket,' said Williams smugly. 'Now they're all tucked up nice and tight in my cosy cell waiting to go before the magistrate in the morning.'

Tommy's relief was so intense that he couldn't help but smile, even though it pulled on the cuts in his lips.

But that smile swiftly disappeared when the

356

two policemen came into the room carrying arm-fuls of shoeboxes. 'We found these in the back of his wardrobe, sir.'

There was a horrified cry from Rosie and an answering yap from Monty as the boxes were deposited on the low table and opened to reveal dozens of packets of cigarettes and tobacco as well as several half-bottles of gin which were clearly marked with the RCA insignia.

Tommy's blood froze. He'd been stitched up – and he knew exactly who'd done it. 'It's not mine,' he protested as he struggled to get out of the chair. 'Someone put all that there to frame me. It's not mine, I tell you.'

Sergeant Williams ignored his protests, and as the evidence was packed away and carried down to the sergeant's car, he indicated that Tommy should be helped to his feet and then handcuffed.

'Thomas Arthur Findlay,' he intoned gravely, 'I am arresting you for possessing goods which you are clearly planning to sell on the black market. You will also be charged with stealing the pro-perty of the Royal Canadian Air Force, and for the robbery committed on Jackson's tobacconist on the night of December the twenty-second.'

'It's not mine,' moaned Tommy as he feebly struggled against the policemen's iron grip. 'I was stitched up.'

Williams carried on with his speech as if Tommy hadn't spoken. 'As you have broken your terms of probation, you will spend the night in my cell alongside your friends, the Copelands, and be transferred first thing in the morning to His Majesty's Prison in Maidstone.'

'No. I can't be banged up with them,' Tommy whimpered through his pain. 'They'll kill me.'

'I must warn you,' continued the sergeant with little emotion, 'that anything you say will be taken down and may be used in evidence against you.'

Tommy felt the cold grip of the handcuffs round his wrists, and he shot a glare of pure malice at Ron. 'I'll get you for this, you old bastard,' he snarled.

'I heard that threat against a law-abiding citizen,' said Sergeant Williams, 'and if you open your mouth again, I'll charge you with intent to harm.'

Tommy cried out in pain as he was man-handled towards the stairs. 'You're hurting me,' he wept. 'For God's sake, don't be so rough.'

But the policemen carried him none too gently down the stairs and out to the police van. The door was opened and he was virtually thrown into the back. He lay there fighting to breathe and to contain the searing pain that shot through his body and right through his head.

But the terror of knowing he would be sharing a cell with the Copeland brothers was far greater than any pain, and he sobbed in despair as the doors were slammed and the van began to trundle inexorably towards the police station and his doom.

'I'm sorry you had to witness that, ladies,' said the sergeant. 'But rest assured, you are quite safe now, Rosie. We've found enough evidence at the abattoir office to finally prove that the Copeland brothers were responsible for at least one murder as well as black-marketeering, grievous bodily harm and aggravated burglary, so they'll be locked up for the foreseeable future. As for your brother, his sentence will be increased to take into account these latest charges, and this time he will serve the full term.'

He turned away from the women and gave Ron a sly wink of thanks for the tip-off as he carefully placed his peaked cap on his head. 'I wish you all a very pleasant evening,' he said, and with the broad grin of satisfaction for a job well done, he took his leave.

Epilogue

There had been a great deal of discussion once the sergeant had left the Anchor, and as the women settled down to explain everything to Barbara Boniface, Ron had sneaked a slice of cake, kissed Rosie goodbye and left them to it. Monty and Harvey were due for their evening walk, and he was looking forward to getting some good clean air in his lungs after breathing in the same atmosphere as Tommy Findlay for the latter part of the afternoon.

The master-stroke in his plan to nail Findlay once and for all had been his purchase of that black-market gin from his mate Bill Fletcher, who always kept a bottle or two of something hidden in his potting shed. Those bottles had condemned the man to at least ten more years in prison, and Ron had no regrets about what he'd done. His Rosie would be safe, and all the unpleasantness that had simmered between her and Eileen could be wiped away in the knowledge that their little Flora had survived Tommy's twisted plotting, and that although she would be leaving Cliffehaven the next day, she was returning home to the people who loved her.

It was heart-warming to know that good things could still happen in these dark days, and there was a spring in his step as he tramped up the steep hill behind the racing, excited dogs.

A month had passed since that day of revelation, and Peggy had been well aware of the need for Rosie and Eileen to set aside their feud and recover from their deep disappointment that Mary had left Cliffehaven to be with Barbara and Joseph before she went to college. She knew that hard work was a good cure for all ills, and had encouraged them to help her remove all trace of Tommy from the spare room.

The walls had been freshly painted, the curtains and bedding thoroughly washed, and the stained carpet which was riddled with cigarette burns was taken down to the corporation rubbish dump. Once the floorboards had been scraped and newly varnished, Rosie had managed to purchase a pink rug from the Saturday market which exactly matched the roses clambering up the pretty curtains. It was now a perfect guest room, and Rosie had confided in Peggy that she hoped that one day Mary might come for a visit.

Peggy had fretted over everyone, for she'd known how deeply saddened Eileen and Rosie were that Mary hadn't wanted to stay and perhaps forge some sort of relationship with them, but Peggy secretly thought she'd done the right thing. Such revelations would take time to absorb and understand, and the girl needed the security and love of the woman who'd more or less raised her to help her through. Barbara had, to all intents and purposes, been Mary's mother, and it was right that they should be together.

As for Rosie and Eileen, they were beginning to pick up the threads of their lives again, their sorrow for what might have been soothed by the many letters that came from Mary, who seemed to understand that it was necessary for all of them to stay in touch.

It was now February, and Peggy was in such a happy mood that she went about the house singing to herself. There was so much to be grateful for despite the absence of Jim and the almost daily air-raid warnings. Cordelia was fully recovered; Fran and Robert had become inseparable; Suzy and Anthony were blissfully happy in their tiny cottage; and dear little Rita seemed to have wings on her heavy boots now she and Matthew were planning their engagement.

She came into the kitchen with a broad smile on her face and picked up Daisy, who was scuttling around the floor on all fours. Giving her a big kiss, she danced round the kitchen and sang along to the music on the wireless.

'Goodness me,' said Cordelia as she came in wearing her best suit and hat. 'Someone's happy this morning.'

Peggy kissed her. 'Oh, I am,' she said. 'It's a beautiful day; I've had another two airgraphs from Jim; Danuta's finally written to say she's

361

well; everyone's in love or at least happy with their lot; and you and Bertram are off to have a lovely lunch at the golf club.'

Cordelia looked at her over her half-moon glasses and tried to look stern. 'You'll get caught out one day with all your matchmaking, Peggy Reilly. And if you think Bertram and I are giddy about one another, then you're sorely mistaken.' She glanced at the clock and frowned. 'He's late – and that's most unlike him. I do hope he hasn't forgotten about our lunch.'

'Of course he hasn't,' said Peggy as she gently placed Daisy back on the floor. 'He's probably just–'

The loud rap on the door made her grin. 'That's probably him now. I'll go and let him in while you put on your coat.'

She was humming as she went skipping into the hall. Opening the door, her smile widened at the sight of Maud from the local nurseries holding an enormous bunch of spring flowers.

'These are for you, Peggy,' she said. 'Picked fresh this morning after I received a lovely telephone call long distance. There's a note with them. TTFN.'

Peggy opened the little card that was tucked between the blooms. 'To dearest Peggy,' she read. 'With many thanks for everything you've done for me. With fondest love, Mary. Xx'

Peggy blinked back her tears and eyed the note and the flowers with the deepest pleasure. It was always good to know that one of her chicks remembered her.

Dear Reader,

I do hope you enjoyed reading *Sealed With a Loving Kiss*, and that you've happily returned to the trials and tribulations of Peggy and Ron and the rest of the family. It's always a joy to return to Cliffehaven to renew my acquaintance with the Reillys and their evacuees, for it's as if I've come back home to a warm welcome – especially from Harvey.

The inspiration for Mary's story was triggered by a photograph of Coventry Cathedral after it had been bombed, and my imagination began to work on a story. At first I was going to set it in Coventry, but I've only visited there once, so don't really know it as well as I know Sussex. The idea of a tin trunk being discovered in the ashes of a bombed-out rectory intrigued me – is this going to reveal something very ordinary, or would it be more like Pandora's Box and once opened, bring only chaos and confusion? Of course it had to be the latter, otherwise there would have been no story and, as it turned out, a great many loose ends that have been running through the series could be tied up, and mysteries explained.

Mary's relationship with her parents also intrigued

me, for no matter how cold or cruel parents can be, a child will always love them and do all they can to gain their approval. This is something that is quite personal to me, as my own childhood was rather fractured, and it is a theme I have returned to several times over the years.

Thank you for reading my Beach View Boarding House series, and I hope you continue to enjoy the stories as we progress through the war and beyond.

Ellie x

A Map of Cliffehaven

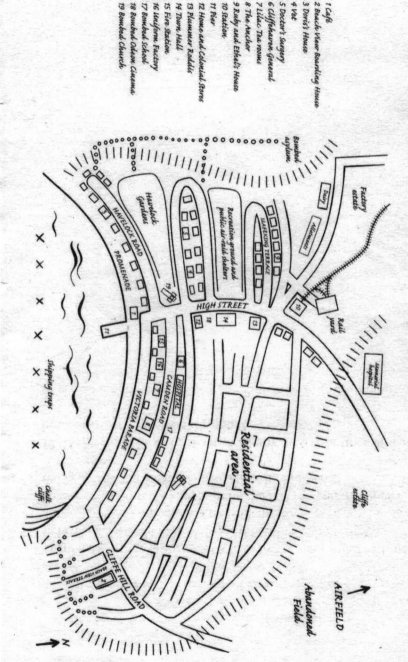

1 Café
2 Beach View Boarding House
3 Doris's House
4 Vet
5 Doctor's Surgery
6 Cliffehaven General
7 Lilac Tea-rooms
8 The Anchor
9 Ruby and Ethel's House
10 Station
11 Pier
12 Home and Colonial Stores
13 Plummer Raddis
14 Town Hall
15 Fire Station
16 Uniform Factory
17 Bombed School
18 Bombed Odeon Cinema
19 Bombed Church

Bombed asylum

Dairy

Allotments

Factory estate

Rail yard

Memorial hospital

Havelock Gardens

HAVELOCK ROAD

PROMENADE

Recreation ground and public air-raid shelters

MAFEKING TERRACE

HIGH STREET

CAMDEN ROAD

VICTORIA PARADE

Residential area

Cliffe estate

AIRFIELD

Abandoned Field

Chalk cliffs

Shipping traps

CLIFFE HILL ROAD

BEACH VIEW TERRACE

N

This Large Print Book for the partially sighted, who cannot read normal print, is published under the auspices of

THE ULVERSCROFT FOUNDATION